Miracle in Las Vegas

A novel by Paul D. Smith

iUniverse, Inc.
Bloomington

Miracle in Las Vegas is a work of fiction. The characters, names, incidents, dialogue, and plot are the products of the author's imagination or are used fictitiously. Any resemblance to actual persons, companies, or events is purely coincidental.

iUniverse books may be ordered through booksellers or by contacting:

iUniverse
1663 Liberty Drive
Bloomington, IN 47403
www.iuniverse.com
1-800-Authors (1-800-288-4677)

Because of the dynamic nature of the Internet, any Web addresses or links contained in this book may have changed since publication and may no longer be valid. The views expressed in this work are solely those of the author and do not necessarily reflect the views of the publisher, and the publisher hereby disclaims any responsibility for them.

ISBN: 978-1-4502-4773-3 (sc)
ISBN: 978-1-4502-4775-7 (hc)

Cover design is the creation of John Daiker

Printed in the United States of America

iUniverse rev. date: 11/16/2012

Miracle in Las Vegas is dedicated to my parents, Ediss Kathleen and Robert McMann Smith.

So many rewarding events were unfolding, it was as if an entourage of guardian angels had chosen Las Vegas as their convention center city.

Chapter One

RICHARD STEWART, THE OMAHA BUSINESSMAN, remembered back to the previous year when he and Benjamin Anderson decided to make a major historic decision on behalf of the Stewart Company. For several months the men considered every aspect, pro and con, of opening a retail store in Las Vegas.

On the morning they made their final decision, Benjamin said, "As long as we're going outside Nebraska for the first time, we might as well get started as soon as the fall promotion season is in place."

"And I am more convinced than ever that Las Vegas is right for us," Richard declared.

The expansion decision was not without philosophical controversy. Richard often recalled the time when his father, who founded the business, had said, "Even though expansion might make us financially stronger, being securely comfortable is a business virtue that should never be taken lightly."

But with the Great Recession over and the overall economy soaring to new heights throughout America, Richard's and Benjamin's outlooks had taken a 180-degree turn. Richard would never make a major company decision without Benjamin's input and approval. The thirty-one-year-old black vice president had been his best friend since they were very young, and he considered Benjamin's business wisdom priceless.

Once they made the decision, Richard was excited to see what the entertainment capital had to offer.

Richard Michael Stewart seemed to have everything. At age twenty-nine he was co-owner and president of the highly successful Stewart Golf and Sporting Goods Company. He was tall and handsome with short, dark brown hair and expressive dark eyes. Many thought of him as Omaha's number one bachelor, and in some social circles he was known as Richard the Invincible. Such lofty nicknames were generally uncharacteristic, however, for he was anything but a typical well-to-do playboy. He was a modest man whose most important goal was to find the woman of his dreams, settle down, and raise some kids.

Richard and his sister Elizabeth were Samuel and Margaret Stewart's only children, and the siblings had many advantages. Their bright, energetic young parents introduced the children to a wide variety of interest areas. Margaret, a University of Nebraska at Omaha music teacher, and Samuel, a successful businessman and avid sports follower, encouraged the youngsters to pursue the interests they appreciated the most. In that positive environment, the children became very close.

Elizabeth Ann was a striking blue-eyed brunette, a French-Italian-Swedish charmer whose personality and vitality enhanced her beauty. Two years older than Richard, when they were very young she carefully looked after him. As they were growing older, their respect for each other was infallible.

She eventually graduated from the university in Lincoln. On her way to becoming a registered nurse, she married Thomas Graham, an intern physician. Later they both went to work at John Hopkins Children's Center in Baltimore. Now 31, she was the mother of three children. Although she was co-owner of the Stewart Company, since the tragic death of their parents Richard handled all aspects of the business.

The year following Richard's decision to open a store in Las Vegas was proving to be the most challenging of his life. Starting in January he intensified his efforts to find an ideal Vegas location for a Stewart store. Soon after the search began, he became closely associated with five very diversiied individuals. They were Paula Summers, gorgeous and talented television newscaster; James Forrester, powerful public relations genius; Juan Gonzales, brilliant and savvy hotel manager; Anita Stevens, spirited and dedicated high school counselor; and Robert McGuire, a recovering alcoholic and former homeless person trying to turn his life around for good. While their backgrounds were different, there were likenesses, too. All were well-educated and independent thinkers, and all but one were highly successful in their chosen careers. Within a period of a few months, these five people managed to change Richard's personal and professional life in ways he never could have imagined. The forces of nature that drew them to him and then so closely united them bordered on the mysterious. And there were times when Richard wondered if a supernatural power, like a guardian angel, had taken control of his destiny.

It was Friday in the second week of August, and the sun was rising on a clear, cool morning, but by mid-afternoon massive waves of heat would penetrate every nook and cranny of Omaha. Dressed casually—

short sleeve, pullover sports shirt, pleated trousers, and tasseled loafers — Richard settled into his United Airlines seat and assumed Las Vegas would also be very hot, just not as uncomfortable as a steamy Omaha. At exactly 8:30 the jetliner lifted from Eppley Airfield into the azure sky. From his window he could see landscapes of sprawling business complexes, residential neighborhoods, and arterial flows of traffic.

The metropolitan sights were soon followed by summer's enriched Nebraska farmlands. Most of the crops were fully grown and with harvest season just around the corner, the countryside was teeming with vibrancy. Soon the jetliner entered a bank of clouds and the lush landscape disappeared.

Opening his *USA Today,* Richard glanced at the headlines: Economic Recovery Soaring ... Fed Stabilizes Interest Rates ... UN Global Warming Conference Begins. Turning to the financial section, he read a portion of an article about the stock market's continuing climb. Next, the sports section revealed his St. Louis Cardinals had blasted three home runs while coasting to their fourth straight Busch Stadium victory.

A sugary voice interrupted his reading. "Something to drink this morning, sir?"

His dark brown eyes lifted to the bright blue eyes of a flight attendant whose lapel pin revealed her name, and he responded, "Make mine an orange juice, Katie."

With a wink and a smile she warmly responded, "Just for you."

On two more occasions Katie stopped to check on Richard, first inquiring if he'd like a pillow and the second time commenting casually, "It's going to be a scorcher in Vegas today, so if you're out and about try to stay cool." *Which should be no problem at all for you,* she thought.

Outside the window, the puffy clouds were separating and the jagged skyline of the Rocky Mountains became visible. Eventually the mountainous terrain was joined with mesas and expansive stretches of brown-pink-gold desert sands.

Richard dozed until the pilot's voice filled the cabin. "We are entering our final descent to Las Vegas. Flight personnel, please prepare for landing."

As the jetliner glided gracefully toward the runway at McCarran International Airport, Richard looked out at a megalopolis in the midst of an ongoing metamorphosis of building, tearing down, rebuilding, and expanding. The craft tipped slightly at an angle before touching down with just a few bumps.

Inside the terminal he rode the tram coach leading to the descending escalator and the baggage claim area. There he removed a single travel case from baggage retrieval and continued walking through the terminal. Outside the building a uniformed attendant motioned to him before opening the driver's door of an oxford white Lincoln MKS, its 273-horsepower V6 engine purring like a contented wildcat. The car's interior was opulently outfitted—parchment leather seats, sunroof, eight-inch navigation screen, Sirius satellite radio with a twelve-speaker surround sound system. As usual, the Omaha businessman's arrival in Las Vegas was flawlessly synchronized.

Twenty minutes later on the Strip he pulled into the Paris resort parking and handed his keys to a valet parking attendant.

Inside the hotel he went directly to the guest reception counter where a guest assistant informed him, "Your suite is ready, Richard, and you have two messages."

"Thanks, Evelyn, and would you have Mr. Gonzales call me when he's free?"

Richard proceeded down a hallway before riding an elevator to his thirty-third floor home away from home. Inside the entryway he took two steps down to the attractive, sunken living area which he called his ER, or entertainment room. The room was appointed in soft pastel colors, cream-colored carpet, and upscale furniture—yellow velvet sofa with a matching recliner, glass-enclosed entertainment center, forty-two inch HDTV, designer tables, lamps, and accessories. Brightly colored drapes depicting Parisian scenes enclosed an entire wall of floor-to-ceiling windows. Across the room a maple leather-upholstered bar with two swivel stools was selectively stocked. Behind the bar a service counter opening connected to the kitchenette.

He walked into the master bedroom with its circular bed, quilted satin coverlet, and matching pillow shams. Invitingly nestled in a corner was an elevated blue-tile spa. The bedroom's bathroom, featuring ceramic tile with gold trim, opened to a walk-in closet.

Moving on to the kitchenette, he poured himself a glass of milk before checking his messages. One was a reminder of his noon luncheon conference; the second came from his good friend Anita Stevens. She requested that he call her after school.

His cell phone chimed and the voice of Juan Gonzales, one of the hotel managers, greeted him. "Ricardo, I've reserved a handball court for five o'clock if that works for you."

"It does, and I'm feeling good, so let's make it for lunch tomorrow."

"Consider it done."

After the call Richard returned to the ER and with a remote control he partially opened the window drapes. From there he could see below the morning-peaceful Paris pool, a busy Las Vegas Boulevard, and across the street a bustling Bellagio resort. On the western horizon just beyond the city, a silvery mist hovered at the base of the Spring Mountains and Richard thought, *Seventeen months from now our family resort's lights will be clearly visible from here.*

Tired from his early-morning flight and his two-day Omaha conference with Benjamin and store managers, and with ninety minutes to spare before the Summer Summit meeting, Richard moved across the room and stretched out on the sofa. Soon deep-sleep visions drifted back to the previous November when he first started coming to Vegas. Back then there was neither a sleek Lincoln MKS nor a fancy Paris suite awaiting his arrival. Back then he was using limited travel allowance, staying in regular rooms, and driving thrifty rental cars.

Chapter Two

FOR HIS FIRST STAY AT Paris he'd requested a room with a pool view but ended up on the hotel's east side. When he went back to the guest reception counter to request a change, he was informed no other vacancies were available.

Standing nearby, dapper daytime manager Juan Gonzales stepped in. "Mary, I'll take care of this. Sorry for the inconvenience, Mr. Stewart." The manager's fingers deftly skimmed the keyboard before he nodded and said, "Ah, as I heard a few minutes ago, there is a cancellation coming in on the west side. Much nicer view, so may we reassign you there?"

"I'd appreciate it."

While accompanying Richard back to the elevators, Juan asked if he could be of further assistance.

"Well maybe. Do you know of a good athletic facility around here, preferably a place where they might play some handball?"

The thirty-three-year-old manager's eyes lit up. "Now this is quite a coincidence, because I play handball regularly at the Las Vegas Athletic Club. We're always looking for new talent, and it's not every day we run into a real live handball player from the Midwest. So are you driving?"

"I am and will gladly travel for a game."

"Excellent. The club is an easy ten to fifteen minute drive from here—east on Flamingo Road and then north on Maryland Parkway. Let me guess; you're an open division competitor."

"Nah, I'm lucky to scrape by in the A's back in Nebraska. And you?"

"I just play to stay fit and have fun. Any chance you'd be free to play later this afternoon?"

Richard accepted the invitation, and Juan called his secretary to reserve a court. Such was the beginning of what would become for both men a rewarding and enduring friendship.

While searching for the prize real estate property, Richard stayed at the Paris hotel several times over the next couple of months. During those visits he developed an overall favorable impression of Las Vegas. As he toured various residential and business areas, he discovered the city was very similar to other American cities. He liked the people he was meeting, found them courteous and cooperative. Although he'd never been to the famous Fremont Street Experience, he'd always been impressed with the Strip's glitz and glamour and its world-wide drawing power. As for dining out and entertainment offerings? Incomparable.

On the other hand he'd seen very little of the Strip's nightlife. That was mainly because attending the best shows alone wasn't very appealing. He also didn't care for the traffic congestion and media reports alluding to the city's rising crime problems. All things considered, however, what most interested him were the 300-plus sunshine-filled days, a bonus which made the city one of America's most popular golfing destinations.

To assist in his property search, he enlisted the services of a well-known Vegas real estate broker. After a series of unsuccessful weekend visits, in early January the broker discovered a choice property in a northwest section of the city. Richard quickly made an offer for the site, but it was just as quickly rejected.

When his counterproposal was also refused, his broker advised him, "I'm afraid your expectations—at least what you're willing to pay in a popular golfing community like Summerlin—might never materialize."

Discouraged with the result and the broker's analysis, Richard decided to postpone his expansion plans at least until spring. By then he and Juan had become good friends, and Richard was going to miss their weekly golf and handball outings, lunches, and coffee-break discussions, not to mention the enjoyable social contacts he'd had with Juan's wife and children. He admired the Paris manager's intelligence and enjoyed his sound common sense often colored by his subtle sense of humor. Those latter traits had developed during Juan's youth.

The third of five children, Juan grew up in San Diego where his Mexican parents worked long hours in low-paying jobs just to keep the family going. In spite of the hardships, they instilled in their children a sense of self-respect and a yearning for academic achievement. Juan's high school accomplishments led to a scholarship at San Diego State University where he earned a degree in hotel management. When he met Richard, he and his wife Maria were busy raising their two children—nine-year-old Mario and five-year-old Juanita. The Gonzales home was in an established Henderson neighborhood, a two-story beige stucco structure with professionally designed desert landscaping. The backyard included an in-ground pool, spa, and overlapping waterfall. The residence spoke well of Juan's successful business career.

On the Friday afternoon following Richard's failed offers, the two men played another handball match, which as usual Juan won easily. A fit five feet nine inches and 175 pounds, he was a savvy player, lightning swift and dexterous on the handball court.

In the dressing room after the match Richard asked, "What is it with Hispanics and handball? You read my mind like an open book today."

"Hey, I'm sweating, and besides, you seemed distracted."

As he pulled off his perspiration-soaked shirt, Richard said, "You know, Gonzales, one-sided victories savored with humility are not consoling."

"To be humble is a family tradition."

"Humble as I will be next time we're on the golf course."

"Golf is for the lazy and retired."

"Anyway, this is the last of our weekend sports marathons for a while. Remember our conversation about the promising property my broker discovered? This afternoon I made not one but two respectable offers, and both were turned down."

"Really. Why was that?"

"Another offer was coming in, and suddenly the original price soared into outer space. To top it off, my broker said what I was willing to offer in a golf-premiere area like Summerlin was not practical."

"Hmmm, well I'm sorry to hear of your disappointment. So you probably won't be coming to town for a while? If not, Maria and I and the kids will miss you."

"More than likely I'll start again in the spring. Oh and before I forget, have you heard of a James Forrester from New Horizon Public Relations? I received a message from his assistant requesting me to call her back. She said it was important."

"Sure I've heard of him. New Horizon is just down the street from the hotel and Forrester's their head honcho. I know both Paris and Bally's regularly use their services for promotions. Before leaving town you should find out what he wants."

On their way to the showers Juan continued, "Too bad you're not going to be around. I had an idea I thought might interest you."

"You were going to spot me ten points the next time we play?"

"Ten may not be enough. No, actually there is an attractive young lady friend of mine I wanted you to meet."

"You mean attractive as in beautiful, fun loving, and looking for excitement?

"Now you're reading *my* mind."

"I'm listening."

"Her name is Paula Summers. She just turned twenty-four and works for KBLV television. She's also completing a master's degree at UNLV."

"Tell me more."

"Her goal is to become a news commentator for a major network. Last fall her station was filming a story on women and gambling in Vegas, and in the process I was responsible for connecting her with the Paris and Bally's casino operations. Our personalities clicked and we became good friends."

"Okay."

"Believe me, Ricardo, my little friend is a triple threat—sweet, smart, and sexy. I've matched her up a few times, but every one of those guys fell madly in love with her. Recently she broke up with the last one, and I know she's not seeing anyone right now. She likes to go out and have a good time, but she's not interested in anything or anyone that might interfere with her career. I thought of you because you've said you'd like to see more of the Vegas nightlife. I figure she should be going out socially again, too, but now with you leaving ..."

While toweling down after their showers, Richard said, "About your triple-threat friend, I'm here until Sunday and haven't anything planned, so—"

"Tell you what. She usually finishes work early on Saturday afternoon, so why don't I arrange a get-acquainted meeting? If you like each other, maybe you'll decide to go out tomorrow night."

"You think she'd be available this late?"

"Actually I already told her about you. I said you were a personal friend of mine, a successful businessman who prefers the company of intelligent, nice-looking young ladies. She seemed slightly interested, so if I can put it together, let's plan on meeting at the Le Café around three o'clock."

"Sounds agreeable to me."

"If she can't make it, I'll let you know."

In spite of Juan's encouragement, arranging a social meeting with Ms. Summers was not a sure thing. His latest recommendations, both regular guests at the hotel, had turned out to be, in her words, "utter disasters." The first was a Hollywood bit player who after only a few dates wanted to tie the knot in a Vegas chapel. The second was a Yale business school graduate who she thought was intelligent and fun to be with, until she learned he was also married with a couple of kids.

When Juan called later to tell her more about Richard, she said, "You know what happened with your last two recommendations."

"They were just acquaintances, but this one I know much better, and I promise you he'll make up for my past mistakes. Hey, the guy owns a successful golf and sporting goods company, and for sure he's never been married."

"How old did you say he was?"

"He's twenty-nine."

"And how is it he owns a very successful company at that age? And why has he never been married? This just doesn't sound right."

"Okay, well, he took over the family business several years ago when his parents died in an airplane accident. He isn't married because he's looking for someone so special he calls her his Dream Princess. So far he hasn't found her, but you know there's a lot of pressure on a young dude handling a growing enterprise."

"Uh-huh, I'm sure. But you say you do know him very well."

"I do, my little friend, and I'll swear by him."

With a little more persuasion she agreed to the get-acquainted meeting.

Later, when Richard returned the call from James Forrester at New Horizon, he spoke with Madelline Taylor, the president's assistant.

She said, "We understand you've been trying to find a property for a golf and sporting goods store. If you can make it, we'd like to meet with you in our office at ten o'clock tomorrow morning. Mr. Forrester said I should tell you the meeting may very well prove to be in your best interests."

Ms. Taylor's remarks, along with Juan's assessment of Mr. Forrester and New Horizon, were encouraging enough for Richard to accept the invitation.

That evening he had dinner at the Planet Hollywood next to Paris. While eating alone at the Spice Market buffet, he considered his options for the night. He'd been to a couple of the Strip's popular late-night spots, but didn't care for the smoky atmosphere or their overdose of hard rock and rap music. The son of a college music instructor and a musician himself, his preferences were mixtures of rhythm and blues, Dixieland, and progressive jazz.

He decided to stay where he was and try his luck in the Planet Hollywood casino. Back in Omaha he occasionally went across the river to Council Bluffs, Iowa, where in one of the city's casinos he would try his luck at craps or blackjack table. With little else to do on weekend nights in Vegas, he found himself gambling more than usual. He remained, however, a conservative player who set limits and knew when to quit. That evening he reached his limit at a craps table early and thought, *There must be something more exciting for me to do in this town besides having dinner alone and losing money.*

It hadn't been a good day for Richard, and he wished he was going back to Omaha the next day instead of Sunday. The pessimism was short-lived as he considered the possibilities of his upcoming appointments with Madelline Taylor and Paula Summers.

Chapter Three

THE NEXT MORNING AFTER BREAKFAST Richard walked from Paris, crossed Las Vegas Boulevard, and just south of the Bellagio complex he stopped in front of a stunningly attractive five-story building. At the center of the nicely landscape lawn, a gold-on-black metal sign read Renzcorp Center. The structure's exterior looked like shiny white stucco but was actually dryvit acrylic foam, completely sustainable during summer's most torrid sunlit days. Each of the building's five stories was surrounded with windows and below them three-foot extended cantilevers. At the fifth level the semicircular foyer with a gold-reflecting glass front curved in an arch to the rooftop. As if suspended in space, glittering gold letters above the curvature identified New Horizon PR & E.

Inside the atrium Richard rode the elevator to the fifth floor and a busy New Horizon outer office. A tall, willowy receptionist greeted him and said she'd inform Madelline Taylor of his arrival. While waiting, he glanced around at other office personnel either on their telephones or absorbed by their computers. Twin glass doors at the back of the office bore a gold-leaf lettered sign, J.D. Forrester, President.

Moments later the receptionist Cynthia Miller, the tips of her fiery red hair bouncing mischievously on slim shoulders, returned and escorted Richard into an office adjacent to the president's.

As she rose from her desk chair, Madelline Taylor offered a gracious smile. "Mr. Stewart, thanks for coming on such short notice. Mr. Forrester is out of the office and has asked me to speak with you. Please have a seat."

She was a strawberry blonde with soft hazel eyes, and in her green mint suit, matching heels, and upswept hairstyle, she looked more like forty-years-old than fifty-three. Her floral-scented office was organized and immaculate, and the only item on her glass-top desk was an open laptop computer.

As he sat in the chair in front of her desk, Richard said, "Ms. Taylor, you said our meeting would be in my best interests. Please tell me what you're thinking."

For the next twenty minutes, glancing first over the top of her glasses, then back to her screen while typing, she asked basic questions that he answered straightforwardly. "Can you tell me a little about your company?" … "How many stores do you have?" … "And your plans were to open a golf and sports equipment store here?" … "We understand you've worked as a consultant for several golf course country clubs."

"I have, and may I ask why Mr. Forrester is inquiring?"

"I can't say for sure, but I do know it has something to do with your plans for opening one of your stores here."

"How does he know about me at all?"

"He heard about you from a real estate acquaintance."

"I see. Well at least for now I've decided to postpone my plans."

"Mr. Forrester was so informed by his acquaintance yesterday."

"It just happened yesterday, and I thought such information was considered confidential."

"Well, you know how stories get around. And will you be leaving the city soon?"

"I plan on leaving tomorrow afternoon."

Once her basic questions were answered, Madelline Taylor removed her glasses and sat back in her chair to engage in more casual chitchat.

Fifteen minutes later she concluded, "I've enjoyed talking with you, Mr. Stewart, and I'd say the chances are exceptional you'll be hearing from Mr. Forrester soon."

"Please tell him I'm looking forward to his call."

As he was leaving the Renzcorp Center, Richard felt that although the meeting had been brief and not particularly revealing, Ms. Taylor somehow made him even more curious concerning Mr. Forrester's intentions. That aside, his next appointment, definitely more pulse quickening, would be with Juan's triple-threat friend.

It was three o'clock when he entered Paris's Le Café and was about to discover Juan's appraisal of Paula Summers was not an exaggeration. She was a natural blonde with chiseled features, sky blue eyes, and a sleek figure. In the spring she would complete a master's degree in journalism and media studies at the University of Nevada, Las Vegas. As for her television news position, KBLV's managers would like nothing better than to keep her as a permanent staff member.

Paula was raised in Mississippi. Her mother was a sales associate in a Tupelo mall jewelry store, and her father was the manager of a major chain grocery store. The oldest of three children, she was consistently praised for her good looks and her achievements. In high school among many other honors, she was editor of the school newspaper, homecoming queen, and voted by classmates most likely to succeed.

Similar distinctions continued at Mississippi State University where in her sophomore year she became editor of the college newspaper. Acting on the advice of her journalism advisor, starting her junior year she switched her major to television news. The next semester she was working for the campus television channel, which in turn led to a weekend news reporting position for a Starkville television station. Upon graduating she turned down several television news reporting offers from regional stations, opting instead to work for a master's degree at UNLV.

As she told her parents, "The university is close to the West Coast television market, and how many twenty-four-year-olds with newsroom experience have a master's degree in media journalism? Catching on with a major station out there would be the answer to my prayers."

Inside the Le Café, Richard noticed Juan and his friend being seated in a booth. He joined them and after introductions Richard said, "Juan's told me a lot about you."

Slipping out of her KBLV windbreaker, Paula said, "He's told me a lot about you too, but y'all don't seem old enough to be the president of a major sporting goods company."

Richard chuckled and replied, "We're actually a mid-size company looking for expansion. We decided to come out here because we think Las Vegas is the ideal city for our type of business."

A few minutes more of relaxed discussion prompted Juan to say, "You two will have to excuse me. Paul McCartney's in the showroom at Bally's tonight. They're having some reservation conflicts and have asked me to help out."

In the next hour Richard and Paula talked about her graduate studies, her television work, his opinion of Las Vegas, his golfing interests, and so forth and so on. When she said she had to leave because she was expecting a call, he asked the question he'd been considering since their eyes first met.

"I was just thinking if you haven't made plans for tonight, may I take you to dinner, or perhaps a show?"

She smiled and said, "It just so happens I'm free."

"Wonderful. Now I must confess I know very little about where we could go on such short notice."

"I think I can help you there," she said before opening her billfold to a laminated media card bearing her picture and identification. "If we were going to a show, this card would provide us with seats reserved for media guests, but it's a little late for that. As for dinner, I have a friend who works at a nice restaurant inside The Venetian, so I'll try there. Could you pick me up around five o'clock?"

On the back of one of her business cards she jotted down her address. After leaving the café, he walked with her outside to valet parking. Minutes later a driver arrived with Paula's older, two-door blue Skylark. Richard said he'd see her soon.

In addition to her television position Paula had a journalism scholarship, but graduate school was expensive, and she'd learned to live within a tight budget. She shared a two-bedroom campus apartment with Sheryl Wilson, a sociology graduate student from Salt Lake City. Because of their differing schedules the women seldom crossed paths for any length of time. Paula used little makeup, styled her own hair, and although she couldn't afford an expensive wardrobe, her good looks made Walmart and Target merchandise look like Saks Fifth Avenue top-of-the-line.

When he arrived at her apartment, Richard was surprised with her quick changeover from cute working girl to sophisticated lady on the town. She'd slipped into a slim-fitting scarlet dress with three-quarter-length sleeves and black pumps. Her makeup was minor—a touch of light pink blush and crimson lipstick—and she'd brushed her pretty blond hair straight down between her shoulders. For the unseasonably warm evening she chose a light tan suede coat. After he helped her into the coat, she told him she'd reserved a table for them at The Venetian's Postrio.

On the way to their destination, he began talking about his limited Vegas experiences. "As I told you earlier, my time in Vega has been mostly confined to business, so I seldom stray far from the hotel. Juan told me you're an entertainment insider, so maybe tonight you could broaden my horizon."

True to her journalistic spirit Paula was ready to respond. After leaving the car at valet parking, she led the way to the bridge over the Grand Canal. From there she described in detail the extensive work and high construction costs of the canal, the Doge's Palace, and the Campanile Tower. As they entered the hotel/casino, she pointed to the domed ceiling with its dazzling frescoes framed with complimentary gold molding. Continuing into the building she talked about the resort's versatile entertainment offerings and the Sands Expo, which she said was "one of the most popular convention centers in existence." They rode an escalator to the next level and strolled along the Grand Canal lined with a variety of attractive stores, restaurants, and boutiques.

"Extraordinary shopping centers like these," she said, "have become a major attraction for every successful resort in Las Vegas." On a canal overpass they paused to watch a young gondolier serenading his passengers.

"As you can see" she said, "they didn't miss a thing in making this place delightfully reminiscent of Venice."

They entered the vast replica of St. Mark's Square where Wolfgang Puck's Postrio restaurant was busy with people waiting in line. Advised of their arrival time, a hostess escorted them to a table overlooking the entertainment-filled square. During dinner a short distance from their table, a female pianist pleased a circle of admirers with a lilting version of *Rhapsody in Blue.* Other spectators tried to detect the minuscule movement of a human statue shrouded in a white robe. In a distant corner of the square, performers in folk costumes danced gaily to a small band's polka rendition.

Richard lifted his palms and said, "Everywhere you look, there's a different type of entertainment going on. It's like a carnival out there."

"It is, and now you can see why The Venetian is universally popular."

"You really do know a lot about this place, don't you?"

"I should. After all, I'm a television news specialist, and The Venetian often serves as my story base."

After finishing their meals, Richard checked his watch and said, "It's still early. Would you mind if we went somewhere else? Maybe we could find a nice place for a drink and more conversation."

"That's fine and I know of a perfect place. Have you been to Wynn's?"

"No, but I've heard a lot about it."

"It's right up the street, so whenever you're ready."

Must be my lucky night to be with this charming little news lady who, like me, isn't in a hurry to say good night. Thank you, Juan Gonzales, wherever you are.

Twenty minutes later as they entered Wynn's, Richard was in awe of the gorgeous floral displays, lighted trees, glass tile columns, and artistically designed patterns embellishing the ceramic tile floors. He responded, "This is without question the most enchanting hotel entrance I've ever seen."

"I think you'll find everything about Wynn's is enchanting."

Paula led the way to the Parasol Up lounge, then down an escalator to the Parasol Down terrace bar. A receptionist seated them at a water front table, and while he savored a glass of merlot and she a margarita, they had a nice view of the Parasol's lighted waterfalls, warmly resplendent in their purple, pink, orange, and silver variations.

Paula said, "Juan mentioned that you two play a lot of golf. Has he told you about the premiere course they have here? Just down a hallway upstairs there's a viewing balcony overlooking some of the playing area."

"He said it's inviting all right, but also expensive."

"He was right on both counts—stunning landscapes with fountains, waterfalls, and exotic wildlife—truly a golfer's paradise. It costs $500 to play a round, but no one seems to complain."

"For five hundred bucks it better be a paradise. Not to change the subject, but being here makes me think back to when the Wynn enterprise lost Danny Gans. Although I never had the opportunity to see him in person, I've heard his show was the best in town. Entertainers like Mr. Gans have always appealed to me, but that's because I'm also an impressionist."

"You are, seriously?"

Leaning over so that only she could hear, he sang in a gravelly voice, "Ya gotta start off each day widda song,

Now even when things go wrong,

Why, you'll look bettah,

You'll even feel bettah ..."

"Jimmy Durante. That really wasn't too bad."

In a scratchy Bill Clinton voice he continued, "I also do former presidents, if, that is, an independent counsel isn't investigating me for falsely impersonating."

"Well, I'll be, another Danny Gans before my very eyes. May I interview you, Mr. Stewart?"

"Inspirations from my Omaha high school talent show days."

The getting-to-know-you dialogue continued until midnight.

While driving her back to her apartment, he said, "My business here is finished, and I'm not sure when I'll be back. When I do return, and I'm sure I will, I'd like to see you again."

"I would like that, too."

Following their unusually interesting first date, Richard was tempted to kiss her good night at her doorstep. Recalling Juan's advice not to take anything for granted, instead he simply took hold of her hands and said, "Thanks for going out of your way to make it a memorable night. I loved the dinner, and The Venetian, and Wynn's, and within a few hours you taught me more about Vegas entertainment than I've learned on my own for a couple of months."

After they said good night, Richard couldn't stop thinking about her. *Juan was right. She really is sweet, smart, and sexy. And there's an air of confidence about her, not arrogance, but a quality of assurance in everything she does. Now I wish I wasn't going home tomorrow.*

Admiring an attractive woman's attributes was not unusual for Richard, but to be quite so infatuated on a first date definitely was.

Chapter Four

O N SUNDAY AFTERNOON RICHARD WAS unaffected by the gloomy cloudiness engulfing the Omaha-bound jetliner. His memory was recalling scenes from Saturday's interesting events—the promising interview with Madelline Taylor, the get-acquainted meeting with Paula, and of course that memorable night on the town. He reminded himself that on Monday morning he'd have to set aside such pleasantries and concentrate on a backlog of company business.

As owner and president of the Stewart Golf and Sporting Goods Company, Richard thoroughly enjoyed the ever-changing demands and challenges of competitive retail sales markets.

In the mid-1970s his father Samuel, a recent graduate from the University of Nebraska, opened a downtown Omaha store specializing in the sale of golf equipment, accessories, and apparel. Although the store was relatively small, profits rose substantially during the first two years, enough so that he considered initiating a mail-order service. Two important factors—golf's increasing popularity and Omaha's central distribution location—convinced him the potential was there. The projected cost for a mail-order department would approach $50,000, a prodigious sum for an aspiring young businessman.

Sam, a former varsity golfer at the university in Lincoln, was highly respected by friends and associates in the Lincoln-Omaha golfing communities. Confident his new service would succeed, he thought of offering investment shares to a number of his colleagues. His expansion package would include an attractive rate of interest and a full return of principal in five years. If his venture failed, he knew he could face bankruptcy and the loss of some good friends. In the end his aspirations won out, and it didn't take him long to acquire the necessary investment capital.

Sam's wife Margaret was a piano and music instructor at UNO. In her spare time she assisted him in the preparation of mail-order catalogs which were sent to golf centers and enthusiasts throughout the nation. The promotional theme promised:

Discount Prices!

Courteous Service!

Prompt Deliveries!

Satisfaction Guaranteed!!!

Response to their promotion was so positive that in the first year they hired five new sales-distribution employees.

In the midst of those busy times Margaret gave birth to their first child, Elizabeth Ann. Two years later Richard Michael was born.

Three years later the company had expanded to include a wide range of sports merchandise. Within six years satellite stores were established in Lincoln, Norfolk, and Grand Island. Within ten years, with all business-connected debts paid, the main retail store moved to a large facility in west central Omaha, and an operational center opened on the twenty-third floor of the downtown Woodmen Building. By then the firm had departments for sales, promotion, production, and distribution. Its reputation for quality merchandise and timely customer service had spread like a dry-grass prairie wildfire.

For more than twenty years the organization prospered without a major setback. Then came the airplane crash that took the lives of Samuel and Margaret, an incalculable tragedy for Elizabeth and Richard, for family, and for close friends. Not the least of those affected were Stewart employees. As Richard stepped into his father's position, they wondered if the firm's reputation for staff integrity would remain. Soon his leadership talents calmed their fears and restored their confidence.

Two years later he chose Benjamin Anderson to be his vice president. They'd known each other since they were children and took pride in their mixed-race, best-friend relationship. Benjamin handled the firm's fiscal policies and often acted as a company spokesman. He also introduced the firm's Internet online sales services, an addition that in time would increase the payroll to seventy-five full-time employees.

With the winter season established, Richard's life was unfolding at its normal pace. Helen Baxter, who lived in a condominium not far from the Stewart residence, had been the family housekeeper for twenty years. She was like a close, caring relative to Richard and kept his life running like clockwork—house spic-and-span, clothes washed and ironed, dinner waiting when he home came from work.

Monday through Friday he was in bed by 11:00, rose in the morning before 7:00, and was in his office by 8:30. His work week consisted of five and a half days. Like his father, he routinely played handball at the downtown YMCA, and on weekends he worked out at a fitness center near the Westroads Mall. He was an active member of the Chamber of Commerce, Sertoma Club, and the more social Happy Hollow Club. Casual entertainment included dating some of Omaha's most eligible ladies and playing his trombone for The Improv, a jazz ensemble that played Saturday nights in Old Market downtown. More often than not on Sunday morning he attended services at the First United Methodist Church.

Being an only son played an important part in his plan to find and marry the woman of his dreams. That was because he wanted several children—at least two boys to carry on the family name.

To assist in the company's clerical operations, he depended on his fifteen-year veteran secretary Melanie Thomas and her two full-time assistants.

On Tuesday afternoon Melanie buzzed his office. "You have a call from a Mr. Forrester on line three."

Richard was greeted by a gritty sandpaper voice. "Mr. Stewart, I'm James Forrester from New Horizon here in Las Vegas. Sorry I missed you Saturday. So tell me, how are things in Omaha these January days?"

"Well, Mr. Forrester, if you don't mind a little snow and below zero wind chills."

"Ouch, don't remind me. I lived with that stuff years ago back in Massachusetts. I called because I'd like to meet with you personally."

"Your assistant said you might be calling."

"As I'm sure she told you, our firm specializes in public relations affairs and entertainment promotions. Right now we're also entering the developmental stages of a new resort, and I think we've reached a level of progress that could use some advice from a person with your background."

"Please go on."

"If possible I'd like for you to come out here to learn about our plans. For now, try to envision a family resort nestled in a breathtaking valley oasis. It truly is a fantastic setting at the base of some spectacularly beautiful mountains."

"Ms. Taylor said you knew I was interested in opening a store in Las Vegas. And please, call me Rich or Richard."

"And me, James or J.D. How about coming out here this weekend? We're having a Friday luncheon, at which time I'll be meeting with my 15-member resort committee. They are a highly specialized group and we'll be discussing our resort plans. If you like what you hear, I hope you'll want to learn more. Naturally we'll cover all expenses."

A picture-in-picture image of Paula Summers prompted Richard's quick response. "I'm sure I can make it."

"My secretary checked the Omaha United flight times, and if you wouldn't mind an 8:30 morning departure, you'd be here easily in time for the meeting."

"That's my usual time for flying to Vegas."

"Very good. We'll have a Hertz vehicle awaiting you at the McCarran car rental. We understand you've been staying at the Paris hotel, so we'll make arrangements there, too, unless you'd prefer somewhere else."

"Paris will be fine."

"I'll look forward then to seeing you this coming Friday."

After the call Richard shrugged his shoulders and smiled. He'd known promoters who could be motivating but were also dominating, and judging from their brief conversation, James Forrester certainly seemed like the type. On the other hand, it was interesting a prominent Vegas promoter wanted him to come all the way out there for a meeting. The possibility of seeing Paula Summers again? Even more interesting.

That evening while catching up on e-mail in his library study, he called Juan to reveal his weekend plans. His next call was to Paula.

"Good evening," she answered in her professional newscasting voice, "this is Paula Summers, on assignment for NBC News."

"Hi, Rich Stewart, remember me? The Venetian and Wynn's? Did you say NBC News?"

She snickered and said, "Sorry. I was sure you were Lynn, a co-worker calling back from the station. How could I have forgotten The Venetian and Wynn's? We were just there. So where are you?"

"In Omaha."

"Omaha is much too far away."

"But I plan to be in Las Vegas this Friday."

"Mmmm, now that sounds much better."

"You said when I returned I could call on you."

"And what brings you back so soon?"

"Fortunately an unexpected business invitation. Any chance you'd be free Friday or Saturday night?"

"I promise to keep *both* nights open."

Following the call Richard took a deep breath, leaned back in his chair, and once again smiled. *This is like June in January. An all-expense paid Vegas weekend and two nights on the town with none other than triple-threat Ms. Paula Summers. Sweet.*

Chapter Five

WHILE WORKING IN HIS OMAHA office the next morning, Richard received a call from Madelline Taylor regarding the upcoming meeting. To allow for his Friday-to-Sunday stay, he worked late a couple of evenings and arrived in Vegas as scheduled. Awaiting him at the McCarran rental center was a shiny red Ford Fusion. Then at the hotel registration counter every guest detail had been attended to. His room would be similar to his last one, but this time his luggage was whisked away by a prepaid hotel steward.

As soon as he reached his room, he called Juan's office, but his secretary said he was out of the hotel. She also said at her boss's request she'd reserved a handball court for them later in the afternoon.

After unpacking, Richard left Paris, crossed the street, and continued walking down the boulevard to the Renzcorp Center. This time inside the New Horizon offices, Madelline herself greeted him.

"Nice to see you back so soon, Mr. Stewart. We have a few minutes, so may I show you around Mr. Forrester's office?"

From the moment they entered the president's workplace, Richard was struck by its spaciousness and state-of-the-art decor—a combination of carpet, tile, and oak flooring, polished oak woodwork, finely textured walls and ceilings. Mr. Forrester's glass-top desk and plush beige leather chair were surrounded by three smaller leather chairs.

Richard said, "This has to be the most expansive and most appealing executive office I've ever seen."

Madelline nodded her head. "And the wall to your right divides it from an equally impressive conference room."

They moved beyond the desk into the rounded dome part of the office. Its features included a light blue velour davenport and matching easy chairs, wall-extended television, and a wet bar with a complete fruit juice dispenser. Sunlight from the circular dome windows cast a relaxing blue-green light, and visible from the wraparound windows were partial views of Planet Hollywood, Paris, Bally's, the Bellagio, Caesars, and the Flamingo.

"He calls this the Time-out Corner," Madelline said, "a place to sit back and unwind during and after long business sessions."

"I've seen mini bars in business offices before, but never one featuring fruit juices."

"Mr. Forrester is an advocate of healthy living and would never mix his business with liquor."

Across from the Time-out Corner, six tiers of shelves, a computer desk, and a table with several chairs served as the office library. The shelves were stocked with Renzcorp and New Horizon texts and manuals, business newspapers, and magazines.

Next to the library was a revolving door with gold lettering on each glass panel: Versailles Conference Chambers.

"That's where we'll be meeting," Madelline said.

Richard asked about the name Versailles and she explained, "As well as being an excellent promoter, J.D. is a serious student of American history. He thinks lessons learned from the past should serve as models for today's political and business ventures. For example, he believes the Second World War would have been avoided had the First World War Treaty of Versailles representatives accepted President Wilson's peace plans. He thinks their unwillingness to act in good faith and unduly punish Germany was the most costly mistake in world history. Such results, he will tell you, should serve as a reminder to 'make decisions that will promote a bright and prosperous future for everyone.' That's a direct quote; hence the name Versailles."

Through the revolving door they entered the chambers. This half of the dome's wraparound windows offered partial views of the prodigious City Center, the Monte Carlo, MGM, and New York–New York. Near the front of the chambers, a U-shaped table was surrounded by fifteen evenly spaced, high-back leather chairs with a laptop at each setting. At the center of the table an oak lectern and a twelve-foot-square high-resolution screen awaited the speaker. Most of the committee and J.D.'s guests were casually moving about or engaged in small group discussions.

Madelline informed Richard, "The committee members are from various locations throughout the Southwest. Each one of them was chosen by Mr. Forrester for his or her talents and organizational skills."

She pointed to a guest chair with Richard's name, and then directed his attention to Mr. Forrester. The New Horizon president was obviously in a pleasant mood as he circulated among his committee members and guests.

Recently turned fifty-two, he was over six feet tall with body builder proportions. His square jaw, broad nose, and a thin scar over one eyebrow gave Richard reason to think he'd probably competed in one or more physical contact sports. Invasions of gray around the temples of his curly dark hair, his thick, but closely trimmed mustache, and his penetrating dark eyes combined to make him ruggedly handsome.

Richard's first impression was he'd rather face a coiled cobra than an angry James Forrester.

Of Italian and Greek descent, James was the eldest of six children raised in a community south of Boston. His father owned and operated a cafe specializing in Italian entrees. Though his parents were caring and compassionate, they were rock-solid firm regarding responsibility. They expected their children to excel in school and when they became teenagers to also work weekends in the café.

James graduated from Boston University and Harvard Business School. His first position was with Atlantic Public Relations of Boston. Three years later he was recognized as the firm's most effective public relations executive. The next year he was lured from APR by billionaire business magnate David L. Renzberg. Headquartering in Atlantic City, Mr. Renzberg's corporation represented a conglomerate of insurance companies that entrusted to Renzcorp enormous investment capital. The corporation's key objectives were (1) to increase their clients' assets through ownership and management of major metropolitan shopping malls, and (2) to establish influential public relations and entertainment centers in prime U.S. locations.

It had been fifteen years since Renzcorp assigned James to preside over New Horizon PR & E. Originally located a few miles from the Strip, its present location on Las Vegas Boulevard was entering its second year.

The Vegas business climate presented outstanding challenges for J.D.'s promotional talents and tireless energy. During the Great Recession years he was a guiding light for many of the resort, hotel, and casino establishments. While gambling revenues were shrinking substantially, he encouraged their leaders to promote other forms of entertainment like shows, shopping facilities, and sporting events. He further convinced them to substantially lower prices for guest accommodations and entertainment events. At the same time he measurably lowered his own firm's promotional rates and fees. Because of his strategies, a major portion of his clients survived the recession and were prospering again.

James was pleased that along with the strong Vegas economic recovery, a less greedy and more regulated business climate had also evolved. The less stressful atmosphere helped him convince David Renzberg and his board of directors that conditions were perfect for the development of a family golf and entertainment resort.

Noticing Madelline's and Richard's arrival, the president walked over and shook hands. "I see by Maddy's complimentary description you're Rich Stewart. Was your flight and arrival satisfactory?"

"They were, and thanks for the accommodations."

"You'll be seated with our other guests behind the conference table. When my presentation is over—if you don't mind—I'll be introducing you to them."

As Mr. Forrester was walking away, his overall demeanor, including his confident athletic stride, reminded Richard of someone familiar from the past. He couldn't quite make the connection, but his memory would continue the search.

During the informal luncheon Madelline introduced Richard to several committee members. However, the moment Mr. Forrester took his place at the lectern, members and guests went as one to their assigned places.

Looking relaxed and confident, he scanned his audience as he said, "I'm honored to be with you once again. Each of you is an accomplished professional in your chosen field, and you are my *sine qua non* team, my commission on a mission, and it will be our unified goal to create America's finest family entertainment resort."

From a table in front of the lectern Madelline activated onto the screen a series of family-oriented golf scenes, and Mr. Forrester continued, "It's difficult to imagine not too many years ago the game of golf was predominantly the leisure choice of doctors, lawyers, and the more affluent. As we know, today's golfing clientele includes factory and construction workers, taxi drivers, teachers, ministers, and an influx of young people that just keeps on growing.

"More and more people are now seeking family-oriented leisure lifestyles. It's an evolution we think will lead to a new and prolonged era. The influences of the old theme 'What happens in Vegas stays in Vegas' will not disappear, but there is also an undeniable momentum building for a more family-friendly option."

As the speaker moved from the lectern to one side of the screen, Richard's memory suddenly kicked in. *Now I know who he resembles— none other than Rocky Marciano, the old heavyweight champ.*

Marciano had been one of his father's favorite sports heroes, and Richard recalled as a child watching his dad's movie collection of Rocky's title fights. *Marciano, whose unbridled intent was to send his opponent far into the outer galaxy. No doubt about it, Forrester looks and moves very much like The Rock.*

Madelline entered more color graphics onto the screen and Mr. Forrester continued. "These illustrations demonstrate why our city is the vacation, convention, and cash capital of the entire United States. With 300 days of sunshine and year-round golfing opportunities, we believe we can also become arguably the undisputed golf capital of America. That's why we're making the sport our resort's central attraction.

"There are already over fifty golf courses located in and around the city, but most are too expensive or inaccessible for our visitors and many of our hometown residents. Our plan is to make our resort's golfing opportunities more accessible and more affordable for everyone.

"The resort will be nestled between two signature golf courses. One will be the Country Club reserved for professionals and more highly skilled golfers. The other will be the Public Links course serving the vast majority of our customers. Each course will be challenging; each will offer breathtaking landscapes; each will offer fees designed to attract average-income folks." He again scanned his audience before he added, "Now wait just a minute. Did I say two golf courses, one for the pros and one for the amateurs? Ladies and gentlemen, that is exactly what we're planning."

There was a pause for audience discussion until a committeewoman from Palm Springs rose to ask, "You said last week the resort will be at a location on the city's west side. Any chance we could see it today?"

"Yes, you definitely can. If you want to see it this afternoon, to avoid school zone slowdowns, drive west on Charleston Boulevard past the 215 beltway to Desert Foothills Drive, and then turn north until you reach Alta. There's not a lot of traffic out there and parking is never a problem. The four beautiful mountains you'll observe can be seen from all over Las Vegas, but believe me when you see the entire area up close, you can just *feel* the resort potential.

"Now if you can be patient, at this very moment road graders are clearing an access road to those mountains. And tomorrow we'll be taking a New Horizon bus directly to the site for your up-close observations. At that time we'll be able to partially drive through the winding valley separating the second and third mountains. Development of this valley will become the focal point of the resort."

Madelline showed an artist's preliminary drawing of the resort on the screen and guided the arrow along the base of the mountains.

"As you can see," J.D. said, "portions of the Country Club course will extend onto the early inclines of the mountain hillsides as high as zoning laws will allow. I'm still working on the finite details, and I'm pleased to report that this morning we learned we are close to acquiring the final five thousand acres needed to begin our work."

He paused for more audience interaction until a guest from Phoenix rose to inquire, "You're saying it will be a golf and family entertainment resort. Just how family-oriented do you mean?"

"That's a good question. While golf is our central theme, we'll have designer swimming pools, lighted outdoor and indoor tennis courts, a twenty-four lane bowling center, and a variety of attractions for the younger folks. There will be movie and entertainment theaters, indoor and outdoor sports arenas. Gourmet restaurants will offer culinary favorites from around the world. One of our most novel attractions will be our shopping mall village which you will see situated along the shorelines of the man-made lake. Some of the village stores will be budget-conscious outlets.

"The last time we met I said I'd have some other important news for you today. In addition to the resort attractions, we will be developing a residential community around and just beyond the golf courses. It will consist of moderately priced single-family dwellings, duplexes, triplexes, and town houses. Even the residences located directly on the golf courses will be priced to attract middle-income buyers.

"What we're not intending is to make the community a rich man's paradise or a pricey senior development. That was the Vegas real estate trademark for too long, and unfortunately it negatively affected the economic base for the majority. Along with our continuing economic recovery, we'll be practicing here in Las Vegas what many of our nation's leaders are working for—namely, a thriving American middle class."

This time there was no interaction from the committee and guests. They seemed mesmerized as the speaker emphasized, "Do these expectations sound too idealistic, like a far-fetched dream? If that's what you're thinking, may I remind you the greatest period of American growth and prosperity came following World War II. In the next three decades the American working middle class enjoyed their finest lifestyles. With that in mind, we intend to make our resort and the surrounding community a twenty-first century middle-class dream come true."

His speech completed, the president opened the floor for more questions.

A committeeman from Los Angeles rose to ask, "Is it true the twin hotels will be designed to match some of the largest and most expensive on the Strip?"

"Not nearly so in either aspect. We'll have two fifteen-story hotels, and each will accommodate approximately fifteen hundred guests. Again, we're striving for quality not quantity, quality along with prices average Americans can afford."

When the question-answer session ended forty-five minutes later, the speaker introduced each of his fifteen committee members. Then he said, "Before we leave, I want you to meet Richard Stewart, owner and president of the Stewart Golf and Sporting Goods Company. Those of you who frequent the fairways may be familiar with his Omaha-based mail-order and Internet marketing services."

In response to the welcoming applause, Richard rose, nodded, and smiled.

"I'm pleased to announce," Mr. Forrester continued, "we will be considering one of his retail stores to be our sports merchandise supplier."

The announcement surprised and thrilled Richard. As committee members stepped up to wish him well, he was still tingling from head to toe. The president was the last to shake hands and said, "We'd be pleased if you'd join us for our official on-site inspection tomorrow."

"I wouldn't miss it, and I want you to know I'm honored we're in the running as your sports merchandise store."

"You definitely are. Oh and by the way, from now on you'll be driving one of our Lincoln MKS cars. So tell me, from what you heard today what is your general impression?"

"I think your resort and community concepts are exciting and thought provoking. If you don't mind, James, I'm curious to know exactly how you heard about our company."

"It happened I was on the golf course with one of our firm's real estate brokers who, by an amazing coincidence, has also been representing you. He said he'd been trying to find a prime property for one of your stores but hadn't been successful. He also said you'd served as a consultant in the building and promotion of golf course enterprises in and around Omaha. That really caught my attention."

"I have been involved with several."

"To be honest with you, Rich, it's not easy to find a person with your overall management experience. I mean someone who could efficiently guide us through the remainder of our early planning. I'm referring not only to the golf courses but to the entire resort. If you will agree to come to work for us in an advisory capacity for a few weekends, I have an office waiting for you right down the hall. Because I'm often out of town during the week, our resort meetings will usually be on Saturday and occasionally on Friday. It would require extensive air travel and time away from home, but be assured we'll do everything possible to make it worth your while."

A new sidetrack vision of Paula encouraged Richard's response. "I'm single and accustomed to weekend flying."

"We could arrange a private jet."

"Thanks, but for personal reasons I fly only with the major airlines."

"That's fine. In our business we represent nearly all of the airlines, and they in turn provide us with special privileges. Except for major holidays or emergencies, securing a reservation should never pose a problem."

"You said the go-ahead depends on the final acquisition of five thousand acres of land."

"Don't worry. I'm confident we'll get what we're seeking. Oh yes, almost forgot, I played with a set of your company's trademark golf clubs last week at Lake Tahoe."

"You did? And your score?"

"Not commensurate with the quality of your clubs. You see, I have these interplanetary drives from the tee, but my approaches and putting game are considerably less inspiring. In response to my frustrations, I've been known to whack a tree or toss one of my irons into the nearest pond. Your company could get rich off guys like me."

The New Horizon president didn't seem so pompous anymore; instead, he seemed more like the personable, highly respected promoter Juan purported him to be. *And his entire resort community will be designed to attract middle-income people. Now that's one for the books!*

Chapter Six

LATER IN THE AFTERNOON AS Richard entered Paris registration, he noticed Juan moving from one assistant to the next. When he spotted Richard, he took a break and they walked over to the Le Café. Over soft drinks Richard revealed highlights of his luncheon meeting.

Juan responded, "So he may want one of your stores at his resort. In their promotional efforts, they must have been impressed with the recent resort successes and decided to join the party. And with golf as their central theme, it could be a promising development for you. All of which means you'll be spending more time here. Very good."

"As I said, while he didn't guarantee he'd choose us, I'm thinking my serving as a consultant might give us the inside track. And if he does select us, maybe he'd be willing to share the costs for building a new store."

"You never know about these public relations whiz kids. They have enormous power and will use it when they really want something. Let him tell you because he might even offer to finance the building of your store."

"Such an arrangement would be entirely acceptable."

"By the way, I've learned New Horizon is the avant-garde public relations firm in the entire Southwest, and Forrester is considered irreplaceable by everyone in the entertainment genre. It's rumored any one of the controlling interests would give him a ton of stock if he'd jump ship."

"That's also encouraging."

Juan changed the subject. "So tell me, how did things go with Paula? Where'd you go? What'd you do?"

"Well, we had a good time, went to The Venetian for dinner, then to Wynn's for drinks and conversation."

"And what did you think of her?"

"Eh, she's okay."

Juan chuckled as he said, "Yeah, right. When she dresses up and walks that slinky cat walk of hers, every eye is keenly focused."

"I agree, she is what you said, a triple threat."

"And exceptionally talented. Wait until you see her on the television screen. Remember I said she produced a story in our Paris and Bally's casinos? It focused on the different roles women play in gambling, and she produced and narrated the entire thing. The *Las Vegas Review* compared her on-camera delivery to an up-and-coming Mary Hart. Incidentally, she's opposed to gambling, became more so after working on the gambling story. During her preparation she said the station's managers told her to stay away from gambling negatives and make it a lighthearted presentation. So she did."

"I can't wait to see her in action."

"So you'll be seeing more of her?"

"I'm planning to, for sure."

"I had a feeling you two would connect. May I remind you, if you find yourself falling for her, don't move too quickly. She's been pursued often and as every one of her would-be lovers discovered, she's not interested in anything or anyone that might interfere with her career."

The moment Richard returned to his Paris room, he called her.

"Hi," she answered, "I was waiting for you."

"How'd you know it was me?"

"You said you'd be calling at four, and Juan said you're always prompt. So you had an interview this afternoon."

"I did."

"Maybe you can fill me in tonight."

"And what about tonight—got everything planned?"

"I do. First I thought we'd go to dinner, and then I'd like to stop by the Forum Shops in Caesars. Along the way, you can tell me all about your meeting. As for dinner, what are some of your favorite menu selections?"

"On Friday night back home it's usually seafood."

"Good, now there's an excellent seafood restaurant across from the Monte Carlo. Their fresh ocean catches are among the best, so I'll make a reservation."

That evening following dinner, they moved on to the Forum Shops. In that setting she was looking forward to showing him how she prepared for one of her television features. Because of its cosmopolitan environment, similar to the Grand Canal Shoppes, the Forum was one of her favorite venues . As they joined the hundreds of shoppers and visitors strolling along the Roman Appian Way, they took time to admire the sculptured

Neptune and Bacchus fountains, statues of legendary Roman gods and goddesses and Roman statesmen.

"Just look at all these people," Paula said. "Many come here and spend way beyond their means—to impress someone, or to endear themselves to someone, or simply because they're caught up in a Vegas spending mood. Next week while you're in Omaha, I'll be working on a story about why so many Vegas visitors come to the Forum. From fifteen to twenty short interviews I'll select the most interesting and screenworthy. Then I'll narrow those down to the best seven or eight."

"Your work requires more preparation than I thought."

"Tonight I'll do those preliminary interviews to show you how I work. You've heard about the power of the media? I'll demonstrate just how true it is. Naturally with a news camera crew I'll attract more attention, but even without them once the person I will be interviewing is informed that I'm a television newswoman, he or she will nearly always be eager to respond. I'll tell them I'm doing a research survey, and if chosen they will be on television. Now if you'll sit down on the bench over by the fountain, I'll get started."

In the next twenty minutes he watched her interview quite a few people. Following the last interview she rejoined him and asked, "So what did you think?"

"You were right. They seemed to enjoy responding. And how long will the finished story be?"

"It will fill a three-minute time frame."

"That's all?"

"You'd be surprised what you can accomplish in three minutes of television time. My one-on-one celebrity interviews with commercials will fill fifteen- and thirty-minute time segments."

"That sounds even more challenging."

"Not really, Rich. I feel comfortable in all of my assignments. I guess you could say television reporting is in my blood."

Continuing their walk, they passed retail outlets including Caesars Exclusively, Tiffany and Company, Louis Vitton, and Estée Lauder. Inside a women's fashion store window, a pair of pink leather heels with narrow, criss-crossing straps captured Paula's attention. With the window display lights assisting, the silver, black, and lavender stones embossed within the straps made the shoes scintillatingly attractive.

"Aren't they adorable?" she said. "They're Manolo Blahnik's, and a perfect match for my very favorite pink evening dress."

"Let's check them out."

Inside the store a sales clerk revealed the price tag to Paula. As they were leaving the store, she said to Rich, "Four hundred and forty-five dollars is just slightly out of my price range."

He made a mental note of the store and the shoes.

At an outside patio along the walkway they stopped for ice cream shakes, and again Richard recalled his afternoon meeting.

"Turns out New Horizon is planning to build a huge family entertainment resort between two signature golf courses. The intriguing news for me is that their president, James Forrester, is considering our company as his on-site sporting goods store."

She looked pleasantly surprised and said, "How exciting. I think everyone involved in Vegas entertainment recognizes Mr. Forrester's promotional successes."

"He also asked me to come here a few more weekends. He wants me to be his consultant for not only the golf courses, but for the resort in general. I've done that several times back in Nebraska, Kansas, and Iowa."

"And what did you tell him?"

"I said I would. What can I lose?"

"It won't interfere with your Omaha business?"

"If assisting him leads to a new store, I'll gladly spend more weekends here. The timing is right because winter is our slowest time."

"So at least for a while you'll be spending your weekends here?"

"It all depends on one final land purchase he's confident he will make. Now I've been thinking, inasmuch as you're a television news specialist and you know so much about Vegas entertainment, would you be willing to act as *my* consultant? If I'm going to assist in the planning of a new resort, I'd like to know everything there is to know."

"Hmmm, it does sound like an interesting assignment. I accept."

"Paula Summers, you just answered my prayers."

Relevant to hopes, prayers, and other inspirations, Richard now was certain a guardian angel was taking direct aim at him. First he met Juan, a good handball partner, and they quickly became good friends. Juan introduced him to Paula, and for Richard it was love at first sight. Then in a city of over two million people served by hundreds of realtors, James Forrester heard about him and his company through a *mutual* broker. Mr. Forrester invited him to Vegas and informed his committee he's considering a Stewart store for his new resort. And to make that little prize more likely to happen, he offered Richard a temporary, but well-paying position.

Mind-boggling events, Richard thought, *yet somehow strangely connected. And because of it all, looks as if I'll be seeing more and more of this charming little lady who just may be my one and only Dream Princess.*

Chapter Seven

IN EARLY FEBRUARY TEMPERATURES IN southern Nevada climbed into the seventies, and Mother Nature responded vivaciously. Mountain slopes and foothills glistened in dew-fresh silvery greens, and the Mojave Desert floors were replenished with color-laden sagebrush and cactus. Overnight the blossoming fruit trees and flowers—larkspur, pink cherry, Indian paintbrush, and shooting stars—contributed their iridescence.

Except for an occasional game of golf, Richard had little opportunity to notice the early renaissance. He spent most of his weekend hours assisting architects and contractors working on resort planning and blueprints.

Upon his latest arrival at Paris, Evelyn handed him a New Horizon envelope marked Priority!!! Inside he found a $2,000 New Horizon check with an attached note.

For services rendered thus far. We're looking forward to more of your invaluable insights.

James Forrester

When the two men met in the president's office that afternoon, Richard said, "I want to thank you for the check, James. Now tell me what I've done to deserve such generosity."

"Consider it a bonus for what our architects are calling your creative and very adaptable concepts."

"Surely not worth that much."

"To be honest with you, Rich, I'm also about to ask a special favor. First, however, let's move into the conference room. I want to show you something new on our latest blueprints."

Inside the Versailles Chambers J.D. activated the big screen and guided the arrow to a resort area circled in blue. "This represents the final parcel of property between the second and third mountains we purchased late yesterday. All that remains will be the removal of minor legal stipulations."

"Which means the real work begins."

"Exactly. I've decided to name the resort the Monte Vista. It's not an uncommon name, but considering the magnificent views our guests will enjoy, it couldn't be more appropriate. I also have some special news for you. With your permission and in compliance with your specifications, we will be assuming the building costs for a Stewart Company store. As we get closer to the construction phases, you and I will decide on the best location."

Richard took a deep breath before he said, "That is without question exceptionally good news."

"I thought you'd approve. Now about that special favor. Would you be willing to act as the resort's temporary program director?" Defensively raising his hand, J.D. added, "Not full time, of course. You'd be here only on the weekends until we find a permanent director. It looks as if it may take us a while, but if you will provide us with your expertise until then, it would be mean a lot to us."

Richard smiled and said, "James, with the construction of a Stewart store at the resort, I'll do whatever's required. Could we set a deadline of, say, June 1? As I'm sure you know, that's crunch time back home."

"By then I'm certain we will have found a competent full-time director."

"Last week at our managers' meeting I mentioned you were considering us for a store."

"And what was their response?"

"They reacted favorably, but naturally had questions I couldn't answer. One thing I'll need will be the choice of staying in Omaha whenever they might need me."

"Certainly. You have tremendous respect for your Omaha staff, don't you? Such a level of appreciation doesn't just happen overnight."

"When my father started the business, he knew selling golf equipment meant dealing with customers who would expect the very best merchandise and excellent customer service. His goal was to establish a sales-oriented, accommodating, and cordial staff. Job interviews, he felt, should be informal, an opportunity to learn not only how the person would serve customers, but also how he or she would interact with co-workers. He considered an outgoing personality and a good sense of humor as job-defining assets. He in turn compensated those who were hired with substantial salaries, benefits, job security, and a whole lot of personal respect."

"Your father was a thoughtful leader. He obviously believed that integrity is at the heart of every successful business enterprise. His hiring principles remind me of the morning I met Madelline. I'd interviewed several people with glowing credentials, and then she came along with that captivating personality of hers. I barely looked at her credentials before taking her to lunch as my new assistant. Since then she's been our behind-the-scenes star."

"I can tell she enjoys working with you. A moment ago you paid my father a compliment, and I want to thank you. Before we lost him, there was an article about the company in the *Omaha World Herald*. The writer praised the firm's integrity, said it was unsurpassed in Omaha."

"To be honest with you, Rich, we know a lot about you and your firm. We know your company continued to expand after you took over. We also know during the Great Recession the Stewart Company continued to prosper."

"In bleak economic times people often turn to recreational pastimes."

"Yes they do. I hope you aren't offended with our probing, but we wanted to know everything about you before seeking your professional advice on such a major project."

"So you don't think our philosophies concerning customer service and staff relationships are outdated?"

"Absolutely not. When I was a youngster, my parents owned and operated a hometown restaurant. As we were growing up, all six of us kids were required to work there. I've never forgotten what they taught us about how customers should be treated."

"I have similar recollections of my folks."

"My parents are no longer living either. I know losing your mom and dad was a devastating loss for you and your sister."

"What never goes away is that they were too young with too much ahead of them."

J.D. paused momentarily before he said, "In my position I'm not directly responsible for the well-being of most of the New Horizon staff, but I do know more business enterprises should be like yours. In the past thirty years we've seen too much of upper management projecting profits ahead of customer service. Consideration for their own employees is also less than inspiring. The work atmosphere your father and you have established for customers and staff could serve ideally as a model for Monte Vista. That's why as part of your upcoming work I'm asking you to organize the resort's personnel guidelines."

"I'll look forward to it."

"So we have a deal until June 1?"

"We do."

"Not to change the subject, but someone said you have a lady friend. She said she saw you two at a Treasure Island show a while back. May I ask who she is?"

"Her name's Paula Summers. She's an acquaintance I made through a friend. You may have seen her on KBLV television."

"She's at KBLV? What does she do there?"

"She calls herself a news feature specialist and concentrates on human interest and interview stories. She's also working on a master's degree at the university."

"I heard from my source she's very attractive."

"I wholeheartedly agree with your source. Through her work she's closely connected with the Vegas entertainment industry, and luckily for me she's already agreed to teach me whatever she can. I'm thinking her assistance would prove to be very useful in my upcoming Monte Vista work."

"What a timely coincidence," J.D. said, and from a desk drawer he removed a leather tri-fold and handed it to Richard. "Inside you'll find dining reservations at some very fine restaurants. I thought you and Ms. Summers could use them."

"I'm sure we will. Thanks again for your thoughtfulness, James."

When Richard informed Paula of J.D.'s decision to build a new Stewart store, she too was delighted. It meant he'd be in town nearly every weekend until June. And with the new restaurant reservations they'd be taking in not just the major shows, but dining at premiere dining establishments.

It seemed as if everything happening was a gift intended to strengthen their relationship. And the fact Richard was in Vegas only during the weekends made their times together seem even more appealing.

By the time the Valentine's Day weekend arrived, he was completely in love with her. Friday evening they went to the Stratosphere's Top of the World. There, from their 1100-foot high window table, they could enjoy choice lobster and shrimp entrees along with magnificent views of the city. However, neither the food, nor the view, nor Paula's latest entertainment revelations were foremost in Richard's mind. He was more intrigued with the woman sitting across from him—mesmerized by her brilliance, her expressive blue eyes and her sensuous lips, and little things like her occasional use of a once more distinct Mississippi drawl. Paula Summers' charms, big and small, were piling up like Super Bowl players on a goal line fumble.

Noticing his distant gaze, she inquired, "Richard, are you listening to me?"

No response.

She waved a hand in front of his face and said, "Hel-looo, Richard, you're daydreaming again."

"Actually I was envisioning you and me on a Caribbean cruise, lounging poolside, soaking up the rays, sipping exotic drinks, and—"

"I will try again. Every weekend I've been telling you everything I can think of regarding Vegas entertainment. Lately there have been times, like tonight, when you seem distracted, as if you're in another world."

"Sorry, and I promise to stay focused from now on."

Following dinner, their next stop was at the Monte Carlo where a song and dance variety show was featuring talented local performers. Paula had promised, "They're called the Lucky Seven and they specialize in rock 'n roll music from the Sixties and Seventies. They're receiving rave media reviews, and judging from the kind of music you've said you prefer, I think you're going to like the show."

And he did, especially during one of the band's lively renditions when they left the stage and paraded through the audience.

Later when he parked in front of her apartment, he reached into the back seat for a sparkly white box wrapped in red ribbons. "I would have given this to you before, but I had to order them."

Quickly she unwrapped the package and opened the box to reveal the pink leather heels with the narrow, gem-studded straps, the same shoes she'd admired the night they were in the Forum.

She slid a slim, pretty foot into one of them and said, "Now how did y'all know I wear a size six?"

"You mentioned it that night."

"Y'all don't miss a thing about me, do you?"

She moved closer to him and he kissed her and they held each other tight.

"I told you that night in the Forum," she said, "I have a dress they're perfect for, and I promise to wear them both only on special occasions. In other words, when I'm with you."

An expensive gift from any man she'd known before not only would have been refused, but would also have been the end of the relationship. That night such a thought never crossed her mind.

Chapter Eight

AND SO THE GOOD TIMES rolled on without a single serious interruption. It wasn't until the third Saturday in March when a confrontation with a stranger on a downtown street resulted in their first serious disagreement. Up until then Richard thought there was little not to admire about his Dream Princess. But there was a side of her he hadn't seen. She was a perfectionist with very little patience for mistakes and shortcomings.

Since he'd been coming to Las Vegas, Richard had never been to the Fremont Street Experience.

"You don't really understand the heart and soul of Vegas entertainment," Paula pointed out, "until you see what's going on down there. To stay competitive with the Strip, they must offer a never-ending variety of crowd-pleasing attractions. Let's pay them a visit this weekend, and you'll see what I mean."

It was a cool and breezy evening, but as usual on the weekend downtown parking lots and street parking were filled to capacity. Steering the MKS through the busy streets, Richard finally found an opening at the corner of Ogden Avenue and Casino Center. From there it was about a two-block walk to the Strip.

Before taking in the Experience, they buttoned up their coats and walked up the street to the California hotel for dinner. The night started out pleasantly in a relaxing restaurant where they enjoyed select prime rib entrees.

After dinner they continued down Main Street to the Fremont intersection. Upon turning the corner they entered the most brilliantly lit, action-filled pedestrian mall in the entire world. Richard had seen segments of the Experience in movies and on television, but they were nothing compared with seeing it firsthand. Tree-like steel tower branches supported the four-block-long, one-hundred-foot-wide steel mesh screen. In the evening darkness the screen looked like a giant white umbrella proudly protecting Glitter Gulch. And every hour the umbrella image came to life when the screen lit up with a variety of colorful psychedelic and musical productions.

Joining the milling throngs of people, the couple was soon immersed in the carnival-like atmosphere. There were assorted cart vendors selling novelty items like flags, banners, and trinkets. People gathered around a man inviting them to pet his two-foot-long lizard. On a portable easel a pencil artist skillfully sketched profiles of passersby. In front of the Pioneer casino was the legendary winking and smoking cowboy. At a corner intersection a youthful violinist's country music coaxed his listeners to dance in the street.

Further down Fremont in front of Binion's Horseshoe, a skilled musician held his audience captive with his bluesy saxophone renditions. Following his last selection, the bright Fremont lights dimmed, and overhead the mesh screen was dramatically filled with the sights and sounds of streaking F-16 fighter jets.

"You were right," Richard said, "the Fremont attractions are never-ending ."

When the show ended and regular lighting returned, Paula said, "Follow me, I want to you to see an amazing sight."

Inside Binion's she led the way to the back of the casino and a glass-enclosed case filled with neatly stacked one hundred dollar bills. "That's a million bucks," she said.

Richard smiled, shook his head, and said, "Wow."

From Binion's they went across the street to the Golden Nugget. This time she showed him yet another glass display, this one holding the largest gold nugget in the world.

"Priceless, I'm sure," he said.

"Maybe not. It seems as if there's a price tag on just about everything in Vegas."

Before leaving the Golden Nugget Richard said, "Juan mentioned you're opposed to gambling, but I think I can show you if you set limits you just might have some fun. I can teach you how to play some basic blackjack in a few minutes, and we'd be using my money, so you couldn't lose. Want to give it a try?"

"Casino gambling of any kind doesn't appeal to me. I think risking money that way is nothing more than a careless waste of time."

Outside the casino they continued down the street past the Fremont, Four Queens, and Fitzgeralds. Along the way they observed more street kiosks, including a spray-can artist skillfully swirling his picture-perfect impressions on canvas. Next, a model clay sculptor entertained his audience with a precise replica of an audience member. During their stroll Paula also discussed several downtown entertainment strategies promoters had tried—what had worked and what hadn't.

By the time they reached 4th Street, cooler breezes were prevailing, and the couple decided to close the night at the Peppermill Lounge at the north end of the Strip. They'd been there before and found the relaxing atmosphere to their liking.

Backtracking to Casino Center, they turned north toward Ogden and the car. Soon the Experience sounds were fading, and although the adjoining streets were well lit, they were also nearly deserted. While waiting for the intersection's pedestrian signal, they noticed a man crossing the street and heading straight toward them.

When he was just a few steps away, he said, "Sorry to come upon you like this, folks, but could you spare me a few moments?"

The unshaven, wan-looking stranger was wearing a T-shirt under his Levi jacket, tan denim pants, a baseball cap, and tennis shoes. Dark hair clustered around his cap was generously mixed with gray, and Richard assumed he was well into his sixties. He also noticed the stranger's steel-gray eyes were clear and non-threatening.

Frightened by the interruption, Paula quickly moved behind Richard as he inquired, "Something we can do for you this evening, sir?"

"As soon as I saw you I said to myself, 'Now those two look like a couple who might be willing to offer some assistance to a damsel in distress.' Seems there's a homeless young lady hiding in an alley just down the street here."

Richard nodded and said, "Okay."

"She's a runaway teenager from Phoenix, and she's afraid the police may have seen a missing person's photo and will take her in. She needs something to eat and a place to stay for the night. And if you could spare a little extra for some shoes to replace the thongs and the light jacket she's wearing, I'm sure she'd be grateful. As tonight reminds us, desert nights around here can be downright chilly this time of year."

"I take it you just met her."

"That's correct, sir. I was taking my nightly walk, and she stopped me and asked for some money. I gave her what little I had, but it won't be nearly enough to cover what she needs. It's too late tonight, but tomorrow I'll try to connect her with the Salvation Army. They're good with kids and will give her some assistance, hopefully will convince her to get in touch with her family or someone who's close."

"May I ask your name?"

Paula said, "Richard, be careful."

"My name's Robert, Robert McGuire, sir, and yours?"

"I'm Rich Stewart. It's nice to meet you, Robert."

Robert tipped his cap and said, "Nice to meet you, and nice to see you, too, miss."

Paula tsked her tongue and whispered, "Tell him to go away."

Richard asked, "How old is the girl?"

"She says she's eighteen, but I used to be a high school teacher and I'm sure she's more like sixteen."

Richard took his billfold from his sport coat pocket and withdrew two twenties and a ten dollar bill. Before handing them over he said, "Now this money will be used for the girl's needs and not for drinking or drugs, right?"

Surprised with the generous offering, Robert said, "You can be sure it will be used completely on the girl's behalf."

"Take this then and do what you can for her."

As Robert slid the fifty dollars into his pocket, he said, "Most considerate of you, and God bless you, Mr. Stewart. You two have a pleasant night now."

Robert turned and hastened across Ogden before heading toward the alley only half a block away.

Richard took Paula's hand as they crossed to the car, but as soon as she got in he said, "Lock up, honey. I'll be right back. I want to see what's going on."

"Richard, don't—"

But he'd already turned and was jogging toward the alley dividing a parking lot building and a closed business. Because a security light had burned out, the alley's interior was quite dark. Peeking around the corner of the building, a short distance into the alley Richard could barely see Robert standing in front of a young girl leaning against a steel railing. Their voices were clear.

"Where'd you get that kind of money?" she asked.

"Luckily I ran into a nice man, and when I told him about you, he said I should use this to get you a good dinner and a place to stay tonight. There's enough here so tomorrow morning I can help you find some shoes and a nice warm coat. Now, Jennifer, I know you're hungry, so let's find you a nice place to eat. You don't have to be afraid. As I told you, the police around here know me, and as long as we're together no one will bother you."

As they started to leave, Richard, not wanting to be seen, turned and jogged back to the car.

The moment he moved into the driver's seat, Paula said, "For God's sake, you should be more careful with these street people. The police are supposed to keep beggars like him away from downtown. And why on earth did you follow him to that dark alley?"

"I don't know; curiosity I guess. I didn't realize you were so upset, but I was where he couldn't see me, and there really was a girl waiting for him. He's using the money to get her something to eat and a place to stay for the night. I also heard him say tomorrow he'll help her find some warmer clothes."

"I find it difficult to believe a homeless person would take money and be thoughtful enough to help another homeless person. He said she was a teenager. More than likely he has an ulterior motive and will take advantage of her." Looking back toward the alley, Paula continued, "He may have a gun or a knife, and if he sees us in this fancy car, he might decide to come back. Let's just get out of here."

Before pulling away from the curb, Richard glanced into the rearview mirror, but Robert and Jennifer were nowhere to be seen.

Aware that Richard's attitude toward the homeless was in stark contrast to her own, Paula was silent as the MKS left downtown bound for the Peppermill. When they arrived, a waitress seated them near the lounge fireplace and moments later returned with their drinks.

In an attempt to end the ongoing silence, Richard started talking about what they'd seen back on Fremont Street.

Paula interrupted him. "I'm fully aware, Richard, that not all homeless people are necessarily bad. There are some justifiable cases, but a majority of them are alcoholics and drug addicts, and I find it difficult to sympathize with them. In my opinion they should be out looking for jobs instead of preying on innocent people. And I'm still wondering why the police aren't doing more to stop them from roaming the streets and frightening people. Maybe there's a good story here."

Surprised with her continuing negativity, he said, "When I was a kid growing up in Omaha, our downtown store was not far from the Salvation Army Rehab Center. There were quite a few poor people roaming the streets near the store, and every once in a while they'd come in asking to work for food. My father often helped them with pickup jobs like vacuuming the store, cleaning the windows, or shoveling the sidewalk after a snowstorm. He always made sure they had enough money for a good meal, and even when there was no work, he'd often give them gift cards for nearby cafes. I also remember him on cold winter nights helping to deliver coats and blankets to the homeless downtown."

"I admire what your father did, but that was long ago. The majority of today's homeless are, I will say again, hopeless addicts ready to take advantage of anything the public throws their way. I wonder how he would have reacted if you'd refused to give him a handout. And fifty bucks! *That* can buy a lot of booze."

"Did you take a good look at him? He may have needed a shave and looked a little undernourished, but otherwise I think he looked very normal. Didn't you hear him say he used to be a high school teacher, and he wanted to connect the girl with the Salvation Army? I think he was telling the truth, and at no time did I think he was a threat to us. Although the girl in the alley was homeless, after our discussion, brief though it was, I don't believe he was."

"He certainly knew how to panhandle, and you sound like a crusader for the entire homeless population."

"Let's just say, like my dad, I sympathize with anyone who's poor."

"That's because you don't know anything," she said, but the tone of her voice and the hint of a smile indicated she wanted the argument to end.

He felt the same way, and like that it was over.

It was their first serious disagreement, but the irony was that deep down Paula admired him for defending without yielding something he truly believed in. Any man she'd known before him would have wilted in such a heated confrontation.

Lying in bed that night, she was restless. *Something's happening to me. I've never felt the way I do about him with anyone else, ever. Lately it seems as if I want him here more than just on the weekends. Maybe it's all the good times we're having. Or maybe it's because I know how much he loves me. Or maybe it's because I know I can't control him. Whatever the reasons, I'm falling in love and I don't know what to do about it.*

Since she could remember Paula had been in control of her emotions and her personal life. She never imagined she would become involved with a man capable of capturing her heart and soul. On the one hand she considered the possibility a guardian angel might be watching over her. On the other there was that element of fear for anything which might interfere with her career plans.

Chapter Nine

PEOPLE FALL IN LOVE IN Las Vegas every minute of every day. There's nothing unusual about that. But Richard's and Paula's was not just another romance. Through the remainder of March and into April their relationship soared to enviable heights. They'd been to the best shows and dined in the finest restaurants. During those times she'd introduced him to agents and promoters, people who in the future could share ideas that might benefit Monte Vista. On several occasions they'd gone backstage to meet star performers she'd come to know through her work. Overall, Richard was more in touch with the Vegas entertainment genre than many of those directly connected with the industry.

By the middle of April, however, Paula's orchestrated weekends had about run their course. They began planning together where they'd go and what they'd do. It really made no difference as long as they were together. Their good looks, friendly personalities, and the exciting times they were enjoying set them apart. People accustomed to seeing them together thought of them as the ideal couple, or a match made in heaven.

Although Paula wasn't wearing a ring, those same admirers figured she would be soon. Some of them probably would have been surprised to learn the perfect couple had never slept together. That was, of course, her decision, not that Richard didn't keep trying. As their love was maturing, several times he'd come close to uncovering her most intimate desires, but she always knew where desire ended and common sense took over. As Juan had said early on, "Don't even think about taking her to bed, 'cause believe me, mi amigo, it ain't gonna happen."

Richard was in his Omaha office on a Monday morning when a call came from J.D. It was quite unexpected for they'd been together at Saturday's resort meeting. He said he was canceling the upcoming weekly meeting, because he'd been asked to attend a conference at Renzcorp's Atlantic City headquarters. He'd be gone until the following Sunday, and in his absence he asked Richard to stay the coming weekend at Mandalay Bay.

"Their promoters are consistently attracting a major portion of the young adult crowd," J.D. said, "and staying there should give you an opportunity to learn more about their promotional planning."

Richard and Paula had been to a jazz performance at the House of Blues and had dined at the Aureole restaurant. Those memorable evenings made Mandalay Bay one of their favorite destinations, and he welcomed J.D.'s assignment.

Friday morning after moving into his upper-level penthouse suite, Richard began his busy day. His agenda included visiting Mandalay's popular attractions, engaging with key personnel, and taking notes.

It was late afternoon when he called Paula. "I have this quaint little suite with a spectacular view of the Strip, and inasmuch as I'm here the entire weekend, why not party over here? By the way, you might also consider bringing along your overnight paraphernalia."

"You know, Richard, you never cease to amaze me. What if people there were to discover I was staying with you? I have my professional reputation to protect, you know."

"C'mon now, darlin', I've been wandering all over this place since this morning. I went to lunch at the rumjungle, and I talked with personnel at Shark Reef and the House of Blues. And you know what? I didn't see a single face I recognized."

"But I am a television personality, and I would not want anyone thinking I was staying there with you overnight."

"Aren't you being a bit overcautious? Even if they saw us going into or leaving the suite, would they presume we were sleeping together? I don't think so."

"I think there's a good chance someone who matters might. We've been on the town every weekend, and there are gossip columnists around, you know. Besides, sleeping together could seriously complicate our relationship. I don't like it when you go back to Omaha as it is. Don't worry; when the time comes, I plan to make you forget every moment we've lost."

Such comments from her lit his nerve pathways like a fiber-optic Christmas tree, but this time he said, "Well, honey, maybe it's time we start looking for an engagement ring."

"A ring, did you say? Need I remind you we've known each other only four months?"

Verbal fencing regarding sleeping together always ended the same—Paula elusive and Richard, though never obtrusive, at least a bit disappointed.

"Anyway, I've decided," she continued, "tonight is your special night. We can go wherever you want, do anything you choose."

"You did say *anything* I choose."

"Well *almost* anything."

"All right, well, we never did have a little gambling excursion on the town, so for something different, let's go casino hopping. I haven't done that for quite a while."

"If that's what you want."

To make him feel it really was his special night, she slipped into her favorite evening outfit—the ankle length, pink satin dress and the fashionable leather heels he'd given her Valentine's night.

When Richard arrived to pick her up, before leaving her apartment she picked up a small briefcase. "There's story information inside," she said, "that I should leave at the station sometime this evening."

"We can do it now."

"No rush, later on is fine. So where are we going?"

"I think we'll start with seafood dining at the Flamingo, and afterward we'll test our luck in their casino. From there we'll have easy access to Caesars, the Bellagio, and Bally's. All in a Friday night's work, okay?"

"And I'm feeling so good this evening," she said, "we might even throw in Paris."

"You *are* feeling good. Okay, now, I'm going to set a cash limit for each casino. That's gambling lesson number one. Do you remember a while back when I offered to teach you how to play some basic blackjack? And do you recall I said we'd be using my money and you couldn't lose?"

"I'm still not interested. I'll just be your cheerleader. I am, however, willing to make you a five-dollar bet. Tonight you will lose more money than you'll win."

"You are on."

Following dinner that evening they moved on to the Flamingo gambling floor where he filled an opening at a blackjack table. The dealer's ID-pin revealed she was Sin Wan Lee from Taiwan. Diminutive and bubbling, Sin had a fetching smile and catchy accent that niftily connected with each player. After Richard won several sequences, she nicknamed him Lucky Boy.

When he was two hundred dollars ahead, he decided to cash in his chips. "Lesson number two," he informed Paula, "is to remember lucky streaks seldom last. Once you build a substantial surplus, take the money and run. See? I told you it can be fun. And have you got your five bucks handy?"

"So you're leaving a winner. Well, I am surprised, Lucky Boy. Ah, but the night is young."

They went across the street to Caesars, where in the casino he switched from blackjack to craps. For a while his winning ways continued, but when the dice turned cold, he quickly cashed in his chips. Wisely he surmised, "Walk away early from a losing streak is lesson number three. It's time we move on."

Up one escalator flight they crossed the pedestrian bridge leading to the Bellagio. Inside they walked through a classic European-style hallway adorned with distinctively decorated Tuscan chandeliers. Flanked by expensive jewelry and clothing stores, the hallway eventually opened to the Bellagio casino. Hoping to re-establish his good luck, Richard found an opening at a blackjack table, but in less time than at Caesars he lost his limit and again decided to move on.

As they left the building, then all the way across Las Vegas Boulevard, and even on the long, moving walkway leading to Bally's, he offered no further gambling tips. He was silently hopeful his missing-in-action good luck would return at Bally's, but inside that casino he lost not only his limit but also the bonus he'd won at the Flamingo.

As they were leaving the gambling area, he said to Paula, "My bad luck streak started at Caesars and didn't relent and now I'm out of cash." He paused before he added, "Now wait, wait just a minute. I can run over to Paris and write a check and—"

"Oh no," she said, "I remember you saying when you lose your limit, you should quit. *Always* you said. So it's over for tonight, done with, kaput. By the way, you owe me five bucks."

Silence again as they followed Bally's walkway dividing the hotel registration counters and the casino.

Halfway to the front entrance Paula said, "Too bad about your bad luck tonight, but I know of something I think you'll find much more interesting than throwing your money away."

He stopped and said, "Which reminds me, you said you wanted to take the information in your briefcase over to KBLV. We can drive over there right now."

Stepping very close to him, she lifted her eyes to his and said, "I have a little confession to make about the briefcase. When I said this was going to be *your* special night, I should have said *our* special night. Because, Richard, there's no story information inside the case. There's only a negligee and some overnight paraphernalia you suggested I bring with me."

It took a few moments for him to recover from the shock waves. He shook his head and said, "Honey, do you mean that?"

"You've always taken me at my word, Rich."

He took hold of her hand and without delay they proceeded out the front entrance, across the street, and through the Flamingo casino. Outside in valet parking an attendant soon arrived with the MKS.

Richard tipped the young woman with a twenty-dollar bill to which she responded, "Thank you, sir, and you two have a wonderful night."

In unison they said, "We will!"

During the drive to Mandalay Bay, however, Paula began having second thoughts. "I think I feel good about this, but I'm also nervous and apprehensive."

Glancing her way he said, "We don't have to go through with this, honey; whatever you say." But in his next breath he added, "Just don't change your mind, however."

"I won't change my mind. I have tomorrow off, and I told Mr. Hamilton I had a personal commitment and couldn't work until Sunday afternoon."

Sunday afternoon! This is unbelievable.

Once inside his suite they held each other tight. Then she picked up her briefcase and said, "I'm going to the bathroom to change. Don't y'all go away now. I'll be right back."

Luxuriating in the excitement of his unexpected good fortune, Richard sat down in a chair and inhaled deeply.

Moments later Paula appeared in the doorway, the bathroom light from behind silhouetting the shapely figure beneath the black negligee— voluptuous breasts tapering to a slim waist and sharply defined hips.

Still wearing her panties and heels, she walked toward him and said shyly, "I've never worn a negligee for anyone, and I feel silly, like a lady of the night."

"You are beautiful, darling."

A few steps closer she shed her shyness and pulled back the negligee. Posing with shoulders back, hands resting on her hips, and slim ankle turned provocatively, she inquired, "How much do y'all love me, Richard?"

"More than you'll ever know."

He rose from his chair, picked her up and carried her into the bedroom. When he placed her down at the side of the king-size bed, she allowed the negligee to fall around her ankles. Stepping from her heels, she moved to the center of the bed and sat with her legs crossed.

By then he'd undressed down to his shorts, and now it was her turn to admire his physique—not that of a body builder but of a well-conditioned athlete—well-rounded shoulders and arms, the legs of a sprinter, and a rock-ribbed stomach.

"I'm waiting for you," she purred.

He moved next to her on the bed, and she pressed her lips to his forehead, cheek, and lips.

After he returned her kiss, she touched his lips with the tip of her tongue.

As he tightened his embrace, with his own tongue he massaged the roof of her mouth. The feel of his sinewy body pressing into her softly textured skin set them both on fire, and he could feel her heartbeat quickening.

"I want you to call me Rene for the rest of the night," she sighed. No one ever calls me Rene, no one except you when we're making love."

Aroused deeply by her intimate responses, he promised, "I will be very careful with you."

She replied, "I know you will," and with a smile she added, "And I will endeavor to do the same."

At first they fulfilled their promises, and she returned his well-coordinated, gentle thrusts with her own measured movements. But soon her most sensuous feminine instincts took over. Agilely she circled her hips faster and faster. then slower, but more firmly, until a dreamlike bursting of stars accompanied a nerve-tingling sensation she'd never known before.

As he gazed into her eyes he laughed softly, and she knew he had also reached the ultimate.

"Paula, I love you," he said.

"And I love you, too, Richard."

Tenderly they held each other and spoke softly, romantically, until they both fell asleep.

Shortly after nine o'clock the next morning, the telephone on the table next to the bed awakened them. Richard answered groggily.

Juan responded, "Did I wake you up?"

"As a matter of fact you did."

Richard glanced at Paula, yawning and stretching, then sitting up with the sheet around her shoulders and covering her upper torso. For the first time since he could remember, her hair was tousled, but it only made her look more desirable. Inquisitively she looked at him, and when he mouthed Juan's name, her expression changed to a half-smile grimace.

Juan said, "Out late with the princess, huh? *Really* late. I've never known you to sleep this late. So tell me about Mandalay Bay."

Richard looked again at Paula and said. "All I can say is the scenery over here can only be described as heavenly."

Coyly she lifted the edge of the sheet so it was like a veil beneath her blue eyes.

Juan asked, "That good, huh? Why not give me the details at lunch?"

"Sorry but I can't. I have a couple of appointments around here this morning that will take some time. Tell you what—I'll call you later to let you know what's up."

"By the way, did you have fun gambling last night?"

Richard sent Paula a wink and said, "Luckily I won considerably more than I lost."

Following the phone call, Paula said, "If he knew I was here like this, he'd have an instant heart attack."

"Don't worry; he'll never know."

They showered and dressed before going downstairs for breakfast at an outdoor table near the Mandalay Bay pool. Still in a state of ecstasy they ate sparingly, more intrigued with each other's eyes and afterthoughts than the food before them. They decided to spend the rest of the day driving around town, doing what they wanted, stopping when and where they chose.

On the way to the Monte Vista site, Richard stopped at the Meadows Mall Macy's store where Paula purchased some personal necessities. From there they walked hand-in-hand down a mall corridor before pausing in front of a jewelry store. Half of the window display highlighted an attractive array of engagement and wedding rings.

She pointed to a glittering center diamond circled by a cluster of smaller diamonds. "Isn't it lovely?" she said, and snuggled her head on his shoulder before adding, "Maybe someday soon?"

Thinking someday soon meant when her parents would be in town for her graduation, he responded, "Whenever you're ready."

Before going out for the evening, they stopped at her apartment. While she changed into a yellow vested two-piece suit, a butterfly-adorned blouse, and yellow French heels, he made reservations for a famous singers' impressionist show at the Golden Nugget.

While they were enjoying the show that evening, Richard leaned over and whispered to her, "Do you have any idea how much I love you, Ms. Summers? What made you change your mind about us, you know what I mean."

She whispered back, "I love you, too, and I guess I just got tired of your begging. Just joshing, Mr. Stewart."

Afterward they went back to his Mandalay suite. Very much in a musical mood after the show, Richard chose an "All-time Romantic Favorites" album from the entertainment center.

During the first song they danced partly seriously, partly playfully around the room.

"You dance divinely, sir," she said.

"As do you, Ms. Summers."

The second selection featured misty-voiced Diana Krall:

" 'Swonderful, 'smarvelous, you should care for me,

'Sawful nice, 'sparadise, 'swhat I long to see,

You've made my life so glamorous,

You can't blame me for feeling amorous ..."

Paula responded, "What a beautiful song, and it fits my mood perfectly, except I think I'm getting tired."

"As am I. It's been a busy two days."

They went to the bedroom and lied down and she snuggled her head onto his shoulder. A few minutes later she said, "I'm afraid little memories from last night are not going to let me sleep. Can we live them again?"

That night they made love twice before going to sleep.

At dawn he awoke to find her sleeping peacefully at his side. His love for her had new meaning now, because he knew this beautiful woman—soon to be his wife and the mother of his children—was as much a perfectionist in the art of making love as she was in everything she undertook; knew her sensuous talents came not from previous experience; knew the passions she felt for him were inspired by the love she felt for him and him alone. She'd taken him into a world of enchantment, and no one could ever take her place. Of that he was certain.

By the time they showered and dressed that morning, it was almost ten o'clock. They thought about attending a church service, but his early afternoon flight would press them. Following a hotel restaurant lunch, she drove him to McCarran where they kissed and said their farewells at security checkpoint.

"I want you to know," he said, "this has been the most memorable weekend I've ever experienced."

"Me too, Richard. Call me as soon as you get home."

Chapter Ten

THE NEXT DAY IN OMAHA, Richard, Benjamin, and Stewart store managers used their morning meeting to review first-quarter sales results. Their findings made them feel like Wall Street brokers learning working-class incomes were rising, retail sales were increasing, and unemployment figures were at a ten-year low. If the remainder of the year produced similar results, the company would shatter all existing sales records.

Richard and Benjamin had lunch inside the Old Market V. Mertz restaurant. Morning optimism aside, Benjamin confessed to feeling uneasy. Though early on he'd been impressed with the prospects of a Monte Vista Stewart store, he was also having reservations. As chief administrator of the firm's finances he was frugally cautious, except, that is, for occasionally increasing staff wages and benefits. Even when expansion and additional hiring became necessary, he considered every monetary angle before acting.

"You're absolutely sure," he asked, "we can trust in Mr. Forrester's projections? Could it be he's moving too quickly and over-speculating?"

"Trust me, the man undertakes only what he thinks is attainable and long-range sustainable. I can assure you, Ben, he has the financial wherewithal to make this resort enterprise happen. I know they reviewed the backgrounds of several firms before deciding on us, and as I've said, he is convinced a store out there could project us into profitable global markets."

"I suppose we could hardly go wrong. If you're that sure of him, it's good enough for me. Not to change the subject, but tell me more about the lady you're spending so much time with, and when are we going to meet her?"

"She wants to meet you, too, but with her television work and finishing her master's thesis, she's very busy. She graduates in just a couple of weeks now, and soon after that I intend to bring her here for a visit."

"So the relationship's gaining momentum."

"It is, absolutely. Now to another matter. Because of the extra load you've been carrying, effective immediately I want your salary increased by 10 percent."

"Ten percent. Isn't that a little extrava—"

"Don't argue with me on this now. Our sales reports warrant the increase."

"You're sure."

"By all means."

"You just made my day."

Tuesday evening Richard called Paula at her apartment where she was working on her thesis. She revealed for him the program schedule for her upcoming graduation ceremonies.

The next evening it was she who called. "Richard, I have the most exciting news. John Hamilton informed me this afternoon KHOL television in Hollywood has been inquiring about me. He said I should expect a call from them at any time."

The news surprised more than pleased him. He immediately wondered how the implications of her moving to Hollywood might affect them personally.

After a pause he said, "I see, well, that sounds promising."

Her optimism, mixed with excitement, continued for the remainder of the call.

Thursday night she didn't return several of his calls, and he assumed something major must have happened.

Upon returning to Vegas the next morning, he tried her cell phone number. *Leave a message.* Then he tried KBLV. *Unavailable.*

Inside the busy Paris guest reception area he pulled Juan aside. "Can you squeeze in a workout later?"

"Sure, I'll meet you at the club this afternoon around five o'clock."

Evelyn then handed Richard a message from Paula, which a few steps away he opened and read:

Richard dear,

I was called early this morning (Thursday) by the news director at KHOL in Hollywood. They want to interview me at the station tomorrow morning and have chartered a private jet, so I have to leave this afternoon. I know how much this weekend meant to you and me, but I hope I'll be returning Saturday. I'll call you tomorrow evening at eight o'clock.

He wondered why she hadn't left her message on his cell phone. And again he was concerned with how her acceptance of a job in Hollywood might affect their upcoming plans.

His next stop was at New Horizon, where Cynthia quickly ushered him into J.D.'s office. The president was leaning back in his chair, phone propped to his ear. He motioned to Richard who took a desk-side seat.

J.D.'s expression indicated he wanted the conversation to end. "Sure, sure, we'll see to that. Make every effort to stay in touch now, and so will I."

As soon as he hung up, he rose to shake Richard's hand. "Am I glad to be back. I tell you, Rich, the Atlantic City resort scene is too elegant for my blood—ritzy New York and New Jersey women strutting around in their elegant clothes and flashing their elegant jewels. Even the menu choices were elegant." As he often did to emphasize a point, he smacked his fist into the palm of his other hand and added, "The wide open spaces of Nevada never looked better."

The latest fist-in-palm gesture prompted Richard to ask, "Just out of curiosity, James, do you remember Rocky Marciano, the old heavyweight champ? Wasn't he from a town near Boston, not far from where you grew up?"

"Yes he was, from Brockton, just down the road about thirty miles. Funny you should mention him, because my father had some interesting stories to tell about the champ, even shook hands with him once at a banquet. Dad said he was a gentleman with a heart of gold until he climbed through the ropes and the bell rang. That's when he turned into a wild stallion blessed with a horse-kicking right hand. Retired undefeated, you know, forty-three knockouts in forty-nine fights."

Why does this not surprise me? Richard thought. "This is a quite a coincidence," he said, "because my father also admired him, even had a movie collection of his title fights. My grandfather came from Italy and was very proud of his Italian heritage. He idolized Marciano and that respect lived on in our family. Every once in a while my dad and I would watch the Marciano movies together. Dad called him the Immovable Force and said he could have licked any fighter in boxing history. Until, of course, Ali came along."

"I know, but wouldn't that have been one helluva barn-burning match?"

"That it would have been."

J.D. chuckled and said, "Would you believe when I was growing up my father said I looked a lot like the champ?"

Sizing up his boss more closely, Richard said, "You know, there are some similarities at that."

Marciano aside, Richard revealed in detail his Mandalay Bay report.

J.D. responded, "Your research will undoubtedly provide the committee with some timely promotional ideas." He paused before changing the subject. "Today I'm afraid I'm facing a serious problem, Rich. It seems we still haven't found a suitable replacement for you. Maddy has contacted several national agencies, even placed ads in the *Wall Street Journal* and *USA Today*. After all was said and done, we came up with only two candidates we felt were worthy of consideration. The fellow from Albuquerque had worked several years as a successful business executive, but he lacked the necessary PR talents. The young woman was a recent grad from Southern Cal, honor student she was, but also lacking in people skills. I personally interviewed both of them, and neither had a clue as to what I was after. They were primarily interested in cutting costs and profit-making strategies."

"So what are you thinking?"

"I'm thinking I'd be relieved if you'd stay on as program director through the summer, but this time on a full-time basis. It's like this: ever since you joined us, your organizational skills have projected us far beyond our expectations. I know I'm asking a lot, but we *really* need you."

"I wasn't planning on an extension, James. I'm sure you realize, along with Christmas this is our busiest season."

"I know it is, but you've told me how efficiently your staff has been handling everything back home."

Richard's thoughts mingled with the realization that Paula would likely be moving to Hollywood. "With each passing day," he said, "the director's responsibilities are going to multiply."

"And that is exactly why I want you here full time for the summer. How does $100,000 with all living expenses paid sound for the summer months? As before, you could return to Omaha whenever required. Any chance you could give me your answer today?"

"For this to happen, relative to what I said, I'd need a full-time assistant and considerable clerical help."

"Regarding the second item, Maddy has efficient secretaries at her fingertips. As for an assistant, she'll help you find that person, keeping in mind the final choice is up to you. All we care about is that he or she possesses promotional talents, is family oriented, enjoys working with people, and loves the game of golf."

Is that all? Richard thought.

J.D. said, "As we talked about earlier, for the summer I want to hire three people to begin preparing model personnel guidelines for the resort. The goal will be to establish a conscientious, service-oriented staff, one that will be highly diverse—men and women, young and old, all races represented—all working at a level of integrity tantamount to what exists in your company."

"What kind of incentives would we be offering my assistant?"

"I'm thinking $60,000 annually, an attractive benefits package, and if the person works out a promise to stay on as the permanent director's assistant. A beginning contract such as that should be attractive to any number of capable candidates."

"I agree. All right, under those conditions I'll make arrangements to stay full time through the summer."

From his desk drawer J.D. withdrew an envelope and handed it to Richard. Inside he found gambling gratuities worth $1,500 playable at several casinos affiliated with New Horizon.

"And tell Ms. Summers we will make her our primary news source for all future Monte Vista stories."

"She'll be honored with your thoughts, and thank you, James. I promise to do whatever I can do for the resort this summer."

When Richard notified Juan of the latest developments, he responded, "Forrester obviously thinks you have the magic touch. Hey, I'm happy you're going to be around for the summer. And I'm sure Paula is thrilled."

"Actually, I haven't had a chance to tell her. She's in Hollywood."

"She's *where*?"

"She interviewed today for a job at station KHOL. She's calling this evening to tell me what happened."

"KHOL is the major West Coast affiliate of NBC. I know some of their execs stay at the hotel. I guess I knew something like this would happen sooner or later."

"She plans to return sometime tomorrow."

"Of course, heaven forbid you two didn't see each other for an entire weekend."

"What can I say? She's my princess."

"I hope this new situation won't interfere with your relationship."

"We'll be fine."

"Good, and when she gets back tomorrow, we should all get together. I'll call our sitter and we can go out on the town, drink tequila, have fun."

That evening when she called, Richard was watching television in his hotel room and waiting.

"Sorry I've been tied up the last couple of days," she said, "but it's been worth it. Can you imagine them flying me here in a private jet?"

"Sounds exciting all right. So tell me exactly what happened and what time you're coming back tomorrow. I miss you already."

"Rich, this is everything I'd hoped for. They showed me around their offices and filming studios today, and I met most of the upper-echelon staff. The news director said I'm being considered for one of two positions, but I won't be permanently assigned right away. Tomorrow they want to discuss contract provisions, and I am *so* excited."

"Before you return here, you mean."

"Oh, I'm sorry, but I won't be coming back tomorrow. They've arranged for me to stay temporarily at a DoubleTree, which is only fifteen minutes from the station. I'm nearly certain I'll be back next week, and for my graduation for sure."

"What about KBLV and your school work?"

"I called my advisor this morning. When I told him my thesis is nearly completed, he said I should not worry and just hand it in as soon as possible. As for KBLV, they're NBC too, so it's all in the family."

He took a deep breath and said, "Look, do what you have to do. I can always come there as soon as you're settled in."

"Thank you, Rich, for giving me the kind of support I need. I'm missing you terribly, but as you said, we'll be together soon. Tonight they're taking me out to a swanky restaurant, and they say I'll be meeting some very important people. But you know what? I'll be thinking of you every minute."

"And me, you. Happens I have some late-breaking news of my own. Mr. Forrester's asked me to remain this summer as his full-time program director. So at least you and I will be close. You know how he is. When I accepted his offer, he gave me gambling certificates worth fifteen hundred bucks."

"For all they do for you they must want not only your store, but you as a permanent player. Anyway, that much play money should keep you busy for quite a while."

"I'd rather be with you."

"I know. I was in such a hurry I left my cell phone in Vegas. I don't think I'll be at the DoubleTree very long, because they said they'd soon have an apartment for me. Please don't try to reach me at the station. I'm sure they wouldn't appreciate me taking personal calls just yet. Don't worry because I'm nearly certain I'll have my schedule straightened out soon and then we can work things out. I'll call you at this time tomorrow. Hopefully then we can discuss possible plans for next weekend."

"Okay, I'll be waiting. I love you very much."

"I love you too."

Richard was more concerned than he'd indicated. He didn't like the sounds of "nearly certain," or "hopefully," or "possible plans." He couldn't help but feel the essence of her message was, "Don't call me; I'll call you."

Chapter Eleven

FOLLOWING A RESTLESS NIGHT BURDENED with a myriad of possibilities concerning Paula, the next morning Richard informed Juan, "It looks as if we'll have to postpone our night out. She's staying in Hollywood and won't be back until next weekend."

"She won't? Hmmm, that's too bad. They're probably trying to close some kind of a deal with her, right?"

"That's what she says."

"As for tomorrow night, come along with us. We can still take in a movie and then stop back at the house."

"Sure, I've nothing else to do."

Saturday's resort meeting was a conference room luncheon featuring a tray of cold cuts and cheeses and assorted salads, rolls, and soft drinks. Afterward, committee members offered their weekly summations followed by J.D.'s comments. He was in one of his ultra-optimistic moods.

"Today I want to thank all of you for your exciting updates. You are off to a tremendous beginning."

Madelline activated a presentation of the latest Country Club blueprints on the screen as J.D. continued, "As you can see, the course layout will blend naturally with the foothills-valley terrain. Our fairways will be landscaped with lovely water fountains and ponds, colorful varieties of palm and deciduous trees, and flourishing floral gardens. Although the course itself will be challenging with its share of sand bunkers, water hazards, and rough grass areas, we want the professionals to look upon it more as a uniquely attractive, masterfully planned dream come true. From all over Las Vegas people will look at those four mountains and say, 'That's where that great new Monte Vista resort is located.'"

His speech continued for forty-five minutes. In closing he said, "At this time I want to thank Rich Stewart for providing us with his expertise in our first-phase planning. I'm pleased to announce he's agreed to stay on as our full-time program director through the summer."

Committee members and guests warmly applauded before lining up to offer handshakes and words of encouragement.

When they'd all left the conference room, J.D. informed him, "We've made arrangements for you to stay the summer in a premiere Paris suite. If for any reason you find it's not what you like, we'll make other arrangements."

Recalling Juan's description of his hotel's high level accommodations, Richard said, "A Paris suite should be fine."

He wondered how anyone—other than a famous athlete, a show biz celebrity, or a corporate CEO—had the power to secure a premiere Paris suite for an entire summer. It seemed as if all J.D. had to do was wave his magic wand and whatever he asked for would be granted.

Later as Richard was organizing files in his office, Madelline stopped by and he asked her, "Would you say J.D. is among the most powerful figures in Las Vegas?"

"As powerful and influential as anyone I know."

"Even as powerful and influential as, say, the mega-resort hierarchy?"

"All things considered, I think so."

"I've never been to his home, but I've heard it's quite the place."

"It is very nice, on a golf course fourteen minutes west of the Strip. Mr. Renzberg offered a more luxurious residence overlooking Lake Las Vegas, but J.D. wanted a location more convenient to his work."

"I've yet to meet his wife."

"Marjorie. You'll like her, I'm sure. Whenever she comes around the office she takes time to speak with everyone. They're active in community affairs and the Catholic Church and they seem to be very happy."

"I understand they have a son."

"That would be Derek. Right now he's following in dad's footsteps at Harvard."

Just as Richard was preparing to leave the office, Juan called. "Sorry, but Maria won't be able to make it tonight. Juanita woke up sick this morning. The doctor says it's a virus, but with adequate rest and fluids she'll recover quickly. Maria will be staying with her, but she insists that you and I go out."

"If you're sure about Juanita."

"She'll probably be well by tomorrow. Ah, a night on the town. It's been a while for me, so what should we do?"

Richard remembered Juan saying as a single man he occasionally went to a casino and tried his luck at a craps table.

"I haven't been inside Wynn's for a while," Richard said, "but I know they have a lively weekend casino. Thanks to my boss I've got some gambling gift money, so why don't we pay them a visit?"

"Wynn's it will be."

Early in the evening they met in Juan's office where the Paris manager was scanning the day's registration reports. His hair was slicked back and in his red-and-navy-striped polo shirt, cream-colored pleated pants, and casual loafers, he looked ready for prime casino action.

"How's Juanita feeling?" Richard asked.

"Better, and she hopes you'll stop by tomorrow."

"Before my flight, I will for sure."

On the drive to Wynn's Richard said, "I've been hearing about a strategy in which a craps player can often beat the house by following a simple set of procedures."

Juan replied, "I think I've mentioned there was a time I could be very lucky with the dice. Memory serving, Lady Luck paid a visit to my table quite often."

Richard was smiling when he said, "I see. Well, if you pick up any vibes from your ghost world, please let me know."

Inside the casino all craps tables were filled except for a $10 minimum, $10,000 maximum game.

Richard moved into an opening and said to Juan, "Concerning the strategy I was telling you about, except for the pass line bet I won't enter the game until a player tosses seven winning numbers. Once that happens, I'll start betting on every toss. By the way, if you feel like trying your luck, there's plenty here for both of us."

"I can only advise you. Maria is like Paula, very touchy when it comes to gambling. Besides, if anyone connected with Paris discovered I was playing with New Horizon gift money, I'd be looking for another job. Trust me."

A perky, auburn-haired cocktail waitress took their beer orders before Richard traded a third of his gratuity for $500 in chips. Through the next series of players, rarely did one of them toss more than a few winning numbers before a game-ending seven appeared.

As one disgruntled player was leaving the table, he muttered, "This table's as cold as January in Duluth."

Juan said, "Well at least your strategy hasn't been too costly. Then again you haven't won anything either. How exciting."

"My strategy, mi amigo, requires diligent patience."

At that moment at the opposite end of the table a middle-aged and well-dressed couple filled another opening. The gentleman, looking quite urbane in his pinstripe gray suit and open collar white shirt, traded several hundred-dollar bills for a stack of expensive chips. At first glance his partner, a petite lady with neatly trimmed brown hair and mini-frame glasses, could easily be mistaken for an English teacher. Like surgeons standing before an operating table, the couple began conversing in low tones and nodding their heads. Eventually the player next to them sevened out, and now one of them would take over.

Focusing on their every move, Juan nudged Richard and said, "Something tells me you should forget your strategy and start betting."

Following Juan's gaze to the couple, Richard asked, "You mean because of those two?"

"They act like pros to me, and I'm thinking there's a good chance Lady Luck came with them tonight."

Richard was half-frowning when he said, "Really."

A dealer placed several dice in front of the couple. Signifying she would be the player, the lady picked up two of the dice and blew softly on them. As she placed the dice back on the table, casino lights from above enhanced the sparkling diamonds in her rings and bracelet. She turned the dice so that the numbers equaled a face-up seven, rubbed them across the table's surface, and tossed them in an arch over the table. Obedient as puppy dogs they bounced off the table's end before tumbling to a four and a three.

"That's a winner on the rollout," the dealer declared. "Place your bets. folks, and let's do it again."

Juan said, "She's got style, Ricardo. Stay with her."

Slightly more impressed, Richard placed two more chips on the pass line.

She rolled an eleven, another winner, then an eight.

Her escort said, "Nice roll, Ivory."

Juan turned to Richard and said, "Did you hear him call her Ivory?"

"You mean ivory as in dice?"

Juan nodded and said, "As in dice. I told you they were pros." Juan called across the table, "Roll them bones, Ivory."

She sent Juan a wink and confidently rolled a six.

Juan said to Richard, "She just gave you a six and an eight, the two best numbers. Would you believe?"

Richard doubled his bets on both numbers.

From that moment forward, with few exceptions Ivory rolled payoff number after payoff number. It seemed as if Juan's Lady Luck, like a flittering Tinker Bell, had cast her spell, and the game-ending number seven was AWOL, incommunicado, on a cruise to Norway. The sound of rising voices around the table was drawing observers like flies to a safari picnic, and waitresses hustled to keep thirsts tossed quenched and brains drenched. Whenever one of the paying numbers began stacking up with chips, Ivory leveled them with yet another winning toss.

Arms folded across his chest, a brawny floor manager arrived to oversee the excitement. His suspicious glances were aimed mostly at Ivory, but she shrugged him off with another wink, this time connected with a nose-wrinkling smile.

Juan, on the other hand, was not pleased. "What is his problem? Does he think the lady's shooting loaded dice or what?"

Nearly twenty-five minutes elapsed before she finally tossed a game-ending seven. Glancing at the players around the table, she raised her hands and said, "Sorry."

But those who'd been betting with her weren't sorry. They cheered and applauded her.

Juan was beaming when he said to Richard, "Mi amigo, you've just won a sweet little bundle."

Richard noticed Ivory and her escort preparing to leave the table, and said, "They're out of here, and so are we. Winning streaks like hers don't come along very often."

He gathered his chips, among them numerous gold-colored Wynn 100s, and moved to the cashier cage.

A female attendant behind the bronze bars inquired, "May I ask you, sir, how much of this did you win?"

"All but $500."

She counted the rest and said, "Congratulations. Your payout profit is $5,435."

Richard said, "May I kiss you?"

She pointed to the bars separating them and answered, "If only it weren't for these."

At her request Richard waited for a casino manager, who a short time later arrived with a check, IRS form, and photo-op camera.

When the picture taking was over, the two friends returned to Paris and stopped at Le Café for hamburgers, fries, and shakes. Their dialogue pleasantly recalled the highlights of Ivory's rewarding run. By the time they finished their snacks, it was eleven o'clock and Juan was ready to get home.

After his friend's departure, Richard went upstairs to his room where his thinking quickly switched to Paula. He felt melancholy as he wondered where at that very moment she might be, whom she was with, and what she might be doing.

Chapter Twelve

RICHARD HAD SPENT MOST OF his adult life looking for the one-and-only Dream Princess. And in spite of Juan's advice concerning Paula's ambitions, following the Mandalay Bay weekend their May graduation engagement seemed a sure thing. Now he had reason to wonder. Excluding her absence, the weekend had been super rewarding. As Monte Vista's summer program director he'd be generously paid. On a much lesser scale, but nonetheless stimulating, was J.D.'s gratuity leading to the five-plus grand he'd won at Wynn's.

Such events helped him to rationalize. *I think I need to cut her some slack. Her actions are the result of unavoidable events, and I think that when the time comes, we'll easily make our adjustments.*

Back in Omaha and throughout much of Nebraska, heavy thunderstorms were occurring with costly frequency. In towns and cities rivers and streams were overflowing their banks, basements were flooding, and sewer systems were backing up. In rural areas farmers looked on helplessly as early wheat, corn, and soybean fields were transformed into sloughs and duck ponds.

As for Stewart Company business, Richard and Benjamin weren't overly concerned. Accustomed to Mother Nature's springtime temper tantrums, they remained confident their customers' spirits wouldn't be dampened for long, and they were right. Reports from the Stewart stores indicated golf and other outdoor sports products were selling as if the weather was Palm Springs perfect.

Benjamin had another concern. It wasn't like Richard to leave the company for an entire summer.

When Richard returned to the office on Monday morning, Benjamin asked him, "What's going on out there anyway? We're going to miss not having you around for three months."

"They're still having difficulty finding someone who can keep the resort progress stable. As before, Ben, for any emergency I'm free to come back here for as long as it takes."

Though still concerned, Benjamin chose not to pursue it further.

Later in the day Richard received an unexpected call from Juan.

"Ricardo, what's new in Omaha?"

"It's springtime stormy here. What's up with you?"

"Paula called me this afternoon."

"She did? And why did she call you?"

"She said she was in town to pick up some personal belongings. She couldn't talk for very long because she was flying back to Hollywood. When I asked for a number, she said she still couldn't find her cell phone, but hopefully she'd be getting a new one tomorrow and—"

"You mean she moved out of her university apartment? Did she say why she hadn't called me?"

"She said she'd call tonight to explain why she wouldn't be back here again for an indefinite time."

"For God's sake, her graduation's next week, and her folks were planning to be here."

"She didn't say anything about them. She didn't want me to tell you we'd talked. She said she preferred to tell you herself, but I knew you'd want to know."

"Right, thanks for telling me. Damn it."

"You know what I think, Rich? I think she knew I'd tell you. That way you'd have time to adjust to the news before she called you. I wouldn't put too much into this. Whoever's in charge out there must be trying to convince her she has to give herself body and soul to her new job."

"Bastards."

"Si, son bastardos. Know what I think you should do?"

"Go ahead."

"Congratulate her. Tell her you're counting the days until you see her."

"It seems I have little choice."

That evening when she called she sounded tentative. "I have both good news and bad."

"Okay, tell me the bad first."

"You're sure? Well, things are happening so quickly, I'm afraid I won't be able to see you for a while—I don't know how long. I've already moved into a nice little apartment not too far from the station, and this morning I went back to Vegas to get the rest of my stuff. I'm on a full news reporting schedule and have been assigned to cover a story in San Francisco this weekend. When I told them I was planning to go back to Vegas for graduation ceremonies, at first they agreed. Then yesterday they—I keep saying they—actually it's our General Manager Sterling Hastings and News Director Seth Greene. Anyway, they informed me a number of newsworthy events were coming up, and they want me to remain on call. I wish things were different, but right now I feel I have to stay focused and flexible. I guess I'll be missing the graduation ceremonies after all."

"But what about your master's degree work?"

"Okay, I contacted Mr. Weatherford at UNLV. He agreed to give me more time and said all I have to do is hand in my thesis as soon as possible. In my spare time—if I ever get some free time that is—I'll be putting the finishing touches on my paper. So that's the bad news. I can't be with you."

"I agree, very bad."

"Now for the good. Remember how I told you there are two available positions? For one I'd be the nightly news co-anchor with Mr. Greene, and the salary is far beyond what I'd expected. But this is even better. This morning Mr. Hastings made a special announcement. You've heard of Allyson Devereaux?"

"The name sounds familiar."

"It should. She interviews well-known celebrities and sometimes appears on the national network. Turns out she's resigning to accept a position with NBC in New York, and they're considering me as a possible replacement."

Finding her latest disclosure anything but good news, but still relying on Juan's advice, he took a deep breath and said, "Honey, it sounds as if your dreams may be coming true. Do what you have to do and whatever else happens, don't be overly concerned about you and me. One way or another we'll work it out when the time comes."

"Thank you again for your understanding, Rich. You know if it was possible I'd be with you at this very moment."

Their conversation, most of it revolving around her exciting new Hollywood life, lasted for over an hour.

She closed by saying, "I'm so relieved you'll be in Vegas all summer because, as you said, you'll be close if I need you."

To be fully prepared for his approaching summer work, the next week Richard reviewed a portion of the resort construction contracts. At first everything seemed to be in order. He also discussed progress and planning with representatives from the main contracting companies and several subcontractors. Friday afternoon he worked with an architect sketching blueprints for the resort's shopping mall. Afterward he and J.D. met and decided to name the mall The Lakeside Shopping Center.

Saturday morning before the weekly meeting, as he was reviewing more of the construction contracts, Richard discovered a discrepancy he knew could lead to serious problems. Two major firms had been allowed gentlemen's agreements to take the place of signed contracts.

When he mentioned his discovery to J.D., he said, "Don't worry about those particular firms, Rich. We've worked with them before, and I want to give them adequate flexibility. Trust me; they're like family, good as gold."

Richard didn't challenge the response, mainly because he didn't feel he should disagree with his new boss. Not yet, at least. In fact, the New Horizon president would have consented to almost anything his program director requested. The better he knew Richard the more he admired him, not just as a businessman, but personally. Madelline had never known J.D. to be so impressed with a staff associate. And similar to Paula she was convinced her boss wanted Richard to become a permanent Monte Vista executive.

Following the luncheon meeting, J.D. was asked to participate in an impromptu conference at MGM Resorts International headquarters. The last-minute request canceled a meeting with Richard, so free for most of the afternoon, he decided to go to a library to find a late edition of the *Omaha World Herald*. He enjoyed the solitude of a library and preferred a hands-on copy of the newspaper to an internet version. He recalled the evening he and Paula visited the Fremont Street Experience, and during their conversation she had mentioned there was a public library located not far from downtown. He decided to try there.

To avoid mid-day Strip traffic he took the I-15 freeway to the downtown exit, turned left on Las Vegas Boulevard, and a few blocks later pulled into the Las Vegas Library parking lot. As he was about to enter the building, he had to step to one side as a group of children burst through the front doors. It was the end of a library visit for twenty-odd church-school second graders, who for some unknown reason went scampering in all directions. Bringing up the rear, their teacher blew a shrill whistle that startled the runaways, and like a flock of ducklings they gravitated back to her. Quickly she herded them up the steps of the church bus. Tickled with the teacher's magical powers, Richard shook his head and smiled.

Inside the library quite a large number of people were engaged in routine activities—some wandering through the aisles in search of a book; others reading at carrels and tables; several concentrating on library computer screens. Judging from their appearances, Richard assumed some were homeless, in the library because they needed somewhere to be.

When a librarian informed him they didn't receive the Omaha newspaper, he took a *USA Today* to a table. As he was scanning the front page headlines, he happened to look up and noticed a familiar-looking man heading for the exit doors. Sure enough, it was the same man who several weeks earlier had asked him for money on the downtown street.

Richard had occasionally wondered what happened to the homeless girl in the alley. Eager to find out, he left his seat and caught up with the man outside the exit door.

"Sir, excuse me, but do you recall one night a couple of months ago when we met downtown? I gave you some money to help a homeless acquaintance of yours."

"Yes, I do remember. Her name was Jennifer and she was in a predicament, just a little teenager in distress. I also fondly recall your generosity that night."

"Curiosity got the best of me and I followed you to the alley. I apologize for eavesdropping, but I guess I just wanted to see for myself. Can you tell me what happened to her?"

"Hmmm, so you followed me. Well, I'm afraid I can't tell you much— Mr. Stewart, isn't it?"

"My first name's Richard, and I believe yours is Robert."

He nodded his head and said, "She was a runaway from Phoenix. Thanks to you she had a good dinner and then I took her to a shelter for the night. I gave her the rest of the money and said I'd come back the next day to help her find some shoes and a warmer coat. Unfortunately, the next day I couldn't locate her and I never saw her again."

"How old was she?"

"She claimed she was eighteen, but I'm sure she was more like sixteen. Kids like her conceal their age because they're afraid you'll call the cops. She had a goddamn drug problem, and people around here don't take too kindly to alcoholics or drug dependents no matter what their ages. She said her parents had kicked her out and told her not to come home until she'd kicked her habit completely. She wasn't willing to make the sacrifice, or more than likely she didn't think she could. She said she'd seen television shows about Vegas and thought it would be a good place to start a new life. It didn't take her long to realize she was as unwanted here as she was back home. Every day kids like Jennifer join the Vegas homeless ranks."

"You seem to know a lot about the homeless."

"That's because I've been there, done that."

"I see. I knew there were some homeless kids around. I just never thought there'd be very many without parents."

"All ages are well represented in the homeless population, Mr. Stewart— old folks, married folks, single mothers with babies, war veterans, and kids without parents. You'll see a heavy cross-section of them in this particular area. That's because places like the Salvation Army, Catholic Charities, and other food and shelter centers are within a concentrated radius of where we're standing right now."

"I thought some of the people inside looked as if they might be homeless."

"Some like to come to the library all right. If they wander too far away from this general area, the police consider them loiterers and will tell them to move on. Still, newcomers like Jennifer often drift into the downtown area."

"So you're saying right around here is where most of the homeless come to eat and sleep."

"Many do, but you can also find them in various locations around town. Years ago they'd set up encampments. When they found an open lot, they'd put together makeshift tents made out of tarps, wood pieces, cardboard boxes, old sheets, whatever they could find. Once they were set up, the population multiplied fast. I'm sure they found safety in numbers."

"I've heard about encampments, and I've always wondered what they did for bathrooms."

"A major problem everywhere for the homeless."

"You said years ago they tried encampments here. They don't do that anymore?"

"I'm sure they still do somewhere, but the public outcry in Vegas has been overwhelming. Not long after an encampment starts, people living nearby complain to the city and soon they are forced out. Because they have no means for cleaning up, the property is littered with soiled bedding and clothing and all kinds of junk. And the public is left with yet another disparaging image of the homeless. One thing about this part of town, around here there's food, and for some, adequate shelter."

To allow new arrivals easier access to the library entrance, Robert suggested they move farther up the sidewalk. As in their first meeting Richard felt there was much more to Robert McGuire than first appearances might allow. He was easy to talk to, seemed knowledgeable, and flashes of politeness spoke of a different time in his life.

Richard noticed the two books Robert had checked out: *The Total Money Makeover* and *How to Make Money in Stocks*.

Glancing at his watch, Richard said, "It's two o'clock. Do you suppose I could interest you in going somewhere for a cup of coffee or a coke? Unless of course you're too busy."

"I don't have transportation."

"My car's right over there in the parking lot. You can ride with me."

Robert took a cigarette from his jacket pocket and lit up before asking, "Mr. Stewart, is there some particular reason you want to talk with me some more?"

"My friends say I'm an inquisitive cuss, and I find you to be an interesting person to talk to."

Robert rubbed the back of his neck and said, "No offense, but you are straight, aren't you, mister? Oh yeah, you must be. I mean, the pretty lady you were with, is she your wife?"

"Not yet, but soon I hope."

"Scared the living bejesus out of her that night, didn't I?"

"I guess you did at first, but she recovered quickly." Then Richard fabricated," Later on she said she admired you for wanting to help Jennifer."

"Well, I guess a cup of coffee sounds okay, but I do have to be at work at the Golden Nugget by four o'clock. Saturday's usually my day off, but I'm subbing for a friend."

Inside the MKS, Robert was fascinated with the soft leather seats, the dashboard's leather and wood accents, and the directional screen. "So this is a new Lincoln. I haven't been inside of one of these for a long time. Not quite as fancy a body style, but much more technically advanced than they used to be."

"It's a lease car from the company I work for. So tell me, what kind of work do you do at the Golden Nugget?"

"I like to think of myself as an assistant manager of sorts." He chuckled softly before he added, "Actually, my main responsibilities are to keep the buffet food stations filled and the tables and booths cleared and prepared."

"How do you like working there?"

"They've been good to me. I've no complaints."

Richard drove from downtown into the north side of the Strip, and just past Circus Circus he pulled into a McDonald's restaurant. Inside he ordered a coke for himself and a cup of coffee for Robert before they sat down in a booth.

Engaging in a serious conversation with a new acquaintance was not out of character for Richard. It was second nature for him to be gregarious, the poor and lonely not excluded. While he was growing up, a spirit of reaching out to them was common throughout the Stewart household. Sometimes the family would host a Sunday afternoon dinner for employees new to the firm. Other guests might include several poor people his father had recently met at his downtown store. On those occasions his mother Margaret and his sister Elizabeth had a busy Sunday preparing dinner for ten or more people, but they enjoyed serving everyone. Richard's compassion for the less fortunate had a solid anchor.

Robert said, "The night I asked you for money, maybe you thought I was homeless, too. As I indicated, I've been in that position many times. You see, Mr. Stewart, I'm a recovering alcoholic, and in the past my lifestyle was one of moving across the country, of finding and losing jobs."

"You said, 'in the past.'"

"Hopefully that's behind me. I want to be like my boss, Jeremy. He's also a R.A. and he once was homeless like me. But he's been sober for more than twelve years, and these days he has a wife and a couple of kids. They live in a real nice home and seem to be very happy."

"I look upon alcoholism as an illness that could happen to anyone. You see a lot of homeless people on the streets these days. One thing that puzzles me is why more of them don't seek shelter in those places you mentioned."

"It's because of the incredible numbers. That situation means a homeless person can be allowed only a limited time in any one shelter. When there's neither a shelter nor an encampment for them, there's no place to go except back on the streets. At night, even though they're off limits, some will sleep along the railroad tracks and underneath bridges, just about any place they can lay their heads for a few hours. Sad because what they really want more than anything is a place to call home."

"Not to change the subject, but when did you start working at the Golden Nugget?"

"I've been there more for over six years now."

"That's a good long spell."

"Since I've been divorced, six years is a record for me. I almost lost my job there once."

"What happened?"

"Well, I had a relapse. After a night of drinking I called in sick, and to my surprise Jeremy showed up at my apartment. One look at me told him what I'd done, and he was very upset, but he gave me another chance, along with a stern warning it was my last."

"How did you happen to get the job there in the first place?"

"I owe it to the Salvation Army and Alcoholics Anonymous."

"You've mentioned the Salvation Army several times."

"It's because I volunteer at their homeless center."

"I would imagine they're very active in Omaha."

"Wherever they are, they do whatever they can to assist the poor and homeless."

The easy-flowing dialogue between the men ended at 3:15 when Richard said he had to leave. From there he followed Robert's directions back into the heart of old downtown.

During the drive Richard said, "I've enjoyed talking to you today, Robert. Inasmuch as my fiancée is away for a while, next weekend I may have more free time. Maybe if you're not too busy we could meet and talk some more. I assume your phone number is in the directory?"

"You really want to talk some more?"

"As I said, I found our conversation today very interesting."

"I don't have a phone, but you can leave a message with the operator where I live."

Near the corner of 8th Street and Carson Avenue, Richard pulled up in front of a long, narrow, two-story beige color building. The place looked fairly neat and clean, but it was in need of a fresh coat of paint and minor repairs. A sign on the lawn read McAllister Rooms and Apartments.

From the glove compartment Richard removed two of his business cards and handed them, along with a pen, to Robert. "On the back of one could you write down the apartment's phone number?"

Robert did so and handed the card back.

Outside the car he leaned through the open window and said, "I've enjoyed talking with you, too, Mr. Stewart, and I'll look forward to seeing you again."

From the moment they parted company, Richard wondered what possibly could have prompted him to tell Robert he wanted to see him again. It had to be more than feeling sorry for someone who seemed lonely. Then it struck him. *He reminds me of my father, different in many ways, yet they're about the same age, and he's intelligent and personable, and his efforts to help the runaway teenager remind me of how Dad would have reacted. He even volunteers for the Salvation Army as Dad did. Comparable in so many ways.*

That weekend he expected Paula to call and when she didn't, he decided not to try to reach her either. *If she's so damn busy she can't take the time to contact me, to hell with it.* The decision was not a remedy that would permanently ease his longing for her, but his wounded pride had to react in some manner. He was lonely and confused, and rationalizations were losing their consoling effect. He figured it was time she forgot about herself and start considering his feelings, too. So far discussing when they were going to be together, and how much they meant to each other, were adding up to nothing more than empty promises and postponements.

Chapter Thirteen

DURING THE THIRD WEEK IN May Richard's most pressing work problem remained—a full-time assistant had not yet been hired. Still a more personal problem persisted. One of the reasons he'd taken the summer position was to be closer to Paula, but now there was no communication between them whatsoever. She'd been gone for almost three weeks, and in the solitude of his spare time Paula fever seemed unrelenting. More than a few times he wished he hadn't agreed to take his summer position.

Musically inclined as he was, whenever he was driving, he'd tune in to his favorite FM station. The music the station played, and the songs he sometimes sang along with, were usually romantic ballads, but never before had he taken their lyrics to heart. These days the words seemed directly aimed at him.

"And I can change the world,

I will be the sunlight in your universe,

You would think my love was really something good,

Baby, if I could change the world ..."

The prospect of a long, hot summer without Paula Summers seemed about as exciting as a weekend wait in a hospital ER.

Following Saturday's mid-day meeting, Richard called Robert who suggested they meet at the at Mary's Donut Shoppe. It was just a few blocks down the street from where he lived.

When Richard arrived, he found Robert seated at the counter.

"I hope you don't mind this place." Robert said. It's probably not like what you're used to."

"This place is fine," Richard said before they moved on to a booth.

After a waitress brought the men their coke and coffee orders, Robert said, "You know, Mr. Stewart, we talked an awful lot about me last week. Today I'd like to learn more about you."

"All right, well, I own a golf and sporting goods company in Omaha. We produce and distribute equipment and apparel throughout the United States, and we're presently in the process of expanding and hiring more staff. I'm in Las Vegas because we're opening a store within a new resort here. I've never been married, but as I told you I hope more that situation changes soon."

"Your fiancée is a beautiful woman, Mr. Stewart. So tell me more about yourself."

"Okay. I grew up in Omaha and attended the university in Lincoln. I majored in business, competed for the varsity golf team, and played my trombone in an off-campus jazz band. I continued my education in law school at Creighton University, but had to quit after a year. Now if I had a wife and some kids, there'd be a lot more to talk about. And please, call me Richard or Rich."

"I'll try to remember. So you own a golf and sporting goods company. I find that very interesting. When I was a businessman in Cincinnati I played golf quite often, and I still watch some of the major tournaments on television. You say your company is expanding and hiring. That means it's prospering."

"Fortunately our retail, mail-order, and online services are more than holding their own. To insure our continued growth, we believe in recycling a major share of our profits back into our business."

"So you're a bricks and mortar, mail, and dot com company all rolled into one."

"You could say that. Now you said you used to play golf and still follow the pros."

"I wish I was in a position to start playing again."

"Once you get hooked, it's a compelling pastime all right. Last week you talked about liking your work and living in Las Vegas. What about your life before you came here?"

"Hold on there. I like my job, but I didn't say I like Las Vegas. Unless you're a person of adequate means, it's no different than any other big city—growing too fast and there's too much goddamn crime. At least around here you don't get a helluva lot of snow. I guess, Mr. Stewart, I'm what you'd call one damned poor snowbird."

"Please don't call me Mr. Stewart."

"It's just out of respect."

"If it's not too personal, may I ask about your life back in Ohio, what you did before you came here?"

Richard was turning the spotlight back on Robert without him realizing it.

He spoke of growing up in Cincinnati and attending the university where he earned a degree in business management. He went on to become an insurance adjuster and then a bank mortgage broker. During that time he married a school teacher, but the marriage ended four years later.

"My former wife Michelle—I called her Shelley—was a beautiful lady and a great mother. The divorce was entirely my fault."

"You said mother, so you had children."

"We had a daughter, Anita Ellen. She'd be twenty-seven now."

"And where is she?"

"I honestly don't know. The last time I saw her, she was three-years-old." A smile lit his face as he recalled, "She had beautiful red hair, and gorgeous green eyes, and was she ever smart."

"Why do you think you caused the divorce?"

"It was primarily because I was overly ambitious and overconfident. I wanted a higher paying position so I could save enough money to buy my own restaurant. Against my wife's advice, I quit my bank job because I was sure I could find something better. Unfortunately, my timing was bad. All of a sudden the entire country was hit with a bad recession, and there were too many qualified people seeking fewer and fewer jobs. I couldn't find a position even close to the one I'd left, and for a long time I was unemployed."

"I assume your wife was working."

"Oh yes, she was a highly respected Hyde Park elementary teacher. One thing about her, she loved the upper-level social life. She thought instead of struggling to pay our bills, we should be moving into a more expensive home and driving luxury cars like yours. I can't blame her for feeling as she did.

"In the summer a business teaching position opened up at Taft High School. Back in college I'd picked up a teaching certificate just for insurance, and she insisted I apply. I was hired but I'm sure it was because of her influence. I did enjoy teaching the kids, but because of tightening school budgets, at the end of the school year I wasn't offered a continuing contract."

"So it was back to square one."

"That's right. My renewed efforts to find any kind of a decent job fell short, and Shelley was becoming disenchanted with me and our marriage. Before I met her, I liked to party and sometimes drank too much, but when we started going together I quit completely. As the problems in our marriage grew worse, I started drinking again, on the sly of course, but it didn't take her long to find out."

"I imagine she was very upset."

"She told me if I didn't stop, she'd divorce me. I promised her I would and for the most part I did. Then one winter night I went to the grocery store. It was a cold and snowy night, and on the way home I stopped at a lounge for a quick vodka. While there I met an old college acquaintance, and unfortunately one drink led to another. By the time I left, I was over the limit. It was one of the biggest mistakes of my life.

"By then it was snowing heavily outside, and at an intersection my car slid through a red light. Before I could stop, I clipped the rear end of a police vehicle, sirens and all, on his way to an emergency call. His car spun out of control and crashed into a light pole. With his vehicle incapacitated, he was furious. Another officer arrived and I was tested, handcuffed, and spent the night in jail.

"At my hearing the judge gave me a thirty-day sentence, but because it was my first offense and I was barely over the limit, they released me after a couple of weeks. Shelley wasn't so forgiving. She insisted I leave our home and have no further contact with Anita. She said she wanted to make sure our daughter would never be in a car with me again. She also made it clear my separation from Anita was permanent no matter what the judge said."

Robert dabbed at his moist eyes with a closed fist. "Sorry, guess I'm acting like a sentimental ol' crybaby."

"From what you've told me, Robert, I can understand your sorrow."

Robert took a deep breath and said, "Before the divorce was final she was already seeing someone else. I remember his name was Gene Stevens. He was a prominent building contractor, a widower, and a member of her school's PTA. One of his kids was a student in her class, and I'm sure that's how they came to be."

"What did you do then?"

"After the divorce I went to Chicago and stayed with my cousin and his wife. I got a pretty good job there and worked for several months. But I was still drinking and as soon as they found out, I was unwelcome at their place, too.

"I'd become a habitual drunk, but I was sneaky, always finding ways to conceal my problem. Some of the jobs I had over the years, though not high paying, really weren't too bad, and I held on to a couple of them for several years. Others were menial and lasted just a short time. Through it all my main purpose was to get enough money to survive and support my problem. But every time it caught up with me. Of course you know the older you get, the harder it is to land a good job. Over the years I moved from one city to another—St. Louis, Springfield, Tulsa, Albuquerque, and a few smaller cities in between. It was during those times I learned what it means to be homeless."

"Where were your parents and family in all this?"

"I was an only child and my folks, like Shelley, thought I was a hopeless case and sided with her. I'm sure they wanted to stay connected with Anita. She was their little angel."

"And where are they now?"

"First my father passed away, then my mother about eight years ago. I didn't learn about his death until quite a while after it happened. My mother moved to Florida to live with her sister, and for a while I tried to stay in touch with her. But she didn't encourage my efforts. I think she figured sooner or later I'd be asking her for money. Older folks have to worry about such things, you know."

"And why did you decide to come here?"

"Like so many others, like Jennifer, it seemed like a good place to start over. Once I got here I was fifty-four-years-old, tired of moving, and I made up my mind to make it in Las Vegas one way or another. As always, that didn't mean I'd left my drinking problems behind."

Though beleaguered again with the recurring memories, Robert perked up when Richard inquired about his Golden Nugget employment.

"As I said before, it was a fortunate turn of events for me. Probably sounds a little melodramatic, but I truly believe getting my job there saved my life."

"And as it's worked out, you've probably said goodbye to being homeless for good."

"I hope that's how it will be, that I won't slip back again. I have no one but myself to blame for my shortcomings. As a young family man I made some bad choices. I should have been willing to stay with the banking position I had, at least until something better came along. And most of all I shouldn't have started drinking again."

"Tell me about the restaurant you were planning."

Robert smiled and said, "Ahhh yes, the restaurant. It was going to be an upscale Shangri-la with plush decor, candlelit tables, and classic artwork and statues. We'd have an exclusive menu featuring delicacies from around the world to be served by highly skilled waiters and waitresses. It would have been a dining experience which I'm sure would have pleased Shelley." He chuckled as he added, "At least at the Golden Nugget I ended up in the restaurant business."

Subconsciously Richard again compared Robert to his father, Sam. *Business majors in college ... each struggling to be independent ... a compelling dichotomy of youthful ambitions ... except, one person's hopes went awry.*

"You know, Robert, not everyone is willing to take the blame for the kind of personal setbacks you've suffered. You haven't blamed anyone but yourself for your difficulties, and I think it takes courage to admit, unconditionally, you were wrong about some life-altering decisions."

"I never thought of myself as being courageous, more like intrinsically stupid."

"You said you don't know where your daughter is today."

Robert shook his head and said, "It may seem strange I don't know more, but because of the litigation threats, I felt both unwanted and handcuffed. As she was growing older, I figured she wouldn't want to hear from me of all people. The last I heard was several years back when I contacted an old friend in Cincinnati. He told me she was married, but that's all he knew. When I called him later to learn more, he acted as if he didn't want me calling him anymore."

"With her in mind, why didn't you seek help to control your drinking?"

"Illogical things came into play. I've always had my share of pride, and I'm afraid a part of me didn't want help. Freeing yourself from alcoholism is like trying to escape from the claws of a goddamn monster dragon which strangely enough seems protective. Alcoholism is an insatiable, unmitigated son of a bitch."

Richard had to smile at Robert's intelligent manner of speaking often spiked with expletives, especially in his references to alcoholism.

Robert lifted the palms of his hands and said, "My life history sounds kinda ridiculous, doesn't it?"

"It does at that. Pretty damned stupid ridiculous if you ask me."

And they both laughed.

Richard looked at his watch and said, "It's nearly three o'clock and I have to leave because I'm going out to dinner with friends. Let me drop you off at your apartment."

"That's all right. It's not that long a walk from here."

Richard insisted and while he was driving, his mind searched for a reason to meet with Robert again. "You say you volunteer at the Salvation Army quite often. My father also volunteered for them back in Omaha. I think it would be interesting to see their operations up close. Maybe next weekend you could take me down to the homeless center and show me around."

"I should advise you, Mr. Stewart, where we'd be going is on the front lines of poverty. If you really want to go there, Saturday normally is one of my days off, and I'll see what I can do."

Chapter Fourteen

ALTHOUGH HIS SUMMER SUITE AT Paris would not be available to him until the second week in June, the next weekend Richard assumed his full-time summer position. Saturday morning his first waking thought was that if things had gone as planned, he and Paula would now be engaged and celebrating in the Bahamas. Lonesome and longing to hear her voice, he decided to break his vow and call her, but voice mail was his only choice.

More than likely on assignment in Hong Kong, he thought, and his message was brief. "Call me when you're able."

His next call was to Robert, also unavailable.

Fifteen minutes later when he called back, Richard asked, "Our resort meeting is this afternoon, so do you think maybe we could go over to the Salvation Army this morning?"

"Sure, no appointment needed there."

"I'll pick you up right away then."

During the drive toward the homeless center, Robert said, "You're an unusual man, Mr. Stewart, I mean because not many folks truly want to know firsthand how the poor live down in the trenches. Far too many have to beg, steal, and pick through garbage cans just to stay alive. Others have lost all hope and have learned how to be comfortable being uncomfortable. They are known as the chronic homeless. Unfortunately, they're also the ones the critics use as models."

"So you're saying there's truth to the notion that many don't want to change the way they live."

"Some don't, but a lot fewer than people assume. I've read a lot about it. Figures from a national coalition for the homeless have determined that as many as 75 percent of those able to work would give anything to be self-sufficient if only the opportunities were there. And why do we let the minority, those who don't want to improve their lives, why do we let them become the stereotype for the homeless in general?"

Just past the library on Las Vegas Boulevard, Richard turned left on to Owens Avenue. Moments later he pulled into the parking lot of the Salvation Army homeless campus. As the men walked onto the grounds, Richard noticed a variety of structures. There was the Day Resource Center, the Safe Haven, and several smaller buildings. The most noticeable structure was a three-story dormitory.

"That's the Lied center," Robert said. "It has living accommodations for adults enrolled in vocational transition classes and for mental health residents. The cafeteria there serves hundreds and hundreds of people every week. That's in addition to another Family Service facility where they supply groceries to many needy families."

"Feeding so many people a day must require an enormous amount of preparation. How many homeless people are there in Las Vegas anyway?"

"It depends on your source. The actual number is indeterminable because so many are transitional—here one day, gone the next. Others are living temporarily with relatives or acquaintances. You hear estimates ranging anywhere from ten to fifteen thousand."

Around the buildings there were people of all ages waiting for assistance of one kind or another. Seeing so many needy folks in a single setting was a saddening, numbing reality for Richard.

The newly arrived—those with their belongings in grocery carts, duffel bags, or backpacks—were asked to remove them from the sidewalks and away from the buildings. Some of the people gathered in small groups, while others sat on benches beneath a shade canopy. Some were conversing in pairs and groups, while others seemed isolated. Cigarette smoking was not uncommon.

Most were dressed in worn and soiled clothing. Some relied on wheelchairs, walkers, and canes. Far too many, even some of the younger adults, were missing teeth, and some had no teeth at all. Smaller tots clung to their parents. Most of the older children looked withdrawn, yearning for something to attract their stymied energies. Most of the people were wearing tennis shoes or thongs. Two older women wore once fancy, sun-shielding hats, now stained and ruffled.

Robert said, "A lot of these folks are clients in the vocational programs. You'll also notice a lot of activity around the Safe Haven building. The staff there works with those suffering from mental disorders. They coordinate with local and state mental health agencies and have access to social workers and psychologists. A general consensus is that one in four of the homeless population suffers from some degree of mental illness. Those close to the situation know one in four doesn't come close to the actual number."

As the two men were touring the different facilities, Robert said, "The needs of the homeless here today are endless, but one of the most immediate responsibilities is assigning cots for the folks who'll be sleeping here tonight."

"And how many will that be?"

"Again, indeterminable numbers every night."

"I'm still wondering about bathroom facilities for so many."

"And as I said before, a never-ending problem."

"So with the homeless population holding steady in Las Vegas, it's little wonder so many have to live on the streets. Something more from city hall should be done."

"Sincere efforts are always under consideration, but there are too many political leaders, not just here but everywhere, who think of the homeless as nothing more than menaces to society. They'd like to give each one of them a bus ticket to another city, the farther away the better. I wonder how many of them realize that more than 40 percent of the homeless are children under the age of six, and at least 25 to 30 percent of the homeless are military veterans, many recently returned from the wars in Iraq and Afghanistan. And of course many are physically and emotionally unstable. Should the very young and veterans be given bus tickets?"

Robert shook his head in dismay as he continued, "Anyway, what happens to homeless kids as they get older can be devastating. When they enter public schools, they wear second and third hand clothing, and they have little or no money at all. Some have only limited communication skills, and once they are in a school environment, there are many students who will tease and bully them."

"Not exactly a self-esteem builder," Richard said.

Robert introduced him to several staff personnel who were polite, but too busy to delay for long.

As they were leaving the Owens campus, Richard said, "More people should see for themselves what's going on down here."

"Yes, they should. It might help them understand that there's a tremendous amount of misinformation about who the homeless people are, and the overwhelming problems they are facing. Now I told Major Benson you wanted to learn about the inner workings of the Salvation Army organization, and he said he'd like to meet you. This morning he's over at the main headquarters, so we can go there if you like. It's about a fifteen-minute drive from here."

"Let's do it."

With Robert's directions, Richard drove several miles south and west through the city before turning on to Palomino Lane. It was a neighborhood of well-kept single-story homes mixed with elegant two-story residences, a few with circular driveways and wrought-iron fences. Several blocks up the street he parked in the Salvation Army administration parking lot.

Inside the building a secretary took the men to Major Thomas Benson's office where Robert handled introductions.

The major, a late middle-aged man and well-dressed in a suit and tie, looked over the top of his glasses and said, "I understand, Richard, you were interested in our Owens facility."

"I am and we were just there."

"Rob is one of our most faithful volunteers down there. He's also our computer expert, puts us back on track when we have problems. He said you'll be moving to Las Vegas before opening a sports equipment store in a new resort."

"I won't be permanently moving here, but we will be opening a store."

"And what was your general impression of what you saw at our Owens center?"

"It was an enlightening visit for me. I didn't realize there were so many homeless people in Las Vegas. Rob said that in addition to caring for their immediate needs, providing vocational training and job placement are the Salvation's most challenging goals."

"That's true, but with outside support and our newer facilities, we're reaching out to more people than ever before."

"My father had a business not too far from the Salvation center in Omaha. I know back there they've always been active in job training programs. The success of those programs in a city as large as Las Vegas must require tremendous organization."

"There's a lot to do all right. We call them our re-entry programs. Our coordinating staff enlists clients and arranges for food and housing. The vocation clients then attend training classes for positions like secretaries, janitors, security guards, waiters, waitresses, and the list goes on. Last year we were able to place hundreds of men and women into full- and part-time positions. Of course, with more financial resources we could do a lot more. Las Vegas is a generous community, but the homeless needs and rehabilitation costs just keep rising."

"May I be your latest donor?" Richard asked before writing a check for $1,000.

It was nearly noon when he and Robert left the headquarters building. During the drive back to Robert's apartment, Richard could see in the distance the skyline of downtown buildings and Fremont Street. He thought of how crowded and energized Glitter Gulch would be on a Saturday, yet how close it was to the area where so many of the poor and homeless congregate. For many of them the main concerns were getting in line somewhere for their next meal, and wondering where they'd be sleeping that night. The contrast of lifestyles, so close to each other, seemed starkly ironic.

For no other reason than to start a conversation, he said, "I have a question for you, Rob."

"Go ahead, Richard." It was the first time Robert, without urging, had called his new acquaintance by his first name.

"I want your opinion. You've lived here for a long time, so you must know something about the dynamics of gambling. Say a person won several thousand dollars and wanted to increase his winnings. Which game of chance do you think would offer the best odds? Silly question, just curious as to what you think."

"Well, the person could get lucky again, but as anyone familiar with the situation knows, gambling luck is fleeting at best. I'd say the person should think of putting the money to better use. Why? Someone you know get lucky?"

"Yeah, someone I know. By the way there's an important business matter developing within our firm, and with your business background, I think I could use some outside advice."

Robert exhaled a sarcastic hiss and said, "You want my advice concerning an important business matter? Seriously?"

"Seriously. If you don't mind, I'll be calling you in a couple of days. You said your other day off was Tuesday, so if you're free that day, I would like to meet with you."

"I'll be sure to make myself available."

Chapter Fifteen

THAT EVENING, THEIR GOAL TO make Richard's leisure time less lonely, Juan and Maria took him out to dinner, then back to their place for conversation. Much of the talk revolved around Richard's rapidly changing life. "Yes, the Monte Vista project was on target ... Yes, he would remain as program director the entire summer ... No, as yet he hadn't spent his gambling winnings ... Yes, when Paula came back they'd have a big celebration party," and so on.

At 9:30 the children, Juanita and Mario, returned home from a movie with Maria's older sister, Christina. As always, the youngsters were excited to see Uncle Ricardo. A month earlier he'd given Mario a set of junior golf clubs and several times at a nearby driving range had worked with him on driving and putting techniques.

Richard told the proud parents, "Mario's a natural, has exceptional timing and coordination."

As for five-year-old Juanita, she was Richard's "dark-eyed senorita," and she loved sitting on his lap while he read to her. Whenever Uncle Ricardo was around, it was the best of times.

Later when he returned to his Paris room, Paula fever stalked him again. Discouraged she had not returned his call and weary of lamenting her absence, he stretched out on the bed and thoughts drifted back to the morning events.

It could have been so different for Robert McGuire. A business grad hoping to succeed, married to a woman he loved, a young father with a daughter he loved, all that going for him. If only seeking a better job would have worked out, eventually he probably would have opened his Shangri-la restaurant. But the disappointments came one after another, and then the drinking problems, and soon all of his hopes and ambitions were detonated, destroyed, disintegrated! Now here he is, twenty-five years later, with little to show for his personal life. Yet in his spare time, because he cares about the less fortunate, he volunteers faithfully for the Salvation Army. He seems to know everything there is to know about the homeless. Probably a major part of his desire to assist them comes from work ethic aspirations he kept losing to his drinking problems.

Seeds of inspiration planted earlier in the day began showing signs of life. *I need an assistant before any more work piles up. There's research to be done, calls to be made, personnel programs to be organized. The job requires an intelligent person with a sound business background, someone with maturity who can take over when I have to be in Omaha.*

Thoughts crystallized. *Why not hire Robert? He has the education and the background. He's quick thinking, has a great sense of humor, and I'm sure he would get along well with others. And he loves the game of golf. But will he accept the position if I offer it to him? Would he want to leave the security he's built into his present job? I wonder what Ben would think of him.*

Richard recalled the afternoon meeting when James Forrester announced that the official Monte Vista groundbreaking ceremonies would take place Monday morning. The committee also approved the final blueprints for the Resort Links golf course.

So I need someone like yesterday.

Pockets of concern intervened. It was true he'd known Robert for only a short time. *He has three DUI arrests, has gone back to drinking before, and admits to being a single drink away from falling back into the abyss. I could be all wrong about this.*

Before Richard fell asleep, the positive thoughts were overshadowing the negatives. *He's well read and speaks knowledgeably about what's going on in the business world. The Salvation Army people praise his volunteering efforts. They even rely on him to solve their computer problems.*

Monday morning Richard called Benjamin in Omaha to share his reasons for hiring Robert.

Benjamin responded, "From what you've told me, he sounds like a very good choice. Trust what that little voice inside is telling you, Rich. She's usually right."

That clinched it. Next he called the McCallister Apartments, but Robert was out. The operator said she'd have him call back, and twenty minutes later Robert was on the line.

Richard didn't delay. "About the business matter we discussed? It concerns a job opening I think you'll find worth considering."

The line was momentarily silent before Robert replied, "Did you say a job opening? Would I have to sell golf equipment or something along those lines?"

"No, no, what I have in mind is not a salesman's job. Any chance we could meet tomorrow morning?"

"Yes, sir, I'm off all day, and I don't have to be to work until four o'clock on Wednesday. I had promised to work at the Salvation resource center tomorrow morning for a while. Could you pick me up at the library around eleven o'clock?"

"I'll see you there."

Richard next informed J.D. "I may have found my assistant, and assuming I'll be hiring him, the orientation may take the next couple of days. By the way, he's an older, but well-qualified gentleman."

"Take all the time you need, Rich."

Tuesday morning when Richard walked into the library, Robert was waiting near the checkout desk. He was wearing his best outfit—gray tweed sport coat, white dress shirt, and well-pressed blue denim trousers. His black shoes were older but polished to a bright shine, and although a barber's trim was overdue, he'd neatly combed his hair and had closely shaved.

Richard said, "You look very nice, Robert."

"Thanks. I don't dress up very often."

Briefcase in hand, Richard asked a librarian for permission to use an unoccupied room. She escorted the men to a vacant classroom containing an instructor's desk, a table, and student chairs unceremoniously scattered about.

Richard asked Robert to have a seat at the table before he said, "I'm sure you recall me talking about the Monte Vista resort. To review, early last winter the person who's in charge of the project gave me exclusive rights for an on-site Stewart store. He also asked me to assist him in the resort's early planning stages."

"I remember."

"This summer I'm carrying a time-consuming workload, which brings me here with you. You have some impressive credentials—a college business degree, valuable experience, and you've stayed in step with today's business climate. I know you once played golf, and you still like the sport. That's an important plus."

"I believe I told you I played regularly with friends and business associates back in Cincinnati, but that was long ago."

"But you said you still watch some of the major tournaments on television."

"Oh, I still love the sport all right. Last spring I went to see the finals of the Senior Master's event here. It sure made me wish I was playing again."

"Good. As the summer program director, I need a dependable assistant, someone with business savvy, someone who can help me with organizational planning, and someone who will work well with a cross-section of people. It won't happen often, but there will be times when I'll have to be in Omaha. During those absences I'll also need someone who can adequately fill in. I'm offering the position to you."

Robert's eyes blinked slowly as he said, "You want me to work for you, for the New Horizon resort enterprise?"

"That's correct. When summer ends, I'll be relinquishing my duties as program director. Don't worry, because if you take the job and you work out—and I'm sure you will—you will remain in the same position with the permanent director. When the resort operations begin, the position will take on even more importance."

"My goodness," was all Robert could muster.

Richard knew if Robert accepted the offer a major overhaul would be in order. He would need new clothes for the job, an apartment near the resort site, an adequate vehicle, and so on.

"Do you have any health problems you know of, any reason why you couldn't handle a steady, mobile-style workload?"

"Healthwise, I've been fortunate. I have a little arthritis, but it's not debilitating. I walk a lot, sometimes late at night 'cause I don't sleep all that much. And of course runnin' from the law hasn't hurt my conditioning either." With a sly smile he added, "Just kiddin' ya, Richard."

Richard smiled back and said, "If you decide to come to work for us, the company is going to ask for a complete physical examination."

"I already had one this year and passed with flying colors."

"Wonderful. By the way, we'll get you a Las Vegas Athletic Club membership. Are you familiar with their facilities?"

"I know they have several locations around town."

"You can come with me to the Maryland Parkway branch, and I'll help you get started in a fitness program. Quite soon I'll want you on the driving range, the next step in getting you back to playing golf again."

For the first time Robert looked apprehensive. "All this sounds terrific, but I really don't have any extra money to pay for golf equipment."

"Golfing essentials are definitely not a problem. Those you can select as gratis from our company catalogue. I don't mean to rush you, but next week in your off-work hours I want you to do some research for me concerning some of the best golf courses. I realize there is your present job to consider."

"I'm real interested, Mr. Stewart, I mean, Richard. If I make the grade, tell me again what happens after you leave."

"A good question. I won't be the program director anymore, but as I said, I'll make sure you continue with my successor. If for some reason those circumstances don't work out, we can transfer you to any number of promising jobs. One of the reasons I keep alluding to you playing golf, is because in the future I'm going to recommend we hire a golf coordinator for senior citizens. In addition to that, before the resort opens I'll need a manager for our satellite store. As you can see, there will be some outstanding opportunities awaiting you."

From his briefcase Richard removed a manila folder and placed it before Robert.

"Inside you'll find a contract stipulating a $60,000 annual salary along with an outstanding benefits package. It includes medical and dental insurance, 401K, a two weeks paid vacation, everything an executive assistant should have."

Robert quickly scanned the three-page contract before looking up and responding, "I accept. I want the job."

"Better read it carefully. You don't have to do it now."

"Oh, but I want to do it now." He reached inside his coat pocket for his older, plastic-frame reading glasses, and this time read the contract carefully before he said, "I agree to everything."

Richard handed him his pen and Robert signed the contract.

"Congratulations, Rob. In a few days you'll be receiving my company's promotion brochures and advertising flyers. Getting a feel for our objectives will give you some perspective of what we'll want for Monte Vista. Oh yes, you'll want to give the Golden Nugget a two-week notice ASAP. We'll provide you with a cell phone, and I've forgotten, did you tell me you have a car?"

"I have a '92 Ford pickup parked in back of the apartments. She needs a new muffler, but I'll get it taken care of promptly."

"Okay, now, you're going to be out in the business world, so you'll also need some clothes to fit various occasions."

"Most of my clothes come from Goodwill and discount stores. What I'm wearing today is my one and only Sunday best."

Richard had decided not to reveal that he personally would be providing the financial means to help Robert. Figuring such an arrangement might make his new assistant feel uncomfortable, he said, "New Horizon will be assisting you monetarily in your transition. They have a slush fund set aside to help new employees."

The real slush fund was the $5,435 Richard had won gambling at Wynn's. He figured there was a viable connection because his original gambling gratuities came through James Forrester. Now the money could be used in the best interests of Monte Vista, so in a roundabout way Richard felt he wasn't misleading his new assistant.

"What about my past, the drinking problems?"

"I think you've learned to deal with the situation. By the way I have a psychiatrist friend back in Omaha who believes that with guidance and self-discipline nearly every alcoholic can permanently overcome his dependency. If ever you would like, I could—"

Robert threw back his head and said gruffly, "I had a shrink once, and I don't need another one."

"Okay, Rob, fine, but there is a risk here for both of us. In this position you're going to face daily pressures. One time off the wagon—I mean one time only—and I'd have to let you go for good. No second chance as you once had at the Golden Nugget." With peremptory force Richard added, "Don't drink at all. This job and drinking do not mix, period."

Robert took a deep breath and said, "I understand."

Glancing at the clock on the wall, Richard said, "Let's see it's almost noon, and since you aren't working all day, we should go shopping for those new clothes you'll need for work."

As was his tendency when in doubt, Robert rubbed the back of his neck as he asked, "Level with me now. Is there some kind of a catch to all this?"

"None at all. It isn't easy to find someone with all-around business experience who's not already tied down. Trust me, there are no strings attached."

Minutes later as the MKS cruised from the downtown area, there was excitement mixed with wonderment in Robert's heart. Complaining of allergies he didn't have, he dabbed at his moist eyes with a closed fist.

Their destination was the sprawling Boulevard Mall on Maryland Parkway a few miles east of the Strip. After the car was parked, Robert seemed uneasy as they entered the mall's front doors.

"Even though I've lived here for years," he said, "I rarely go inside a large shopping mall like this one. If you're my age and not dressed quite well, some of the security guards always seem to be watching you."

"I don't think you'll have to be concerned about such circumstances anymore. Now if you don't mind, we're going to get you a haircut."

Down the hallway leading to Macy's they stopped at a hair salon. Inside, a receptionist advised there would be a forty-five minute wait. They decided to leave Robert's name with her and moved on to the food court. Because it was the noon hour the court was busy, but the men ordered a soup-and-sandwich special and found an empty table.

Forty-five minutes later they were back in the salon where a young stylist had been assigned to them. Her name tag revealed she was Charlene Carlson. Her bleached mixed-color hair was piled in a twist, and she wore sparkly makeup and ruby red lipstick.

In the midst of vigorous gum chewing, she asked, "Do both of you want a haircut?"

Robert said, "Just me, unfortunately."

Charlene proceeded to wash and blow-dry his hair. After surveying its thickness and length, she offered several trimming options. Robert glanced across the room at Richard, seated in a chair and glancing through a magazine.

"I think I'd like it short, about like his," Robert said.

Promptly the stylist's shaver sent generous amounts of dark-mixed-with-gray hair tumbling onto the apron.

"Miss, you're really whackin' away up there, ain't you?"

Charlene's no-nonsense glance reflected in the mirror as she replied, "You said short, you get short." Then she turned the chair so that they were face-to-face and added, "Don't worry, Mr. McGuire. You remind me of my grandpa, and I'm going to make you look really good."

Changing to clippers, her rhythmic movements resembled an artist applying final touches to a portrait. In finishing, she shaved behind his ears and trimmed his eyebrows.

Confidently she handed him a mirror, which he feared would reveal irrevocable damage.

Instead he nodded as he said, "Hmmm, never had it cut quite that short before, but it's really not too bad. Looks as though you got rid of a lot of the gray."

Charlene said, "I'd say you look pretty snazzy there, sir, like a sportsman, or perhaps an executive."

The short trim had sharpened Robert's features, and if he gained a few pounds he would be a very handsome man. Richard paid for the bill with cash and included a sizable tip for Charlene.

They returned to the main corridor and continued on to Lenscrafters where Robert selected new reading glasses in a handsome black-and-gold frame. Richard wrote a check for them and told Robert that New Horizon would reimburse him later.

Next stop, Macy's department store. There in the men's department a sales clerk approached Richard and asked, "Sir, may I help you?"

"Not me, I'm an accountant and apparel advisor for Mr. McGuire here. Would you please show us some of your most popular dress suits?"

Basking in sheer delight, Robert merely grinned and shook his head.

The salesman, Cory Langston, asked, "What size do you wear, Mr. McGuire?"

Robert rubbed his chin and said, "Well, I used to take a forty-two medium, but these past few years I've lost some weight."

Cory sized him up and proceeded to lay out several suits on a table. They were from Alfani, Calvin Klein, and Ralph Lauren.

As Robert touched their smooth textures, Richard said, "Try the Ralph Lauren first. That tan color should look good on you."

Minutes later as Robert emerged from the dressing room, Richard had to smile. The rolled-up pants and sleeves were too long, and when Robert looked into the full-length mirror, he said, "Makes me look like an old time Charlie Chaplin or Groucho Marx."

Richard nodded to the salesman and said, "Size it for Mr. McGuire."

Cory quickly pinned the trousers and coat sleeves.

With Richard assisting, Robert chose another suit, two sport coats, and two pairs of coordinating trousers and shirts. Cory said the tailoring would be completed in a few days.

They moved on to men's shoes where they picked out two pairs for dress and two pairs for leisure.

Richard said, "Now we need to get you some more casual wear."

Several aisles away Robert tried on a bright-color Hawaiian polo shirt and plain khaki pants, both of which required no alterations. He asked Richard if he could wear them along with his new Rockport casual shoes.

"Of course, they're yours. You know, Charlene was right; you really are quite a distinguished-looking fellow. In fact if you go out tonight, you better be on the lookout for wild women."

"Take me home. I want an early start."

The shopping spree took the entire afternoon, with a time-out for ice cream sundaes in the food court. It was nearing the dinner hour when Richard said they were almost finished. Their last stop was Foot Locker for workout tennis shoes.

Robert's new wardrobe consisted of the new suits, shirts and ties, and two sport coats; Geoffrey Beene and Dockers slacks; shirts by Hilfiger, Tommy Bahama, and Izod; London Fog raincoat and a windbreaker; a Seiko watch; Bostonian, Calvin Klein, Rockport, and Nike shoes; several pairs of socks and shorts; and a workout outfit. At Richard's insistence, included was a bottle of Eternity cologne. In all, he'd written checks amounting to more than $2,500.

Outside the mall they wheeled their loaded cart to the car where they placed the packages inside the trunk. The fresh, floral-scented air, surfing on the waves of springtime breezes, briskly awakened their appetites. Richard noticed an Applebee's restaurant at the north end of the parking lot, and they stopped there for dinner.

A young receptionist warmly greeted them before seating them at a table in the restaurant's Greenhouse addition. At a nearby booth waiters and waitresses were singing "Happy Birthday" to an shy-appearing young man.

"Never been to an Applebee's before," Robert said, "sure is a lively place."

In the next hour while eating their chicken and rib dinners, the two men seldom stopped talking, smiling, and laughing along the way. They could have easily been mistaken for father and son.

At one point Robert said, "I wonder what my friends around the apartment will think when they see me in those slick new threads?"

"Which reminds me, what are the lease terms for your apartment?"

"My landlord doesn't believe in long-term leases. Some of his renters aren't too dependable, so short-term agreements make it easy for them to part company."

"I want you to move to a new location near the resort site as soon as possible."

"Now that, I'm afraid, *won't* be possible."

"Sure it will be. What time did you say you work tomorrow?"

"My evening shift starts at four o'clock."

"Good. Yesterday a couple of the committee members and I spent some time at the resort site. On the way back, over on Charleston we passed a couple of nice-looking apartment complexes and I called them. They said we could see their models tomorrow morning after ten o'clock. How about if I pick you up?"

"Except I can't afford to move into an expensive apartment. Maybe after I start receiving a paycheck, but until—"

Raising his hand in a halting gesture, Richard said, "Once we find an apartment you like, we'll pay your first month's expenses and cover whatever your present landlord requires. Along with our Monte Vista mobile home office, the apartment will also serve as your workplace. Don't worry, because a month from now you'll be responsible for your own bills."

"Whatever you say."

"Now for the telephones. In addition to your home phone, you'll need a cell because you'll be on the go, and I'll be in touch with you often. When we were talking to Major Benson, he said you are familiar with computers. Do you have one?"

"No, but I've been using them in the library for years."

"We'll be ordering you a new laptop, printer, and fax."

"Mr. Stewart, how adequate is the New Horizon fund anyway?"

"Adequate enough to get you started."

"Do I have to pay this back? I'd certainly be more than willing to."

"No, just consider it a bonus for signing with us. Tell me again about your pickup."

"It's an older Ford. She looks good enough, but she is a little rough mechanically."

"Maybe we could get you a company lease car. I know they have several in the reserve pool. I'm not familiar with their overall employee policies, but I'll find out. You'll definitely need reliable transportation."

"Another problem is that I have only a limited insurance policy on the truck. Full coverage on a newer car might be a problem."

"Car insurance through New Horizon shouldn't be a problem."

"Except my driving history will be disclosed, and I'm sure their insurance people wouldn't appreciate my blotchy record. My license is restricted because of the three violations—one in Cincinnati, one in St. Louis, and one here. Another violation of any kind and the state of Nevada has advised me they will revoke my license."

"How long ago was the last one?"

"When I first came here about seven years ago, but sure as hell none of the citations will go away."

"I'll see if I can handle matters with the insurance people."

Robert had to pinch himself to be sure what was happening was not a dream. For a long time he hadn't believed in spiritual forces or any type of momentum that could dramatically change his life. Now it was he who was wondering if a guardian angel was watching over him.

Wednesday morning the two men traveled on West Charleston Boulevard to the Peccole Ranch area to see the two apartment complexes. The first was attractive and efficient enough, but the second offered a beautifully landscaped courtyard, three swimming pools with spas, and a complete weight and Nautilus facility. There were two vacancies available, and Robert chose the ground-level one-bedroom unit.

When they returned to the McCallister Apartments, Richard said, "Give your notice here tomorrow. I'll be in touch with you in a couple of days regarding the research information I'll need from you." He opened the glove compartment and withdrew an envelope. "Inside there's a two-week paycheck. Along with all the changes you're making, I want to pay you in advance for your upcoming work."

Robert paused before he said, "You know, Richard, it's been a long time since I've worked in the real business world, and I'm afraid I'll make some silly mistakes."

"Just remember, the resort project is new to all of us. We all make mistakes, and we'll just take things as they come." Richard had one final question. "Just curious, what was your daughter's name again? Anita?"

"Yes, Anita Ellen."

"Pretty name."

Chapter Sixteen

A COUPLE OF DAYS LATER in his New Horizon office, Richard was sorting through his Monte Vista daily worksheet when Cynthia Miller buzzed him.

"There's a call from Ms. Summers on line one."

Richard reached for the phone so quickly his elbow collided with the edge of his desk. Paula's voice, smooth and sweet as a Chopin sonata, quickly nullified the pain.

"Richard, honey, I've been missing you terribly today, and I'm sorry I haven't called you."

Like the pain, past anger and regrets also swiftly vanished. "I know they're keeping you busy," he said, "so don't worry about it. Hey, it's great to hear from you."

"So much is happening, I can't keep track. I had to call you from here at the station, or I might not get another opportunity. By the time I get home at night I'm ready to collapse, but I keep reminding myself the sacrifices are going to be worth it."

"Tell me what's going on."

"For starters, they've set me up in my own private office, and I have a lovely view of Sunset Boulevard."

"And do you have the position you wanted?"

"Well, no, not Allyson Devereaux's job, not yet anyway."

"How soon until you find out?"

"No one is saying for sure. I do know Allyson will be here until the end of next month. Before she leaves, I'll have worked with her on three interview stories. There are two other candidates also working with her, and my main concern is they both have more experience. I think the powers that be want to find out if I have the ability to make up for my inexperience. The good news is that within the next several weeks a final decision will be made."

The prospect of yet another lengthy postponement instantly aggravated him. "You did say several weeks, didn't you? Paula, how can you possibly consider several weeks as good news? I don't want to wait several weeks until I see you. Last week you should have been here for your graduation, and I thought after the ceremony we'd be telling your folks about our engagement. Wasn't that the original plan?"

Surprised with his terse response, she said, "You need to understand, Rich, I have no control over what's going on with management. They have to do whatever is best for the station, and it would be unwise for me to be impatient with them."

"Look, if I came over there for just a couple of days, I'm sure you could manage your career and still spend some time with me. I want to see you, Paula."

"I've thought about you coming here, but during the spring you were always on my mind. It just wouldn't work out with you here right now."

"You know what I'm beginning to think? All you need from me is an occasional phone call."

"As I said, I can't control what's happening."

"You need to set aside some time for your personal affairs. You should make that clear to those who are dominating your life these days."

"But that—"

"But that might mess up your damn career."

"Richard, I know you don't mean that. Before today you've always understood what's being required of me."

"You and I have two completely different points of view, and you're going to do whatever you think is right for you no matter how it may affect us."

"I know I miss you and I love you and that's why I called."

"I believe you do, but we were too close to stop seeing each other completely for an indefinite time. Look, there's an important staff meeting and I can't be late, so I have to go. I'll have to call you another time."

His disconnecting click surprised him almost as much as it did Paula, and it didn't take him long to regret what he'd done. His sudden outburst, he realized, might give her reason to end their relationship for good. He almost called her back, but pride interfered. He knew if the situation was reversed, a swarming SWAT team couldn't stop him from seeing her.

Minutes later Cynthia again buzzed him, and he hoped it was Paula calling back.

Instead, Robert said, "Hi, Rich, just wanted to let you know my cell phone sure is a handy little gadget. I used to think people who used these things thought they were hot stuff. Now here I am talking to you outside Smith's grocery store."

"So tell me what's going on."

"Well, this morning I've been over to the apartment complex lookin' around. Earlier I picked up my clothes from Macy's, and as you said might happen, ever since I got all duded up women are showing me some real respect—even got a wink from one of them in the store here a while ago. Foxy looking thing she was."

"Avoid women. They're a dangerous commodity."

"Huh, you're telling me? Seriously though, yesterday I went to the library and researched *Golf Digest* and other publications for articles concerning some of the most popular golf courses."

"Tell me more."

"I found a story in *Barron's* predicting by the year 2020 more than fifty-five million Americans will be playing golf. Five million of those will be teenagers and younger. That will make golf the USA's number one family recreational pastime. I'd say Mr. Forrester was right on making the sport Monte Vista's central theme attraction."

"Timely fact-finding on your part, Rob, and also excellent promotional information. You can tell me everything when I see you. And you'll be moving within the next few days?"

"I'll be moved in by Sunday. I don't have too much stuff, and one of the workers at the homeless center offered to help."

"How about your pickup?"

"I had a new muffler installed."

"You informed the Golden Nugget?"

"I did that. They were supportive; said a one-week notice would suffice. They were also kind enough to say I could come back if the new job doesn't work out. They said they'd find something for me."

"No chance of that, right?"

"No, sir, no chance whatsoever."

Hearing Robert's energized responses was heartwarming. Following the call, the lingering afterglow somehow made Richard think of Robert's separation from his daughter. *That was more than twenty-five years ago, and he still feels she's heard only the worst about him. For fear of being rejected, chances are he will always be afraid to reach out to her.*

He rose from his desk and walked over to the window. Gazing into the cloudless blue sky he thought, *What if I was to contact Anita? I wonder how she'd react were she to learn her father was a responsible person holding down a good job. What if once she knew such information, she'd want to know more? And what if I could arrange for them to be in touch with each other? That would be nothing short of a miracle for him and possibly for her.*

Returning to his desk, Richard jotted a few notes on a memo pad before calling Cynthia. His written request was simple: *Find out what you can about one Anita Ellen, childhood name McGuire. Age twenty-seven, Cincinnati, Ohio, I think. I want to know whom she's married to, where she works, anything you can uncover concerning her personal life. And find me an address and number where she can be reached. Thanks.*

A short time later Cynthia returned with her findings. "Her last name is Stevens, her stepfather's name. She still lives in Cincinnati, was married at one time but is no longer. She's been divorced for a couple of years and has no children."

Really, divorced with no children. Her marriage must have ended quickly. I wonder why.

"She graduated from University of Cincinnati, taught for three years in a public high school, and then went back for her master's degree. She's currently a counselor at Walnut Hills High. I have her address and home telephone number." Cynthia placed the information on his desk.

"Thanks, Cyn, thanks so much." *A high school counselor. Robert will be pleased to hear that.*

When he finished his afternoon work, Richard started to write what he hoped would be an interesting letter to Robert's daughter.

Dear Ms. Stevens:

After the introduction, however, nothing he wrote seemed satisfactory, and several attempts were tossed into the recycle basket. Finally he decided to make his message pure and simple and hope for the best.

My name is Richard Stewart and I'm president of the Stewart Golf and Sporting Goods Company in Omaha. Please understand I am writing this letter on my own volition.

Recently in Las Vegas I hired a man to work within our company interests. His name is Robert McGuire, and I understand he's your father.

Apparently he hasn't been in touch with you for about twenty-five years. He told me he's always wanted to reach you, but there were compelling reasons why he couldn't.

Again, he did not ask me to write this letter, nor did I inform him I would. I thought I'd let you know about him and that he's doing well. He has fond memories of you as a child. He's always felt because of his past mistakes you would never want to hear from him. I've taken it upon myself to think perhaps you would.

If you'd like more information about your father, please write or call me.

Sincerely,

Richard M. Stewart

He personally typed the letter on Stewart Company stationery he had in his briefcase. The official letterhead and his Omaha business card, he figured, would remove any doubts about his authenticity.

As he was about to seal the letter, he wondered if Anita would consider his correspondence an intrusion into a very delicate matter. Because Robert wouldn't know of the letter either, he had to be concerned with the reactions of both parties. He decided to tear up his letter and mind his own business, but a heartbeat short of that he sealed and stamped the envelope. *Just maybe this could be a giant first step in bringing them together. If nothing else it will serve the purpose of letting her know her father is alive and doing well.*

As he walked to the outer office, stomach butterflies were in furious flight, but he shrugged them off before dropping the letter into the tray labeled Outgoing Mail.

Chapter Seventeen

EARLY MONDAY MORNING ROBERT ANSWERED Richard's latest call.

"This is Robert McGuire, welcoming you on behalf of the future Monte Vista Golf and Family Resort. Please tell me how I may be of assistance."

"That's an outstanding greeting. Sounds to me as if you've been reading my company's customer service guidelines."

"I read them front to back yesterday. By the way I'm all moved in and I love my apartment."

"Excellent. The reason I called is because I want you to come to a special committee meeting with me tomorrow morning."

Robert's voice was noticeably strained. "Uh-oh, getting me into trouble right away, huh?"

"At that time you'll be meeting James Forrester, the person most responsible for Monte Vista."

"My goodness, I'm going to meet the gentleman you're always talking about?"

"One and the same."

"I should wear a suit and tie, or maybe a sport coat?"

"Whichever you prefer. I told him I'd hired a top-notch assistant, and he's looking forward to meeting you."

"Goddamn, I hope I don't screw up."

"Oh and regarding swear words like goddamn, son of a bitch, etcetera?"

"Sorry, guess I slip up sometimes."

"Remember, although Mr. Forrester may look as rugged as, say, a Rocky Marciano, he's a Harvard Business School honor graduate and a first-class gentleman. Whether he's presiding over a corporation meeting or addressing his resort committee, his language is very selective. Even behind the scenes he doesn't swear much, not at all in the presence of women. So around him, use your normal conversation minus the swearing. Okay?"

"I'll be careful."

"You'll also be meeting his assistant, Madelline Taylor. Your paths will cross regularly and as you'll soon discover, she's a sweetheart."

"I don't have to give a speech, do I? If I have to review my research in front of Mr. Forrester and all those people, I'm afraid it could be embarrassing for both you and me."

"You won't be giving a speech, but a successful promoter like James Forrester knows mistakes are often stepping stones to improvement. I can pick you up at 9:30, unless you want to drive."

Concerned his old pickup would be out of place, or might even break down in busy Strip traffic, Robert replied, "You can pick me up at my old apartment. It'll make it easier for you, and maybe I'll see some of my friends there."

The next morning when Richard arrived, Robert, looking businesslike in his tan suit, light blue shirt, striped tie, and dark cordovan dress shoes, was waiting outside on the McCallister front steps. In one hand he carried a clipboard with the research notes he'd gathered for Richard.

Complimented on his appearance, Robert replied, "Thanks, but as I thought might happen, people around here are looking at me as if I just robbed a bank, or might be dealing drugs."

On the drive to New Horizon while reading excerpts from his research, Robert interjected, "Maybe highlights from some of these luxurious golf courses are not what Mr. Forrester wants. Some of their amenities are quite extravagant."

Richard said, "Though his resort will be targeting average-income customers, J.D. will take into consideration the best money can buy. Keep in mind, he has unlimited resources. Think of him as a public relations genius who could take a church choir soprano and make her an opera star at the Met. Or transform desolate desert country and mountain foothills into a popular family resort. The man is blessed with the unbeatable combination of brains, talent, and a warm heart."

"I know you think a lot of him. How many people will be there?"

"There'll be fifteen committee members and counting guests about thirty-five in all. I'll be introducing you to many of them."

"Does Mr. Forrester know about my illustrious past?"

"I told him the best parts. The rest are irrelevant."

Inside the New Horizon offices they went directly to the Versailles Chambers. While a few of the committee members remained at their seats to review their upcoming reports, most of them were moving about or engaged in one-on-one discussions. Robert was fascinated with the ebullient business atmosphere, especially the U-shaped table with its fifteen high-back leather chairs, laptops, and agenda notebooks.

Richard led Robert to the podium where J.D. was glancing through his own speech outline.

Robert's first thought was, *He really does look like Marciano, Marciano with a mustache, that is."*

J.D. looked up and said, "Nice to see you, Rich, and who might this gentleman be?"

"This is my new assistant, Robert McGuire. Robert, I want you to meet James Forrester, president of New Horizon and founder of Monte Vista."

With feigned confidence—in reality hoping the ensuing exchange would be brief—Robert shook hands firmly as he said, "I've been looking forward to meeting you, sir."

"We're pleased you're joining us, Robert. Richard speaks highly of you."

"He's speaks well of you, too, Mr. Forrester."

"Hey, no misters around here. You're one of us now, an official member of our Monte Vista team."

Pleasantries aside, as they were walking away, Richard said to Robert, "You handled that situation gracefully."

"To tell you the truth, I'm still in a daze."

After the remaining committee members and guests took their seats, the speaker scanned the faces of his audience. "Each of you looks bright and enthusiastic this morning," he said, "as well you should, because a year and a half from now you will have played a vital role in the creation of the most attractive, exciting family resort in Las Vegas. Did I say Las Vegas? Make that the entire United States. Did I say the entire U.S.? Make that the entire world."

From then on his address centered on his latest projections and expectations. At one juncture he said, "We're thinking of sculpturing all-time golf stars on the sides of the two highest mountains—legends like Ben Hogan, Arnie Palmer, Babe Zaharias, Nancy Lopez, and so on. They'd be known as Monte Vista's twin Mount Rushmores."

The Mount Rushmore reference incited muffled laughter along with scattered side comments. The speaker smiled too, but when he said, "Well, this is Las Vegas, you realize," audience discussions shifted to which golfing stars would be most appropriate.

He motioned to the back of the room where two staff members wheeled a ten-by-five-foot rectangular model into the middle of the U-shaped table.

As soon as the men removed the model's cloth cover, members and guests left their seats for a closer look.

Moving to the front of the model, J.D. said, "Ladies and gentlemen, this is our updated resort model. Look it over, and we are officially open for discussion."

The thought provoking question-answer session continued until the noon hour.

As they were leaving the conference room, Robert said to Richard, "You were right about him being a dynamic speaker, and he really does look like Marciano."

For lunch they walked across the street to the Paris hotel, where Juan was waiting at a cafe table near the swimming pool. All he knew about Robert was Richard's description of him as "an intelligent, older gentleman with a sound business background. I think you two will like each other."

Richard's assumption was correct. Right away their personalities blended. Each man was highly intelligent, and each possessed a catchy sense of humor—Juan's dry and subtle from his near-poverty upbringing; Robert's more brittle from his street experiences.

Following lunch the three men went to the Maryland Parkway athletic center for a workout. Although it was Robert's first visit, his efforts on the treadmill, bicycle, and step climber drew praise from his younger companions.

During a break at the water fountain Juan said, "You're in pretty good shape there, Roberto."

"Richard wants me back on the golf course in the near future, so at night when I'm taking my walks, I've been going further and jogging a little too."

Early the next morning, Richard called Robert. "Turns out you won't have to be concerned about your pickup anymore. Madelline informed me there's a Chevy Malibu waiting for you in the firm's parking lot."

"Did you say a Chevy Malibu? Man, that's one fine lookin' set of wheels."

"I understand it's white with a blue velvet interior, sunroof, and all the goodies. One thing you might not approve of are the red and gold New Horizon monograms on the doors."

"Oh well, I can't accept it then," quickly followed by, "Just tell me when and where do I get the keys?"

"You can pick them up from Madelline any time. One other thing, I did something of a personal nature you really might not approve of."

"Whatever you did, I staunchly approve of."

"Maybe not. I wrote a letter to your daughter."

There was a long pause before Robert asked, "And why did you write to her?"

"I figured you might want to be in touch with her. I'm sorry, Rob, maybe I shouldn't have, but I thought—"

"It's okay. How'd you find her address?"

"Cynthia in the office researched for me."

"And what did you find out?"

"She's still in the Cincinnati area, a guidance counselor in a high school there. Does the name Walnut Hills sound familiar?"

A smile pressed the corners of Robert's mouth. "Yeah, I know the school very well. So she's in education, just like her mom. Imagine my little girl counseling high school kids. Man, that's really something." Another pause before he continued, "I may have told you that a few years ago I'd heard from someone back there she was married."

"She's not married anymore."

"She's not?"

"She's been divorced for a while now and assumed her stepfather's name. She's Anita Stevens again. Did your contact tell you anything else about her?"

"He didn't seem to know too much. Did you find out if she has any kids?"

"Apparently she doesn't. Anyway, I wanted you to know I wrote to her and asked her to write back or call if she chose to. My ulterior motive was to see if she'd like to know more about you. So what if I do hear back? Would you like to be in touch with her?"

"I guess that would be all right, but remember, Rich, in all likelihood she doesn't want to hear from me. As I told you, her mother made sure I was legally off-limits, and since then I'm sure Anita has heard only the worst concerning my character."

"I thought about that, but things have changed."

Robert's voice quavered, "Yes, they have. For many years I wouldn't have wanted her to know about me, but now, because of you—"

Trying to swallow his own walnut-sized lump, Richard interrupted, "Hey, Rob, you had your life back on track long before you knew me."

"I'm just sure she won't want to be in touch with me."

"Let's let her decide. It may not make any difference anyway. She may just ignore the letter."

"Sorry I'm acting this way, but you know me."

"Yeah, I know, you're a sentimental crybaby."

"It really would be amazing if I could be in touch with her."

"We'll see what happens. Now, back to business. This afternoon I'm going to Omaha to work with Ben for a couple of days. You know about the committee's focus on the golf courses, but J.D. wants progress on all fronts. I'm leaving you with basic information concerning the retail stores scheduled for leasing in the shopping mall. If you recall the model, the complex will be situated along the shores of our man-made lake. With that in mind, Madelline can provide you with more pertinent information. I want you to come up with good promotional strategies for the mall itself and for some of the major stores. Since its location is in such a picturesque setting, you can allow your imagination to go to work."

Before they disconnected, Robert said, "I hope you won't think I'm prying, but what's happened to Mystery Woman?"

"Paula, you mean. She's still in Hollywood, still in the process of securing a major position at the television station."

"I see. I assume you and Paula are still a big thing."

"Sure, without question."

"As serious as ever?"

"Well, yes, but right now she has a rare opportunity with no other choice than to give it her undivided attention. Why do you ask?"

Detecting a shade of frustration in Richard's tone, Robert said, "No reason, just curious. By the way, I'll be working at the homeless center later this afternoon."

"So even though your new apartment is quite a distance away, you're going to continue your Salvation Army work?"

"Of course. With my new transportation, getting there won't be a problem."

"I still think about the people we saw that morning. I would imagine New Horizon is already contributing to the Salvation Army. If not, we should talk to J.D. about the firm becoming a major contributor."

"Good thinking. Be assured, they're grateful for everything that comes their way."

On his way to the air terminal, Richard thought back on his discussion with Robert and how steadfastly he'd defended Paula's reasons for staying focused in Hollywood. It made him realize he loved her as much as ever. *I'll wait for her 'til hell plays host to the winter Olympics. She's in my blood forever!*

Chapter Eighteen

THURSDAY IN OMAHA RICHARD AND Benjamin met with Stewart store managers. Their main objectives were to plan summer sales promotions and deal with expansion. The overall company payroll was now ninety full-time employees.

The following afternoon Richard had just returned from lunch when Melanie informed him, "You have Anita Stevens waiting on line three."

Well, I'll be damned! Pulse quickening, he prayed he'd say precisely the right things.

"Hi, Rich Stewart here."

A sandy-textured voice said, "Mr. Stewart, this is Anita Stevens. I received your letter."

"I'm glad you did. It's nice to hear from you, Ms. Stevens."

"About the letter. I really don't know what to think. I don't know anything about my father. I didn't know if he was in the country or even alive anymore."

"He's very much alive and, may I add, in very good health. I'm glad you called because I'm sure he'd like to be in touch with you."

A prolonged silence before, "So where is he right now?"

"In Las Vegas."

"Las Vegas."

"Yes," Richard affirmed.

"A gambler, I suppose."

"No, I'm sure not."

"Can you tell me more about him?"

"All right, well, since his divorce from your mother he's never remarried, and he works for me. Our Omaha company has business interests in Vegas, and he's presently my assistant in the development of a new resort."

To be sure the person really was her father, Ms. Stevens said, "Tell me specifically about him; for instance, what college he graduated from."

"University of Cincinnati, class of 1975. I know he worked in Cincinnati as a businessman and also taught in a high school there."

"Hmmm, what I best remember about my father was he deserted my mother and me long ago." Another pause before she added, "I know he was an alcoholic and had problems with the law."

Fearing from the tone of her voice she might hang up, Richard weighed his words carefully. "I don't know all the details—and please forgive my intrusion—but from everything he's told me, he never really did abandon you or your mother. He closed his eyes, hoping he would not hear a click.

Although she was tempted to hang up, Anita allowed Richard to continue.

"It is my understanding that because of his drinking problem, it was legally impossible for him to get near you. Because he couldn't find work, he felt he had to leave Cincinnati. As for breaking the law, the only jail time he served was an abbreviated sentence for driving under the influence. I can assure you he's not a drinker anymore, and from everything I know he's a fine, upstanding citizen."

Another prolonged silence until Richard said, "Would you like to be in touch with your father?"

"Be in touch with him? Hmmm, I can't honestly answer that right now. Tell me more about what you *personally* know about him."

"All right, well, he's in good physical and mental condition. He's well read, knows a lot about the business world, and he has a variety of interests. I find him to be a kindhearted man who blames himself for losing your mother and you. When you were a child, he admits to making a succession of mistakes that turned out to be, in his own words, unintended but disastrous. He said he was overconfident and irrational, but that's all in the past. Sorry if I sound repetitious; guess I'm a little nervous."

She tsked her tongue and said, "Why should you be nervous? You seem to know a lot about him. Did he ever tell you why in all these years he's never made an effort to contact me?"

"He said in the beginning he tried, but your mother kept a restraining order active and also threatened him with legal action. In light of those circumstances he was afraid you'd never want to hear from him, even when you were older."

"My mother had her reasons, Mr. Stewart. You know, this is coming at me from out of the blue. I don't know what to say."

Richard's mind searched for another way to keep the conversation alive.

Then she abruptly said, "Thanks for writing to me. I may call you back," and she was gone before he could reply.

God, I think I blew it. One thing he'd discovered. *Rob McGuire's daughter certainly has a lot of spunk!*

The rest of the day and part of the next, several times he second-guessed how he could have handled the situation better.

Then Friday afternoon she called again.

"Mr. Stewart, Anita Stevens."

"Thanks for calling back, Ms. Stevens."

"A friend of mine and I have been thinking about a summer vacation. After you and I talked, we decided Las Vegas would be an exciting place to visit, so it looks as if we may be coming there for a few days."

"Very good. If you will put your trust in me, I will—"

"Oh don't worry, as far as trust is concerned I've already checked on you and your company. Other than informing Mr. McGuire of our plans, we shouldn't need any more assistance from you."

Realizing with the gravity of the situation she had reason to be touchy, he said, "I was just thinking, it would be easier for everyone if I made the arrangements for him to meet you. I assume school's still in progress there."

"Counselors have been out of school for several days." For the first time she laughed softly as she said, "My friend Melissa is also a counselor and has caught the Las Vegas fever."

"Hey, wonderful. I'm sure you'll find it, as you said, an exciting place to visit."

"When we talked about going, she called a travel agency and was informed the Luxor hotel has a special discount package. Melissa's not here right now and she has all the information. If everything holds together, I think we'll be leaving here Tuesday and coming back on Sunday."

"That should work."

"What does Mr. McGuire think about you contacting me? I'm assuming it was he who asked you to get in touch with me."

"No, as I wrote to you, it was my idea. When I first told him I'd written to you, I think he was concerned about what your reaction might be. I know he was excited about me contacting you, but as for the opportunity of seeing you, well, that would be far beyond all expectations. When you get a specific flight number and time, let me know and we'll work it out from there."

"This is nerve racking," she replied.

"I can imagine. Please call me as soon as you talk to your friend."

The next morning as Richard was preparing to leave his Omaha residence, his cell phone chimed.

"Mr. Stewart, this is Anita Stevens. I have our American Airlines flight times. We'll be leaving next Tuesday morning and will arrive there at 2:30 in the afternoon."

"I'll let your father know."

Richard then called Robert who drowsily answered, "Rich, you're early today. It's only a little after six o'clock here."

"Did I get you up?"

"It's all right. I've been at the resort site every day. The excavating companies are progressing on schedule, and this afternoon I'm meeting with a top foreman."

"That's good. I want you to be acquainted with as many of the crew as possible."

"I've been doing that."

"Now, I have some special news. Are you ready for this?"

"I hope I'm ready. What's up?"

"Your daughter's coming to Las Vegas Tuesday and she wants to see you."

There was a muffled sound as if Robert dropped his phone. Seconds later he said, "You mean she's really coming here next week, and she wants to see me?"

"I just talked to her and she said she'll be arriving early in the afternoon."

"God almighty, how'd you ever accomplish that?"

"She seemed reluctant at first, but I think she's warming up to the idea. She and a girl friend are staying at the Luxor. Tell me where you'd like to meet her, say some place later on for dinner, or possibly the next morning?"

"Now damn it, Richard, be serious. I want to see her the moment she arrives, okay?"

Richard chuckled and said, "I understand. By the way did you get your new vehicle?"

"I picked her up yesterday afternoon, and I tried to call you but you were tied up. White Chevy Malibu with blue velvet seats—just like you said—and has she got a lot of zip or what? After I left the tavern last night, I revved her up to eighty over on the Desert Inn Road." He paused before adding, "Just kiddin' ya, Rich. I love the car, though, and those bright red and gold New Horizon monograms make me feel prestigious. My goodness, I can't believe she's really coming here, and I'm going to see her and be with her."

"On the day of her arrival, I better drive. You might be too preoccupied and crash on the way to the airport."

"Yeah, it's about twelve miles out here from where I used to live, and you're probably right. I'll need you to steady me no matter what."

"Just remember, even though I'll be with you out at the terminal, once she arrives you're on your own. You'll want to wear something that will make you easy to identify. I'll tell her what to look for."

"How about my navy blue polo shirt with the gold Stewart Company insignia?"

"That would be a great choice."

Next Richard called Anita and said her father would be meeting her at the airport.

"How will I recognize him?"

"He'll be wearing a blue shirt with a Stewart Company logo. And you?"

"I'm five foot three, have short red hair, and I'll be wearing glasses. Melissa is a brunette, taller, and a little heavier than I. We should be easy to recognize."

"Okay then, we'll see you Tuesday afternoon."

In Omaha, as Richard hung up the phone, he felt thrill-chills as rambunctious cherubs played hopscotch on his spinal cord.

In Las Vegas, Robert McGuire was experiencing similar sensations.

In Cincinnati, Anita Stevens was struck with a deluge of conflicting emotions.

Chapter Nineteen

W HEN RICHARD ARRIVED AT THE Paris guest reception counter on Monday morning, Evelyn said his summer executive suite was vacated and ready. She went on to describe its various features. "And you're going to love the blue-tile bedroom spa."

Juan appeared and said, "Suites like yours are normally reserved for entertainment celebrities or foreign dignitaries. May I have your autograph, *Monsieur* Stewart?"

"About time you treated me with some respect around here, Gonzales."

Juan shook his head and said, "Treat him royally and right away it goes to his head."

He escorted Richard to his new suite. In the beautiful entertainment area, the sunlight entering through the floor-to-ceiling windows enriched the beige-pink-orange color accents. They went into the master bedroom to check out the elevated circular spa.

"Ah, I can see it now," Juan said, "romantic music playing, you and Paula-baby relaxing in the swirling blue waters."

"That's absolutely amazing, because I'm having the same vision."

The day before Robert's daughter was due to arrive, he accompanied Richard to the Monte Vista site. There they found water trucks spraying segments of the desert floor and mountain foothills, a preliminary task before the bulldozers, dump trucks, and graders moved in. A foreman offered to show them around the area in his open-air Jeep, and while Richard remained keenly attuned to the foreman's informative comments, Robert was obviously daydreaming.

Finally Richard said, "Don't worry, Rob. Tomorrow's going to be a piece of cake."

Tuesday afternoon after entering the McCarran terminal, the two men checked the flight schedule and found that Anita's plane was arriving on time. Twenty minutes later near the baggage retrieval area they searched the faces of the newly arrived passengers descending on an escalator.

Robert also glanced at himself and asked, "How do I look?"

"She's going to think you look like a respectable gentleman."

"Is my hair messed up?"

"Your hair's short, remember?"

Robert touched the top of his head, "Oh yeah, that's right. I also sprayed on some cologne and I'm chewin' Breath Savers. Take a whiff and give me your honest opinion."

Richard leaned over and said, "Not too bad, except did you have some garlic and onions for lunch?"

"Garlic and onions! Are you serious?"

"Nah, just kiddin', you even smell respectable."

"Tell me the appropriate way to greet my daughter. Should I say, 'Hi, and you must be Anita, sure good to see you,' or 'My goodness, Anita, you look very nice today,' or—"

Richard chuckled, "Don't try to memorize anything or you might really screw up. Just say whatever comes natural."

"How can you be so calm?"

Truth be told, Richard's heart was also palpitating.

Suddenly at the top of the escalator they spotted two young women wearing slacks, tank tops, and sandals. The taller of the two was a brunette. At her side an auburn-haired woman was wearing narrow, metal-framed glasses.

As the women rode the escalator down to the landing, Richard said, "There you go, Rob."

Robert took a deep breath, walked over to the ladies, and said, "I'm looking for Anita Stevens?"

Bright emerald eyes met his steel-gray gaze as she replied, "I'm Anita, and you must be Robert."

Her companion said, "I'll wait for you over there, Anita," and she moved near to where Richard was standing.

He in turn stepped closer to her and said, "My name's Rich Stewart. I'm here with Anita's father, and you must be her friend. I hope you two had a pleasant flight."

"I'm pleased to meet you, Mr. Stewart. I'm Melissa Sanderson. So you're the gentleman who wrote to Anita." Glancing at Anita and Robert she added, "That's quite a meeting going on between those two."

The father-daughter reunion was joined with occasional nods and faint smiles until Anita stepped forward and gave him a little hug.

"Wow, what a touching scene," Melissa said.

"Very much so. He's been excitedly waiting for this moment."

Robert and Anita joined them, and following introductions the men retrieved the newly arrived luggage. From there, all four continued through the terminal and outside to short-term parking. While the men loaded the luggage into the trunk of the car, the women moved into the back seat.

As they were leaving the airport area, Richard asked, "How would you like a drive through the famous Vegas Strip?"

Melissa quickly responded, "We would *love* to see the Strip, Mr. Stewart. I had a dream about this place last night, and now we're really here."

Anita nodded in agreement.

Soon they passed the UNLV Thomas & Mack Center and Melissa inquired, "So you two gentlemen are in business together?"

Robert answered, "Richard owns a golf and sporting goods company in Omaha and will be opening a store in a new resort here. He's also a central figure in the planning of the resort and I'm his assistant."

Melissa said, "A new resort. Ummm, now that sounds intriguing."

Emotionally overwhelmed by the reunion with her real father, Anita once again merely nodded.

Shortly after turning on to Paradise Road which would eventually connect with the north end of the Strip, they passed the Hard Rock resort with its giant trademark guitar.

Richard said, "This place is popular with the young hip crowd, including many movie stars, especially the younger ones."

Melissa, for whom inquisitiveness was second nature, leaned forward and said, "So how long have you two been working together?"

Robert answered, "Actually we started just recently. Before Richard hired me, I worked at the Golden Nugget. It's one of the premiere downtown resorts, on a par with some of the biggest and best places you're about to see on the Strip."

"And what was your position there?"

"I worked in culinary services. I liked it there, but Mr. Stewart offered a better opportunity."

Glancing into the rearview mirror, Richard caught Anita's eye and said, "And what about you? How long have you been teaching, or should I say counseling?"

"This was my second year. I was a teacher for a couple of years before going back to school for my counseling certificate." Her eyes turned to Melissa.

"I've been a counselor for six years. And do you, Mr. Stewart, have a family?"

"No, I'm single."

The women exchanged glances before Melissa continued, "Have you ever been married?"

"Not yet."

She shook her head and said, "Amazing."

Anita's eyes scanned the vehicle's ceiling.

Robert remarked, "But he's got a steady gal, a real beauty."

Melissa said, "I would imagine. And you live in Omaha?"

"Yes, I do."

"Mr. McGuire, you're single, too?"

"Correct, Melissa, and would you please call me Robert or Rob."

"And me Rich or Richard."

Melissa asked about the overhead monorail following Paradise Road, and Richard explained, "This one joins this end of the Strip to resorts almost four miles south to the MGM Grand. It's fast and convenient for those who need it."

To the right were the sprawling Las Vegas Convention Center and the huge Las Vegas Hilton. Richard described the center as "one of the very finest convention centers in the world."

Melissa noticed a bus stopped at an intersection light, and she said, "Anita, that's the *Wheel of Fortune* bus! We watch Pat and Vanna almost every night."

"They're in Vegas this week," Richard said, "and if you would like, I can provide you with reservations."

Melissa said, "Wonderful," and Anita added, "That would be nice."

Anita's main focus, however, was less on the passing sights and more on her father. And whenever he turned around to speak, she gave him her undivided attention. As for Robert, just being in his daughter's presence was all he could ask for.

At the Sahara Avenue intersection, Richard turned west and just to the right was the towering Stratosphere hotel. He mentioned the Top of the World restaurant's "panoramic views and marvelous menu selections."

Continuing south on Las Vegas Boulevard, they approached the Circus Circus resort, and Melissa asked, "Is that the scariest looking clown you've ever seen, or what? Oh look, Anita, down the street, there's a bungee jump. I want you gentlemen to know my little friend here might just take one of those jumps."

Richard said, "That would take some real courage."

Robert turned and asked, "You'd do a bungee jump?"

"I doubt if I would. Just in case, I prefer soft landings."

Melissa clarified, "Heights this woman fears not. She was a one- and three-meter springboard diver at University of Cincinnati. And her folks had to talk her out of the ten-meter platform competition."

Robert asked, "You were on the varsity diving team?"

Anita answered, "I was, both in high school and college."

Robert glanced at Richard who nodded respectfully.

As the car entered the heart of the Strip, Richard provided tidbits of information concerning Wynn's and Encore, Treasure Island, The Venetian, Mirage, and so on down the boulevard.

Approaching the Flamingo Road intersection, the girls glanced back and forth at the towering edifices of the Flamingo, Caesars, Bally's, the Bellagio, and Paris. Just past the Bellagio, traffic thinned and Richard slowed his speed so his passengers could better see the Renzcorp Center building.

Robert said, "See the New Horizon sign above the Renzcorp's top floor? That's the firm we work for."

"I love the circular glass foyer and those shimmering gold windows," Melissa said.

"Very attractive," Anita added.

While passing the City Center, Richard said, "You're looking at one of the Strip's most prodigious production of residential towers, an all-inclusive resort, many shopping venues, and restaurants ready to satisfy everyone."

The center was followed by the Monte Carlo, MGM Grand, and New York–New York.

Past Tropicana Avenue Melissa spotted a sphinx statue in front of a bronze-reflecting glass pyramid. "There's the Luxor, Anita."

Moments later Richard parked in the Luxor guest arrival area. As the men stepped out of the car to unload the luggage on to a cart, Robert inquired, "Where did you learn all that stuff about the Strip?"

"Last spring Paula showed me around and taught me everything she knew."

Inside the hotel near the guest reception counters the girls thanked the men and accepted Robert's offer to take them to dinner.

Robert asked Richard, "Would it be all right if I act as their chauffeur and guide for the next few days?"

"Of course."

When the men returned to the car, Robert asked, "Well, what do you think, Rich?"

"About what, the Luxor?"

"Come on now, you know what I mean."

"About your daughter you mean. I'd say she's a very interesting young woman."

"And pretty, and intelligent, right?"

"Okay, she's got very expressive green eyes and she's a little doll. Her friend seems like a sweetie, too."

"By the way I think I spoke out of turn about my acting as their chauffeur and guide. Except for downtown, I really know very little about the best places to go."

"It shouldn't be a problem. Compliments of New Horizon we can arrange reservations for any number of restaurants and shows. As for tonight, I'll be happy to reserve a guest table at a Luxor restaurant known for its service and menu selections."

A half hour later in his apartment Robert tried to take a nap, but lingering recollections superseded all attempts. He thought of how Anita's delicate facial features, her red hair and her green eyes resembled his mother Kathleen … considered how in the coming days and nights he would try to convince his daughter he never wanted to leave her or her mother … pondered ways to explain why he'd never contacted her, and so forth and so on.

Meanwhile back at the Luxor as Anita was unpacking, she also was immersed in flashbacks. She liked the way her father looked but thought he should put on some weight … appreciated his gentlemanly manners and his efforts to make her feel at ease … was glad he'd offered to escort her and Melissa around town. Nevertheless, her mother's long-term ambivalence toward him could not easily be dismissed. Whether in her work or her personal life, Anita possessed an innate ability to separate truth from lies, fact from fiction, sincerity from deceit. In the coming days she intended to learn exactly why her father had disappeared without a trace and why he'd never contacted her.

Those matters aside, after a challenging and at times hectic school year, she and Melissa were looking forward to five exciting days and nights in Las Vegas.

Chapter Twenty

THE LADIES BROUGHT ALONG SEVERAL outfits that would work for different occasions. When Robert called Anita to inform her they'd be eating at an exclusive Luxor restaurant, she wanted to know what they should wear.

"I haven't been there myself," he said. "but Richard says you should feel free to dress comfortably."

Wanting to look his very best, Robert chose a pink polo shirt, double-pleated white trousers, and tasseled tan loafers. As soon as he strolled into the Luxor lobby, he spotted Anita and Melissa waiting for him. In their bright summer dresses and French heel sandals, the ladies looked youthfully adventurous. Anita had substituted contacts for glasses, and her father thought she looked even prettier than before.

Melissa said, "You look dashingly handsome, Mr. McGuire."

"*Very* debonair," Anita added.

"And you two look like a couple of summer fashion models."

One on each side, the ladies put their arms through his and followed signs pointing to the designated restaurant. Once inside he ordered a filet mignon, and the ladies chose items from the seafood menu.

While enjoying the superb service and their delicious meals, Anita lifted her glass of wine and toasted her friend, "Ah yes, Missy, we do deserve such delicacies, do we not?"

Toasting her back, Melissa said, "Of course, dah-ling. We are, after all, esteemed counselors at the highly acclaimed Walnut Hills High."

Robert was feeling good because Anita seemed more at ease than earlier. After dinner he offered to drive back on the Strip for a closer inspection of the world-famous sights. By the time they left the Luxor, darkness had overtaken the final rays of sunlight, only to be replaced by the Strip's preternaturally bright neon and flashing lights. In the distance Anita noticed the Paris hotel's Eiffel Tower. She said back in their hotel room she'd read an interesting article about the famous French street, the Rue de la Paix, and Robert made Paris their first stop.

The walkway inside the hotel soon converted to a cobblestone street lined with restaurants and lounges, specialty boutiques, and lighted, simulated second story apartments. After an hour of walking and browsing through several shops, the ladies asked to move on so they could observe other Strip attractions.

As they stepped outside the Paris entrance, the warm summer air was invigorating, and at the ladies request Robert left the car behind so they could join the throngs of people walking northward on the boulevard.

Across the street, inspired by the resounding voice of Luciano Pavarotti, the Bellagio fountains lifted high into the nighttime sky, and around the lake a variety of dancing water configurations completed the captivating scene. The three observers watched until the show ended.

They crossed Flamingo Road and walked past the Flamingo resort, and several smaller business establishments. Farther down the street in front of Harrah's, an outdoor lounge's band music blended naturally with other Strip sounds.

Suddenly, across the boulevard in front of the Mirage, the nighttime sky was invaded once again, this time by the soaring, golden flames of a mini volcano. Eager to go inside the resort they'd seen in the movies and on TV, they crossed the boulevard and entered through the front doors. Their attention was immediately drawn to the beautiful aquarium overlooking the hotel's guest arrival desk. Inside the vast display there were countless mixtures of rare and colorful ocean species.

They continued walking through the Mirage's tropical rain forest. Next an atrium's signs pointed the way to popular Mirage sites and attractions. However, the adjoining sights and sounds of a Mirage casino were too tempting for the ladies to ignore. As Robert looked on, they tried their luck with penny and nickel slot machines. Soon losing more than they were winning, they decided to quit, but with a promise to do better the next time around.

Anita glanced at her watch and said, "It's eleven o'clock, Missy, but back home it's three hours later. If we don't get back to the hotel and get some rest, we'll probably sleep until noon."

By the time they walked back to Paris and Robert drove back to the Luxor, it was midnight. They agreed to meet for more activities at ten o'clock the next morning.

So ended their first night on the town.

In spite of their late-night outings, each morning before breakfast the ladies slipped into running shorts, tank tops, and tennis shoes before jogging from the Luxor all the way to Flamingo Road. During the return they crossed the street and stopped at a sidewalk convenience stand for bottled water and pastries. Back at their hotel they showered and changed clothes in time for Robert's ten o'clock arrival.

Every day their requested destination was a shopping mall. The excursions ranged from the exclusive Wynn Esplanade and the Planet Hollywood Miracle Mile to the Boulevard Mall and the Las Vegas Outlet Center.

Thursday as the ladies were shopping in the Outlet Center, Robert, waiting for them at a food court table, used his cell phone to call Richard. "Those two are relentless shoppers," Robert said, "but they've made only a few of what Melissa calls 'irresistible' purchases."

"So are you tiring of the shopping excursions?"

"Absolutely not. As a matter of fact I'm loving every minute. Those two are really quite a pair. As you probably already realize, Missy's a bundle of energy. Anita is more reserved but, I've discovered, is quite the independent little gal. Her folks may be well off, but Missy told me since college Anita has refused any financial assistance from them. During our conversations, it is obvious she's seriously into a number of social issues, especially where children are concerned. I'm proud of her attitudes."

"She seems like the social issue type, all right. Anyway, I'm glad you're enjoying yourself."

Each day lunch was of the fast-food variety, but thanks to Richard's New Horizon complimentary passes, evenings found them dining at well-known restaurants. In those settings the ladies quickly discovered that dietary restraint was at the top of the Vegas most-endangered list.

Wednesday and Thursday the after-dinner shows were for Celine Dion at Caesars and David Copperfield at MGM. Friday, as Richard promised, they had second row seats for the *Wheel of Fortune* show at The Venetian. Afterward, they again tried their luck with slot machines and added a few rounds of roulette. As happened on the first night, they ended up losing, but this time they swore off gambling for good.

Robert wanted Saturday night, their last night, to be outstanding. Richard did his part with reservations at the eleventh-story Eiffel Tower restaurant. Along with a spectacular view of the Strip, they enjoyed exquisite French cuisine and wine. Most of the discussion revolved around the ladies' vacation experiences.

Anita summed it up. "I'd say it's been the most *fannntastic* vacation I've ever experienced."

Melissa said, "May I add, simply *maaagnificent*."

And Robert, "Ah, and for me, absolutely *mahhhvelous*." More solemnly he added, "I only wish it didn't have to end so soon."

Their after-dinner show reservations were for the Parisian Folies show in the Paris Theatre.

Earlier in the day Richard called Robert to inquire, "I forgot to ask you Thursday, but how are you and Anita getting along?"

"On a scale of ten I'd say around seven. Unfortunately I haven't had an opportunity to talk to her personally very much. There have been times when she seems moody, probably recalling negative things she's heard about me."

"Don't be overly concerned, Rob. She's bound to have doubts with a mother who's unwilling to forget the past."

"Yeah, I suppose. Incidentally, last night when we were out, Melissa said I should ask you to join us tonight for dinner and a show."

"And Anita?"

"I'm sure she'd also like for you to be there, so how about it? Your dinner and show reservations are for four."

"I appreciate your offer, but I've been swamped with work, and I think tonight I'll turn in early."

"I told them you were busy, but I have an alternative. They don't leave until tomorrow afternoon, so I thought we could all go some place for brunch. I'm sure they'd be thrilled if you'd join us."

"Tell me when and where."

"Well, we haven't been to the Fremont Street Experience, so maybe we could treat them to a nice place down there."

"In that case may I suggest the Garden Court buffet? Paula and I went there a few times and their Sunday brunch is superb."

"Good idea. Oh and before I forget, something's been running through my mind. You know how we need three people to help develop the Monte Vista hiring guidelines? And you know how you've been saying it could be difficult to find three qualified people for only the summer? Well, two-thirds of the solution may be right in front of us."

"Okay, go ahead."

"Hire those two. They're high school counselors who interview people all the time. I would think two young women with master's degrees in counseling could easily adapt to writing personnel manuals."

"They'd have to come back right away and work into August. I didn't think to tell you, but Wednesday we hired a male pre-med student. Then yesterday Maddy said she had a lead on a promising candidate through the college placement bureau. I haven't interviewed her yet, so the two jobs are still open. Did you mention the possibility to the girls?"

"No, I wanted to know what you thought."

"You're right in that they should easily adapt to the work, but would they be willing to come back here on such short notice? I would imagine they've made plans for the summer."

"Tomorrow when we're all together, why don't you ask them if they'd be interested?"

"Why don't you find out tonight?"

"I don't think that's the best way to go. Anita might think I'm trying to convince her to come here for myself or asking for favors on her behalf. It would be much better coming from you. As I said, she's *very* independent, and I don't think at this point she's looking for any favors from me."

"So you want Anita here for the summer, huh? You sly fox, you."

"Guess I am that, all right. Are you sure you can't make it tonight?"

"No, but I will be with you tomorrow."

The next morning Richard handled the driving and parked near 4th Street and Fremont. From there the ladies could stroll the Experience's entire four blocks. It was a sunny, quiet Sunday morning, and while taking in the sights several times they stopped to take pictures. By the time they arrived at the Garden Court buffet, they were all hungry and happily filled their plates.

As they were eating, the women recounted their vacation highlights for Richard.

When they finished, he said, "It sounds as if you have some great memories. Now one of the reasons I wanted to be with you this morning is that I have a proposition I want both of you to consider."

The ladies exchanged puzzled glances.

"I'm sure Rob's told you about the resort our corporation is building. In that undertaking we'll be hiring hundreds of employees. To make the transition run smoothly, we're going to need three people who can organize and write preliminary hiring guidelines. The work would include writing personnel screenings and interview procedures. I'm looking for people with work backgrounds similar to yours, so how would you like to come back here and work for a couple of months? You'd put in a forty-hour week, and although it will be concentrated work, we'll pay each of you $1,000 weekly, plus all your living and transportation expenses will be paid by the company. I will continue if you're interested."

Melissa answered first. "It's a dreamy idea, but in July I'm teaching a summer class at the university."

Robert said, "Can you find a substitute?"

"It's too late. It's a new discipline management course the state is requiring for all teachers, and my section is filled. If I'd known earlier, I would have loved to, but now damn it—pardon my French."

Robert's anticipation teetered on a faint hope as his eyes turned to Anita.

"I might be able to," she said. "Tell me more, like—"

Melissa interrupted, "I thought you were going to New York in July."

"I was, but I can visit New York anytime. Actually there's a New York just down the street from our hotel."

"You're so funny. I think I'm jealous."

Richard went on to explain more about the job expectations and responsibilities.

"Just do it, Anita," Robert said. "School's out. You can go home, pack up, and be back here in a few days."

"But where would I stay?"

Richard answered, "Our New Horizon personnel department takes care of the hiring details. Yesterday as I got to thinking about you two, I figured finding a nicely furnished two-bedroom apartment for a couple of months would be a problem. So I talked to the director, and she said they regularly reserve temporary apartments for newly hired staff. She said they're nice and located in a desirable area. Not that I was taking anything for granted, but I wanted to know, just in case. She said to consider it done if I needed it, and in line with company policy all expenses would be covered. So an apartment unit is yours if you want it, Anita."

"By 'desirable area' you mean—"

"She said it's located in a popular Green Valley location with easy access to where you'd be working. Is transportation a problem?"

"No, I'd be driving my car back here."

Hoping to clinch it then and there, Richard said, "We have a deal then?"

"I would have to be back in Cincinnati before the second week in August."

Richard said, "That should work."

After a pause she said, "I'll let you know in a couple of days."

Melissa said, "I hear the summer weather out here is torrid."

Anita smiled as she said, "Now, now, if I decide to take the job, you can come back when your classes conclude. Then we'll party some more."

It was noon when Richard took them back to the Luxor and they packed for their flight. As Robert drove them to the terminal, Anita would only tell him she would consider the offer and call him as soon as she made up her mind.

Before the women passed through the security boarding gate, he gave each of them a hug. His parting words to Anita were, "I'll be eagerly awaiting your decision."

Chapter Twenty-one

WITH MIXED EMOTIONS—HOPE, OPTIMISM, AND anxiety—Robert left the McCarran International premises. Since he had first heard Anita was coming to Las Vegas, he'd been floating on a silver-lined cloud. If his daughter decided not to return, that cloud would swiftly disappear. He prayed Richard's generous offer would tip the scales in his favor.

In the next couple of days, Anita envisioned the job as an exciting summer adventure, but her main objective would be to spend more time with her father. He didn't seem like the undesirable character her mother had portrayed him to be, at least not anymore. On the other hand, the prospect of working for Richard Stewart stirred uneasy feelings. She'd known men like him before—the All-American type, oozing with good looks, money, and charm. True, he'd treated her respectfully, but at times he seemed overly accommodating. *Beneath the outward appearances, he's probably a hopeless narcissist. Oh well, things are never perfect.* Because he was her new boss, and wanting to keep their relationship formal, she would continue calling him Mr. Stewart.

Tuesday morning she called Robert to say she was taking the position. "I'll be leaving Cincinnati early Friday and should be there Sunday afternoon."

Robert immediately notified Richard, who in turn asked the personnel director to reserve a one-bedroom apartment. It would be in the Desert Delight development just off Green Valley Parkway in Henderson. In addition to the apartment units the complex consisted of condominiums and town houses, some of which were situated along the boundaries of a municipal park. Anita's ground-level apartment was in the center courtyard, at the top of a gentle slope overlooking a swimming pool.

The next day Robert called on the Desert Delight manager. In a touring cart she showed him around the entire area before taking him to Anita's apartment. The unit had been freshly painted and the carpet shampooed. He was also pleased that the contemporary furniture looked fairly new. That evening he called Anita to tell her of his inspection.

She in turn said her Internet travel guide mapped out the best overland route to Las Vegas. "The distance is about nineteen hundred miles. Allowing for a few stops, I should be on the road for thirty-five hours. I'll be driving to St. Louis, Kansas City, and then across Colorado to I-15."

Robert advised, "Have your car serviced beforehand, drive carefully, and beware of strangers. A pretty young woman like you—"

"Don't worry about me. I'm driving a year-old Toyota Camry, and I have my cell phone, you know."

Thursday evening as she was preparing to leave, Richard called her to say, "I think it's great you're taking the job, Anita. I think you'll like the other two team members. Try to get a good night's sleep now."

"Thank you. I'm going to bed soon. It's been hectic getting ready so quickly. Oh, Melissa says hi, and if you need her next summer she'll make herself available."

"Tell her the new resort will always need good summer help." He paused before adding, "Being here this summer will give you and your father the opportunity to know each other much better."

"Well, Mr. Stewart, he's not exactly my father. I mean he is, but not really. If I sound bewildered, it's because I am. I appreciate that you took the time to bring us together, but I still have reservations. The last time he was in my life I was three years old, and I believe you've heard the rest of it."

"What does your mother think of your decision?"

"I didn't tell her when we went on vacation I'd be seeing him, only that we were going to Vegas to relax. Naturally I had to give a reason for returning for the summer."

"And what was her reaction?"

"She was upset and said she'd never misled me about him."

"Except about him not wanting to reach you."

Anita's voice turned scratchy. "Whatever my mother did back then she thought was best for us, and she must have had sufficient reasons for reacting as she did. We talked a lot about him last night, and I almost changed my mind about coming. Last week so much was happening, I didn't have time to consider everything. Her story and yours concerning his character just don't match. She says he was a complete slave to booze and we were secondary."

"What then made you decide to take the summer job?"

"He's called me three times, and I decided to find out for myself why he did what he did. As Mom said, when I was older he could have contacted me if he wanted to, and remember it was you, not he, who contacted me."

"I respect your thoughts. I know him to be a kind, considerate man and a dependable worker." Anita did not reply and he added, "I'll look forward to seeing you Monday morning in the New Horizon offices."

Friday night she called Robert from a Hampton Inn in Topeka, Kansas. She'd finished a fast-food meal and was tired. In the morning she'd be up early and would try to cover a similar distance.

Saturday night she called from her motel room in Richfield, Utah. She described Colorado's and Utah's mountain scenery as glorious and breathtaking.

At three o'clock on Sunday afternoon her call came from a convenience station twenty miles north of Las Vegas.

Robert advised her, "There's some roadwork going on in out there, but stay on the interstate past downtown and the Strip all the way to the East 215 turnoff, then go north on Las Vegas Boulevard. I'll be waiting on the roadside by the Sunset Road intersection. You know my car. And yours?"

"My Camry's an aqua-colored four door. See you soon."

Thirty minutes later she spotted his car and followed him east on Sunset Road. Across from the McCarran runways, he pulled into a Postal Service Center parking lot before walking back to her car.

"That was quite a trip for you," he said, "but you look great."

Glancing over the top of her sunglasses, she said, "Thanks for meeting me. Jeez, it's even hotter here than before!"

"Your apartment complex is not far, so follow me."

After they arrived at the Desert Delight office, the manager took them to Anita's unit for a walkthrough.

As she stepped outside onto the patio, Anita looked down the rise at the swimming pool and said, "This place seems to have everything I'll need."

After helping move her belongings inside, Robert took her several miles south to an outdoor shopping mall. The complex included a large Smith's grocery store.

From there he drove to the Strip and the Renzcorp Center where he showed her through the New Horizon offices, her destination for the new team's first gathering the next morning.

On the return they stopped at the Hard Rock Cafe for dinner. By the time they got back to her apartment, she was ready for a good night's sleep.

Before parting, Robert said, "As I understand it, Richard's orientation will take just a few days. He's an interesting speaker and I'm sure you'll enjoy the training sessions."

Anita thought to herself, *His final session cannot come too soon.*

The next morning, wanting to look the part of a young businesswoman, she wore her newly purchased light blue two-piece suit, white blouse, and white French heels. The first team member to arrive at New Horizon, she was greeted by Madelline.

"The other team members are Janelle DeYoung and Jeff Parsons. You'll be known as the Monte Vista Personnel, or MVP, team," Madelline told her.

Next to arrive was Janelle—athletically built, a freckled redhead with alert but friendly blue eyes. From Las Vegas and spending the summer with her parents, she was an English major at Northern Arizona State in Flagstaff. Her resume revealed a 3.5 GPA and exceptional writing skills.

Richard and Jeff Parsons entered the office together. Jeff had just completed pre-med training and in August would enter medical school at the University of California in San Francisco. The future physician was tall and lanky with mischievous dark eyes. He combed his hair in a short ponytail, wore small diamond earrings, and dressed casually for nearly every occasion.

Richard knew Jeff had once participated in basketball and track, but during his interview he had said, "I no longer participate in sports because they interfere with studying, and also time I could be out dancing and partying with beautiful women." As for his choosing to spend the summer in Vegas? "Las Vegas seems like the best place to have my final fling before med school."

Richard liked everything about Jeff, including his exuberant confidence. Judging from his scholastic and work histories, he'd completed commendably every major task he'd undertaken.

Richard and Madelline agreed they couldn't have asked for a more capable team. All three possessed different personalities and talents: Jeff was bright, liberated, progressive; Janelle was studious, an English perfectionist with writing skills; Anita was also well-educated and experienced in interviewing and counseling.

Richard did have one concern. Anita seemed uncomfortable in his presence and always called him Mr. Stewart. Before the training got underway, when he reminded the team after Wednesday he'd be seeing them only on occasion, her expression was one of relief.

He hadn't miscalculated. Anita had made up her mind to *think for myself* and *openly disagree with Mr. Stewart whenever the occasion arises.*

For their first official meeting Richard drove the team several miles to their workplace in a small strip mall on South Paradise Road. J.D. had decided the team's office should be a comfortable distance from the Renzcorp Center. As he told Richard, "We don't want our resort clients to look upon us as an overly aggressive competitor."

The office had previously been occupied by a tax accounting firm and had been vacant for several weeks. When Richard turned on the lights of the long, narrow office, the team members were surprised to find three work stations fully equipped with desks, chairs, file cabinets, laptops, and telephones. A conference table with a lectern, a screen, and fax and copy machines were in the middle of the room. Toward the back an eating area had a microwave and refrigerator. Also in the back were two bathrooms.

Richard went right to work. After asking his team to be seated at the table, he handed out his orientation schedule before projecting onto the screen a corresponding study preview. Step-by-step he discussed the team's responsibilities and goals.

Halfway through the preview he asked his team, "Does this seem like a lot to accomplish in a couple of months?" Noticing their faint smiles and shrugs, he said, "Without question, it will require organization and teamwork, but we know from your past work performances how creative and productive each of you are.

"Keep in mind we don't want you to come up with standardized hiring procedures. We want guidelines that will discover people who will take personal pride in pleasing customers, and who will collaborate well with other staff members."

That afternoon the team watched a ninety-minute video entitled, "Hiring Practices in Today's Changing Markets." Following each model scenario, the team offered their impressions and suggestions.

Before the first day was over, they realized Richard was a highly knowledgeable personnel dynamics instructor. His direct, fluent style was spiced with humorous tidbits, and frequently he sought responses from the team. Anita's skepticism was gradually replaced with respect for his ability to arouse spirited reactions. Early on when she challenged one of his own firm's hiring procedures, he praised her criticism and improvement suggestions. Such interplay set the tone for controversy, and soon positive and argumentative give-and-take were commonplace. It was exactly what he wanted from his team—to agree, disagree, and strategize before coming up with workable solutions.

Both days he took them to lunch at a Strip restaurant, and he was pleased his three workers both respected and liked each other. Wednesday at a New York–New York deli cafe he announced the orientation was completed. He then presented each of them with complimentary dinner and show reservations. He said he'd return Friday afternoon to review their early progress.

Anita's father later informed Richard that she'd been selected team leader by her co-workers. At the review meeting on Friday, she submitted for Richard's inspection several pages citing a cross-section of job descriptions and hiring procedures.

After reading through their summaries, he told the team, "You're coming up with the kind of solutions we're looking for. Good thinking and excellent teamwork."

Within a couple of weeks Robert told Richard that Anita and Jeff were dating. Richard appreciated the information, for he'd been concerned she might become homesick for family and friends back in Cincinnati.

Chapter Twenty-two

JUNE, JULY, AND AUGUST SERVE up the hottest days of the year in Las Vegas. The Vegas Valley is 2,174 feet above sea level and regularly becomes a punching bag for the sun's most powerful summer workouts. That summer the fiery orange ball was in full-blown resplendence 88 percent of the daylight hours. For most of the population it was as if a giant magnifying lens had been positioned between the sun and the city.

On a late June Saturday afternoon Richard was staying cool in his Paris suite, dozing now and then during a Twins-White Sox game. His cell phone chime surprised him, but Anita's scratchy voice was even more awakening.

"I want to meet with you as soon as possible, Mr. Stewart."

"Anita, is there a problem at work?"

"It's quite another matter."

"I'll meet you at the MVP office first thing Monday morning."

"No, we need to talk before that, preferably today. You name the time and place."

He gave her directions to a neighborhood Italian restaurant located not far from where she lived. He'd been there before with Juan for lunch.

"May I buy you something to eat while we talk?" he asked.

"That won't be necessary."

"I'll be there then before the dinner rush, say in an hour?"

Richard presumed Anita's anger had to be about her father. In the role of re-uniting them she was the critical link, and Richard had taken care not to make her feel uncomfortable in any way. Regarding Robert, it was true he'd disclosed cherry-picked information, much of which could be construed as misleading. *He must have told her more about himself which may have conflicted with what I told her. And just when everything was working like a charm.*

At four o'clock he settled into a booth toward the back of the restaurant. A few minutes later Anita arrived. She was wearing jeans, a sleeveless pullover blouse, and sandals, but not a smile.

He rose to greet her, but before he could speak, she snapped, "I'm very disappointed with you, Mr. Stewart."

Lifting his palms he said, "Please tell me how I've offended you."

A waiter arrived and took their soft drink orders. The moment he left, Anita continued, "Do you take pleasure in lying to me, Mr. Stewart? Do you think I'm a fool?"

"I don't understand."

"I feel betrayed. At lunch today my father told me a completely different story than what you've been telling me. Not long before you contacted me, he was working at the Golden Nugget all right—not in management, but filling buffet stations and cleaning tables. Not that there's anything wrong with that, but I was misled." With each new declaration her voice elevated another scratchy notch. "And he doesn't claim to be free from drinking. And there's more you didn't tell me. I do not appreciate being lied to."

"It wasn't as if I was trying to deceive you, Anita. I never really had an opportunity to tell you what kind of work he did at the Golden Nugget. As for the other matter, he doesn't drink anymore and probably never will. Surely you know an recovering alcoholic can never be sure he's completely free. He sometimes tries to put a lighter side on a serious issue. That's all he intended, I'm sure."

After the waiter returned with their beverages, for a while the conversation alternated between Anita's terse assertions and Richard's calm replies. His self-blaming responses gradually had the effect of defusing her anger.

"Anyway, he thinks you're some kind of a saint," she finally said. "Why don't you tell me what really happened between you two, how you *really* got to know him."

Richard briefly recalled the episode downtown and the unintended meeting in the library. "We sat down and talked, and I found him to be not only very intelligent, but also someone who finds purpose in helping others. I'm sure you're aware he volunteers regularly at the Salvation Army. His work there ranges from serving meals to assisting staff members in various activities. We met several more times, and in the process he recalled having difficulty finding work in Cincinnati, his drinking problems, and losing your mother and you. I think I mentioned before it was after a DUI accident that your mother divorced him and wouldn't allow him to have anything to do with you. He left Cincinnati lonely and brokenhearted. From there he wandered from city to city and town to town."

"He didn't go into too many details, just said he was drinking too much and was to blame for the divorce." Anita's brows narrowed. "Mother has never forgotten he was arrested and served time in jail. She's also never wanted to discuss the subject at length. "

"He told me about it. On a snowy night after drinking one too many with a friend, his car slid through a stop sign and struck a police car."

Spears of gold pierced her emerald eyes as she responded, "He struck a police car?"

"No one was hurt, but after the arrest it was more difficult than ever for him to find a decent job, and so he left Cincinnati. One thing he didn't leave was his drinking problem. In the ensuing years he held a few jobs, but in time none of them worked out. And there were times he was homeless. He went to quite a few homeless centers for food and shelter back then, but he never sought employment guidance from any of them. He tried to find better jobs on his own, but as he said, 'Being broke with jail time leaves you with very poor credentials.'

"When he first came here he got a job working in a newspaper circulation department. He worked there for more than a year, but when they discovered him drinking on the job, he was of course fired. That left him broke and he was homeless again.

"One morning he woke up on a bench in a children's playground park bench not far from where many of the homeless congregate. A daycare supervisor's van had broken down near the park, and while waiting for assistance, she had her children playing there. At first she didn't see your father, but as he got up to leave he started talking to some of the children. When she noticed the situation, she became very upset and stepped between them. She told the children to keep their distance and said the law should put drunken perverts like him away for good.

"He said her comment cut straight to his heart. Discouraged and distraught, he wandered away from the park and just down the street passed by the Salvation Army center for the homeless. He'd been there the day before for a meal, and one of the staff members recognized him. Noticing your father in disarray, he caught up with him and convinced him to stay there for the rest of the day and night. The next morning a member of the Salvation's Safe Haven staff talked to your dad and arranged for him to meet with a social worker. When your father later admitted he'd lost his desire to live, they talked him into staying for further consultation with a psychologist.

"After a few sessions the psychologist encouraged your father to continue staying there for counseling, and also to begin attending Alcoholics Anonymous meetings. With nowhere else to turn, he took the advice. That opened the door to a Salvation job training program. With a place to stay and regular meals he earned a diploma, and soon he was hired by the Golden Nugget. That's where he worked for the several years before I met him."

"You seem to have all this memorized."

"The way he tells it makes it easy to remember. Just think, Anita, counseling through the Salvation Army and AA led to a job, and hopefully the permanent end to his alcohol dependency."

"Tell me again how you first met him."

"Okay, I was downtown one evening last spring with my fiancée, and he stopped us and asked me for some money. He said he wanted to help a homeless girl hiding in an alley down the street. I believed him and gave him enough to help her out. After the second meeting in a library, I just couldn't get your father out of my mind. He's about the same age as my father would have been, and I don't know, he just reminded me of my dad in so many ways. I'd been offered my summer resort position and I needed an assistant with a business background. I decided to offer him the job, and that was only a few weeks ago."

"But he'd been away from business management for a long time. Didn't you think the challenges would be too much for him?"

"The more I thought about it, the more I figured hiring him might be good for all parties. He had what I was seeking—a degree in business administration; and he'd stayed current with the business world; and he had a good personality."

"And you wanted to give him an opportunity."

"That's true."

"But where did he get his nice clothes and his apartment and the new car?"

"As for the clothes and his apartment, I'd just won some money gambling and decided to use it to help him get started. I'm sure you've noticed the car has New Horizon signs on the doors. It's one of their lease cars."

"You used gambling money to help him?"

"I'm not a steady gambler, but one night I got lucky and won a few thousand dollars. I decided not to chance giving it back to the casino, but instead put it to good use. Please don't tell him I used gambling winnings on his behalf. He thinks the money came from a New Horizon transition employee fund, and I don't want him to feel he owes me."

Her eyes turned frosty as she said, "Do you make a practice of lying?" But then she shook her head and said, "Forget I said that."

"All I know is I wanted to do everything I could to benefit your father. Besides, I know he's going to be a sound investment for us."

"I see, Mr. Stewart."

"Anita, could you please drop the formality?"

"All right, but you are my boss."

"And I hope, your friend. There's another matter that should be cleared up. When I learned how he felt about being separated from you, it was my idea to bring you two together. As for you coming here to work, that was his idea. He suggested it the day before we all went to breakfast."

"I figured as much."

"I apologize for the way I've handled the entire situation. At various points I took the easy way out. I hope you can forgive me."

"Well, perhaps," she said, but her expression told him he was completely forgiven.

When saying goodbye in the parking lot, each person felt a sense of relief knowing important pockets of mystery regarding Robert McGuire had been revealed and resolved.

Chapter Twenty-three

RICHARD HAD BEEN ON THE job for more than a month and he was on a roll. Construction work at the resort was progressing as expected, encouraging news for J.D. and the committee. In Omaha Benjamin was receiving glowing reports from each of his managers, rewarding news for everyone there. Robert and his daughter were enjoying each other's company, and that was ideal. For the Omaha businessman only one thing was missing. If only Paula Summers were back in Las Vegas, it would be a perfect world.

With the resort operations and New Horizon offices closed on the Fourth of July, Richard found himself with little to do. He thought of contacting Juan and Maria, but then remembered they were with relatives in San Diego. As for Robert, he was planning to spend the afternoon with Anita. Richard considered playing a round of golf, but the afternoon forecast for 111 degrees canceled further consideration.

Were he back home, he'd be sailing and water-skiing with friends at a nearby lake. In the evening he'd be dining at the Happy Hollow Club, and afterward, somewhere in Omaha there'd be a colorful fireworks display.

Just before entering the Le Café for breakfast, his cell phone chimed and to his surprise Paula said, "Hi, I've been thinking about you and keeping my fingers crossed you're not upset anymore."

"Well, Paula, what a pleasant way to start my day. Hey, I just happened to be thinking about you, too."

"Lovers' mental telepathy, right? I was planning to come over to Vegas today to see you, but at the last moment was informed I'd be expected to work for an impromptu AIDS benefit rally. It's at the Hollywood Bowl this afternoon, and Seth Greene volunteered most of the news staff to assist in televising it. I'm not too disappointed, because he says I may be doing spot interviews with Antonio Banderas or Renée Zellweger or Matt Damon. Can you imagine lil' ol' me interviewing one of them? I can't wait."

"Sounds like a promising opportunity all right."

"It's so good to hear your voice again," she said. "I thought perhaps after our argument you might not want to hear from me, but then I remembered how much we've always meant to each other. And after all doesn't everyone have a little disagreement now and then?"

"We've had very few, that's for sure. So why don't I just drive over there? I could probably make it in time to watch you work this afternoon, and I might even stay over for another—"

"Which sounds wonderful, but we've been through this before, Rich. It's simply too complicated for you to be here right now. I'm afraid you'd feel stranded."

"I haven't seen you for over two months, Paula."

"And I miss you, too. My folks also want to come out here, but I had to tell them not for a while, so don't feel I'm singling you out."

Realizing the discussion could turn into another fiasco he'd later regret, he took a deep breath and said, "Whatever you think."

"Just be patient a while longer, okay? Now tell me about your work at the resort."

"So far our progress is ahead of schedule."

"Thanks to you I would imagine. I still think they want you with them permanently."

"J.D. just needs someone to help him through the summer. I think I owe him that much."

"And what have you been doing in your spare time?"

"Words to describe my social life. Hmmm, how about uneventful, nondescript, and boring. Juan and I work out at the club, and we play a little golf, and occasionally I go over to their place. I've made a few acquaintances at work, but most of my leisure time I spend thinking of you."

"Good, because if I thought one of those beautiful showgirls was trying to cast a spell on you, I would scratch her eyes out. I suppose I could say go ahead and have a woman friend—a wrinkled grandmotherly type that is—but I'm afraid even she would make me jealous. I guess you'll just have to wait for me."

"But seriously, shouldn't we set a specific time for when we can be together?"

"What I know is Allyson's leaving soon, but there are no immediate plans to fill her position. I thought they were procrastinating, you know, having fun watching their three little princesses dance around the fire. Now it's rumored major program changes are underway, and that's why they're taking so long."

They talked for a long time before Paula closed by asking him to stay in touch now that she'd taken the first step.

Following their conversation, Richard was relieved he hadn't lost his cool and pressed her further. *Another blowup like before and I could lose her for good.* At least after her reconciling call, he'd be more content spending the afternoon nursing a cool drink and catching up on some reading at the Paris pool.

Upon returning to his suite, his cell chimed again, and this time it was Robert. "If you don't have anything scheduled today, why don't you join Anita and me at her place? We're going to have a light fruit and veggie snack, lounge around the pool, and jump in when needed. We'd like some company, so meet us there around two o'clock. Okay? Fine, done!"

"I don't want to intrude."

"You mean where Anita's concerned? She suggested I invite you."

"Well then I will."

"I could pick you up on the way."

"That's all right. I know where she lives, and I want to stop by Walmart to pick up a few items. I'll see you at the pool."

It was a perfect afternoon for poolside leisure—a deep azure sky touched with a few thin streaks of cirrus clouds and soft breezes.

The first to arrive, Richard went to the men's dressing room and changed into his swim trunks. As soon as he stepped outside, he noticed Robert and Anita walking from her patio. Carrying a picnic basket, Robert was wearing Bermuda shorts, a T-shirt, and tennis shoes. Anita wore a short terry cloth robe over her swimsuit, and beach sandals. Inside the crowded pool area they joined Richard before moving to a tree-shaded picnic table.

As the men sat down at the table, Anita took her towel and went to the pool to swim a couple of laps. Minutes later as she emerged from the pool, the sight of her toweling down in her cherry red bikini surprised Richard. He knew she'd been an accomplished diver and was well-proportioned, but a light bronze tan acquired during after-work swimming had toned her shapely figure, the sharp contours in her back and shoulders, her slim waist, and her beautiful legs.

"Your daughter looks as if she could still be competing for the university."

"She takes care of herself all right; says she swims daily and also works out in the apartment gym."

Returning to the table, Anita set out pitchers of lemonade and iced tea, along with the bowls of the sliced vegetables and fruits.

Not long after eating, Robert said he was tired and stretched out on a lounge chair. Hoping to nap, he placed a towel over his eyes. His companions, in turn, remained at the table and discussed work, the latest news, movies, and what was going on back home.

"Your dad," Richard said, "tells me you're extremely dedicated to your profession."

"I feel fortunate to be working with young people. Perhaps it's because I feel I have something special to offer them, especially those going through difficult times. I'm sure a much of my inspiration comes from being a rebellious teenager myself. Those times left me with deeply emotional experiences to draw from."

Pushing his sunglasses onto his forehead, he said, "All I've heard about you is that you were an outstanding student and a diving medalist."

"Not always an outstanding student, and who's been saying those things?" She glanced at her apparently slumbering father and said, "Never mind, I know."

"He said Melissa told him when you were on the university team, you did some pretty fancy diving."

"I competed in the one- and three-meter events."

"She also said you were one of the university's best."

"Melissa exaggerates. I was a third-level competitor on a five-woman team."

Richard's comment, "Memory serving, my best was a cannonball off the low board," made her chuckle.

Several times they took time to cool off in the pool before continuing their conversation.

Robert, meanwhile, was only pretending to sleep. Instead he was listening to every word his boss/best friend and daughter had to say.

"Tell me more about your life in Cincinnati," Richard said.

"Okay, well, Missy and I share a town house apartment, and I visit my folks quite often. I work out at a fitness center, and sometimes on the weekends I fill in as a counselor for a firm called Family Consultants. I have a few friends I consider quite close, and occasionally I go out on a date."

"Occasionally means there's no one special in your life?"

"No, I'm fairly recently divorced, you know."

Later in the afternoon as the pool crowd numbers were dwindling, Richard offered to buy his friends dinner at a nearby Mexican restaurant. While there, he also asked them to accompany him to a fireworks display at the north end of the Strip. Again they agreed.

Darkness had settled when he parked the MKS in a vacant lot near the Stratosphere complex. After stepping from the car, they leaned back and watched the starry, tranquil night transform into thunderous explosions and cracklings, brilliant streaks of flames, and bursting showers of sparks.

It was nearly eleven o'clock when he dropped Anita and Robert back at her place.

On his way back to Paris, Richard opened his moon roof and inhaled the fresh desert air. He smiled to himself as he recalled a day that turned out much better than expected. First there was Paula's call, then a relaxing afternoon at the pool with Rob and Anita, a tasty Mexican dinner, and finally, a good old-fashioned fireworks display.

Couldn't be much better, he thought, *unless, of course* ...

Chapter Twenty-four

O NE DISTINCT TRAIT THE MONTE Vista Committee shared was a hero-sized respect for James Forrester. He'd shaped his fifteen talented associates into an organized team ready to promptly fulfill his requests. Not that the New Horizon president was faultless. There were times he could be overreaching in his expectations and demands. That became all too clear during a mid-July meeting when he made a surprise announcement.

"People, we are off to such an incredible start, the Renzcorp board wants us to fast-forward next year's grand opening to September. I know that's four months early, but your initiative and progress make it possible for me to honor their request for a Labor Day weekend PGA tournament. I'm asking that accelerated operations begin immediately."

The announcement stunned everyone. Committee members were already working overtime, and there were times Richard was in his office into the evening hours. Not a single committee member had ever openly disagreed with a Forrester decision, but this one was sure to stir discontent.

Richard recalled his boss's insistence concerning unsigned contract agreements with two of the major construction firms. "Don't worry about those particular companies," J.D. had said. "They're like family, no signatures required."

So the unsigned contracts give him the flexibility to follow his own time schedule without the possibility of legal reprisals, which is exactly what he's doing.

Informing the companies' representatives of the new deadline was Richard's responsibility. From the moment he met with them the following Monday, he was on the defensive.

"To meet such demands in unrelenting desert summer heat," one of them argued, "we'd have to hire many more workers in addition to contending with overtime allowances," and so on.

When Richard went back to J.D. with their complaints, he countered, "The board doesn't want more labor costs and overtime. All they want is for the new target date to be set into motion. I think we should proceed, Rich."

During the week the opposition's displeasure intensified. Friday morning inside the site's mobile home headquarters, Richard was at his desk while glancing over the day's schedule. Suddenly the door slammed open and standing before him was a broad-shouldered, angry construction superintendent.

Sam Beesley's curly blond hair was ruffled and his piercing blue eyes unyielding as he spat out his anger over the new demands. "Who in the hell is responsible for this? If you sons a bitches think you can pull this off, you're wallowing in it up to your ears!" Following several more angry comments, he crashed his fist onto the desktop, turned on his heel, and stormed out.

It happened so quickly, Richard was left speechless and dazed. Never in all his business dealings had he encountered such a violent outburst. Later in the day, still feeling the emotional fallout, he called Juan to tell him of the incident and the surrounding circumstances.

"Make no mistake," Richard said, "Sam Beesley was boiling mad."

Juan responded, "From what you've told me, I agree with him. The new target date made possible by gentlemen's agreements opened the door to unreasonable expectations. You were in law school. Wouldn't such contracts be considered illegal anyway? I think you'd be wise to tell Forrester he should reconsider."

Richard felt trapped between the likes of Beesley, former LSU linebacker, and Marciano, the heavyweight champ. He called Madelline who promptly arranged for a meeting with J.D. the next morning.

When they met, Richard revealed in entirety the Beesley encounter and the committee's unified discontent. He concluded, "I think the accelerated target date is impractical for all parties, James, and we need to reconsider."

Although Monte Vista was the president's prize jewel, he also realized his program director was completely frustrated. After a brief pause J.D. responded, "All right then, let's consider an alternative."

Richard replied, "To maintain the level of work performances we expect, we should reinstate our original January 1 opening. Look at it this way, the following April we can host a grand opening golf tournament the likes of which this city has never seen. We'll call it the Monte Vista All-American Easter Classic."

No further encouragement required, J.D. said, "Go ahead and reconcile our differences. I'll handle the Renzcorp board."

Richard promised to immediately prepare revised contracts for all parties. "Only this time everything will be specifically spelled out, and we'll need signatures across the board."

"Your legal instincts, Mr. Stewart?"

"Yes sir, something like that."

Revising the contract language took most of the weekend, but by Sunday evening Richard was able to call Sam Beesley and request a second meeting.

At site headquarters the next morning, Richard was apologetic. "Look, Sam, our unreasonable expectations were the result of improper contract agreements. We were wrong and it won't happen again. The contract before you can only be consummated first of all with your written approval, and then those of the two major contracting companies."

The changes reinstated the original deadline, but in Monte Vista's interests the revised contract also called for monthly guidelines citing specific work completion dates. In addition, more direct lines of communication for all parties were established.

As he read the contract's highlighted alterations, Sam nodded his approval and his expression softened. Fifteen minutes later his signature was followed with a firm handshake and some friendly dialogue.

That afternoon the companies' reps also signed on to the new provisions.

While peace was restored in the Monte Vista camp, a week of disruption and a time-consuming weekend left Richard visibly stressed.

Juan noticed and advised him, "You know, Ricardo, I think it's time for you to start having a social life—with a lady friend I mean—someone to take to dinner or to a show, someone you can relax with."

"You mean as on a date? Are you serious?"

"A friendly relationship might be good for you, at least until you and Paula can be together again."

"I'm fine."

That evening following a shower and preparing to spend an uneventful evening watching television, he reconsidered his friend's advice. *Maybe it is time to have a more social life.* He considered the two single secretaries in the New Horizon front office. Then there was Nicolle, the Paris reservation assistant who was more than friendly. He eliminated her because all he was looking for was a companion, not someone who might have deeper intentions.

He recalled the Fourth of July he spent with Robert and Anita. *Now she's an intelligent woman and easy to talk to. Maybe I should call her.* Realizing she knew about his relationship with Paula, he'd have to think of a logical reason for wanting to see her. *She said she sometimes works weekends for a family counseling firm. I could take her out for a drink and ask her what she thinks about my long-distance situation with Paula. It would be interesting to hear another woman's perspective, especially that of a professional counselor.*

Finally he called her. "I was wondering if you might have some free time. There's something I'd like to discuss."

"Uh-oh, did we mess up at work this week?"

"No, no, nothing like that. Actually, I'd like your professional opinion concerning a personal matter."

"My professional opinion? Sure, I have time right now."

"I'd rather talk to you in person. Any chance I might stop by in a half hour and we could take a drive?"

"That's fine."

Although they'd talked at length on the Fourth, from the moment he picked her up, he felt uneasy and spoke rather aimlessly. After opening the car's moon roof, he said, "Ahhh, that fresh air feels good. I get tired of this town's arctic air-conditioning. How about you?"

"Mmmm, me too. At night I shut off the air and sleep with my bedroom window open."

"Anyway, I felt like cruising around and sharing some thoughts with you. On a Wednesday evening, Strip traffic should be relatively light."

As the MKS sailed northward on the boulevard toward the Strip, Anita noticed the world famous sign: Welcome to Fabulous Las Vegas, Nevada.

"I've seen that sign in movies and on television all my life," she said, "but the word 'fabulous' falls short of describing what's going on in this town."

"After you've been here for a while, though, life becomes almost as routine as anywhere." Approaching the Luxor, he continued, "The blue-white light above the apex of the pyramid rises ten miles into the sky and is the most powerful beacon in the world."

"Can you believe it's been over six weeks since Missy and I were there? I wanted her to come back when her class ends, but now she says she can't afford it."

"You two had quite a time."

"Thanks to my father. He took us everywhere."

"So tell me, how do you like your summer job?"

"It's been interesting and Jeff and Janelle are fantastic to work with."

As they were passing the Excalibur he said, "Did you know thirty-six of the thirty-eight largest hotels are right here in Las Vegas, and over forty million people visit here every year?"

"That's remarkable. Now tell me, how is it you know so much about Las Vegas?"

"To help me adjust to my summer job, my fiancée—Paula Summers is her name—taught me everything she knew about Vegas entertainment. Back then she was a television news reporter for KBLV and *very* knowledgeable."

"I see."

In front of the Bellagio the fountains were soaring and dancing to the voice of Gene Kelly.

"I'm singin' in the rain,

Just singin' in the rain,

What a glorious feelin',

I'm happy again—"

"I haven't been inside that place yet," Anita said, "but I hear there's nothing quite like it on the Strip."

"Lavishly artistic in their many attractions, yet somehow they manage to create an inviting atmosphere for everyone."

He turned east on Flamingo Road until he spotted a Starbucks. "Mind if we stop for a drink?"

"Sure, something cool sounds good."

Inside they ordered iced lattes and took them to an outside table where Richard asked, "So how do you personally feel about this town by now?"

"I like it here but of course there are times I miss my family and friends."

"You've changed your father's outlook on life, you know."

"I think where he's concerned, you deserve most of the credit. Now you said you wanted my opinion regarding a personal problem."

"Yes, well, when we were at your pool on the Fourth, you said you've done some adult counseling."

"Back home I sometimes work on weekends for a family consulting firm."

"Unfortunately, I'm having problems in my relationship with Paula. I thought perhaps you could give me some professional advice."

"I heard a little about that situation, that she's in Hollywood and has been gone for quite a while?"

"Another reason I thought of you is because she's about your age and you're both well educated and career minded."

"Okay, let's start with how did you two meet?"

"A good friend introduced us."

"And when was that?"

"Last January."

"And how long since you've seen her?"

"I haven't seen her since early May. We talk on the phone but not enough, not for me at least."

"And it's been well over two months without any direct physical contact?"

"Therein lies the gist of my problem."

"You didn't know each other very long. I'm assuming it was love at first sight, or at least nearly so."

"More for me than for her."

"You've never felt the way you do about her with anyone else, ever?"

"Back in my hometown I've had several close relationships, but nothing too serious ever developed."

"I understand. Perhaps you were concerned the parties involved might be more interested in your community and financial status than you personally."

"There's some truth to that."

"And then along came Paula."

"She wasn't like anyone I'd ever met and as I said, it didn't take me long to realize I loved her very much. I had to keep in mind her goal was to have a successful career in television news and her job could cause us to be separated."

"Father said something about her being a talented newswoman."

"She calls herself a news feature specialist. You may have heard of Allyson Devereaux?"

"I've seen Allyson on television."

"It turns out she's leaving her position at KHOL in Hollywood. Now Paula and two others are in contention to replace her."

"Your fiancée is ambitious and must be *very* talented. Can you tell me a little more about her?"

Gazing above Anita's head as if an actual image of Paula had appeared, he said, "She's very beautiful, a natural blonde with fascinating blue eyes. Oh, and in addition to her work, she's completing a master's degree in journalism."

"My father said he saw her once, and I see what he means when he says you adore her."

"And what else did he say about her?"

"Like you, he said she's beauty pageant gorgeous. He calls her Blondie and Mystery Woman."

Richard smiled and said, "Mystery Woman applies because in our situation she was here one day and gone the next."

"And now she's concentrating on the television position in California."

"She's already signed a contract with KHOL, and these days her bosses are sending her on assignments all around the country."

"She's doing what she set out to do. Isn't that good?"

"Except before she left we were nearly engaged. Now she can't find the time to come here and she doesn't want me to come there either. She thinks with all of her responsibilities I'd feel stranded. What it comes down to is the engagement's on hold indefinitely."

"Do you think there's a possibility she may have changed her mind concerning your engagement plans?"

"She says she still loves me, but doesn't want anything to interfere while she's trying to land the Hollywood position."

"Hmmm, an indefinite delay after you were both sure of a commitment. Your concern is understandable."

He shrugged and said, "My story sounds a little like a country western love song, doesn't it?"

She smiled and said, "Perhaps, but let's go back to the beginning. She didn't contact you to explain why she left so abruptly?"

"She did."

"And you said you've told her you'd come there?"

"I told her many times I would. The other two newscasters who want Ms. Devereaux's position are more experienced, so I know she's dealing with some pressure. To complicate matters the station's top guns are taking their time. She says they'll make a decision soon and then we'll be together. Soon, however, has become a nebulous word which keeps getting postponed."

"In addition to being frustrated, do I detect a degree of anger?"

"More like disappointment. So what do you think?"

"If you want my professional advice, I'll need to know more. I'm expecting a call, Richard, so I should be getting back to my place."

"Then let's meet again. May I call you?"

"Of course."

A couple of days later he did call her again. That evening they stopped for soft drinks and a much longer discussion at another Starbucks, this one located near the UNLV campus.

Anita's final question surprised him. "To help me in my evaluation, I need to ask a very personal question. Were you and Paula completely intimate?"

He paused before he replied, "Just before she left, we were."

She appreciated his frankness and said, "Okay, I believe I have enough information to come up with some choices for you to consider. I'll need a couple of days to wrap it up."

"Good. Now I've been wondering if I've been taking up too much of your time. I understand you've been dating Jeff and—"

"How did you know about that? My father again, right?"

"Is there any reason he shouldn't have told me?"

"I didn't think he would, but I can't keep up with Jeff's weekend partying anymore. He's fun to be with and a great dancer, but you know places like the popular night dance clubs? They don't really get going until late, which is fine for him, but I need more rest. I was planning to tell him this week I have to leave his late-night party circuit. I'm sure it won't take him long to find a new dancing partner."

"Well if you're going to be free, I'd like to take you out to dinner Saturday night. If that's okay, please bring along your final analysis and also a bill for your services."

"A bill? No. Please consider my service as partial payback for all you've done for me this summer. You mean we're going out, as in dress up, get my hair fixed?"

"I'm looking forward to it."

Chapter Twenty-five

ALTHOUGH THERE'D BEEN ONLY TWO counseling sessions, Richard found them both interesting and therapeutic. And there were times Anita had him wondering if he was taking matters too seriously. He'd always held Robert's daughter in high regard, first because she was his daughter, and second for her impressive MVP leadership. Now she was much more than someone he respected; now he considered her a good friend.

Friday morning he called her. "All clear for Saturday night where Jeff is concerned?"

"I told him yesterday I can't keep up with the weekend marathons anymore."

"And what was his reaction?"

"As I said, Jeff can't be derailed for long, so guess what? He's taking Janelle dancing this weekend. If they have a good time, and they probably will, I don't think she'll be taking her weekend early morning jogs anymore. She'll probably be getting home not too long before that."

Richard chuckled and said, "By the way, I remember you saying you'd never been inside the Bellagio, so I thought we might have dinner at Picasso's. I'll pick you up early. It will give us time to look around."

Anita took the opportunity to wear her new black chiffon dress with cheetah print underlay and black patent leather heels. She was also wearing the half-carat diamond earrings her father had recently given her.

Upon entering the Bellagio lobby, she admired the tiled Roman columns, cupid fountains, and especially the dazzling backlit cascade of multicolored flowers hanging from the ceiling. They moved on to the Conservatory and Botanical Gardens with its lavish floral displays. Enhancing the settings were vine-covered lattice archways and classical statues and statuettes. A bridge over a brook led to an oversized white gazebo which opened to another garden setting where members of a wedding party were posing for pictures.

Richard pointed to a balcony overlooking the Gardens, and he said, "The Gallery of Fine Arts used to be up there, but they've moved it somewhere else on the premises. If you're into Renoir, Monet, and other famous artists, we could come back another time."

"You mean you don't think Paula would mind if we continued seeing each other?"

"I wouldn't think so. It's not as if we were out on a date. You're my counselor and my friend."

"I assume she doesn't know you're taking me to dinner tonight?"

"We still haven't talked, but it shouldn't matter. Even her close friend Juan has been encouraging me to have more of a social life."

For the first time Anita wondered if Juan's recommendation was the real reason Richard had sought her counseling advice.

They followed a walkway through the main lobby, then down a stairway leading to Picasso's lakeside restaurant. After they were seated and placed their orders, Anita noticed there were several Picasso art treasures on display. "I remember studying him in a humanities course I took at the university," she said, "and I've always admired his work."

Richard didn't reply, and from his expression Anita knew his mind was somewhere else. She touched his hand and said, "You've been here before, with Paula, right? And you're remembering back to those times."

"You must be psychic. Actually, we were here once last spring."

"I see. Anyway, I have a surprise. I was waiting to tell you over dinner, but now is as good a time as any. By chance I saw your fiancée on NBC's news program last night."

"She was on national television last night? I had no idea. With my busy summer schedule, except for late night ESPN I seldom have time to watch television."

"She was interviewing students from USC and UCLA in regard to the strong job markets on the West Coast. You were right about her being photogenic."

"Well great, I'm glad you had the opportunity to see her. And what did you think of her television personality?"

"She seemed very professional to me."

As the waitress was serving their meals, Anita noticed her accent and said, "Sandra, you're from the South, aren't you?"

"Indeed Ah am, ma'am, born and raised in Chahlston."

Following a friendly exchange, as Sandra moved on, Richard said, "Her accent reminds me of Paula's southern accent. She seldom uses it anymore, but it's always charming."

Anita smiled faintly and shook her head. "From every angle, Richard, Paula Summers dominates your thinking."

"Guess I'm hopelessly in love."

While indulging in their Julian Serrano dinners, Anita offered the first of her counseling strategies. "If things don't improve soon you might consider just ending the romance and getting on with your life."

"You mean end it on my own. Be assured, that will never happen."

"I would think, though, if the status quo continues too much longer, it might be better for both of you. My second suggestion is that you force the issue. Call and tell her you're coming to see her. Tell her any further postponements are unacceptable. Don't pussyfoot around; be firm. Tell her to get some time off because you'll be coming there the next weekend, period."

"I tried a watered-down version of that once but didn't accomplish anything. Maybe I wasn't firm enough."

"Remember, a woman who possesses an overload of self-confidence may inwardly want to be challenged. She's always had her way with men, right? You, however, show some backbone. Before she can offer a postponement, tell her you have to break away for an emergency and you'll call back later. But don't call her back for several hours. When you do, tell her a critical resort problem has come up, and you won't be coming after all. Make it a cancellation without a rain check and then politely say goodbye. Such reverse psychology could drive her absolutely mad."

"And if that doesn't change her attitude?"

"Would you be any the worse off?"

"I'll take it under consideration."

"My final analysis. Whenever you talk to her, she says she misses you and she loves you. With all she has going for her, she would never say that unless she meant it. Her actions may seem inconsiderate to you, but you have to remember what's at stake for her. Replacing a television star like Allyson Devereaux? Possibly a once-in-a-lifetime opportunity. So you accept things the way they are. Keep calling her, even if you're only leaving messages. You don't have to overreact, but occasionally send her flowers."

Richard thought, *Similar to what Juan said, but with professional follow-up.* He said, "I think I prefer your final suggestion."

"You mean you've made up your mind already?"

"I'll just have to be more patient and supportive."

"This was easier than I thought."

After finishing the main course, they passed up dessert but the wine bottle was still half full.

As Richard was filling their glasses he said, "Now, Ms. Stevens, during the three times we've met, our discussions have been all about me. I think it's time we concentrate on you for a change."

"Me? Now that doesn't sound good at all. I already told you a lot about myself at the swimming pool."

"Actually I know very little about you personally. For starters tell me how are things progressing with you and your father?"

"We're having some good times. I think Mother overstated his mistakes, and I sometimes wonder why she painted such a bleak picture of him."

It was the first time Richard had heard Anita take a position on the side of her father. He replied, "It's difficult to understand why people react the way they do. From what both you and your father have told me, your mother is a woman of impeccable character and judgment."

"Thank you for that, Rich. She can be demanding, and she's far from perfect, but she is my idol. She and Gene married when I was four-years-old. He was a widower with two little boys of his own, and the year after they married she quit teaching, which she loved, to become our full-time mom. It helped make us a close-knit family. Gene has also always been a caring and supportive parent."

"So you have two brothers."

"Jamie and Travis, and we're like blood siblings. Jamie works with Gene and will one day take over the construction business. Travis is a district manager for several convenience stores in and around Indianapolis. They're both married with kids."

"It sounds as if you grew up in a healthy home environment."

"I definitely can't complain. It was my parents who had their hands full with me, in particular when I was a teenager."

"You a problem? I doubt—"

"Remember what I told you before? I was a major problem."

"Because?"

"I'd rather not get into the specifics."

"Hey, I told you everything you wanted to know about me."

"That was different; you're not my counselor. Okay, but don't say I didn't warn you." Slowly sipping from her wine glass, she recalled, "As I was growing up, I was involved in a variety of activities, and always I was expected to be a high achiever." One by one Anita touched her fingers. "In high school I was on the honor roll, member of the Student Council, secretary of the French Club, and as you know, a varsity diver. Most of my friends were also high achievers, a situation that fit exactly with our parents' expectations."

"You were a busy young woman."

"Definitely. Then in tenth grade my school counselor asked me to chaperone a new student from Chicago through her first few days of classes. Her name was Paige Munson and she was bright and cute and friendly. But she had a wild side, too. Like me, except my rebellious nature was deep down where no one could see. We quickly became friends.

"The next summer we started meeting at a neighborhood swimming pool. We were sixteen, both had gymnastic training, and just for fun we starting doing trick dives off the high-diving boards. Soon we were challenging each other and became the pool's major attraction. One day the aquatics coach at Walnut Hills High was also watching us go through our antics. When he learned we were students at his school, he approached us and insisted we try out for the diving team. We did and we made it.

"By then Paige and I were best friends, a situation that didn't please Mom. Paige didn't come from an affluent family and definitely didn't fit in with my elitist friends. It made no difference to me. I liked her better than any of them.

"She was the oldest of five kids and often took care of her brothers and sisters. In time she confided in me that her father was using drugs and was abusing her. She said her mother was afraid to intervene, and Paige made me promise to tell no one.

"In the second semester of our junior year, her home situation worsened. She was faltering in school and insubordinate with her teachers. I wanted to help her, you know, try to set an example. But instead of her following me, I started following her. I no longer wanted to be at or near the top of every challenge I was involved with. Soon my grades and my attitude were also heading south, and when Paige quit the diving team, I followed."

"It must have been a trying time for your folks. How did they react?"

"Mom was beside herself, and we quarreled a lot. She wanted me to get some counseling, but I refused. Father tried to be the mediator. He said I was merely going through a teenage phase and would be back to normal soon. They were relieved when Paige was sent to an alternative school."

"And that separated you two."

"No, it didn't. Whenever possible we met at a nearby mall and other places. We were mixing with kids with similar attitudes because it seemed unique and daring. Our new activities included drinking, smoking pot, and skipping school. I kept hoping I'd be sent to Paige's alternative school, but it wasn't to be."

"What a dramatic change in your life."

"Then Paige was caught shoplifting, and her dad slapped her around. I'm talking bruises and a black eye. She told school authorities she'd been in an accident. Then she asked me to run away with her to Portland, Seattle, somewhere far away."

"Like the teenage girl your father ran into downtown."

"Yes, like her. The school year was ending, and my folks decided to take an extended vacation at our Kentucky lake vacation home. Their unspoken strategy was for the family to be together without interruptions. They were hopeful in such an environment I'd come to my senses. I didn't want to go, but I was only seventeen and they gave me no alternative.

"From the moment we left home, no one in my family made a reference to my surly attitude. After a few days at the lake they were all having so much fun, I got tired of moping around and started boating and water-skiing with them. I also joined in their late-night conversations. Before long we were the way we used to be.

"By the time we returned home three weeks later, I'd decided to put my life back on track. I wanted to have a good senior year and rejoin the diving team. What was equally important to me was to convince Paige we should do it together. The first night I called her she said she'd been fighting with her dad, and he wanted her out of the house. She said she'd joined a real gang. She said they were people who really cared for her. She also said since I'd been gone she'd experimented with ecstasy and meth, and she wanted me to join the gang. That scared me."

Richard shook his head and said, "By then she was completely out of control."

"I asked her to meet me in the food court in the mall that evening. Then I went to my folks and revealed everything Paige had told me. I said I wanted to bring her home to live with us. I said I knew if she was in a good, safe environment, with encouragement from me and from them, there was an outstanding chance she'd come to her senses just as I had. I told them I believed it was her last chance. I was surprised when Mother offered no resistance; nor did my father. Perhaps they thought if they said no, they would lose me again. Mom said I should bring her home that night, and they would welcome her into our family.

"I was so excited I couldn't wait to see her, to tell her she had a new home with us. I drove my father's car to the mall and waited for her right up to closing time, but she never came. When I returned home, my parents were waiting for me at the front door. Their expressions—a mixture of anxiety and grief—frightened me.

"Father put his arm around me and said one of my friends had called because Paige had been in a bad car accident. My memory flashed back to the food court where I heard people talking about an accident that had happened near there. They said two people were killed when their car missed a corner and crashed into a tree. At the time I didn't think beyond that, but when I looked into my mother's eyes, I knew all too well what had happened."

"Anita, I'm sorry."

"For the next few days my family tried to console me, but except for the funeral I seldom left my room. As time passed, however, it was so very important to me that my parents had agreed to openly welcome Paige into our home. After that my mother and I were closer than we'd ever been."

"May I assume Paige became your inspiration for working with young people?"

"Yes, definitely."

They'd been in the restaurant for nearly two hours when Anita said, "I think we're the object of some impatient glances from the hostess."

"I think you're right. Before we go, I want to offer you the leadership position of the permanent MVP team. We're prepared to offer you an outstanding salary and benefits, substantially more I would think, than you'd make in education. At least you could compare."

"But it wouldn't be the same as working with young people. That's where I belong."

When they said good night, she encouraged him. "Paula loves you, Rich, and I feel confident you'll be together soon and will work everything out." She lifted on her toes and kissed his cheek and said, "That's for good luck."

Chapter Twenty-six

NO ONE COULD HAVE BEEN more inspired and delighted with the metamorphosis of Robert Fitzgerald McGuire than the man himself. That he could have come so far in such a short time would have been a commendable achievement for anyone. Yet, easy to remember were the mistakes he'd made and the losses he'd endured. Well aware a single drinking binge could erase all his gains, he prayed such a setback would never happen again.

As for the present, his work performance was far exceeding expectations. At times his efforts may have seemed obsequious, but he was determined to protect his new life. He was receiving preferential treatment from Madelline, not just because he was Richard's new assistant, but because she personally liked him. Whenever he needed clerical assistance, she prioritized his requests. And lately when he came to the New Horizon office, the two would exit to the rear outdoor balcony to smoke and talk. Since his divorce he'd had virtually no prolonged social contact with a woman, so befriending someone like Madelline was yet another plus. He was working out regularly at the athletic club, eating healthier, and putting on those much needed pounds.

On a Monday afternoon Anita called him to ask, "Will you be coming to my twenty-eighth birthday party?"

"Your birthday? Honey, that's not until December 7, Pearl Harbor Day."

"You remember, good job. Anyway, this year I thought we might celebrate together."

Robert paused before responding, "Either I'd have to fly to Cincinnati, or you could come here, which would be great, except you'll be in school, right?"

"That's true, except I'll be counseling in a school only about fifteen minutes from where I'm now standing."

"What school do you mean?"

"I mean Grant High School in Las Vegas."

Robert's voice wavered between disbelief and exhilaration. "You did say a school right here, didn't you? What about Walnut Hills?"

"Well, it's like this: I'm taking a year's leave. It all came together this morning."

"For sure, you're going to be here for an entire year."

"I decided a change would be good for me, and I'll also be able to spend more time with you."

"Those are two damn good reasons. Ooops, sorry, but this is *incredibly* good news. How did you ever manage that? I remember the school board back home being very inflexible when it came to altering contracts this late."

"It all started last month. In the newspaper want ads I saw this high school counselor opening for an entire year. I decided I'd give it a shot."

"You never said anything."

"I didn't want to build your hopes too high. Anyway, when I applied they seemed interested, and I contacted Kyle Hampton, my principal back home. I explained how you and I were reunited after twenty-five years, and I might have an opportunity to counsel here for a year. He said it was all right with him, but I'd have to talk directly to Dr. Tim Sutherland, the district's personnel director. When he heard my story, he said if I was offered the position he'd see what he could do. In the meantime I applied for, and a few days ago received, a Nevada secondary counseling certificate."

"That's absolutely amazing."

"I imagine someone else would have refused such a late summer request, but Mr Hampton was right. If I had any chance at all, I had to start at the top with Dr. Sutherland. He has a reputation for bending the rules if he thinks the cause is just."

"Bless Dr. Sutherland. That took some guts on your part, young lady."

"Well, whatever. I really didn't think my chances were all that promising. Then this morning Natalie Carter, the Grant High principal, called and said I could have the job, but it required immediate acceptance because she had another eager applicant. I accepted and called Dr. Sutherland. He said he also had an interim counselor in mind for my position, so I could take the job. He even went out of his way to say he knew my mother and had heard of you, too." She paused before adding, "I wonder what he heard."

"Yeah, I wonder too," Robert replied, and they both laughed.

"So you see, Mr. McGuire, things are looking quite spectacular on this glorious July day."

"This is too good to be true, except I'm pinching myself, and glory be, Annie, it is true."

After hanging up he called Richard to convey the news, but he was unavailable.

Earlier, Richard received an urgent request to meet Juan during his morning break at Le Café.

When Richard arrived, Juan was waiting in a booth with a magazine on the table in front of him. He looked up and said, "I'm very annoyed."

"You look very annoyed. What seems to be the problem?"

"A couple of days ago one of the managers from the Hollywood Hilton stayed at the hotel. We usually have lunch together and compare notes. Some time ago I'd introduced him to Paula, and he always asks about her."

"Okay."

A waitress brought their soft drink orders before Juan continued. "This time it was him telling me about her. Apparently she's going over big out there. I asked him how he knew, and he said for one thing she'd been seen on the town with a well-known advertising executive."

"What?"

"That's what he said."

"What did he mean? Dating her?"

"He said they'd been seen together."

"Why didn't you tell me right away?"

Juan lifted his hands defensively as he said, "I figured there was probably nothing to it, and I also felt you had enough on your mind."

"Go on."

Juan opened the *People* magazine to a story with pictures taken at a star-studded Hollywood party. He pushed the magazine in front of Richard, who was shocked to see a picture of Paula in a strapless evening gown and standing next to her a tall, graying man in dressy attire. He looked suave and confident, like a typical veteran Hollywood playboy. The caption identified them as *Paula Summers, KHOL television news newcomer, enjoying the Hollywood party circuit, and Carlton Smith, Conn-Net advertising executive.*

Richard said, "He looks older, but this is the person your friend said she'd been seen with?"

"One and the same."

"Not good, not good at all."

Following a few moments of reflection, Richard said, "Maybe the picture's misleading. You know, she's there, he's there, the photographer asks them to get chummy."

"Maybe so, but I must admit I'm beginning to wonder. She's says she's too busy to see you because of her work obligations. Yet we have living proof she's not always running here and there on assignments. Want to know what I'd do if I were you?"

"Go ahead."

"You have a few weeks left here, and it's time to get Paula out of your system for a while. Do you remember me mentioning Nicolle, the cute little blonde who works for me in guest services? I know for sure she'd be pleased if you would call her."

Richard didn't hear the advice. Juan's shocking disclosure and his own need for a logical explanation were swirling in his mind.

Finally he said, "Want to hear some silly stuff, Juan? I love her so much I can feel her pulse beat in my veins 24/7."

"But she's not available, and you need someone to get your mind elsewhere. What about Robert's daughter? You told me she's an intelligent, interesting person."

"Actually I have been with Anita a few times, not of course on an official date."

"Well good, and?"

"We got together for a few friendly discussions, but that's over with now."

"Why is it over with now?"

"Nothing more to discuss. Besides, she's going back to Cincinnati in a couple of weeks."

"A couple of weeks can be a long time. I would think she'd make an ideal short-term platonic partner."

Richard didn't comment further. As the men were leaving, he picked up the magazine and before dropping it in a disposal barrel outside the café door, he asked his friend, "Do you mind?"

"Nada, good riddance."

For Richard, concentrating on work the remainder of the day was like trying to read a Dostoevsky novel while riding the New York–New York roller coaster. It wasn't until evening Robert called him to tell him of Anita's new job.

"Well, Rob, what terrific news—a dream come true for you, right?"

"Make that a honey-coated dream sent from heaven."

After hanging up Richard tried to call Paula on her cell phone. When her voice mail greeting came on, instead of leaving a message he called the KHOL newsroom.

A night newsman informed him, "She's on special assignment in Dallas and won't be back for a couple of days. If it's an emergency I can notify our news director, and he'll probably call you back."

"Never mind, it's not life threatening. I'll reach her when she returns."

Chapter Twenty-seven

J.D.'S MENLO PARK WAS MADELLINE'S pet name for her boss's workplace, not because of the uniqueness of the Time-out Corner, or the compelling business atmosphere within the Versailles Chambers, or other thought-provoking office stimuli. She simply believed he was the most imaginative public relations genius in all of Las Vegas, and Thomas Edison himself would have admired J.D.'s ingenuity and initiative.

Nevertheless, with the days of summer flying by, the New Horizon president was facing a problem even he might not be able to solve. His program director would soon be relinquishing his duties, and a replacement was not being seriously considered. When Richard asked Madelline about it, rather than make excuses she arranged for a meeting between the two men.

In J.D.'s office the next morning before discussing his concerns, Richard presented two new recommendations for the resort. Both came from committee members. The first pertained to the amusement park.

"Jason is ready to present his plans for a futuristic park. He's proposing an elaborate carnival midway including go-cart tracks and a miniature golf course which he wants to be an exact replica of the resort. Sally wants fluorescent billboard signs to be strategically placed along Interstate 15, the 215 Beltway, and all major city thoroughfares. The signs' flashing message will be, 'All Roads Lead to Monte Vista, America's Foremost Family Entertainment Resort.'"

Leaning back in his desk chair, J.D. said, "Hmmm, I like both of those suggestions. I personally have been thinking each of the indoor showroom theaters should seat no more than six or seven hundred, and we'll make sure there won't be one bad seat in the house. As for weekly entertainment, one will feature stars appealing to more mature audiences, such as Frankie Avalon or Kenny Rogers. The other showroom will headline entertainers appealing to younger generations, and not only will we be offering lower prices, half the seats will be sold the day of the show."

"Which will avoid the sold-out performances which disappoint so many Vegas visitors."

"That's the idea. During next Saturday's meeting, would you present all three proposals for discussion and approval?"

"You know, Maddy's right about you, James. She said you never get bogged down with analysis paralysis."

"She said that? I'll have to order her a bouquet of flowers today. Speaking of her, the last few times Rob's been in the office the two of them have been going out to the balcony to converse and smoke, and they're out there for quite a while. Have they got a thing going?"

"Not that I'm aware of."

"She lost her husband a few years back, and except for her kids and grandkids coming to visit, she's pretty much by herself. I think it would be nice for her to have a good friend like Rob."

"And nice for him, too."

"By the way, what happened between him and his former wife?"

"They divorced about twenty-five years ago is about all I know."

"And he's never found someone else. Life can be lonely."

From his briefcase Richard removed his latest progress report, placed it before J.D., and said, "As you will see, everything is progressing in accordance with our time schedule. By early September the golf course landscapes will be equipped with fully operating water systems. You were concerned about work delays during the monsoon season. Rob has calculated in the worst scenario the number of days we could lose and still remain on schedule."

J.D. barely skimmed the report before he said, "Rich, I think everyone in the entire organization is grateful for what you've accomplished here this summer."

"I'm fortunate to be working with a highly specialized team. Now, Maddy said I should talk to you about my replacement."

Frowning for the first time, J.D. said, "As was our problem last spring, we just can't find anyone who can replace you. Believe me it isn't because we haven't tried. I do know having you here, even if it's only over the weekends, is far better than having anyone else we've seen. That's why today I'm asking you to remain as program director until the first of the year. I don't mean full time, just on the weekends, just as you did last winter and spring. With Rob as your assistant, don't you think you could make it work?"

"He's certainly dependable."

"I've said this before, but by the first of the year I'm sure we'll have found someone with the right qualifications. If you think—"

"Don't give it another thought, James. I'll work here on the weekends, at least until a couple of weeks before Christmas."

With a sigh of relief, J.D. said, "Thank you. I know everyone connected with the resort will be pleased with your decision."

They moved into the Time-out Corner where J.D. poured two glasses of grape juice on the rocks. From their swivel chairs they had a perfect view of Las Vegas Boulevard's bustling activity.

As an afterthought to their working agreement, Richard said, "With my new schedule after Labor Day I'll have to spend some extended time in Omaha. I'll be visiting our stores and meeting with managers in addition to helping with promotional planning for the fall season. It could take me a couple of weeks."

"As before, you're free to be in Omaha whenever it's necessary."

"There's something else I want you to consider. Before our grand opening, what would you think of creating a position for a senior citizens coordinator, someone to handle senior golf and other senior activities? In my opinion Rob would be an ideal choice."

"A senior citizens coordinator. What a terrific idea, and I agree that Rob would be ideal."

"This week he discovered a major Las Vegas golf course enterprise was forced to relinquish its license to host sanctioned professional tournaments. Several of the fairways were in the direct path of frequent mountain wind flows, disruptive enough, they soon realized, to eliminate the course from championship competition. Even though we've been following strict regulation guidelines, I think we should invite PGA officials to come out here and inspect every aspect of our Country Club layout. I don't foresee any problems, but we'll want the course to be as flawless as possible."

J.D. nodded and said, "So if any changes have to be made, minor though they may be, now is certainly the time. Go ahead and extend invitations."

"I think we should also contact several of the best players. Let's get their suggestions for making the Country Club the most inviting course in the nation."

"I know it's a ways off, but maybe we should also include some of them as public relations spokespersons for our grand opening."

"Top performers would be costly."

"I'm giving you the green light."

"I'll go to work on it."

Later when Richard returned to his suite, he remembered Robert's call and he wished he'd been more enthusiastic about Anita's new position. Instead of calling him, he called her.

"Congratulations. Your dad told me about your new job. When did you find out?"

"They called me early yesterday morning."

"You never said anything about wanting a counseling position here."

"I considered my chances quite remote, but just in case I stayed in touch with Ms. Carter, the school's principal."

Richard revealed how excited her father had been. He then told her about Paula's picture in the magazine and how upset he'd been.

"You know, Rich, a photograph taken out of context can be misleading. If Paula had seen a picture of you and me having dinner and drinking wine at Picasso's, what would she think?"

"I agree, a picture can be misleading. Well, I intend to find out."

"Yes, you certainly should."

"I did try to call her at the station, but she was on assignment in Dallas."

"So why didn't you call her there?"

"I thought about it but didn't." Feeling a sudden impulse to speak face-to-face with Anita, he said, "I was wondering if you and I could get together again. Perhaps we could discuss this latest situation a little more?"

"And when would that be?"

"How about Saturday night?"

She paused before she said, "I'm not sure, Rich. I may have a conflict. Could you call me tomorrow?"

Surprised by her uncertainty, he said, "Sure, I'll call you then."

The next afternoon she answered his call in a more subdued voice. "I have a problem."

"And what is that?"

"To be honest with you, Rich, I really don't think I should advise you concerning Paula anymore."

"You don't? I see. Had enough of my silly romantic escapades, right?"

"There's really nothing more I can tell you about what she might be thinking or how you should react. If it's true she's seeing someone else, you definitely should follow the first strategy and go your separate ways."

"I understand, Anita. Look, I'm sorry about this. I'm afraid I've been taking advantage of your time and professionalism."

Her voice quavered as she said, "It's all right. I've always enjoyed our discussions."

The line was silent until he remembered a show he and Paula were planning to see the weekend she left for Hollywood. "Wait just a minute," he said. "I just had a brainstorm. Would you consider going out with me on an official date Saturday night, no counseling whatsoever allowed?"

In a less subdued voice she answered, "You mean there'll be no discussion whatsoever about you and Paula?"

"Sounds doable to me. What I'm thinking is Bellagio has this highly acclaimed aquatic show called 'O.' It's all about aerial gymnasts, acrobats, trapeze stars, and oh yes, daredevil diving athletes. It should be something you would really enjoy."

Her voice cleared completely. "I've heard it's wonderful."

"Let's make it Saturday then."

"All right."

The moment he hung up, Richard felt a new sense of respect for her. It was understandable she didn't want to be involved with his Paula problems anymore. Keeping her name out of the conversation wouldn't be easy, but he'd do his best.

Saturday evening Anita was spellbound as the aquatic performances unfolded in the "O" Theatre. And as promised, not once all evening did Paula's name come up.

As he was driving Anita back to her apartment, Richard said, "Next week Chicago's playing over at the Orleans. They put on a great instrumental show, and I just happen to have a couple of reservations. So would you like to go?"

"I love Chicago."

The next Saturday night during the intermission at the Orleans Showroom, she said, "You seemed captivated with the music tonight. Are you by any chance a musician?"

"Yes, I am. I play my trombone in a jazz group back home."

"You mean professionally?"

"We're called The Improv. We play a mixture of jazz, jitterbug, and close-up dance music, whatever suits our audiences."

"And you play with them regularly?"

"I did until last January when I started spending the weekends here. I plan to rejoin them whenever I'm in Omaha for an entire weekend."

"May I ask why you chose the trombone?"

"My mother was a music teacher at the university in Omaha. When we were very young, she started my sister and me on the piano. Both my parents loved music ranging from symphonies to Dixieland to rock and roll. They had a sound system installed throughout the house, and as a child I liked it best when they played Louis Armstrong and his All Stars. I was fascinated with the talents of Trummy Young, their trombone player. So in seventh grade my folks bought me my first slide trombone. I've been playing ever since. And what about you? Are you a musician?"

"Well, I did take flute lessons for a few years, but remember me telling you about my rebellious teenage days? One of the casualties back then was my future as a musician. My boss playing his trombone in an Omaha jazz band. Now that I would like to see!"

Chapter Twenty-eight

ON WEDNESDAY IN THE SECOND week of August, Richard had returned to Omaha for a two day sales conference with Benjamin and Stewart store managers. Friday morning he was back in his Paris suite with time to spare before the preliminary Summer Summit meeting. Exhausted from his three-day trip, he stretched out on the sofa and quickly fell asleep. Before his wake-up call an hour later, delightful dream flashbacks took him back to the first time he came to Las Vegas, his affair with Paula, becoming friends with Juan, J.D., and Robert, his Monte Vista good fortunes, and his friendship with Anita.

Sitting up on the edge of the sofa, he rubbed his hands across his face before reading again the messages Evelyn had given him—one from Madelline updating the Monte Vista luncheon; the other from Anita asking him to call her after work. A glance at his watch told him he'd have to hurry to be on time for the meeting.

Eight weeks of concentrated work had passed quickly for the MVP team. They'd completed their goals, and now Jeff would be moving on to Berkeley, while Janelle would return to Flagstaff.

When she left her MVP employment, Anita moved to a different apartment only a few doors down from her New Horizon unit. Grant High School was only eight miles away, and whenever possible she visited the school. Although structural repairs, classroom cleaning, and floor polishings were still underway, she wanted to familiarize herself with the campus and meet as many school personnel as possible.

The first official counselors' meetings would be a week from the following Monday morning. On Tuesday she'd attend a workshop for all new faculty members. For the remainder of the week counselor responsibilities consisted of meeting with principals, an all-faculty meeting, and then meetings with teachers, either in team settings or individually in their classrooms.

Anita had experienced the start of school five times in Cincinnati, so she was familiar with the routine. Once school officially opened, her main chores would be assisting new students with their schedules before guiding them on tours. Cecily Fontaine, a French teacher, and Penny Thornton, who taught American Literature, assisted her in making other adjustments.

One of Anita's most challenging tasks would be working with Hispanic youngsters needing help with English. Two years of college Spanish were not enough to make her fluently bilingual, but two other counselors, Manny Hernandez and Carla Emmanuel, promised to step in when needed.

Back in his office, Richard was busy with current Monte Vista affairs and preparing for the summer wrap-up conference.

Several evenings a week Richard and Anita looked forward to spending some of their leisure time together. Their discussion included a wide variety of topics.

Any reference to Paula remained off-limits, as was anything related to Anita's former marriage. Shortly after learning Richard and his daughter were becoming very good friends, Robert offered Richard some advice. "Avoid discussing her former marriage. She doesn't like to be reminded of him."

Still, curious soul that he was, Richard wanted to know why the marriage lasted only six months. One night after they'd been to a movie, he parked in front of her apartment and as usual they reclined their seats and began conversing.

On this night, without preliminaries, he surprised her when he inquired, "You never talk about your former husband."

Anita looked directly at him, and said, "That is a *very* personal matter, Richard, and not one I wish to recall."

Pulling down the skin beneath his eyes, he turned to her and said in a Rocky Balboa voice, "Aw, gee, Adrian, gosh, Ah'm sorry. Uh, Ah didn't mean to upset ya or nuttin' like dat. Here, plant one right here, right in de ol' kisser."

Her frown converted to a half-smile as she said, "Where'd you learn to do that stuff anyway?"

"I told you, I'm a natural born copycat. Well?"

"Why do I let you corner me like this?"

"C'mon now, I've told you a lot about *my*self."

"You always use that excuse. Okay, go back to when I was in college. His name was Daniel Ramsey Collinsworth. He was the All-American type—president of his fraternity, busy political activist, just a regular campus hero."

"So how did you come to meet him?"

"He introduced himself at a football social hour and asked me to dance. Later he took me home and we started dating."

"You must have liked each other right away."

"He was tall and handsome with smiling brown eyes and wavy blond hair, the type most women find irresistible. His dad had been a lobbyist in Congress, and they lived in Alexandria, Virginia. Right after high school he was appointed as a page for a Virginia congressman. He said his father pulled some strings there, a not unusual occurrence for Danny boy."

"How did he happen to end up at your university?"

"The school has an outstanding political science curriculum. Anyway, he was extremely ambitious. He figured after he graduated, he'd become a lobbyist, then a congressman, and eventually a senator."

"Really."

"Mother was thrilled with the relationship. She figured he probably would be a senator someday."

"I get a kick out of your mom. So what happened?"

"Going into our senior year he thought we should live together, but I told him absolutely not. The trouble with Danny boy was he was so enamored with himself, the more I told him no, the more insistent he became."

"Why did you marry him then?"

"In his dominating way he made me believe I really did love him, and we were married two weeks after we graduated. It was a big church affair with all the bells and whistles.

"He started working in Senator Cauldron's office, and I started teaching English at Walnut Hills High. So there I was, twenty-three-year old, a faculty member in my old high school, and married to this man whose main purpose in life, or so he said, was to fill mine with joy and happiness."

"Obviously he loved you very much."

"I wonder. Before long I realized he was jealous if I so much as talked to another man. I thought his attitude would change, and Mother said not to worry. She said he was just going through an early marriage adjustment. One night we were waiting in the lobby of a movie theater, and while he went to the men's room, a young man bumped into me and spilled some of his pop on my jacket. He apologized and I told him not to be concerned. Just then my husband returned, and when he saw the man dabbing at the spot with a napkin, he pushed him back and ordered him not to touch me. Fortunately, a theater manager stepped in and called security. Before they arrived, my ex grabbed my arm and led me outside to the car."

"An embarrassing moment for you."

"Definitely. I told him I was humiliated and would not tolerate such a scene ever again. He promised it wouldn't happen again, but there were other incidents. Beneath all the hoopla he was an insecure person who had very little interest in anything that didn't elevate his self-image. Six months after the marriage I filed for divorce."

"And where is he today?"

"I heard he was selling insurance. I'm just thankful I never became pregnant. I mean, I want to have kids, but—"

"So you do want children."

"Of course. I want at least a boy and a girl, if, that is, I ever meet the right guy. I keep hoping. And you?"

"Two of each sounds good to me." Richard felt a sense of regret for Anita's ex. *To lose a woman like her because of unwarranted jealousy was nothing more than dumb-ass stupid.*

At her doorstep when Richard said good night, she lifted on her tiptoes and for the first time pressed her lips to his. Then she said, "Call me as soon as you're able, okay?"

The kiss was completely unexpected. Although he didn't immediately display his reaction, from the moment he left her he wondered what he'd said or done to cause her to misjudge his feelings. Even though he knew Paula might be seeing someone else, he wondered how she would react if she knew another woman had just kissed him. Causing Anita any embarrassment was the last thing he wanted to do but now, one way or another he'd have to tell her he considered her a good friend but nothing more.

The next afternoon in his office he received a much different surprise when Paula called.

She sounded impatient. "Richard, would you please tell me what's going on? I haven't heard from you for an eternity. Why haven't you called me?"

"I could ask you the same question. This is one of the rare times you've called me."

"You know I've been working and traveling. At least you used to leave a message."

"Paula, I saw your picture in *People* magazine with an advertising executive, Calvin, or Charles, or something Smith?"

"Carleton Smith? The picture in the magazine? That's what's bothering you?" She snickered softly.

"I said something funny?"

"As a matter of fact you did. Carleton Smith works for Conn-Net, an advertising agency representing our station. He's highly respected, and he's been very gracious to me. He's also in his mid-fifties and likes to be *seen* publicly with the opposite sex, but they're not his personal preference. Along the Hollywood party circuit our paths have crossed a couple of times, as they did when the picture was taken. Don't you realize I'm expected to be congenial to important people in the television industry? Why didn't you call me when you saw the picture?"

"I thought about it, but you're never available."

"So you presumed the worst, and now you know the picture meant nothing. Do you really think I'd cheat on you, Rich? You know what? I think we've been apart way too long."

"Amen to that."

"The reason I called is because I have some late-breaking news I think you'll like."

"Go ahead. I could use some good news."

"It turns out I have the Labor Day weekend off, and I plan to be in Las Vegas late Friday afternoon. If that works for you, we'll be spending the rest of the weekend together."

Richard took a deep breath. "You are coming here Friday, and there will be no mix-ups, no cancellations."

"None that I can foresee."

"That is indeed good news."

"It has been a while."

"Paula, honey, I can't wait to see you. We have a lot to talk about, you know. And I have some good news of my own. This is my last full-time week here, but I will be going back to a weekends-only schedule. They still can't find someone with enough experience to take over as program director."

"Right. As I've said before, they want you with them permanently. It's good to know you'll be in Vegas on the weekends, but for now I just can't wait to be with you."

After a long time discussing less important matters, she closed by saying, "I'll call you Friday as soon as I arrive."

"I'm already counting the minutes."

Now his Labor Day weekend would be even more crowded—Friday's Summer Summit Conference, settling matters with Anita, but most important of all, *This time Paula really is coming back.*

When he informed J.D. of Paula's plans, even he seemed excited.

"Why don't you convince her she should come to work for us? With her good looks and talent we could place her in any number of Monte Vista positions. Tell her we are prepared to offer incentives she may find too tempting to pass up. Which station is she working for again?"

"She's at KHOL, but trust me, nothing—I mean nothing—could lure her away. I think she's heading straight for stardom with the parent NBC network."

"You know her best, but tell her we're interested."

Partly because he was so busy, but more so because he was procrastinating, it was Wednesday afternoon before Richard called Anita.

In a noticeably subdued tone she answered, "And where have you been? I haven't seen you for several days and I left you several messages. I know you've been busy, but—"

"Sorry I haven't called, but busy doesn't come close to describing my schedule these days. So tell me how school is going."

"It's a time of adjustment and confusion for everyone, but we're making it."

"I don't have a lot of time, but may I see you for a while this evening around eight o'clock? There's something we need to discuss."

"I'll be waiting."

For the first time since the counseling sessions began, he was feeling uneasy about seeing her. How to tell her what he must tell her wouldn't be easy. *I'll just say Paula's coming to town Friday, and I can't wait to see her. I'll say it is a dream come true for me. That in itself should clearly reveal how I feel.*

It was a beautiful evening—a huge, full moon rising slowly over the eastern mountain skyline and gentle summer breezes—so enchanting that Richard suggested instead of stopping somewhere, they just cruise around town, listen to music, and talk.

Her first question was, "Now tell me, why haven't I heard from you? Let me guess. Mr. Forrester's dominating your time again, right?"

"Putting closure on a busy summer has been time consuming for all of us."

"To be honest with you, Rich, I think he puts too much pressure on you. I find Forrester to be much less impressive than you do. The one time he visited our MVP office this summer, it seemed to me he was more interested in promoting himself than anything else."

"If you knew him better, I think you'd feel differently. He's the most versatile, talented promoter I've ever met, and highly respected by everyone he works with. I could cite some examples."

"Sometimes you sound as if you worship James Forrester."

"In business dealings *and* in his personal life, I do look up to him."

"Okay, but I missed you this week, and every day I waited for you to call. So why didn't you?"

"As I said, I haven't had a moment to spare."

Richard's less-than-accurate sidetracking made him feel awkward and he strayed from his *We can only be friends* message. Instead he asked her to tell him more about school.

"Well, a few students were dropping classes and others wanted to switch subjects. This week we also had two runaways. It seems as if whenever I'm ready to meet with a teacher, or inform another team how I'll be working with them, a new problem arises. Yesterday a tenth grader came to my office and revealed her friend was despondent and was talking about suicide."

"In most cases not too serious a threat, right?"

"Richard, there are times you can be so naive. Recent school tragedies should remind you, every violent threat has to be taken seriously."

On the car radio Shania Twain was singing,

"My dreams came true,

Because of you,

From this moment—"

"You know," Anita interrupted, "that song reminds me of how close you and I have become this summer, and I, Mr. Stewart, have a fantastic idea. Why don't we go out Friday evening and celebrate our summer together? This time I want to take *you* to dinner, and when we finish—I know you like to play that dice game—maybe you could teach *me* how to play. I think it would be interesting. So will you? Can we?"

"I'm afraid Friday and the rest of the weekend I'm going to be very busy and—"

"What do you mean you're going to be very busy? You told me last week your Friday conference will be finished by mid-afternoon, and I think you should enjoy yourself afterward. At least we can have dinner together."

Her spirited request made his *friends only* message seem even more awkward. *I just don't feel like telling her right now. It'll be much easier if I call her from the office first thing in the morning.* "Tell you what," he said, "I'll check my schedule and let you know."

Later as they said good night in front of her apartment, before he could turn to leave she put her hands on his shoulders, lifted on her tiptoes, and pressed her lips to his again. Not passionately, but with noticeable warmth.

That does it. Tomorrow morning I will tell her, tomorrow morning for sure.

At ten o'clock the next morning when he called the high school counseling office, the secretary informed him, "Ms. Stevens will be in conferences until noon. May I take a message?"

"That's okay. I'll call again."

The rest of the morning he and three members of the Monte Vista committee visited the resort site to add the final touches to their Summer Summit reports. As they walked onto a rise overlooking the developing landscapes, Dan Albright, the architect from Albuquerque, set up a portable table and studied his blueprints. Clifton Shapiro, the shopping mall interior design analyst, reviewed his checklist on a clipboard. Darlene Severson, the landscape specialist from Palm Springs, conferred with Sam Beesley who told her the golf course water and irrigation systems were ready for an official inspection."

When Richard returned to his New Horizon office, his phone light was blinking.

Paula's message was brief. "Sorry, but I won't be able to see you this weekend after all. One of our newscasters is ill, and Mr. Greene wants me to cover her story assignment in San Diego. I feel awful about this, but I was left with no other choice. I'll be leaving here soon and won't be back until Sunday. I'll be sure to call you then. Please don't be too upset. Love you."

Discouraged and angered, he assumed she hadn't tried his cell phone because she didn't want to talk to him directly. He touched her cell number and left his own message. "Why didn't you call me on my cell phone? To use a no other choice excuse is pure nonsense. Please listen to me carefully, Paula. Don't bother calling me again until either you are coming here or you want me to come there."

In an attempt to calm his surging emotions, he searched for some other way to spend the weekend. He considered flying to Omaha to participate in driving, as he had for many years, his '57 Ford Thunderbird convertible in the Labor Day parade. *No, it's too late to enter now.*

Another thought appeared. He still hadn't talked to Anita. *So she wants to go out and celebrate tomorrow night. Well then, that's exactly what we'll do.* He called her office again, and this time the secretary was able to put him through.

"Just wanted to check with you concerning our pending dinner date," he said. "It turns out I will have some time, so if it's okay with you, we'll eat at MGM's Rain Forest. It's a fun place with intriguing jungle settings and aquariums. And remember to bring along a voracious appetite because they have delicious dinner entrees and absolutely sinful desserts."

"Ahem, Richard, are you a little nervous? You're running on like my father has a habit of doing."

"Hell no, I'm not nervous, just in one helluva good mood. That's possible, isn't it?"

She snickered and said, "I see, well, whatever you say. It does sound like fun. By the way, it's good to hear you in a more upbeat mood today, definitely less withdrawn."

"And you said you wanted me to teach you about the craps game and I will. While we're eating I'll even teach you how to roll the dice. Then we'll find ourselves a lucky dice table. Okay?"

"I'm dying to find out why that game stirs up so much excitement."

"Something else you might consider. MGM is a hot and sassy place on a Friday night, so feel free to slip into your most exotic dress."

"*Exotic* dress, did you say? Let me look around. I think I may have just the little number for such an occasion."

When the call ended, he felt better. *Dinner at MGM, then rollin' the dice with my friend Anita.* It was a far cry from what he'd been looking forward to. *But it's better than being alone and feeling disenchanted with life in general.*

There was something else. *Spending the evening with her will give me ample time to explain how much I appreciate our friendship. I'll tell her gracefully, give her a chance to read between the lines, help her realize I'd like to be her good friend forever. But nothing more than that. Once she understands everything, we will be ready to have the kind of a night only two very good friends can have..*

Chapter Twenty-nine

NEARLY SIXTY PEOPLE GATHERED IN the Versailles Chambers for the Summer Summit Conference. The afternoon program ran smoothly with committee progress reports taking less than two hours, followed by Richard's thirty-minute summary. During the speeches J.D. listened with approving nods and smiles before delivering his summation.

"In conclusion," he said, "for the extraordinary summer accomplishments, I want to extend my heartfelt thanks to each and every one of you. Because of you the Monte Vista resort is going to fulfill our highest expectations."

Following his speech he mingled with his audience, shaking hands and offering words of encouragement to each resort-connected person.

When he came to Richard, he reminded him of their Angel Park front-nine golf match the next morning. "And while we're enjoying our game, I'm going to tell you about a proposal I think you'll find delectably inviting."

Later when Richard returned to his suite, there was a brief message from Paula. "Your call shocked and disappointed me. I'm sorry you feel the way you do. I think it would be better for both of us if we put our relationship on hold, at least until I know for sure what's going to happen here."

The finality of her response was his first major jolt of the day. It would not be his last.

The second came when Anita answered her door for their evening out. Standing before him was not the high school counselor friend he'd come to know quite well. She'd been replaced by an alluring woman wearing a black sequin dress with shoestring shoulder straps and bordered across the top and the hemline with an inch of sexy black lace trim. The snug-fitting dress, slightly slit above the knee, and her two-and-one-half-inch black heels accented every inch of her curvaceous figure. That afternoon she'd had her hair styled in short, snappy curls, and she'd carefully applied her makeup—a touch of blush pink rouge, lavender eyeliner, and parsimony pink lipstick.

Slowly turning in a pirouette before him, she lifted her eyes to his as she said, "You suggested I wear something exotic. Do you think I look all right for tonight? Or is this a little overdone? I can change into something less exotic in a jiff."

Taking a step back, he scanned her from head to toe, and said, "No, you're fine. I asked for exotic, and you gave me exotic. I should warn you, you could get into trouble looking the way you do."

She smiled slyly and said, "But you'll look after me, won't you?"

After they arrived at MGM, as a friendly hostess was escorting them to a Rain Forest table, Right away Richard was smiling to himself because Anita in her strikingly attractive dress was drawing glances from men and women alike. Even after she passed by, the glances followed her. Not surprising because one of Anita's strongest assets were her legs, the kind women would die for and men could not keep their eyes from.

Soon after being served their dining selections, she reminded Richard, "You said you were going to teach me how to play your dice game."

"And I came prepared."

From his sport jacket pocket he took a craps instruction page. placed it on the table, and between bites took time to explain the basic rules of the game. To her delight, at the side of the table he also showed her several ways she might throw the dice. She was silently hoping she would get the opportunity.

Once dinner was over, he checked his watch and said, "We're a little early before the heavy casino action starts, so what don't we go outside for some fresh air before we start playing?"

"Mmmm, that does sound refreshing."

His underlying motive for the fresh air interlude was to finally divulge his elusive *friends only* message.

Leaving the restaurant, they rode an escalator up one flight and then walked onto the bridge connecting MGM and New York–New York. To one side they had a close-up view of the Statue of Liberty, and on the other side the Gotham city skyline. Suddenly between the statue and the city, a chain of yellow-and-gray Manhattan roller coaster cars, rackety sounds and wild screams included, plunged down a steep descent.

They moved to the bridge's protective steel railing to observe below them the smooth-flowing boulevard traffic. No *friends only* message from Richard yet, but the moment Anita moved closer and slid her arm through his, he turned to her and said, "Annie, there's something we should discuss this evening."

"Before we do, Rich, I want to confess something. I've never liked being called Annie by anyone before, but coming from you or my father, I don't mind at all. This summer you two have become my most treasured friends, and if at times I seem overly emotional in our relationship, please understand it comes from the feelings of friendship I feel for both of you. Now, you were saying?"

Her *treasured friends, deep feelings of friendship* struck like twin lightning bolts. They awakened the distinct possibility it was *he* who had misjudged *her* feelings. With a surge of hope mixed with elation he thought, *Maybe those good night kisses were nothing more than just a friendly show of affection. If only this is true.* He decided to let the night play itself out without having to deliver his dreaded message. *And when I take her home, I'll thank her for thinking of me as her friend. Then I'll say a simple good night and give her a friendly kiss on the cheek. Hallelujah!*

"Richard, you didn't answer me."

He checked his watch. "Actually, what I have to say can wait because it's time to play." He took hold of her hand and with a spring in his step he added, "C'mon, my exotic little friend, let's see if we can win some money."

Upon re-entering MGM, they followed a walkway leading to the casino's table games section. There were players at every table, but one of them was completely surrounded and invitingly noisy. Richard decided to wait there for an opening.

While Anita was looking between the players to see the table's activity, a dealer cried out, "Place your bets on the box cars, the big six, and the big eight."

"What does he mean?" she asked Richard.

"He's encouraging players to bet on some of the numbers I showed you in the illustration. If you recall, I said they were high-risk bets favoring the house."

During a lull in the action in which several players tossed losing sevens, the man standing directly in front of Anita was preparing to leave the game. At the same time two young women—a tall, slender blonde and a shorter, heavier-set brunette—moved next to Anita. Looking on the tough side, but still attractive, they both wore tight, short-sleeved knit dresses, glittering costume jewelry, and stiletto heels. The blonde's hairstyle was a boy cut, while the brunette's hair was swirled to a twist on top of her head. Along with Anita and Richard, the women wanted the departing player's opening.

As the man was leaving his spot, Anita and the blonde both moved for it, but Anita was a step quicker. Her place secured, she turned to the blonde and said, "Sorry, but we here before you."

The blonde tsked her tongue and said under her breath, "Bitch."

Looking past her, Anita reached for Richard's arm, but her hand accidentally brushed the brunette's shoulder.

The brunette said to her friend, "Can you imagine the rudeness of this little redhead? Make that *slutty* little redhead. She bullies her way into the opening and then she hits my shoulder."

The blonde shook her head. "No, I really can't. She *is* very rude."

Anita didn't verbally respond; instead she looked squarely first at the brunette, then the blonde.

Attempting to calm the rapidly deteriorating situation, Richard said, "Look, if you ladies want this place, we can—"

Anita interrupted, "Richard, we were waiting before they arrived. I didn't mean to touch her, and she knows it. They're the rude ones. We're fine."

Glancing at his left hand and noticing no wedding band, the brunette moved very close to him, and said, "You seem like a gentleman, so for you we'll let your little bitch brat have her way."

Without further comment, the two women moved on, but when they turned back to glare at Anita, she sneered and sent a hiss their way.

Richard was chuckling as he asked, "What was that all about?"

"You can't let bullies like those two push you around. They acted as if they'd had too much to drink."

"They sure were unhappy with you."

"And they're gone, and it's time to play the game."

The table's betting range was $10 minimum, $5,000 maximum, and Richard traded $300 for their playing chips.

In the next fifteen minutes three more players sevened out early, and Richard informed Anita they were down over fifty dollars.

"That was fast," she said

"Not unusual in this game, but it can change just as quickly."

The player next to them was also unlucky, and now it was their turn to roll the dice.

When the stickman pushed several dice in front of them, Richard said to Anita, "How about you doing the honors?"

"Oh good, I think." Anita said.

"Remember how I showed you? Toss them in a little arch, just high enough so they bounce off the end of the table."

She selected two of the dice and said, "I will do my best."

He placed a chip on the pass line and Anita tossed a five.

A dealer declared, "Five's the rollout number. Place your bets."

Richard placed two more chips on the number five.

"So now if I roll another five," Anita said, "we'll double our money. How exciting!"

"The shooter's a natural southpaw," the dealer declared. "Let's keep it going, pretty lady."

She rolled a four, then a six, and betting around the table picked up.

But three rolls later, the dice rolled to a five and a deuce.

"Seven and out; sorry, ma'am," the dealer said.

As another dealer cleared the chips from the table, Anita said, "Oh, no."

Richard said, "Don't worry because we didn't lose too much that time, and hey, we're just getting started. Could you excuse me while I run to the men's room? I won't be gone long, so hold on to our spot until I get back."

Soon after he left, across the main walkway and a short distance down a cross walkway, inside an open-front restaurant three members of a leather jacket motorcycle gang were in an argument with the manager and several customers. With voices rising, a physical confrontation seemed likely, and security guards, joined by other casino personnel, were rushing toward the scene. Two of the more experienced personnel at Richard's table promptly ordered two younger dealers to close the table for playing until they returned.

As Anita and the man next to her discussed the cafe commotion, the two women who had confronted Anita had returned and now were directly behind her. Without a word of warning, the stocky, dark-haired woman reached out and grasped two fistfuls of Anita's hair.

In a seething voice the woman said, "You were very rude to us, lady. Do you still feel like being rude?"

Fearful that if she tried to free herself she could lose those two fistfuls of hair, Anita closed her eyes and took a deep breath.

Arm muscles flexed, the aggressor continued, "Not so tough without your boyfriend, are you, sweetie?"

Players and spectators around the craps, roulette, and blackjack tables immediately shifted their focus from the cafe skirmish to the immediate sight of a stocky woman holding a smaller woman captive.

The blonde brazenly stepped forward and in a clear voice said, "You people need to step back and give these two some room." Then she tongue-lip spat in Anita's face before sliding a closed fist across Anita's chin.

Like most of the crowd, the young dealers were awestruck and hesitated interfering.

However, the player who'd been talking to Anita stepped forward, and said, "Now just a moment here, ladies."

Quickly the blonde grabbed the gaming stick from the table and placed it firmly on the man's chest. The look on her face revealed she was very upset, and after he moved back a couple of steps, she brandished the stick like a baseball bat and warned the crowd, "I said, give these two some room and do not interfere. The redhead needs a lesson, and Jessie is going to be her teacher."

Trusting in her threat, the crowd as one moved back to allow a half circle opening at the side of the craps table.

Anita inquired of Jessie, "What is it you want from me?"

"What I want is for you to get down on your knees and apologize to both of us, right now, on the floor." Tightening her grasp with each syllable, she continued, "Do you un-der-stand!?"

Through her pain, Anita asked, "Why don't you be a real woman and go face-to-face with me?"

Jessie grinned and said, "Face-to-face did you say? Fine!"

The moment she released her hold, Jessie grasped onto Anita's shoulders and spun her around. Tilting her head back as is preparing to launch a head butt, Jessie said, "And this is for—"

The sentence ended when a lightning left hook landed squarely on Jessie's jaw. Forced backward by the blow, a shocked Jessie shook her head to clear the cobwebs.

"Why, you little bitch," she said. "I'm going to make you pay for that." She yanked the combs from her stacked hair and it tumbled down around her shoulders. Looking wilder than ever, she kicked off her shoes and Anita did the same.

With fists clenched, the combatants circled each other, and Anita's early expression of helplessness and pain was now a mixture of anger and determination.

After Anita's left hook the crowd sensed the possibility of an upset, and someone said, "Let's get it on!"

With that, Jessie charged forward with both fists flying. Anita stood her ground, but could only partially deflect a fist to her mouth. At the same time she countered with another left hook, this one glancing off Jessie's forehead.

Stopped in her tracks again, Jessie brushed the top of her hand across her forehead and saw a trace of blood from an eyebrow cut. Encouraging a continuation of the fight, Anita squared off again, only this time she confidently circled her clenched fists.

In a desperate attempt to regain control, Jessie again rushed forward, but this time she lowered her shoulder into Anita's midsection. The momentum carried both women to the floor. Furiously they wrestled across the carpet, first one on top, then the other, slapping and punching at every opportunity.

When they abruptly collided with the side of the craps table, each woman quickly rose to her feet.

Moving to within striking distance, Jessie said, "Let's see how you look with the straps torn off that flimsy little dress."

Deeply incensed by the threat, Anita ducked under Jessie's thrusting arms, lifted up, and swiftly secured a headlock. Angling her body for leverage, Anita pulled her struggling opponent down to the floor. Now firmly in control, Anita locked her hold and held fast.

Minutes before, Richard, on his way back from the men's room, noticed the tightly knit crowd near the craps table. As he reached the outer circle of the crowd he was informed, "Two women in one helluva catfight."

Recalling Anita's earlier exchange with the two women, he pushed his way near the front of the crowd just in time to see Anita secure her headlock, wrestle her adversary to the floor, and then render her helpless. The sight of Anita in that position took his breath away and quickened his pulse beat.

"Enough," Jessie declared, and the crowd unanimously cheered.

When Anita looked up and saw Richard, she looked away but by then he'd broken through the front of the crowd. Moving directly over her, he took hold of her hands and lifted her up.

Jessie also rose, but wouldn't look at Anita. Instead she glared at the crowd, picked up her shoes, and left with her no-longer-belligerent girl friend.

Anita's makeup was smeared and her hair disheveled. She smoothed the wrinkles in her dress, glanced around, and said, "My purse, Rich, I don't see my purse!"

The man who tried to stop the fight walked up and said, "I believe this is what you're looking for, and you better pick up your chips. I put them in the tray underneath the table, and I've been watching them. By the way, miss, you sure have a pretty left hook."

While Richard went for the chips, an middle-aged woman approached Anita and said, "Here's an earring you lost, honey. That bully met her match tonight, all right."

Anita went to the side of the craps table and slid her feet into her shoes.

By then the disruption in the restaurant was settled without blows being struck. Now the craps table personnel, along with two security guards, were on their way back to see what the commotion was there.

Noticing them approaching, Richard advised, "I think it's time we leave."

A safe distance down the walkway, Anita stopped and said, "I am so embarrassed. She came up from behind me and grabbed my hair, and she was going to head-butt me, and we fought, and I look a mess, and—oh God, Richard."

He used a handkerchief to wipe away the traces of blood from around her lower lip and then her tears.

She looked up at him and asked, "What if someone connected with the school was here and saw what happened?"

"I would say that's extremely unlikely."

She spotted a ladies lounge sign and said, "I'm going in there, and I don't know when I'll be back."

"I'll cash in the chips and wait for you," he said.

Inside the lounge two women were standing in front of the mirrors. So involved were they in touching up their makeup and chatting, they barely noticed Anita hastening to a corner mirror far in the back. With wet facial tissues she cleaned away her smeared makeup, reapplied it, and arranged her hair as best she could.

Fifteen minutes later when she returned to his side, Richard said, "Ah, you look much better."

"You're lying. I look awful."

"Hey, that little mouse under your eye and your swollen lip make you look even more exotic than before. So tell me, what can I do for you?"

Her green eyes flashed. "Richard, don't patronize me!"

"All I can say is the next time you step into the ring, please let me know 'cause my money's on you."

His remark lifted the corners of her mouth to a faint smile.

He put his arm around her shoulders and said, "I think what you need is a drink."

"Somewhere away from here."

Leaving MGM, and thinking she'd be more comfortable in a familiar atmosphere, he drove the short distance to the Luxor. Inside a quiet lounge they found an isolated back corner table and he ordered a beer and a strawberry daiquiri.

A few sips of the daiquiri seemed to calm her nerves enough for him to inquire, "Where'd you ever learn to scrap like that?"

"Whenever anyone tries to take advantage of me, my Irish temper takes over. Back in my rebel teenage days, my brother—as brothers will do—sometimes teased me. Travis was on the high school wrestling team, and one time when the folks were not home, he got me so upset that I slapped his face. He took hold of me and told me to work my way out if I could, and I did. He said I was fast as a wildcat and started teaching me how to defend myself. He said I needed to know, given the way I was acting those days. When that witch finally let go of my hair and faced me, I knew exactly what to do."

Richard wanted to know the details of what happened after he went to the bathroom, and Anita provided a blow-by-blow description, cute body language included. Her lighthearted, histrionic review had him chuckling.

Later when he was taking her home, he said, "Look, I'm not leaving until Monday, and I'd like to see you again before I leave."

"Don't you remember? Sunday you and my father are coming over for dinner."

He'd completely forgotten her invitation made two weeks earlier. "Oh, that's right, dinner on Sunday. Well, what about tomorrow night? Have you made plans?"

"Are you still feeling sorry for me? I thought you were going to be so busy this weekend."

"Well I was, but with today's meeting things cleared up considerably. Since our evening celebration was so unexpectedly interrupted, why don't we try again tomorrow?"

"If you really want to, definitely."

In saying good night in front of her apartment, he placed his hands on her shoulders and kissed her, first on her cheek, then her lips.

While driving back toward the Strip, Richard's memory recalled the remarkable evening: his original plan to tell Anita how much he loved Paula, and she could only be his friend ... how beguiling she looked in her shimmering black dress ... how relieved he was to learn she thought of him as a treasured friend ... how exciting she looked holding the dark-haired woman helpless ... and how he wanted to comfort her afterward.

It had been an unusal day and night for Richard, one he would never forget. He couldn't wait to see what the next day would bring.

Chapter Thirty

J.D.'S PROPOSAL HAD TO BE important because except for Monte Vista meetings, weekends and holidays were reserved for family matters. To present the idea he chose the beautiful Angel Park Golf Club. From there, visible on the mountain foothills to the west were the rising structural outlines of the Monte Vista development. The morning skies were cloudless and mild breezes caused the club's outdoor flags to flutter but lazily.

When Richard arrived, the recreational grounds were quickly filling with golfing enthusiasts and families. He checked his golf bag at the clubhouse before going to the restaurant where J.D. was waiting for him at a table. With nine holes of golf ahead, both men ordered full-course breakfasts, and the first topic of discussion was the previous day's Summer Summit conference.

J.D. was in high spirits. "The Renzcorp people are thrilled you're staying on until January, and David Renzberg's looking forward to meeting you."

"Tell him I'm looking forward to meeting him, too. Now, James, please tell me about your 'delectably inviting' proposal."

"Of course, but let's wait to discuss the highlights until we're on the golf course."

Richard was familiar with his boss's enticement strategies: *Stir up interest, tempt, lure, delay. Wrap the proposal in a pretty red bow and place it on the doorstep of the person's mind.* It would be futile to try to hasten further disclosure until the time and setting were to J.D.'s liking.

Following breakfast, they went to the clubhouse where J.D.'s VIP status earned him a golf cart already loaded with the men's golf bags and a refreshment cooler. After donning their caps and sunglasses, J.D. drove the cart to the first tee.

In previous matches Richard had been the more proficient golfer. Nevertheless, true to his competitive spirit, J.D. felt that with a little bit of luck he could overcome even his fourteen-stroke handicap. His opening drive sailed over 300 yards down the fairway.

Richard chuckled and said, "Whew, that was one mighty stroke."

His own drive fell in the 265-range, but from then on he used his irons and putter well enough to finish the first hole with a two-stroke lead.

Halfway through the match, J.D. steered the cart up to a rest stop picnic table. Shaded by plum and peach trees, the setting offered a relaxing respite for stretching their legs and drinking Gatorade.

As he surveyed the scenery and inhaled the invigorating mountain air, J.D. pushed his cap back and asked, "What other sport, I ask you, Rich, is played in heaven?"

Richard had to smile. *If golf's most critical success factor was inspiration, Jimmy Forrester would be on the pro tour.* He also knew his boss was ready to disclose his proposal.

"Rich, this morning I'm going to make you an offer I want you to consider carefully. I've been thinking about this for quite a while. I have tried to put myself in your position, have considered the pros and cons, and have come to the conclusion it would be advantageous for you, and for us, if you would move your company's central operations to Las Vegas."

Surprised by the magnitude of the proposal, Richard nonetheless responded quickly, "To be honest with you, James, there's no way we'd ever move from our Omaha base. We like being right where we are, and why shouldn't we? We're enjoying a record-breaking year."

"I know your Omaha operation is close to your heart, but think about the prospects. As our Renzcorp resort interests expand in the U.S. and overseas, your company would be our partner. Don't be overly concerned about your upper-level staff moving out here. As I'm sure you've discovered, Las Vegas is a family-based community blessed with excellent schools, churches, recreational opportunities, and well, just about everything a family or a single person could desire. Every year businesses from all over America successfully relocate their central operations here."

"My problem is that folks back home think of Las Vegas as a great place to visit for a few days, but then they want to return to their normal Midwestern lifestyles."

Aware that Richard was uncomfortable with his offer, J.D. said, "Well, if you should ever want to learn more about our expansion plans and what they could mean to you, just let me know. So, you were with your fiancée last night."

"Unfortunately I wasn't. Her boss gave her a last-minute story assignment and she cancelled."

"I'm sorry to hear that. I know you were looking forward to seeing her. I've been thinking more about Ms. Summers' overall potential, and wouldn't she make an outstanding Monte Vista promotions director? Tell her for me she'd have unlimited radio, newspaper, and television exposure."

"I'll be sure to mention it."

When they finished the match, the scorecard revealed Richard's eight-stroke advantage, but the result was inconsequential. J.D. had accomplished what he set out to do: Plant fertile seeds of temptation in Richard Stewart's mind. Further enticements were sure to follow.

The rest of the day Richard thought little about the offer. Although he knew the New Horizon president was 90-plus percent sure to get whatever he was seeking, the chances of moving the Stewart front office staff to Las Vegas would completely reverse such odds. As for Paula leaving a promising future with NBC to become Monte Vista's promotion director? That was about as likely to happen as Mike Tyson teaching English Literature at UNLV.

Besides, Richard's thoughts were more focused on events from the night before. Several times he tried without success to reach Anita.

Late in the afternoon she finally answered. "Oh, I'm so glad you called. I want to apologize for what happened last night."

"You mean the fight? Hey, you were forced into it, and to tell the truth I was rather proud of you."

"You're really not upset?"

"Did I seem upset last night?"

"No, but I thought perhaps you were feeling sorry for me. Anyway, I went to a masseuse, and she smoothed out most of the rough spots. I wonder if that witch felt the way I did this morning."

"Considerably worse from what I saw. As for this evening, how does dinner at Kokomo's in the Mirage sound? Say I pick you up around seven o'clock?"

"That's fine and by the way, it's nice to hear from you again today."

That evening when he arrived, she looked once more like his high school counselor friend—light makeup, casual summer dress, and sandals.

He checked her face for aftereffects of the fight and noticed her lower lip was still slightly swollen.

"She got me a good one there, all right."

As they were traveling down Las Vegas Boulevard toward the Strip, Anita said, "I really did think you might cancel our date for tonight."

"I thought of you several times today, but canceling our date never crossed my mind."

Following a moment of contemplation, she said, "Well if that wasn't how you felt, how about this? I would like to make love to her, I mean me."

As had happened when he came upon the previous night's fight scene, her words took his breath away and hastened his heartbeat.

He paused before he said, "You know what, Ms. Stevens, you're something, you know that?. Now why would you think I would be—"

"Because of the way you looked at me last night. I've never seen that look in your eyes before, and when you kissed me, I could feel your warmth."

"You're very sure of yourself, aren't you?"

She leaned close to him and in a sultry tone said, "A woman knows when a man kisses her like that."

"Knows what, may I ask?"

"Knows that he desires her?" She brushed her lips across his cheek and touched the tip of her tongue to his ear. Softy she inquired, "Am I right?"

"You've never been to my Paris suite."

"You know I haven't, and you know what? I really don't feel like going out to dinner."

The sizzling exchange caused him to ramble. "We can skip going out. Let's just go to my place and order in. The restaurants downstairs offer a variety of menus. Then after we eat, we could watch television and relax. Do you like baseball?"

"Not particularly."

"All right, well, there are some good in-house movies, and there's a bottle of complimentary champagne in the fridge."

"Ummm, now the latter sounds very good."

When they reached his suite, he showed her around and in the process she said, "This place is—what's that word you like?—oh yes, *exotic*, it's very *exotic*, especially the blue-tile spa."

"I use it only occasionally, not something you regularly do by yourself. Can I get you that drink?"

"Sure, I like champagne."

While she moved onto one of the swivel barstools, Richard went behind the counter, filled two wine glasses, and switched on the radio to his favorite mood music station. After growing comfortable with the music, wine tasting, and idle conversation, he came around the counter and turned her stool so they were facing each other.

Looking into his eyes she said, "So here we are and—"

He leaned over and pressed his lips to hers before she finished, "—and you're going to make love to me now, aren't you?"

"I'd like nothing better."

Richard kissed her again, and this time she slid her arms around his neck and her legs around his waist.

He lifted her from the stool, and as he was carrying her into the bedroom, she said, "I haven't made love for a long time."

"Nor have I."

After placing her down at bedside, they undressed, she down to her pink lace bra and panties and he down to his shorts.

She turned around and said, "Could you unfasten my bra?"

He did so, and when she turned again to face him, he said, "You look even more exotic than you did last night."

Anita was not the type to make love for physical desire alone, or to break up a romance. She was falling in love with Richard, and she felt their deepening friendship meant he was beginning to feel the same way. She believed his love for Paula was waning on its own, and not because of her.

When they were on the bed and caressing, Richard's thoughts flashed to seeing Anita's eye-fetching figure at the swimming pool, and the alluring fit of her black sequin dress the night before, and the stirring emotions he felt for her during and after the fight. His need for Anita was definitely more for physical satisfaction than everlasting love. He figured, all things considered, she was going to make a very interesting bed partner.

Whatever the inviting elements were, their love-making encounter that night was ultra-physical and satisfying to both parties. In the aftermath, as timely as could be imagined, from the radio Renee Olstead's captivating voice was singing,

"What a difference a day makes,

Twenty-four little hours,

Brought the sun and the flowers,

Where there used to be rain ..."

The lyrics made them both chuckle.

He went to the closet and brought back two hotel bathrobes. "Come with me," he said. "I want to show you a magnificent sight."

They walked into the entertainment room where he opened halfway the floor-to-ceiling window drapes. Then he turned off the lights, and the distant bright lights from the Strip invaded the room with a moonlit-like glow. Moving directly to the front of the windows, they could see clearly the busy Las Vegas Boulevard traffic and the pedestrian-congested sidewalks.

Simultaneously feeling renewed passions, they turned to each other and embraced and kissed.

She said, "Make love to me again," and they removed their robes, laid them across the carpet, and he fulfilled her request.

This time when they finished, they showered and moved into the spa's swirling blue waters. Finally hungry for food they went to the kitchenette and prepared ham and cheese sandwiches, chips and dip, and cold glasses of milk.

Richard said, "And to think for the last few weeks we could have been enjoying nights like this one."

Her green eyes flashed. "You mean back when I was counseling you, and all you could think about was Paula Summers? Don't be so sure of yourself, Richard. In all the time I've known you, making love never once crossed my mind, not until last night when you kissed me good night." She glanced at her watch. "It's almost one o'clock. I have to leave."

"You can stay. Tomorrow's Sunday."

"I can't stay here all night. Besides, I have to get up and prepare afternoon dinner for you and my dad, remember?"

That night sleep would not come easy for him because thoughts of Anita dominated his thinking. He thought of Paula, too, but found it easy to reconcile his conscience. *As long as Paula chose not to be here, Anita certainly made these last two nights interesting.* He was relieved he hadn't delivered his *friends only* message the night before. He'd come so close.

The next day he was the first to arrive at Anita's apartment, soon to be followed by her father. It didn't take Robert long to detect a deeper friendship existing between his boss/best friend and daughter. They were smiling at each other all too often, and at one interval he saw Richard place his hand on her hip. *Only briefly,* Robert thought, *but nonetheless!*

For dinner Anita served southern fried chicken with all the trimmings, including apple pie with ice cream. The men complimented her cooking and agreed she could have been a gourmet chef.

After dinner she drove them to her school where she took them on a tour of the library learning center, the tech center, and indoor athletic facilities. Inside her counseling office she fondly discussed her relationships with several students whose pictures were on her bulletin board.

When they returned to her apartment, Robert said he had to leave, but Richard stayed on, supposedly to discuss with Anita some of the permanent MVP team's early personnel samplings.

Chapter Thirty-one

O N THE FLIGHT BACK TO Omaha on Labor Day, Richard leaned back in his seat and closed his eyes. So here he was, Omaha's cool and collected bachelor, formerly Richard the Invincible, completely in love with one woman, yet physically attracted to a very good friend. No sleight of hand intended where Paula was concerned, he'd inadvertently stumbled into his unusual situation, however temporary the circumstances might be.

He assured himself he couldn't be blamed for what happened. *It just happened. Without question, I love Paula as much as ever. Anita and I are just a couple of fun-loving friends having a temporary little fling, and no one has to get hurt.* The fact that it was Paula who had distanced herself from him allowed his conscience to offer only minute resistance.

Recollections and justifications aside, his concentration shifted to new promotional strategies his stores could use for the fall season. He'd be away as much as ten working days, but he was confident Robert would capably handle the resort responsibilities.

Back in Las Vegas, Anita was going to miss Richard, and in her away-from-work hours she tried to stay busy. Frozen dinners were her mainstay, or she'd go a movie with her father, or to a shopping mall with Cecily and Penny. Through school activities and shopping the three women had become good friends. Later in the evening Anita took time to read and send e-mails. Several times she talked by phone with her parents and Melissa.

She and Richard also talked a couple of times during the week, but when he tried to reach her Friday after school, she and other staff members were at a TGIF party at the Hard Rock lounge.

Later when she returned his call, she said she wished he was back in Vegas. "For the first time since I came here, I'm feeling homesick."

"Turns out," he said, "I'll be back earlier than expected. This morning Madelline and your father informed me a critical Monte Vista problem is developing."

The next two days he spent with Benjamin, primarily calling on managers and staff personnel at each Stewart store. During their trip to Lincoln, Ben wanted to know more about the latest Monte Vista commitment.

"People in the office were surprised to learn you'll be continuing your work out there, even if it's weekends only. We were under the impression you'd be finished by the end of summer."

"It seems finding a replacement has been more difficult than they anticipated. What with our new store and J.D.'s other generous overtures, I felt obligated. I'm sure they'll have someone by the first of the year. And remember, I'm free to stay in Omaha whenever I'm needed."

While Benjamin didn't pursue the issue, he was thinking, *I hope they find someone by then.*

Thursday morning Richard was back in his New Horizon office. Because J.D. was attending a four-day Renzcorp conference at Lake Tahoe, Madelline and Robert took turns explaining the problems at the site. Robert revealed that two major companies were responsible for the slowdown in the construction of the twin tower hotels. It was Sam Beesley who told him that for the last couple of weeks the two firms had been dispatching segments of their workforce to another project.

"Our investigation," Madelline said, "confirms the diminished workforce numbers are responsible for the slowdown. J.D. is furious and wants those companies to return to full capacity at once. He didn't want to bother you in Omaha, because he knew you were busy, but Rob and I have made no progress with their representatives, so we're glad you're here."

To determine if his recent contract alterations could in any way be legally challenged, Richard carefully reviewed the revised language and found nothing of a questionable nature. What was applicable was the revised paragraph from the payment schedule section: *Each month, except for inclement weather conditions, or other acts of nature, for all unfinished work New Horizon has the authority to withhold payments to the responsible company or companies. Delays will be subjected to substantial fines, etc.*

He asked Madelline to contact the firms' representatives for an emergency meeting. That afternoon in his office the reps remained uncompromising, and Richard offered little resistance. He remembered a Creighton law professor's philosophy: *In a difficult case listen with an air of polite acquiescence to an overzealous opponent. In so doing your adversary*

*may overstate his or her position, thereby revealing incongruities that
could very well reinforce your rebuttal.*

The reps openly acknowledged decreasing their workforce numbers.
They furthermore declared they should, at their own discretion, be allowed
to split their workforce "as long as the final projections are completed on
time." They went on to threaten the "probability of legal intervention if you
continue to challenge our timeline procedures."

When they finished, Richard requested a twenty-minute recess.

During the time-out the opposition, not anticipating a serious rebuttal,
went to the outside balcony to bask in their presumed success.

Richard, meanwhile, was unable to reach J.D. in Lake Tahoe, but
did leave a message. "We are adequately and legally protected, and I am
confident the problem will be resolved in our favor."

When the parties reconvened, he calmly presented a detailed review
of Rob's documented work slowdowns.

Then his tone of voice deepened. "Gentlemen, you've confessed to
ignoring the revised agreements, and we will not accept your long-range
assumptions, projections—however you classify them—for work that will
be completed at your discretion. If all current deadlines are not met by the
last day of each month, no payments to your firms will be forthcoming.
Read the contract. With any unfinished work we are legally protected
month to month. If you choose not to reconcile our differences, *you* are the
ones who will be subjected to sizeable fines. That, along with the distinct
possibility we will be negotiating with other companies to take over your
construction responsibilities." Then he fabricated, "I've just spoken with
Mr. Forrester, gentlemen, and there are no negotiable points whatsoever."

Stunned by the unrelenting demands, the reps asked for another recess
to re-review the contract. Upon their return a short time later, they agreed
to re-assign the full workforce to the site.

Richard wasn't finished. "We're not talking about starting next month.
We expect you to begin immediately recovering for time lost. Start at the
break of dawn. Hire additional workers. Work Saturdays and Sundays. If
necessary, install floodlights to make certain *all* specified work agreements
are up to date by the final day of this month."

After the reps left, Robert was ecstatic. "Thanks to your contract
revisions, they were ravenous tigers reduced to slinky kittens."

Earlier when Richard was unable to reach J.D., he called Anita at her
school.

"Your father and I are in the middle of some serious negotiating, but
it should wrap up shortly."

"When will you be stopping by?"

"I have some other business to attend to here at the office. It may take a while, and I know you have school tomorrow, but I'd like to see you. This evening, why don't we just take a walk and compare notes? I remember you saying you'd like to see the Bellagio fountains up close at night sometime, so maybe—"

"Which is about all I'll have time for. I want to be well rested for a serious parent conference early tomorrow."

Although they'd talked several times by phone, nearly two weeks had passed since they'd seen each other, and from the moment he picked her up, all attempts at normal conversation fizzled. The underlying problem was that they were each wondering how the other felt about the unexpected events of the Labor Day weekend.

After leaving the car at Paris, they walked across the street and followed the sidewalk circling the Bellagio lake. Across from the hotel's main entrance they joined scores of spectators gathering on the fountains' spacious observation platform. Luckily they found a nice viewing spot overlooking the lake. Moments later, the rumbling of underwater hydraulic engines was the prelude to a thousand jet heads spraying water configurations 50 to 250 feet high. To the crowd's appreciation, circling spotlights transformed the water crystals into kaleidoscopic gems.

The voices of Frank Sinatra and Celine Dion joined the spectacle.

"When somebody loves you,
It's no good unless she loves you,
All the way,
Happy to be near you—"

"Couldn't be much prettier than that," Richard said.

"And even more beautiful up close than I had imagined," Anita agreed.

Such abbreviated dialogue was still about all the couple could manage, and neither person was able to end the awkwardness. The moment the display was over, Anita reminded him she should be getting back to her place so she'd be rested and ready for her morning meeting.

In front of her apartment door they said a simple good night, but as he was turning to leave she placed her hand on his arm and said, "If you knew what I've been thinking about you and me while you were in Omaha, I'm afraid you'd think I'm a wanton woman."

Her comment at long last ended their awkwardness.

He turned to her and replied, "It's not very late, Anita, and I could come in for a while."

"But then I might be poorly prepared in the morning. We have tomorrow night, don't we?"

The next morning as soon as Richard entered the New Horizon headquarters, Cynthia ushered him into Mr. Forrester's office. The president was standing in front of his desk, arms crossed, a contented look on his face..

"Maddy gave me the great news last evening," J.D. said. "How'd you manage to settle the problem so quickly?"

"I simply reviewed the contract language to be sure there was no wiggle room for misinterpretation. I learned long ago back in Nebraska that agreements with contractors should be written to anticipate not only the worst *can* happen, but all too often *does* happen. The building industry has few rules and regulations to live up to. With that in mind many of their head honchos, if they think they can get away with it, will take advantage of oversights."

They moved into the Time-out Corner where J.D. poured their usual fruit juices on the rocks before changing the subject. "Now I don't want you to think I'm prying, Rich, but there've been rumors floating around the office, rumors I think you should be aware of."

"Rumors concerning?"

"When I came in today, it was mentioned that you've been seen out and about with someone new lately. She said the lady was none other than Robert's daughter, the teacher?"

Richard shrugged and said, "Your source is wrong on both counts. Ms. Stevens is a counselor and not a teacher. She's also become a good friend of mine, but nothing more. With Paula away indefinitely, I felt I could use some companionship."

"Well, of course, we all need companionship now and then. And it is true, Paula's been gone for quite a while now."

To clarify his position, Richard said, "By the way the next time I talk to her, I'll try to convince her she should meet with you concerning the resort position you once talked about. I'd give anything to have her back here permanently."

Richard wondered who might have started the rumor. *J.D. said 'she' told him, so it was probably Madelline, except how would she know unless she'd seen us together and that seems unlikely.* He recalled J.D. speaking of Maddy and Rob going outside on the balcony to smoke and talk. *So Rob must have said something to her, yet all he knows is Anita and I get together as friends. Damn, this place is as gossipy as the office back home.*

That evening he and Anita had dinner at Paris's Mon Ami Gabi outdoor restaurant. They were more relaxed and talkative than most of the night before, but beneath the calm, each person still wanted to know if what happened two weeks earlier was anything more than a few fleeting hours of intimacy which could never be recaptured.

As soon as they finished dinner, they went directly to his room. One major change from that exotic weekend would be significant. When Richard's full-time resort position ended, so did the plush Paris accommodations— no ritzy furnishings, no blue-tile spa, etc. His room was a regular Paris accommodation, but the moment the door closed behind them, they turned to each other and embraced and kissed. That was followed by a longer kiss and she dropped her purse to the floor. With heartbeats accelerating, the third kiss preceded the shedding of clothes as they moved to the edge of the bed.

Down to his shorts, Richard said, "Last night you said you'd been thinking a lot about us. Well, I found myself doing the same thing."

Down to her panties and bra, Anita said, "Then I'll have to make this a night you won't easily forget. Wait for me a minute; I need something from my purse."

When she returned, he was lying on his back on the bed. In one hand she was holding a tube of moisture cream. Turn over," she said, "I want to make you feel exotic."

He did so and soothingly she rubbed the cream across his shoulders, arms, and back. She asked him to turn over again and continued massaging across his chest and stomach. A few moments later she leaned over and kissed him before she said, "I'd say you're ready to make love to me now, wouldn't you?"

Clearly, the Labor Day weekend was more than a fleeting intimacy that couldn't happen again.

Fifteen minutes later when their renewed lovemaking was over, he laughed softly.

"What?" she inquired.

"I was just thinking what a fantastic lover you are."

"You make me do things I never before dreamed of."

After driving her home early the next morning, he once more justified what had happened. *It isn't as if she's taken Paula's place. No one could ever do that.* He recalled soon after he and Paula met, his primary goal was to place a ring on her finger. With Anita it wasn't the same. He wasn't falling in love with her, but he did enjoy making love to her. *And I'm sure she feels the same way.* He also re-assured himself, *And no one has to get hurt.*

The next day when Juan returned from his week-long family vacation in San Diego, Richard called him to reveal Paula's version of the *People* magazine photograph.

"I guess I shouldn't have jumped to conclusions," Juan responded. "So you two are back on again?"

"Actually not. She called to say she was coming to Vegas over the Labor Day weekend, but at the last minute, déjà vu. I let her know I wasn't pleased, by voice mail of course, 'cause she's never available. Her return message said we should postpone our relationship until further notice. So now I don't know what the hell to think."

"The love saga continues. I'm sure she still loves you."

"I wonder."

Juan suddenly started asking a range of questions.

"How's Robert doing these days?"

"He's doing great."

"And how is the resort progressing?"

"We're on track."

"How about the company in Omaha?"

"Also doing well."

"Well good, and now what's this I hear about you and Robert's daughter? Is she still your innocent little platonic partner, or are things heating up?"

God, more rumors. "We've been seeing each other within the framework of a friendly relationship, which you yourself encouraged, mi amigo."

"Ah, Senor Stewart, you wouldn't bamboozle an old friend like me, would ya?"

"You know, Gonzales, you sound like a reporter for the *Enquirer.*"

"Rumors are flying."

"I can't help that."

"Well, inasmuch as you're still in love with Paula, and she still loves you, pray she doesn't hear about Anita. The rumors, I mean."

"She'd know better and so should you."

"I realize you need a friend, and Paula really shouldn't be opposed to such circumstances. I'm assuming *friend* is the proper word."

"Look, I'll call Anita and we'll get together for a social visit. If you're not busy, maybe we could make it tomorrow at your place. I want you to see for yourself we are good friends and that's all. And if you should happen to talk to Paula, you can tell her I have a social acquaintance."

"Right. As for getting together, that's fine. As for telling Paula, I haven't talked to her for a long time, and if I did I wouldn't mention Anita."

"What can I say?"

Mid-day Sunday he did take Anita to his friend's home for a visit which included lunch and pleasant conversation, children included.

Later Juan told him, "Maria and I think your friend is a sweetheart. She was a major hit with the kids, too."

Before he left to catch his afternoon Omaha flight, Richard asked Anita, "What does your dad think of us spending so much time together?"

"He's happy because he thinks we're good friends. He once told me I should do everything possible to take your mind off Paula. Little does he know, Paula Summers is history."

It was one of the rare times she'd made a definite reference to Paula, or for that matter mentioned her name in any context. Although he didn't respond, her comment made Richard feel uncomfortable.

Chapter Thirty-two

ANITA STEVENS HAD A LOT to think about. In one sense she was uplifted and inspired, experiencing emotional feelings she'd never before known. She was deeply in love with Richard and was confident he loved her, too. Now it was her turn to wonder if a guardian angel was watching over her.

Along with her inspirations, however, here were concerns which couldn't easily be dismissed.

On Monday afternoon Anita was alone in her office. School was out and most of the 2,400 Grant High students had left the campus. While filing notes taken during her last student conference, she glanced above her desk at the calendar's patchwork pictures of Yellowstone Park scenery. Penciled in the calendar below were her daily assignments for the coming week.

Her thoughts meandered. *Hmmm, I've been in school for almost three weeks and I feel wonderful. Thank goodness I decided to spend the year here.*

William Dempster, bald and portly senior counselor, stuck his head in the doorway and said, "Good night, Anita, I'm out of here. Have a pleasant evening now."

Awakened from her daydreams, she answered, "I will, and you do that too, Bill."

She took a deep breath, and again her memory began turning back the pages of her changing life.

First there was Grant High School. She loved her job and the students she was working with. Second, in the past few months she'd come to know her father, who for years she thought was probably deceased or worse. *He is an intelligent man who's become an important part of my life. I don't care about his previous existence anymore.* Third, she'd discovered the people she met within the school environment were as friendly and likeable as folks back in Ohio. In fact, several were from that part of the country.

And then there was Richard. She cherished the good times and the passions they were sharing. Ironically, it was their intimacy that made her think, *What if, just what if, he still loves Paula, and I'm nothing more than a convenient sex substitute?* She recalled seeing Paula on television. *She looks like a movie star, and she's brilliant and talented, too.* Thoughts drifted to the summer counseling sessions when he called Paula his Dream Princess, the woman he'd been looking for all his life. Anita also recalled how much he cherished their exciting nightlife. *Now he's taking me to some of those same places, and what if it really is because they remind him of her? What if I am just a glorified stand-in. God, how awful!*

She looked across the room to a wall mirror revealing her bespectacled, tired-from-work reflection. *Then there's Paula Summers, about to become a television star for NBC.* She tsked her tongue and sighed, "Oh, well."

If it was true she was no more than what she sometimes imagined, she knew she'd have to share the blame. After all, she'd made it clear to him she didn't want him to even mention Paula's name. Now she wondered if her insistence had been a mistake. *I wish I knew exactly how he does feel about her, yet it isn't something I want to ask him. Suppose the worst; suppose making love is his primary motivation. I truly believe he loves me for much more than that. But if we're going to make it to a higher level, maybe I should be thinking of new ways to strengthen our romance.*

Continuing her thoughts, she remembered him speaking of summer vacations spent at northern Minnesota lakes and snow skiing in Aspen, Colorado. *Without question, he does enjoy the great outdoors.* Although she hadn't lived in Las Vegas very long, she'd learned the city was much more than the entertainment mecca portrayed in movies and on TV. In fact, staff members at school seldom talked about going to the Strip or Fremont Street. They were more involved with school and community events. They also talked about being participating in a variety of outdoor activities.

Maybe I should be taking him away from the things that remind him of her. Maybe it's time to diversify, to put some new and exciting pizzazz into our relationship.

The next day in the teachers' lounge and during lunch, she asked other staff members how they spent their leisure time. She also went to a neighborhood book store and purchased a Las Vegas travel brochure.

When Richard called Thursday night, she was prepared. "I've been listening to people at school, and do you know how many exciting things there are to do out here? I mean besides dining in upscale restaurants and going to shows every weekend. They talk about boating, camping, skiing, exploring the wilderness, and well, you just can't imagine. And most of the activities fall within only a fifty-mile radius of the city. I know you love all the outdoor stuff, and I do, too, so maybe *we* should be trying something different."

"I've heard about the outdoor activities, but except for playing golf I never really looked into any of them. I think we should experiment. Now I know I'm going to be busy, I should be able to find some free time, especially if I come a day early and finish some of my work."

"Good, it's settled then."

Anita had chosen the perfect season for outdoor enjoyment. Autumn in southern Nevada translates into the usual sunny days, but with more moderate temperatures and less wind than in any other season. With that in mind she began making her plans, plans that would take them to new places to see and new things to do.

Following Saturday's Monte Vista meeting, they drove thirty-five miles south of the city for a tour of Hoover Dam. Their guide informed them, "You are standing at the base of one of the Seven Man-Made Wonders of the World ... It took seven years and five thousand workers to complete this project ... There's enough concrete here to build a highway from San Francisco to New York," and so forth and so on.

A week later Richard placed two Gonzales family bicycles in the back of a New Horizon pickup. He and Anita then traveled a short distance west of town to the Red Rock Canyon National Conservation site. After parking the truck near the canyon's entrance, they rode the bikes on an interesting journey through tall, rust-red sandstone peaks, limestone formations, and rock-climbing areas.

Anita had done her canyon promotion research well. When they stopped to rest at an observation lookout, she read from her notebook, "This breathtaking setting rose from a seabed 225 million years ago. As the water receded, sea creatures died and the calcium from their bodies combined with minerals. Over time, wind and water erosion created the fabulous formations we're seeing today. Some of these elevations you're observing rise to over 2,500 feet."

Feigning a look of surprise, Richard quipped, "That's absolutely amazing."

She continued, "The canyon is home to forty-five species of animals, one hundred species of birds, thirty reptiles and amphibians. Beware of rattlesnakes, scorpions, and tarantulas because they're out there."

"I'll be watching. Crawling things *really* bug me."

"Pottery fragments, stone tools, and petroglyphs are proof human beings settled here around 3,000 BC."

He added, "And at night the pathfinders of the future gambled with glittering stones and trinkets while topless women danced by the firelight."

"Richard, be serious. This is very educational."

"I'm listening to every word."

"Good, because there may be a test."

The next weekend they drove forty-five miles northwest through the desert and pine and fir forests to the Mt. Charleston Lodge. Following a cafe lunch, they observed Lee Canyon's ten ski runs, chairlifts, and other snow ski amenities.

Anita said, "Skiing enthusiasts say when it snows up here in January, it's the same as being at a resort in Colorado. We should try it next winter."

The following weekend they traveled fifty miles northeast to Lake Mead's Valley of Fire State Park. There they hiked on trails with vistas overlooking more sandstone, limestone, and rock formations. In the afternoon sunshine the formations became a spectacular inferno.

One of their busiest days came at Bonnie Springs Old Nevada a few miles past Red Rock Canyon. In the morning they visited a petting zoo. Following lunch they walked down the street of a resurrected Old West mining town complete with saloons, gunfights, a country music band, and a staged melodrama. Later in the afternoon they rode horses on a guided trail leading through the surrounding mountain foothills.

Early in November, just below Hoover Dam, they joined other sightseers on a large Colorado River raft. Within the eleven mile journey to Willow Beach, they glided through the Black Canyon's steep inclines interspersed with tall, narrow waterfalls. Along the way they saw many wildlife species including bighorn sheep, osprey, and falcons. .

Anita's planning wasn't confined to outdoor activities. They went to the movies with Juan and Maria and Cecily and her fiancé Cal. On separate Friday evenings they attended the Grant High Lynx homecoming football game, and a Lady Lynx volleyball match. Halloween night Anita invited her father and friends to the Desert Delight party room to celebrate Richard's thirtieth birthday. On several Sunday mornings they attended church services at the Green Valley Methodist Church.

If most of their previous conversations were usually casual, the nature of their new activities allowed time for deeper insights concerning their likes and dislikes, their opinions on a variety of issues, and their ambitions and goals.

He talked about growing up in Omaha, the schools he attended, the camaraderie he shared with his staff, and in particular his relationship with Benjamin.

On one occasion Richard recalled, "Ben and I have belonged to the downtown YMCA since we were kids. Several years back he noticed some of the teenage boys and girls hanging around the Y were out of touch with the mainstream activities. Quite a few of the kids lived close to downtown and were from lower-income families. Ben approached them and offered to organize a boys and a girls basketball teams. Our company furnished the kids with uniforms, tennis shoes, and whatever else they needed. The Y immediately entered the two teams into youth leagues.

"Because it's only a few blocks from our offices, Ben found time to coach them a couple of times a week. When he couldn't be at a practice session, another of our company staff filled in. In the process Ben also got parents and guardians into the mix. His only requirements were that the kids come to practice and maintain a C or better average in school. The kids loved the attention they were getting, and they weren't out of touch and isolated anymore."

Anita's recollections also included growing up in her hometown and her closeness to her family and friends. But her favorite subject was education. While Richard knew she was dedicated to her work, he soon discovered she was also an informed and outspoken critic of social, economic, and political forces affecting public school policies.

Once when he asked her about the growing criticism of public schools, she said, "Everywhere our schools are facing enormous pressure from sources like slanted politicians and media talk-show hosts. I think what they really want is to end public school education and privatize our schools. These critics consistently denounce public education policies. The truth is they know little about what is, or what should be, taking place in the classrooms. Unfortunately they have millions of followers who believe everything they're told. The discontent these critics generate puts tremendous pressures on school administrators, teachers, parents, and, of course, the children.

"A good example was the No Child Left Behind policy which the government forced upon public schools. It was a business-oriented philosophy requiring young people to memorize answers for standardized tests, and the tests represented the main criteria for evaluating progress. Experienced teachers and counselors knew such testing would be unreliable and had little to do with discovering a child's overall potential. But they had no power to discourage the policy. So the government withheld funds to schools with test scores they, not classroom teachers, determined were unacceptable? It was a ridiculous ransom for everyone."

"It sounds as if from the start you didn't think that particular policy was reliable."

"Definitely unreliable. There are many capable, bright kids who freeze at the mere mention of a test. Before schools were forced into the testing process, the best teachers I knew evaluated students based on criteria like work ethic, attitude, and creativity. While testing had some value, it was not nearly as important as learning how to research, teaching inductive and deductive reasoning, and inspiring creative thinking. The moment you entered those teachers' classrooms, you could feel the atmosphere of learning excitement. What people need to do is to keep the government out of the classrooms and put qualified educators in control. Don't think the critics won't continue trying to make public schools look bad every way they can. As I say, they want people to think that privatizing our schools is the best choice."

Richard responded, "You really take this school business to heart, don't you? Helping people must be a family character trait. With your dad it's helping the underprivileged. With you it's doing whatever you can to help kids discover their potential."

Another time he said, "Counseling high school students must be frustrating. I think back to when our folks were in school, the bad stuff was drinking beer and smoking cigarettes. When you and I were that age, add liquor and marijuana. These days there's meth, heroin, ecstasy, and who knows what tossed in. Each new generation of children is exposed to deeper dark-side temptations."

"Which means now more than ever we should be aware and reaching out."

"Liz and I were fortunate. When I was growing up, my parents came to every debate, music performance, and golf tournament I participated in. It was the same for Liz."

"Your parents were exemplary, Rich, but you should remember, yours was a close-knit family—financially, socially, and emotionally secure. That's quite a contrast from conditions existing in all too many of today's homes, especially those of single parents. More than 60 percent of today's youth come from dysfunctional families facing increasing demands on parents. The only chance a large percentage of those kids will ever have has to happen in classrooms, classrooms which are flexible and compassionate with teachers who are determined to discover and develop *every* student's potential."

Richard never tired of listening to Anita's philosophies and convictions because he knew they came from her heart.

By the time the days of autumn drifted into November, she felt she'd accomplished what she set out to do: put some new and exciting diversification into their relationship. Through it all she made sure of one thing. Not once during those two months did they go to a show or restaurant on the Strip or downtown.

One aspect of their relationship did not change. The intimate passions they felt for each other were totally unaffected.

Chapter Thirty-three

IN EARLY NOVEMBER JAMES FORRESTER was called to Memphis to help streamline a promotional campaign for Renzcorp's Riverboat enterprise. He informed his committee he'd be gone the entire week and was canceling the weekly meeting. Because Veteran's Day was the following Monday and schools were closed, Richard decided to stay in Omaha and asked Anita to spend the weekend there. Several times she had mentioned she would love to visit Omaha. He looked upon his invitation as a thank you for her versatile and entertaining autumn weekend planning.

Anita had a much different viewpoint. Although he had never before officially committed himself in their relationship, she felt the invitation meant he was ready to do just that. She had an appointment with working parents who could only meet with her on the holiday, so she'd have to return to Vegas on Sunday. To prolong her visit, she requested and was granted a Thursday afternoon leave. Richard handled airline reservations, and two nights before her flight she called him.

"You said Omaha's going to remind me of home."

"I think you'll find it quite comparable to Cincinnati—a thriving river city with scenic hills and valleys and rich in historical tradition. By the way I told Helen, my housekeeper, to take Thursday and Friday off, so she's spending her weekend with relatives in Kansas City."

"So give me a preview of events."

"Sure. On Friday and Saturday I'll show you around town, then Saturday night we'll have dinner at the Happy Hollow Club. You've said you wanted to see The Improv performing, so later in the evening you will."

"Now that should be the highlight of the entire trip."

"I've been away from the band so much, I think I should practice these next few days."

"And what time will I'll be leaving Sunday?"

"Your plane leaves at 5:30 in the afternoon."

"Then let's go to your church services in the morning."

"That's fine. I want to advise you, the weather here can be unpredictable this time of year. It might even snow. Are you sure you want to come?"

"Richard, of course I want to come. Back home we have ice and snow, tornadoes, the same stuff Omaha has."

He chuckled as he said, "Okay, we'll see you soon."

Earlier he'd informed Robert he was staying in Omaha for the weekend. He didn't mention Anita was coming there. He felt such a disclosure was better left to her.

Anita would find Omaha in its most colorful autumn attire. Two weeks earlier Mother Nature, paintbrush and palette in hand, had dramatically transformed the entire countryside. Most impressive were the apple, elm, and birch trees, now dazzling mixtures of yellow, pink, red, and orange.

Thursday night when Richard met Anita inside the Eppley Airfield terminal, he was pleased that she was wearing a bright red University of Nebraska sweatshirt purchased the night before in Las Vegas.

"I want you to know, Annie, you're right in step around here. The university's playing an important conference game Saturday afternoon."

"I know. I heard about it on television."

During the drive to Omaha proper, from Richard's car window Anita could see outlines of deep sloping, flowing hills sprinkled with various lightings emanating from the ranch homes, farms, and small communities.

Within the city limits he took the Dodge Avenue exit heading east off the highway and across from the Westroads Mall entered the Regency Park community. As he cruised through the quiet neighborhoods, she could see lighted interiors of beautiful homes, some of them mansions.

"My father Gene," she said, "builds exclusive homes like these in Cincinnati. You know, whenever I think of Omaha, I think of Warren Buffett. I like his attitudes."

"Because of his wealth and his generosity, he really is perhaps our most highly respected citizen. My father thought well of him, too."

Richard pulled into the driveway of his two-story, red-and-white-brick colonial home. Though not as expansive or as elaborately designed as some of the residences Anita had just seen, it possessed a distinct charm of its own—full front porch with Corinthian columns, a variety of custom-styled windows, and a front entry with stained-glass double doors.

After parking in one of the three garage stalls, he showed her through the house. During the viewing she said, "I love your home, Richard. It's unique in its structure and layout. My father would *definitely* approve."

Richard saved his favorite place, the first-floor family room, for last. The spacious room was tastefully furnished and featured floor-to-ceiling, sliding glass doors on two separate walls—one opening to a patio, the other to the park-like backyard.

A glimmering black Steinway piano was situated at an angle from the patio walkout .They walked across the room to the fireplace bordered with ceramic tile and gold trim. In the recessed space above the fireplace, overhead puck lights shone on a lovely oil portrait of Sam and Margaret Stewart.

"I can see you in both of them," Anita said. "How long have they been gone now?"

"It's been more than six years."

"Can you tell me what happened?"

"Every spring they went with their friends Randy and Clare Severson to a lake in northern Minnesota. Randy was a commercial pilot, and they'd fly in his private plane to Duluth, then drive to their cabin on a lake near the Canadian border. For several days they enjoyed hiking in the woods, fishing for perch and walleyes, and just having fun in general. In the evenings they'd shop at stores in a nearby town, watch movies, or play cards. Good music was welcome, but no newspaper, television, or radio news was allowed.

"The accident happened near Alexandria, Minnesota. When the plane's engine began missing, Randy contacted the airport and requested an emergency landing. Investigators later said a fuel line was not functioning properly. It was a windy day, and a downdraft carried the powerless plane off its course and into a grove of trees. The report said everyone died instantly."

"How horrible for you and Liz."

"A couple of days after the funeral, Liz and her husband had to return to their jobs in Maryland. As for the family business, although half of it was in her name, it was up to me to take over for my father. Through the years he'd taught me practically everything about company procedures. Plus my business degree and a year of law school helped me adjust. But it was mainly our staff who kept the firm running smoothly.

"I know Dad was hoping I'd take over the business one day, but you know how it is when you're young. You think you have to discover your own destiny. My goal was to become a defense lawyer, while his dream was for me to eventually take over the business. We joked about it, but I never really gave him any hope that I would. To this day I wish I'd handled that differently."

"He'd be proud of what you've accomplished. You were so young to be taking over an entire company."

"Ben's father Ken was the firm's vice president, and without him I don't know what would have happened. The following year he underwent triple bypass surgery, and his doctor advised him to retire, which he did. Ben was a loan officer for an Omaha bank, and I asked him to take his father's place. Since then Ben has played a vital role in the firm's success."

Richard and Anita sat down on the davenport in front of the fireplace to continue conversing, but Anita was tired and soon they retired to the master bedroom.

The next morning they were showered and eating in the kitchen breakfast nook before nine o'clock. Over coffee and cinnamon rolls Helen had made the day before, they discussed in detail the day's agenda.

Their first stop was the company's central retail store located in a mini mall near 84th and Center.

While walking her through several aisles of his store, Richard explained, "Most of the products we sell in our stores are name brands, but we also have a small production plant in West Omaha. They supply all of our stores with specialty promotion items. They're the items you see with the red tags."

They continued into the back portion of the store reserved for golf equipment, apparel, and carts. Suddenly through a door marked Employees Only, a short, balding man wearing thick glasses nearly collided with them.

"Well hello, Rich," he said, "sorry for my haste, and who may this charming lady be?"

"Anita, I want you to meet Billy Goldstein, the best retail store manager in all of Omaha. Billy, this is Anita Stevens, a good friend of mine and a high school counselor from Cincinnati. This year she's on leave and working in Las Vegas."

"My pleasure, Anita, and I appreciate the kind words, Mr. S. Which reminds me, I was going to talk to you about a raise and a few more vacation days?"

Richard grinned and said, "He's such a kidder."

Throughout the store Richard introduced Anita to other employees as, "My friend, a high school counselor from Cincinnati, etc.," or "My friend, who's an interim Las Vegas high school counselor, etc." Anita noticed that each and every introduction was accompanied by the word "friend."

After spending an hour at the store, their next destination was Stewart Company headquarters downtown.

Along the way Anita said, "The people who work for you not only respect you, they obviously like you. Father said your staff's positive attitudes can be traced to your grandparents. He said they came here during the Great Depression and went through rough times."

"My mother's Swedish parents owned a section of land in southern Iowa, and they were prosperous enough to send her through the university in Lincoln. He's referring to my father's family. Grandfather was from Naples, and she was from Paris. They were very young when they met at an art festival in Paris, and a couple of years later were married there. When he was only twenty-two-years-old, to escape serving in the Fascist army he fled with his family to America. By then they already had two children.

"They arrived in New York with very little money, and with the depression in full swing, finding work was difficult. To make matters worse, many people who discovered his background were prejudiced against him because of the impending war with Germany and Italy. When he heard the Union Pacific was hiring railroad field workers in Omaha, they somehow made their way here. Not long after they arrived, he was hired as a switchman."

"So with two children, where did they live?"

"They found a downtown apartment. It had only two bedrooms, so they were cramped, but the location was ideal. The apartment was close to the central station, so she was able to work at home as a seamstress for several downtown clothing stores."

"Considering the times, I'd say they were quite lucky."

"Yes they were. Over the years he worked his way up to become a station manager, and eventually they bought a house not far from downtown. I'm sure my dad was an unexpected addition, because my grandparents were in their forties when he was born. Anyway, Grandpa never forgot how the Union Pacific people took care of him and his family. My father always said his respect for those who worked for him was inspired by the way his father was treated."

"You know what I'm thinking, Rich? There must be a magic formula in the Omaha atmosphere that makes people so generous—your grandparents, your mother and father, people at the Union Pacific, Benjamin, Warren Buffett, and maybe you, too?"

"Don't include me in such company. I haven't earned it. Anyway, my father went to the university in Lincoln where he met Mom."

Driving north on 72nd Street, they eventually turned east on Dodge and passed many business firms and mini malls, apartment houses, churches, and the sprawling University of Nebraska at Omaha campus. In the downtown area he pointed out the historic Orpheum Theater, the newer Union Pacific Center, and the First National Bank Tower.

Returning to the central part of downtown, he parked his car on the second level of a parking facility across from the Woodmen Tower. From there they followed the crosswalk into the tower, and then rode an elevator to Stewart Company headquarters on the twenty-third floor.

Advised earlier of their arrival time, Melanie Thomas and co-worker Jill Larson were waiting for them. Richard again introduced Anita as, "My very good friend who's working this year as a high school counselor in Vegas."

Melanie said, "We understand you're originally from Cincinnati."

"That's home, but I'm on a year's leave of absence. Thanks to Richard I've been reunited with my father in Las Vegas."

Jill said, "My daughter and I are planning to vacation there next winter, and we can't wait to see some of the entertainers. We hear they're wonderful."

With the conversation proceeding smoothly, Richard excused himself to find Benjamin. When they returned, he introduced Ben to Anita as, "Our vice president and as you'll discover tomorrow night, he also plays a wicked bass guitar." Anita was introduced as, "My good friend, who is a Cincinnati high school counselor working in a similar capacity this year in Vegas."

A bit annoyed this time, she thought, *Close friend, good friend—same old, same old.*

The two men showed her around the office before taking her to lunch in the Old Market. They parked the car near 13th Street and Farnam, and from there they followed a cobblestone street flanked with antiquated and renovated retail stores, bars, and restaurants.

Anita said, "Old Market is charmingly nostalgic."

Richard said, "By the way the Century Club, where we'll be playing tomorrow night, is only a couple of blocks away. I think you'll find it's also charmingly nostalgic."

Around the corner of 10th and Farnam, they arrived for lunch at the Spaghetti Works.

During their luncheon Benjamin said to Anita, "Mindy and I are concerned about our children growing up in the increasingly hostile school environments. We live in a suburb, but there are problems there, too. Maybe you could tell me, from a counselor's viewpoint, what should be done."

"Well, Ben, youngsters everywhere are growing up in less than desirable environments. Consider the fact that most young people spend more time in front of television sets and computers than they do in classrooms. A majority of them come from broken homes that are unsupervised, so they are often exposed to uncensored violence and sex. The movies they see, the songs they listen to, even some of the sports heroes they look up to are sending the wrong messages."

"There must be educational motivations that would help them make better choices."

"There are, but they're not organized or outreaching enough. I believe from the elementary grades on up, every school curriculum should include courses dealing with individual and group character development. Every student should learn to treat everybody with respect and dignity, adults as well as his or her classmates. I don't mean just in regard to race and gender, but no matter what their differences might be."

Richard thought back to the time Robert said homeless children in public schools are often harassed by bullies.

Anita continued, "And schools at every level should make sure every student has at least one family member, a teacher, a mentor, someone he or she can turn to in the good times as well as the bad. I'm simplifying what's needed, but—"

Ben interrupted, "Do you know what I think you should do, Anita? Conduct educational seminars and publish your philosophies. They make sense."

Richard said, "She's too busy working with kids."

Following lunch they took Benjamin back to the tower, then drove on to Memorial Park in central Omaha. At the park's highest elevation near the War Memorial, Richard took a blanket from his car and spread it on the hillside. The warm, sunlit afternoon and fresh autumn air were invigorating, and from their vantage point they could see at the bottom of the hill a number of students from the nearby university. Many were on blankets and engaged in conversation, or studying from open textbooks. Other park patrons were picnicking or walking their dogs.

By six o'clock they were back at his place where they changed clothes for the evening. From there he took interstate exchanges that led them across the Missouri River to Council Bluffs.

After driving past a mini-version of Las Vegas hotels and casinos, they stopped at Harrah's for dinner. Inside the hotel, they rode an elevator to the twelfth floor and the 360 Steakhouse. From their dinner table they could see across the river the city of Omaha's beautiful nighttime light display.

Following dinner they decided to return to his place where in front of the fireplace they sipped wine, watched television, and talked.

Chapter Thirty-four

SATURDAY'S AGENDA INCLUDED VISITING SOME of Omaha's most popular sites. Those included the famous Henry Doorly Zoo and Scott's Kingdom of the Seas aquarium; TD Ameritrade Park where the talent-filled College World Series unfolds every June; CenturyLink Center, where world renown sporting events are held; Creighton University, nostalgic in its seasonal splendor; and Nebraska Furniture Mart, largest and most popular furniture store in North America.

In the days before she arrived, Richard was concerned Anita would feel awkward staying with him for three days in Omaha. Instead she was pleased with every new experience. She felt comfortable meeting his friends and realized how much Richard cherished those friends, his business, and his city.

Following a Creighton cafeteria lunch, while walking on campus sidewalks strewn with fallen leaves, she said, "I think Omaha is spectacular, Rich, and you were right—it does remind me of home."

What she was most looking forward to were the evening events. First there would be dinner at Richard's social club, and afterward she'd see him performing with The Improv.

Back at his place an hour before dinner, their preparations for the evening alternated between the master bedroom and bathroom. When he finished dressing, he pulled up a chair and watched her observe in a full-length mirror the fit of her sparkly white, single-strap evening dress.

Making eye contact with him in the mirror, she asked, "Didn't you miss your business and friends back here last summer?"

"There were times, but once you came into my life, my overall outlook changed considerably."

She walked over to him and ran her fingers through his hair, but when he rose and pulled her close to him, she said, "And if we don't leave here right now, we're going to miss our dinner reservations."

The Happy Hollow Club was crowded with members and guests mixing socially in The Pub before dining in the Starlight Grille. Only occasionally had Richard brought a woman to the club, and their arrival caused heads to turn and gossip to churn. After all, not only was he a long-time club member and owner of the Stewart Company, he was also Richard the Invincible, arguably Omaha's number one bachelor.

As friends stepped up for introductions, he used his standard line. "I want you to meet Anita Stevens. She's a friend working this year as a high school counselor in Las Vegas," or something similar.

The introductions were followed by courteous exchanges, along with attempts by several to more closely observe Richard's attractive friend.

After dinner the socializing continued until Richard said they had to leave for another engagement. During the drive to the Old Market, he said, "I wondered what you'd think of some of my socialite friends. You seemed to be enjoying yourself."

"Déjà vu. Remember, my parents belong to an exclusive country club back home. When I was younger, I thought some of their friends were snobs, but in time I realized most of them were just hardworking, honest people. Naturally there were a few snobs, but doesn't every segment of society have its share of snobs?"

"I guess they do at that. I wonder what your dad would think of Happy Hollow."

"I think he'd rather be helping out at the homeless center. I know he goes there whenever he can."

"As one who has been homeless, I think he finds personal satisfaction in doing what he can for the poor."

Suddenly more upbeat, Anita said, "And now we're going to the Century Club." Wanting to learn more about The Improv, her questions came one after another. "Who started the band? How many musicians are there? Do you have a vocalist?"

"Actually the group originated several years ago when a touring band canceled a Saturday night engagement. The owner back then was, and still is, Harry Prendergast. He contacted his friend Alonzo Moore, a semi-retired piano player who rounded up some musician friends to fill the vacancy. The seven who showed up that night had a lot of fun improvising, and the crowd was receptive enough that Harry asked Alonzo and his friends to come back every Saturday night.

"Realizing those same musicians wouldn't always be available, Alonzo contacted Susan Devine, a music instructor at UNO. Together they organized a nucleus of Omaha musicians who also liked the idea, but at times would have other commitments. Susan, however, always has enough for a performance. She'd been my mother's colleague in the music department, and that's how she knew Ben and I had previous band experience. When she contacted us, we were more than willing to join. So the band's a mixture of young and old. Alonzo is well into his sixties, but our drummer, Nick Theophilus, is only twenty and in his second year of college. To join, you must belong to the Omaha Musicians Association and pass a challenging audition. You asked about a vocalist. That would be Starr Simmons. She's forty-nine and sings with our group nearly every Saturday night."

"With such a diverse group, how do you arrange for rehearsals?"

"Except for special occasions, we seldom rehearse. It's one of the reasons Alonzo decided to call the band The Improv, and why Susan has to be selective in her auditions."

Near 13th and Jones in Old Market Richard pulled into the parking lot of an older, two-story brick building. The marquee's red-and-blue neon lights introduced "The Century Club, Music with a Touch of Class."

For more than fifty years the club had been a popular hangout for rhythm and blues, jazz, and progressive jazz fans. The building's interior consisted of a horseshoe bar, two levels of tables and booths, a performing stage, and a midsize dance floor.

Soon after Richard and Anita went inside, Benjamin and Mindy arrived. Petite and becoming in her two-piece, peach-colored suit with matching French heels, Mindy was sales manager of a print advertising firm in northwest Omaha.

This time Benjamin handled introductions. So that the women could get to know each other, hopefully without too much distracting noise, the men took them to a back booth on the second level.

Before leaving to join other band members, Benjamin with a sly wink said, "Now you two try not to talk too much, so you can fully appreciate our music."

Mindy replied, "We'll be quiet as little mice, right Anita?"

"We will, Ben, quiet as little mice."

A few minutes later eight Improv musicians opened with an interpretative jazz selection. In the booth next to Anita and Mindy, a group of football fans were noisily recalling highlights of the afternoon Nebraska game. In fact, throughout the club many customers, seemingly oblivious to the music, were roaming about and being social.

Noticing their inattention, Anita said, "These people are doing exactly what Ben was joking about. I've been to rock concerts where audiences were more respectful."

"Pay no mind to it, Anita. The band always warms up with this kind of music. It's designed to make their listeners feel free and relaxed. People seem to enjoy it and by ten o'clock every Saturday night this place is filled."

Starting the second session, Starr Simmons walked onto the stage. The spotlight sharply contrasted her shoulder-length blond hair and her navy blue, ankle-length dress. Her singing career spanned over three decades, and her voice was as captivating as ever. The audience greeted her with applause and whistles, and she acknowledged them with a happy smile and a fetching wink before singing,

"Fly me to the moon,

And let me sing among the stars,

Let me know what spring is like on Jupiter and Mars,

In other words, hold my hand ..."

One of Starr's selections was "Cry Me a River," during which Richard's solo trombone accompaniment drew another round of applause.

Anita said, "He didn't tell me he could play like that."

"Haven't you noticed, darlin'? The man doesn't talk about himself."

All evening long the only time the conversation between the two women stopped was when Richard and Benjamin joined them during intermissions. Once the men returned to the stage, the ladies were talking non-stop again. It was as if they'd been friends for a long time.

"Rich tells me Ben's been his best friend since they were very young."

"Their fathers were close, too. I don't know if he's told you, but they met when Ben's father was laid off as a packing plant supervisor in Council Bluffs. Ken and Sarah had five kids, and he needed a good job right away. Fortunately, Sam hired him to manage his mail-order department. The two quickly became friends and started going to the YMCA to play handball, a very popular sport in those days. A couple of years later, Ken became the company's first vice president.

"Ben and Rich didn't attend the same elementary schools, but often came with their dads to the downtown office. Ben's a couple of years older and was like a big brother to Rich. The Y is only a few blocks away and they went there to swim, play basketball, and do all the things kids do at the Y. While they were in high school, like their fathers, they started playing handball together."

It wasn't until the band started their final session that the audience energy level began fading, and the music was entirely for slow dancing.

This time as the women started talking, a frown creased Mindy's forehead. "I want to share something with you, Anita, and would you keep what I'm about to say strictly between us?"

"Of course I will."

"To be frank, Ben and I have been concerned, and there's an undertow of uncertainty circulating through the company these days."

"Why is that?"

"We were surprised when Rich left the company for the entire summer. Now it's nearly every weekend again, sometimes for three days. We're wondering how many more extensions will there be? We know he treasures having a store at the resort, and that's understandable."

"Okay, I know that too, but I must admit, Mindy, part of the reason for his long weekend absences is my fault. We've been doing a lot of things together these past couple of months."

"That's fine, but we also know that Rich, weekends only or not, has become a key figure for the entire resort project. It seems as if they keep expecting more and more from him."

"It's because they rely on his experience."

"Maybe, but something is different in his attitude. Always, I mean *always*, he's been up front with Ben in business matters. Lately he seems distant concerning what's going on out there."

"I know he's been busy, and they haven't been able to find a replacement for him."

"In the past he's helped quite a few golfing enterprises get started in Nebraska and Iowa, but we've never known him to be so distracted from company business. I'm just curious: Does he ever say anything to you about his association with those people?"

"He talks a lot about his involvement with James Forrester. I'm sure Ben's told you Forrester's the motivating force behind the resort."

"Ben's mentioned him and says Rich trusts him completely. Perhaps we're reading too much into it, but has he ever talked about the possibility of moving the business to Las Vegas? It's even been suggested he might sell the company so he could work for them permanently. Heaven forbid that either happens."

"I've never heard him mention anything pertaining to either of those. I don't know what Forrester's game plan is, but I've always suspected he has a hidden agenda where Rich is concerned."

Mindy's frown deepened, and Anita quickly amended her statement. "I don't think I'd worry about it, though. He's been showing me around Omaha all weekend, and I can tell you for sure he loves everything about his business and his friends and this town."

"The thought he would even consider moving the company to Las Vegas would in itself be very worrisome. Remember what I told you about Ben's dad? Ben's mother passed on several years ago, and since then Ken lives by himself. He's suffered two heart attacks, and three of his children and their families have moved far away. So now it's only Nyla's family in Lincoln and us. Ken's life is right here, near his remaining children and grandchildren. The thought of us moving away would be devastating for him, as it would be for most of the operational staff. They've invested their hopes and dreams in the company, and we know what happens when a company moves. There are layoffs and downsizing, never mind selling the company. That would—"

"Mindy, given the years of dedication Rich and his family have put into the company, and the way he feels about his life here, I'd say there is no chance he would consider moving or selling."

With a faint smile Mindy replied, "I need to hear stuff like that."

"I'll make you a promise. If I hear anything related to this, anything at all, I'll call you immediately."

"Thanks, Anita," Mindy said, and the two clasped hands.

Starr closed the night with an encore rendition of "How Do You Keep the Music Playing?" When the applause ended, the men returned to the booth where the couples agreed to meet at the Andersons the next day.

On the way to Richard's place, Anita said, "I had a wonderful time tonight, and Mindy's my new bud. And you, Mr. Stewart, never told me you were such a talented musician. I loved The Improv. Such virtuosity."

"Thank you, Anita, I knew you'd like Mindy. She originally came here from New York City as a purchasing consultant for a large department store. At first she didn't like Omaha and she couldn't wait to get back to New York. Then she met Ben and everything changed. Now she loves it here as much as he does."

As promised, Anita didn't mention Mindy's concerns about Richard's Vegas connections. She did, however, promise herself she'd be listening carefully the next time he talked about James Forrester's plans for the future.

Chapter Thirty-five

ANITA'S WEEKEND IN OMAHA HAD been gliding along as smoothly as Red Wings skates on ice. She'd been inside the heart of the Stewart Company ... met and talked with many of Richard's staff and acquaintances ... made two terrific new friends ... dined at his social club ... watched him perform with The Improv ... and best of all, day and night she'd been with the man she loved on his home turf.

In spite of it all he hadn't offered anything remotely close to what she was hoping for. *To everyone we meet he keeps referring to me as "my friend from Cincinnati," or "a friend I worked with last summer"—always his friend, friend, friend!* She was counting on something more meaningful, such as, *"This is my fiancée,"* or *"soon to be fiancée,"* particularly to Ben and Mindy. As the weekend progressed, it obviously wasn't going to happen. Sunday morning she decided, *It's time to confront him.*

Well aware Anita needed something more secure in their love affair, Richard wondered how he'd react when the matter came up. He hadn't talked with Paula for a long time and wasn't sure how she felt anymore. If she didn't love him, he certainly didn't want to change his situation with Anita.

On the way to church Sunday morning, Anita seemed calm and collected enough. "I've never seen you wearing a white shirt and tie, and you look very distinguished."

Meanwhile her subconscious was contemplating something entirely different. *When church is over, at the right moment I'll strike like lightning. I'll tell him exactly how I feel about this "friendship" nonsense. I'll tell him I need to know exactly where our romance is heading.*

As the couple entered the First United Methodist sanctuary, most of the congregation was already seated. An usher led them past a baptismal marble fount and down an aisle to second row seats in front of the pulpit.

After they sat down, Anita leaned over and whispered, "I think people are looking at us."

"They're probably admiring you in that pretty lavender dress and thinking I'm a lucky guy."

What followed was a typical Sunday service—weekly announcements, the singing of hymns, the children's lesson, and the passing of collection plates. The sermon centered on hopes for peace, and churchgoers' obligations to be faithful and give generously during the Thanksgiving and Christmas seasons.

Following the benediction, in a scene similar to the night before, a number of folks stepped forward for introductions. And still on automatic introduction, Richard said, "I want you to meet my friend Anita Stevens from Cincinnati. This year she's working as a high school counselor in Las Vegas," and other "friend" connotations.

This is becoming downright disgusting, she thought.

He, on the other hand, was feeling good about life in general. After leaving the church, while heading for the car, he sang in his Jimmy Durante voice,

"Fame, if you win it,

Comes and goes in a minute,

Where's the real stuff in life to cling to?

Love is the answer—"

"You own Durante," she said.

As he was driving away, however, her more serious sentiments emerged. "You know, Rich, this entire weekend I've been your escort, your lover, and—may I quote you?—'your *friend* visiting here.' You keep referring to me as your *friend.*" Sliding the palm of her hand across his thigh, she asked, "Just a visiting friend, am I?"

"Anita, honey, it's just a way of keeping people from probing into our personal lives."

"Wow, that was one fine cop-out. So you don't want people to think we're more than just friends?"

"Well sure, sure I do. It isn't that I don't want people to know we're very close. I wouldn't be opposed to that—no, not at all."

"Are you a little nervous about this subject?"

Before he could answer, she spoke again. "I think it's time for us to have a serious discussion about you and me."

Glancing her way, he said, "I thought we were doing just fine."

Cruising through the 72nd and Dodge intersection, her prolonged silence told him some kind of an ultimatum was near.

Finally she asked, "How much do you really enjoy being with me, Richard?"

"Enough so that I miss you even when we're apart for only a few days."

"That's another evasive answer. Let's see, we've known each other since June, and we've been making love since September. I enjoy the good times we're having, too, but I've never felt this way about anyone else, ever, and I don't want to get hurt."

"You must know I don't want you to be hurt either."

"In all honesty, I don't want you thinking of me as a friend who is also a convenient little bed partner."

"Anita, honey, I think of you only in the highest regard."

Silence again as he followed the I-680 ramp that would take them to a suburban exit and on to Ben and Mindy's.

Gazing at the passing interstate scenery, she said, "This is what I think. Christmas would be an ideal time for us to be engaged."

Cornered and fumbling for a reply, he took a deep breath before he said, "Hmmm, well now, that's an interesting idea."

"You think so too? I'm glad you do."

Wondering how she could have interpreted his reply so positively, but hoping to avoid further interrogation he asked, "Anything else on your mind?"

"As a matter of fact there is something else we need to discuss. Do you believe engagements should be a time when two people allow their romance to mature, a time to make some intimate sacrifices?"

Wondering where she might be going with this latest ultimatum, he said, "I think all relationships should be prepared to make some sacrifices."

"Because when we become engaged, I think we should agree to a new challenge."

"A new challenge?"

"Yes. Let's say we become engaged at Christmas and set the wedding for sometime in the summer. I think during the months of prenuptial preparation, we should stop making love—I mean all-out passionate lovemaking—until the night of our wedding."

"And why would we do that?"

"I know it would be difficult, but I think it would strengthen the character of our relationship, perhaps even the passion we feel for each other. I mean for a long time to come, Rich." She turned and looked directly at him before she added, "I think it's something we need to do."

"And you think abstinence between us is possible?"

"I think we should make it work." Her tone of voice made him realize she'd made up her mind.

Outside the city limits he followed the turnoff ramp that connected with a county road. He turned left and a mile further entered a suburban neighborhood consisting of recently constructed homes. The Andersons' Cape Cod residence was in the middle of a cul-de-sac—a four-bedroom, three-bath ranch with a lower level walkout opening to the backyard.

Benjamin and Mindy greeted them at the front door and showed them through their home. In several rooms there were pictures of Richard's godson Michael, age seven; Kyle, five; and Misty, three. Grandpa Kenneth had taken the children to visit his daughter Nyla's family in Lincoln.

Following a sandwich and salad luncheon, the couples moved downstairs to the family room. While the men watched the Minnesota Vikings-Green Bay Packers game, the ladies paged through family photo albums in search of pictures of Richard and Benjamin when they were younger.

Allowing ample time for Anita's flight, the visitors left at three o'clock. On the way to Eppley Airfield, thick clouds brought premature darkness and chilling winds were reminders of the approaching winter season. Their conversation did not include any further reference to her Christmas expectations. At the terminal's security gate he kissed her and said he'd see her Friday.

As the jetliner lifted from the runway and above the clouds, Anita settled back in her seat, closed her eyes and thought, *Richard is an incredible man, and this will not be the way it was before.*

During his drive home he also was thinking of the future. He wondered what he would do if Paula landed Allyson Devereaux's job and wanted things to be the way they were. *If that does happen, could I turn her down?* It was a question he couldn't truthfully answer anymore.

Chapter Thirty-six

UPON ARRIVING IN LAS VEGAS, Anita was surprised to find her father waiting for her near the passenger arrival escalator.

"The only message I left for you," she said, "was I'd be busy all weekend, so you must have talked to Richard."

"I called him a while ago. By the way your dress is very becoming."

"Thanks. I wore it to church in Omaha this morning."

He picked up her single suitcase from baggage retrieval.

On their way through the terminal toward short-term parking she said, "So, since I was with him for the last three days, you must know we are more than just good friends."

"Honey, I figured given the amount of time you were spending together, and the way you were carrying on, it had to be more than friendship. I was going to ask, but I figured maybe this is the way young people act in this day and age. I also decided it wasn't any of my business or at least not until you decided it was. So tell me, how serious is it?"

"Very serious, Father. I was reluctant to tell you about us, because we hadn't decided on anything definite. That situation has changed."

"You know how I feel about Richard."

"You really think he's a prince, don't you?"

"Yes, I do. He doesn't talk about Mystery Woman anymore?"

"You once told me I should do everything I could to take his mind off Mystery Woman."

Robert chuckled softly as he said, "I remember; sounds as if you have."

The next day at Grant High School first quarter grades had been distributed, and counselors were receiving a variety of phone calls. Most of the inquiries came from parents or guardians wondering what steps should be taken to help their youngsters improve. A few negative callers wanted to know what was wrong with the school's philosophies in general, or with this or that instructor in particular. Trying to answer such complaints could be difficult and time consuming.

When circumstances involving a student required an additional separate conference, Anita would lead those affected in a roundtable discussion, assist in drawing conclusions, and then make recommendations. Positive results usually could be obtained, but to the detriment of conference goals and the students, a few parents remained uncompromising. Under such circumstances Anita would not hesitate to set the parents straight.

Back in Omaha Richard and Andrea Fialkowski, the company's advertising director, were organizing sales promotions for the Christmas season.

Thursday night Anita called. "My father wants to meet with us over the weekend. He would only say it was a matter of importance, so if it's okay with you, Saturday I'll fix a salad and order in pizza at my place."

As soon as the men arrived Saturday afternoon, she called in the delivery order. During the wait Robert asked his two closest friends to get comfortable on the living room sofa.

He took a seat in a chair across from them, leaned forward and said, "I didn't mention this earlier because I wanted to ask you two together. I have a special favor to ask. A few days ago I was talking to Major Benson at the Salvation Army. You remember him, Rich."

"I remember him well."

Robert glanced at the wall calendar above the phone and said, "Next week the Salvation is celebrating a special day. Think now."

"Thanksgiving you mean," Anita said.

"Exactly. It's coming very early this year, and it's their biggest dining event of the year, even bigger than Christmas. The day before Circus Circus will be serving their special dinner for the homeless. Then on Thanksgiving Day the Salvation takes over. With so many needy folks expected this year, they're going to need a few extra hands."

"Before you go any further," Richard said, "I'm returning to Omaha tomorrow and won't be back here until Friday."

"I was hoping you'd consider coming back Wednesday. That would make you available early Thursday. As for me, I'll already be helping out at the banquet hall, *both* the night before *and* the next morning."

Anita said, "Father, you are such a diplomat."

Robert turned to Richard and asked, "Well, what do you think?"

"I'm afraid I—"

"They're thinking there'll be a record-breaking number of the poor and homeless to feed, Rich."

"You're right; he is a diplomat. I'll think about it."

"I'm sure you'll find a way to be there. We'll count on both of you then?"

Anita said, "You're taking my presence for granted?"

"Sorry, but I assumed you, inasmuch as you won't be working, would automatically volunteer."

"It seems I have no choice."

"Okay, I thought about it," Richard said. "If I work late a couple of nights, I should be able to catch a late Wednesday flight."

"Wonderful. Now I want to caution you, Annie, the word volunteer sounds nice and cozy a safe distance from reality. It's an entirely different set of setting when you come face-to-face with large numbers of the poor. Many of them are trying to cope with overwhelming physical and emotional setbacks—like a fragile soul who can't stop the voices pounding in her head, or a frightened child-turned-adult still running from abuse and neglect, or a—"

"Father, when it comes to homeless people, it's not as if I've been in a closet all my life."

"I know you're a considerate person, Anita, but soon you'll see for yourself."

Richard said, "A lot of what I saw the day I was at the homeless center was indeed thought-provoking."

Anita said, "I've read about and have seen on television stories concerning the growing homeless problems. Besides the Salvation Army, I know there are missions, churches, and outreach programs available for them."

"There are many helpful hands out there," Robert said, "but trying to keep up with the steadily increasing numbers is a never-ending struggle. Only a small percentage will have a shelter bed on any given night. That includes the children."

"Surely there are special allowances for them," she said.

"But only so much can be done. Most shelters can offer sleeping spaces for only a couple of weeks. Conditions for the rest of the year worsen when shelters run out of funds as early as May."

Anita shook her head and said, "The problems homeless people face sound like a hopeless nightmare. Can't the government step in and do more?"

"In the many places I've lived, their efforts have been mostly patchwork. They targeted the symptoms and not the causes, and soon the programs were abandoned. The only way to permanently improve conditions would be to get those able to work into jobs. I don't mean just temporary jobs. I mean full-time, self-sufficient jobs. As I told Rich, experts say as many as 75 percent of the homeless able to work would gladly do so if the opportunities were only there. Should such a goal ever be reached, the problems facing the rest of the poor population wouldn't seem so overwhelming."

Anita said, "Finding jobs for that many would require a miracle sent from heaven."

Richard said, "I know, but isn't history filled with miracles people said could never happen?"

Robert nodded his head. "I agree with both of you. It would take a miracle, but miracles do happen."

Anita said, "I remember you talking about the Salvation Army's efforts to find jobs for people."

Richard added, "Major Benson said their training programs place hundreds of the homeless into good jobs every year."

The sound of door chimes signaled the arrival of the pizza. After Richard paid the deliverer, the food and conversation moved to the kitchen table.

As she sat down, Anita said, "I really can't imagine what it would be like not to have a place to stay night after night. That's without considering adverse weather conditions, the dangerous elements, and the sheer hopelessness of it all."

Robert said, "Being homeless is like being lost in a deep, dark cave. You have little or no resources, and no one to ask for help—unless you beg, and you will beg because hunger has no pride. When you seek a way out of the darkness, the cave only gets deeper. Think of it. If you try to get a respectable job, every hiring agent expects you to wear nice clothes, look confident, and have in your possession an updated work resume with promising recommendations.

"And if you have a history of alcoholism or drug dependency, what then? Do you say to the person, 'Well, the record will show I have had an addiction problem, and I haven't worked for a while, but I'm all right now. And I promise you, I will be a reliable worker.' Trust me; it doesn't work.

"Anyway, getting back to Thanksgiving. When you work on a food serving line, you'll want to make your guests feel that you truly enjoy serving them. They'll appreciate your attitude."

"All right then," Anita said, "what time should we be there?"

"Rich, do you remember the Lied center we visited that morning?"

"I do."

"You can check into the dining hall before eleven o'clock for a meeting and preparatory work. Because of the predicted large numbers, dinner will be served earlier than usual. If you want to work a full day, which shows you really care, you won't be finished for quite a few hours. So I'll enter your names for a full day?"

With Robert's latest challenge the couple smiled and shrugged, but agreed to his request.

"Good, two young people like you should be able to work like horses. Just be sure to get a good breakfast before you arrive. You full-time people won't be eating until the last guest is served. Fear not, because the food will be great for you also, eventually that is."

Typically on Thanksgiving Day Richard and Anita would be with family and friends. They'd be enjoying the traditions of cooking and socializing and watching televised football games. Then everyone would gather at the table for grace and the delicious turkey feast. This year such family events in Omaha and Cincinnati were not to be. This year the couple would be part of a volunteer team working to make the day a pleasant one for many of the less fortunate people in Las Vegas.

When they arrived at eleven o'clock Thanksgiving morning, Richard and Anita found the Salvation Army volunteer parking lot nearly full. Checking into the dining hall, they were given name tags before their instructional meeting. When it was over, Robert, decked out in a long kitchen apron, assigned Richard to assist crews setting up tables and chairs. Anita joined other women separating plates and placing silverware and other accessories on the tables.

Soon the catered food, made possible from countless donations, was ready and team members were placing the offerings on the serving line tables. Menu choices included beef, turkey and ham, mashed potatoes and gravy, sweet potatoes, cranberry sauce, several varieties of salads, fruits, vegetables, relishes, and dinner rolls. There were dispensers for milk, hot chocolate, coffee, tea, and soft drinks. Dessert specialties were pumpkin, apple, and rhubarb pies, chocolate and carrot cakes, all by choice à la mode.

Major Benson appeared, and after being introduced to Anita he said, "So you're the little lady we've been hearing so much about. We are pleased to have you with us today."

Before the dining hall doors opened, the waiting line outside the building extended far down the sidewalk. First in line were those requiring assistance—people confined to wheel chairs and those using crutches, walkers, and canes.

Wearing aprons, plastic caps, and gloves, Richard and Anita were side-by-side in the serving line, each one offering their guests cordial greetings and generous portions of food.

The first hour ran smoothly. Hungry though they were, most of those waiting to be served seemed carefree and talkative. After the tables were filled and people were well into their meals, the servers left their positions, and with beverage carafes in hand they circulated to refill cups and glasses. Others filled bread trays with fresh rolls. Soon workers were assigned to new serving places, and Richard and Anita were separated.

During one interval, while taking a coffee decanter to fill cups around a table, Anita's dimpled smile ignited return smiles. She came to an elderly woman whose hands and wrists were so crippled by arthritis she couldn't slice the turkey breast on her plate. As she looked up at Anita, the woman shrugged her shoulders.

Anita sat down next to her and asked, "What is your name, dear?"

"I'm Gwen Walker, and I see you're Anita."

As she was slicing the turkey, Anita asked Gwen about her life and her loved ones. She said she'd recently suffered the loss of a family member she'd been living with. Now only a few relatives were left, and they lived in other parts of the country. The conversation lasted several minutes.

When Anita rose to continue her work, Gwen placed a hand on her arm and said, "I haven't seen you here before, but if you come back again, maybe we could talk some more."

Anita leaned over, gave Gwen a hug, and said, "I have a feeling we will be seeing more of each other."

Filling bread baskets several tables away, Richard noticed the hug and when Anita's eyes met his, he sent her a wink and a smile which she returned.

By the time the last guests departed from the hall, it was well past mid-afternoon, and now it was time for the servers to fill their plates. Before they finished, Major Benson announced a record number of guests had been served.

As the volunteers were leaving, the major bade each of them farewell at the door. To Anita and Richard he said, "I want to thank you again for coming. You are responsible for spreading a whole lot of happiness around here today."

Richard said, "Best Thanksgiving I ever had, Mr. Benson."

"I'll second that," Anita said.

As the couple left the center, Richard said to her, "Tell me what you're thinking."

"Father was right. Those people appreciate everything you do for them."

"And as he points out, except for some unfortunate turns, most of them wouldn't be in the position they are in today. I met a man who'd been the vice president of a bank and without warning lost his job, insurance, everything. Within a few months his wife left him and took the children. Then of all things he suffered a heart attack. His main concern now is finding a job that can help pay for his daily necessities and the uncovered medical expenses."

Anita recalled, "A young woman told me that last spring a drunk driver crashed into their car and killed her husband. There was little insurance to provide for her and her two daughters. She said her job pays too much for her to receive government assistance, but not enough to cover the mortgage, day care, transportation, and the rest of it.

"After my father talked to us last week, I did some research and found one source pointing out that over 40 percent of the homeless are, amazingly, less than six-years-old. More than 40 percent of those 18 and under have been physically abused. Of those coming out of foster care and juvenile justice systems, 50 percent do not have social support and will be homeless very soon. Nearly one in three of those same children will attempt suicide at one time or another."

"Unfortunately, information like that the critics of the homeless simply ignore."

Continuing on the drive toward Anita's apartment, they traveled on Las Vegas Boulevard through light Strip traffic past the flashing signs of the mammoth, world-famous resorts. On this night all the promotional grandeur seemed dull and meaningless.

For the rest of the weekend, the recurring memories of Thanksgiving reminded the couple they were living in a world where the only sure prognosis for any human being is the unpredictability of life itself.

Chapter Thirty-seven

W HILE SORTING THROUGH HIS MAIL in his Omaha office Monday morning, Richard came upon a letter from Paula. Hastily he opened it before carefully read each word.

Dear Richard,

Because I have so much to tell you, I decided not to call or leave a message, that the best way to convey what I have to say would be in writing. So here goes.

Our waiting at last is over, except I don't even know if you want to see me anymore. You may not want to read this letter or to reply, but I'll take my chances. I want to come to Las Vegas this Friday to see you and spend the weekend with you.

I'm deeply sorry for the way things happened last May, and for everything that has happened between us since then. In retrospect I wish I hadn't left so abruptly. I thought of postponing my leaving until I talked to you, but as you know, the powers that be said I had to leave immediately.

For quite a while I figured our being apart would only be temporary. You were only hours away, and we could work something out. However, it soon became clear I was going to be under a lot of pressure with the late hours, spontaneous traveling, and so forth. I was so busy I knew having you here would be unfair to you. And when they announced Allyson Devereaux was resigning, I realized my efforts would only intensify.

Twice I tried to take advantage of what I thought were opportunities to see you. I didn't want to break those plans, especially after you indicated you wanted to give me an engagement ring. But things just didn't fall into place. Last September when I had to cancel our weekend plans and you were so upset, I felt it would be better if we postponed further contact until my future here was decided.

These past six months I've been on assignments throughout the country—Miami, San Francisco, Dallas, and so on. They treated me royally and assured me I'd have a good position one way or the other. Their promises convinced me I had to postpone my personal preferences, and there could be no distractions.

Friday afternoon I was called into the office of Sterling Hastings, our general manager. He and Seth Greene informed me they'd decided to divide Allyson's position into three separate positions. At first I didn't know what to think.

They said in addition to being a special features contributor, which would be similar to my position at KBLV, I'd been selected to pilot, starting in February, a Monday through Thursday thirty-minute late-night show. It will be called "Close-up with Paula Summers." In the beginning the show will focus on exposing lies and slanderous information that are the gravy train of popular tabloid magazines. As we know, their stories target the rich and famous, especially those within the entertainment and political fields.

For example, take a story about a celebrity supposedly having had an illicit affair. The story will be visible on newsstands wherever tabloids are sold, and the character damage can be career-threatening. Our investigators—if they smell a rat, and there are a lot of them out there— will go behind the scenes to search for the truth. When they uncover story falsifications or unsubstantiated exaggerations, we'll strengthen our findings, build rebuttals, and have on-camera interviews with the party or parties in question.

In other words we will be crusaders taking on the bullies, right versus evil, fighters against journalism terrorists! The consensus is that a large portion of late-night audiences are looking for more high-profile personality programs, and mine will offer a unique perspective. If we succeed in attracting enough viewers on the West Coast, Mr. Hastings thinks the parent network may add my show to their nationwide menu of late-night offerings.

This will require a lot of work, but I've already been assigned three assistants, including Sabrina Corbett, a terrific scriptwriter. When the tabloid topic runs its course, Sabrina and I will have prepared a new human interest topic ready for programming.

There's so much more I have to tell you when and if I see you, but I couldn't have planned what is happening here more ideally. This means I'll have a regular schedule with many weekends free. I'm hoping these latest events will translate into us being together once more.

My folks are thrilled and are planning to come here over Christmas. I'm excited about them meeting you.

During Friday's meeting they said my impromptu roving reporter days basically are over, and I should take some vacation time. I made it clear this time nothing will interfere with my going to Las Vegas. My only obligation will be to meet with representatives from several resorts regarding a late January special telecast.

The rest of the time I want to be with you, to show you how much you mean to me.

I love you,
Paula Rene
P.S. Call me as soon as possible—if you want to, that is.

Richard placed the letter on his desk. He thought back to the day she said they should postpone their future plans until her job situation was settled. Now her decision seemed much more practical than it did then. *And typical for her, she's accomplished what she set out to do, and she loved me all the time, and life is beautiful!*

He rose and walked over to the window and gazed into an overcast sky. *At times she might have seemed inconsiderate where we were concerned, but she was right. If I'd gone to Hollywood, it would have been awkward for both of us.*

Returning to his desk, he glanced at her postscript. *Please call me as soon as possible.*

He touched her cell number but had to leave a message: "Great to hear from you. I'm thrilled with your spectacular news and can't wait to hear the details. I'll be in the office all of the afternoon and should be home by six o'clock. Call me when you are able."

Thin clouds of guilt formed as he wondered what Anita would think of the letter. The clouds dissipated when he reminded himself how long he'd waited to hear from Paula, especially when she'd written a letter like that.

Minutes after reaching home his phone rang. When he answered, Paula said, "Hi Richard, thanks for your message."

"Paula, thank you for the letter. Congratulations, I'm happy for you."

"Isn't it exciting?"

"It is. Hey, it's been a long time since we've talked."

"Too long," she said.

"I guess we finally gave up trying to be together until you knew for sure."

"And thankfully it's all behind us. I assume you'll be in Vegas this weekend?"

"I will be. Tell me precisely when you're coming."

"We'll be leaving here in a station vehicle early Friday and should be there before noon. I'm traveling with two production crew members who will be assisting me in preparing for the January special. It will not in any way interfere with our weekend. Being with you is my first priority."

"You've made hotel reservations?"

"My secretary reserved a suite at the Bellagio, so I'll be right across the street from you."

For a long spell they talked about whatever came to mind. Not once did Richard make a reference to Robert or Anita. Any mention of Anita in particular would open a Pandora's box of difficult-to-explain questions. *And Paula's only recollection of Robert would be the night he, in his own words, scared the living bejesus out of her. Feeling the way she did then, would she believe he is now my Monte Vista top assistant?* He had to chuckle at the irony of it all.

Not long after they disconnected, the phone rang again, and this time it was Anita wondering why his line had been tied up for so long. The sound of her voice following Paula's scrambled his thought processes, and try as he might to hold a normal conversation, he seemed distant.

Finally she asked, "Is something wrong? You're responding the way you do when your mind is drifting." She shrugged it off, assuming something definitely was bothering him, more than likely a business concern, and she kept the call short.

The next morning discussions around the Stewart office centered on reports of a blizzard sweeping across central Nebraska and heading straight for Omaha. Forecasters were predicting more than twelve inches of snow. By mid-afternoon Melanie had relayed the message that all Omaha Stewart employees should leave for the day.

Soon Richard was the only one left in the office. Looking down from his Woodmen Tower window, he could see snow accumulating and miniature white tornadoes swirling around the street corners. He wasn't overly concerned because he'd be traveling most of the way home west on Dodge, one of the major routes kept open by city snowplows. Besides, the deserted office provided an ideal atmosphere to do some constructive thinking.

Returning to his desk chair, he leaned back and closed his eyes. *Now, I've got to stay focused and be sensible. Spending the weekend with Paula will give us the opportunity to know how much we really mean to each other, because I really don't know anymore. As for Anita, I can't tell her Paula's coming to see me, especially on such short notice. She'd be devastated, and I do not want her hurt in any way. So much for telling the truth.*

I need to think of a logical reason why I won't be able to be with her very much. Like I've been called into an important Monte Vista conference with J.D., which could possibly take the entire weekend. No, she knows he wouldn't do that. Or one of the Renzcorp board members is coming to town to review with me all aspects of the resort progress. Hmmm, a board member coming here. Now that could understandably take most of the weekend. Not bad, not bad at all.

Just as had happened when he starting making love to Anita, his conscience was again awakened, only now its concern was for Anita. The concern was short-lived as he reasoned, *It isn't as if I'm trying to deceive her. Bending the truth a little in a touchy situation like this seems like my only choice, especially when the intent is to avoid someone getting hurt. Weekend meetings with a board member is the best way to go, and that's what I'll tell her.*

When he left the Woodmen building shortly after five o'clock, usually it would be darker outside, but the steady snowfall was creating its own ghostly glow. Traveling several miles west, he came to the crest of a hill that gradually descended to 72nd Street. Between the rhythmic snapping of the windshield wipers, he could see the flashing lights of accident-emergency vehicles at the middle of the intersection. To avoid a traffic tie-up, he turned into a delicatessen's parking lot and left his car near the front entrance. Inside he ordered a bowl of chili, a grilled cheese sandwich, and a cup of hot chocolate.

By the time he finished his meal, the accident scene had cleared enough for him to continue his journey to Regency Park. The minute he reached home, he went to the family room and switched the television channel to WOWT. A news flash showed a city resident shoveling a sidewalk, along with a caption warning people to avoid overexertion.

The telephone rang and Paula said, "I see on television you're having a blizzard out there. NBC just showed pictures of interstate traffic problems outside Omaha."

"Same thing here in town, heavy blowing snow with sub-zero temps."

"Sounds awful. It's sunny and sixty-five degrees here. I called to verify we will be in Vegas Friday before noon. My crew members will be staying downtown. They said they previously had good luck gambling there. I am getting so excited, Rich. I can't wait to see you, and my professors, and my friends at KBLV, and of course, Juan."

Hearing Juan's name triggered the possibility of complications. *For sure I'll need to clear matters with him.*

Following several moments of silence, she inquired, "Richard, are you there?"

"Sure, sorry, I was thinking about my weekend schedule. As soon as you arrive, call me at my office and we'll have lunch together."

"Until then."

By morning the fast-moving storm was well into Iowa, but because of the massive snow clearing on Omaha streets, it took Richard nearly ninety minutes to reach his office.

At his desk he listened to a phone message from J.D.: "When you return, I want to meet with you early in the afternoon. If that doesn't work, please call me at home. Thanks."

Still ahead: Inform Anita he could see her over the weekend only for short periods, if at all. Once that was accomplished, he'd be able to fulfill his long-awaited dream—to be with Paula, the woman he'd wanted so much to be his wife and one day the mother of his children.

Chapter Thirty-eight

T O GET THINGS IN ORDER, Richard left Omaha Thursday morning. By the time he reached Las Vegas, he was confident his master plan, to be with Paula most of the weekend, was flawless. For lunch he met Juan inside Le Café, where he revealed the latest concerning Paula's return.

Juan listened intently before responding. "And what is Anita's reaction to all this? You told me a while ago she spent the weekend with you in Omaha."

"I haven't told her about Paula coming here. Nor do I intend to, at least not for a while."

"So your princess got what she wanted, and now the day you've been waiting for has finally arrived. What a sweet arrangement for both of you."

Richard shrugged off his friend's sarcastic tone. "This weekend should give us the opportunity to find out how much we really mean to each other."

"Sounds as if you may be able to put everything back together the way it was, or should I say the way it's always been?"

"To tell you the truth, I really don't know. A lot has happened."

"I agree with you there. And what about Anita? Or do innocent little platonic partners just up and disappear when the princess returns?"

"Now wait a minute, my friend, don't blame me for what's happening. I realize how this could be interpreted, but you have to consider every angle. I haven't seen Paula since last spring. She was my fiancée, remember?"

"Right, but then along came Anita."

"Anita and I are as close as friends can be, and I love many things about her. But there are some important unanswered questions, and this weekend I intend to give Paula every consideration. In the long run I only want to do what's best for everyone."

"You know, Senor Stewart, you've become one helluva rationalizer. I think you're in love with both of them, and now you're going to have to choose one and lose the other." Although Juan's analysis was not what he wanted to hear, Richard allowed him to continue. "Let's say after this weekend you still aren't sure. What happens if Anita finds out what you've been doing? How will you explain your decep—or pardon me, your strategy to her?

"Glad you asked, because I may need your assistance. I'm going to tell her that after Saturday's Monte Vista meeting you and I are playing a doubles handball match with a couple of your buddies from Tucson. Afterward, and for most of the weekend, my time will be confined to informing and entertaining a Renzcorp board member."

"So none of it will be true."

"Well, except for the meeting, not really. What I'm asking is, if by any chance she can't reach me and decides to contact you, just tell her—"

"Whoa, whoa, wait a minute. I don't want to lie to Anita. I respect her very much."

"Juan, it isn't as if—"

"Look, if she ever found out I'd lied to her, she'd never forgive me or you. Why would she call me anyway? I'm sure she trusts you completely. Rich, listen to me. I think you'd be wise to reveal to each of these women exactly what's going on."

"Let me explain why I'm handling things this way. Anita refuses to even mention Paula's name. It's been that way for a long time."

"That's beside the point. You need to tell Anita, and if she doesn't like what she hears, then make up your mind what to do. I will say again, if you don't tell her, knowing her as I do, you will lose her, even as a friend, I'd say permanently."

"Look, I can't pretend Paula isn't important to me. She wants to see me and I owe it to her, and damn it I don't want Anita to know until after we've been together and my thinking is clear."

In a sagely confident tone Juan said, "It seems to me you're more concerned with Paula. May I remind you, last summer when you were frustrated and lonely, Anita came into your life and everything changed. What you're planning is simply not like you, Rich."

Juan was right. The master plan was an anomaly, way out of sync from Richard's normal character. As far as Juan was concerned, his friend's romantic roller-coaster ride with Paula had numbed his common sense. Juan also thought, *In this situation fate may very well have the final word, and fate has a fickle nature, can be glorious or—*

Richard interrupted Juan's thought. "Tell me something. Am I caught up in a complicated set of circumstances or what? Another thing, have I placed a ring on either woman's finger? If you were in my position, wouldn't you want to find out what's best for everyone?"

"Granted, but it's *how* you're finding out that puzzles me. By the way, have you seen Paula recently on television?"

"I haven't seen her since she was here."

"I didn't say anything because I thought probably it was over between you two. Maria and I did see her on television the other night, and she's even more of a knockout than when she was here. I won't say any more. You'll soon see for yourself."

"How she looks will have nothing to do with how I'll feel about her."

"Okay, look, right now I know you're confused, but allow me. If it turns out Anita is the woman you really love, you better be positively sure she doesn't find out on her own what's going on."

Richard found to his liking the latter part of Juan's advice: "Be positively sure she doesn't find out."

"Thanks for your thoughts," Richard said, and hoping to avoid further confrontation, he added, "Incidentally, Paula's looking forward to seeing you."

"She's been a close friend for quite a while. At first after she left I gave her the benefit of the doubt. But as time passed, I realized her main objective was to land that television position with little consideration for how you felt. She should have realized you were hurting. Maria and I knew it, and Anita knew it."

"We also know Paula had valid reasons for her actions."

For no particular reason Juan said, "What a contrast in those two. Paula, of modest means, gives her heart and soul to become a television star and is probably headed for fame and fortune. Then there's Anita, from a well-to-do Cincinnati family. She chooses a career dedicated to helping kids, especially those in need, and that's it. Ironic little twist."

Richard said, "It is at that."

In parting Juan said, "*Vaya con Dios,* Ricardo. I think you're going to need Him."

When Richard returned to the New Horizon offices, Cynthia ushered him into J.D.'s office. Her haste made Richard wonder if a serious new problem had developed. As the two men sat down, however, J.D. seemed serious all right, but also relaxed.

"You'll recall, Rich, our Labor Day weekend golf match when I talked to you about relocating your company here."

"Certainly."

"Yesterday I spoke at length with David Renzberg about the situation. Today I'm prepared to make you the official offer I could only allude to back then."

Wondering if his boss ever gave up, Richard said, "With all due respect, James, nothing will change my mind. There are too many reasons why I would never move our operations from Omaha."

"I think what I have to say may change your mind. Just consider what this could mean to you. First of all, your central staff would join us here at our Renzcorp Center. The move would put the Stewart Company into subsidiary partnerships with Monte Vista, New Horizon, and Renzcorp. In the transition your company operations and procedures would not change, and you'd maintain complete control. We also want you to be chairman of the resort's golfing operations, a position which would ideally coordinate with your company's interests. As chairman, we're offering you a one million dollar yearly salary."

Richard took a deep breath. "Whew, that is an outstanding offer. I'm not saying I'm interested, but go back to the term partnership. Within such an agreement, what about the Stewart Company name?"

"Your company has an established reputation, and we wouldn't think of changing your name or any phase of your organization. Mr. Renzberg said when our resort becomes established, our planning will be the model for future resorts. That means as sports merchandise supplier for our future enterprises, your company will be competing to be number one in both the United States and overseas."

Richard's contemplation was brief. "Were it up to me alone, I might consider your offer. The way things are, it just isn't practical. There are my twelve upper-level managers and their co-workers to consider."

"I understand, but small, medium, and large businesses successfully relocate here all the time. And don't worry, we have experts who would make the transition run silky smooth."

"Just for discussion let's review what you're proposing. The Stewart Company would incorporate with your corporation interests, but our staff and our operations would remain as they are. And for supervising the resort's golfing operations, I'd receive a million dollar salary."

"With more incentives as we progress. Quite simply, we want you and your company with us. With the economy soaring as it is, just think of the potential for new Stewart stores and your leadership role. Now those are downright intriguing prospects."

"It really is an incredible offer. I'm wondering what Ben Anderson's reaction might be."

"You think a lot of Mr. Anderson, don't you?"

"He's our vice president and my best friend."

"With the kind of faith you have in him, I'm sure he's exceptional, as would his future be with us. Any idea what his initial response might be?"

"When you and I discussed this earlier, I didn't mention it to him. My gut feeling? In spite of all the positives, I'm sure relocating would create major obstacles for him and the rest of our staff. As I've said, folks back home are reluctant to change their lives, especially when they're content being right where they are."

"I have a suggestion. To see what Ben's impression would be, have him bring his family out here for a week-long visit right after Christmas. We'll arrange for them to stay in a comfortable resort suite near Summerlin. We'll take them to see some of the community's new housing developments, show them through a couple of the newer schools, pay a visit to the church of their choice. I feel confident they'll find community life here is family-oriented enough to satisfy their most discriminating requirements."

"I'll ask him what he thinks. By the way, I have some personal business to attend to that may take the rest of the weekend. I'm sure I'll be at the meeting, but other than that—"

"Not a problem; do what you have to do."

J.D.'s parting words were, "Seriously consider my offer, Rich. If you decide to join us, I am confident you will never regret it."

Chapter Thirty-nine

CONVINCING ANITA HE'D BE COMMITTED most of the next three days would be a touchy task. He decided to lay out his Renzcorp board member story over dinner at the Red Lobster restaurant not far from her apartment. To set the stage he first asked about what was going on at school.

"Well, much of today I spent trying to solve the problem of two tenth-grade girls conspiring against Angela, who they figured was being overly friendly with one of their boyfriends. A while back words were exchanged in the hall and a near physical confrontation had to be broken up by a teacher. One way or another they discovered Angela's locker combination and left threatening notes inside.

"When Angela came to me with her problem, I called the girls into my office, but they angrily denied it. I notified the parents and asked one of our assistant principals to step in. He warned them he was considering calling the police for breaking and entering charges and that instantly scared them. Angela was called back in and apologies went around the circle, an enforced truce you might say. Usually though, for teenage girls when it's over, it's over, and in the end they might even become good friends."

"Problem solved, good job. Now, I'm glad I have the opportunity to talk to you. J.D. informed me this afternoon that none other than Maxwell Danforth is coming to town for the entire weekend. He happens to be the Renzcorp board member most closely connected with Monte Vista. J.D. wants me to take him on a tour of the site, show him through our progress reports, and reveal step-by-step our future plans. In addition, I'll be accompanying him to dinner and entertaining him afterward. Unfortunately, it could run late both nights."

"You mean you're responsible for him the *entire* weekend?"

"Sorry, but I'm afraid I am. J.D. wants him treated royally. I understand he's single and quite the socializer, so I've been asked to keep my evenings open. I guess it means most of the next couple of days may be a question mark for you and me."

"You mean we'll be seeing very little of each other. Richard!"

"I'm sure I'll see you sometime. I just can't say when. Tomorrow will be difficult, and Saturday Mr. Danforth is the guest speaker at our meeting. On top of everything else, Juan called a while ago to remind me Saturday afternoon we'd agreed to play a doubles handball match with a couple of his buddies coming up from Tucson. He made the appointment a few weeks ago, but I forgot completely. I told him I'd have to check with you, so is it all right?"

"No, it is not all right. And another thing, surely we can get together when your Danforth dinner engagements are over."

As if unsure, Richard frowned when he said, "As I said, both nights may run late. J.D. also wants the three of us to have early breakfast together, so I'll need some rest. You know how you feel when you have a student-parent conference the next day."

She tsked her tongue and said, "Okay, if you'd rather spend the weekend with Forrester and his b-o-r-e-d member, go right ahead. I suppose I could call Cecily to go shopping, but I want you to do me a favor. Tell Mr. Forrester for me, personally for me, weekend nights should be off-limits for corporation, resort, or any other official business. They almost always seem to be for him. He's taking advantage of you, Rich."

Hoping to avoid further fabrications, he changed the subject. "I didn't say anything to you before because I wasn't sure there was anything to it, but are you aware your father and Madelline are growing increasingly fond of each other? For instance, whenever he's in the office they go out on the balcony to smoke and talk and they're out there for quite a while. Word is circulating it's more than just friendly."

"My father and Madelline? I know he thinks a lot of her, but my goodness, I think that is so sweet. She's a classy lady, and he should have someone he personally cares for, especially someone like her."

"I agree." Back on more secure footing, Richard said, "About the weekend, although I'm sure we'll stay in touch, don't count on us being together for any length of time until Sunday."

"Until *Sunday*! I hope I see you a lot before then."

When they returned to her place he stretched out on the sofa, and she massaged his shoulders, arms, and back. "Oh, that's good," he said, "keep doing that."

He was relieved the part of his master plan he dreaded the most— clearing matters with Anita—was essentially done with. The preliminary pieces had fallen neatly into place: *Paula covered; J.D. covered; Anita covered.* He wouldn't have to worry about Robert either. He'd already said the colder weather meant there'd be growing demands at the homeless center and he'd be there much of the weekend.

Nevertheless, Richard's conscience again questioned the story he'd been telling Anita. Again the interrogation didn't last. *The most important thing for the three of is for Paula and me to find out if the magic is still there. Once that's accomplished, I'll know how to handle the situation. Although Juan has made me realize someone will be hurt, it is the only way to solve it.*

Friday morning Anita called him at his New Horizon office. She said she'd be shopping later in the day with Cecily and their friend Penny in the Galleria mall. She suggested he call when he knew the details of his weekend schedule.

After the call he attempted to stay busy, but all he could think about was Paula's arrival. As he wandered into the outer office for a coffee refill, Cindy motioned to him that he had a call waiting. Quickly he returned to his desk and picked up the phone.

"Hi, Richard, it's me. I'm here."

"Paula, wonderful. Exactly where are you?"

"I'm in my suite on the fifteenth floor at the Bellagio. I have what should be an excellent view of the lake and Bally's and Paris, but it's drizzling and cold outside."

"If you're free, I'm coming right over."

"I have so much to tell you. I'll be waiting in the lobby near the guest service counters."

In hurrying through the outer office, he left his raincoat behind. Glancing over his shoulder, he told Cindy he wasn't sure when he'd be back.

Even the descending elevator seemed stubbornly slow, but once outside he jogged steadily through the light drizzle to the Bellagio hotel entrance. Once inside the lobby he scanned a sea of faces until his eyes met Paula's. Swiftly closing the distance between them, they smiled at each other for only a moment before they embraced and kissed. Passersby smiled and shook their heads as they politely stepped around the romantic scene.

"I've waited a long time for that," she whispered in his ear.

"Let's see, the last time I kissed you was six months, three weeks, and six days ago. Want the exact hour and minutes?"

"I've missed you, too."

"So are you all moved in? Is there anything I can help you with?"

"Take me to lunch at the cafe next to the gardens?"

He took a step back and scanned her from head to toe, every inch appealing in her chartreuse pants suit, gold chain belt resting on slim hips, and black leather pumps with gold trim.

He chuckled softly as he said, "You look absolutely fantastic."

"Thank you, sir, and you look great, too."

On the way to the cafe they walked through the Botanical Gardens. The scenery had recently been transformed to a seasonal theme of glittering yuletide trees, reindeer and sleighs, flourishing arrays of red and pink roses, green poinsettias, and silver garlands of tinsel.

They paused in front of a snow-surrounded white sleigh encircled with blooming rose vines.

Turning to him she said, "I can't believe at last we are together again."

"Pardon me, but may I say again how fantastic you look."

There was indeed a new radiance about her—brows finely penciled, longer lashes, slightly lifted eye corners, and lips a glossy red. But the most noticeable change was her magazine-cover-model style platinum blond hair.

He continued, "And you've changed the color of your hair, very becoming by the way."

"They want me to look, in Seth's words, 'distinctive, not like just another television news blonde.'"

"And you didn't need to, but you've lost some weight."

"I actually weigh about the same, but my physical trainer is a muscle-toning expert. Seems I'm surrounded by makeover specialists. They've even asked me to get rid of all traces of my southern accent."

"I love your southern accent."

"They think my occasional slipup sounds folksy, not professional enough."

Adjacent to the gardens a long line was waiting outside the cafe. To avoid an extended wait, they accepted the hostess's offer for seats at the front counter. From her chair Paula glanced around at the surrounding decor—Roman columns circled with blossoming flowers, sculptured white chandeliers, walls finely textured with padded fabric panels.

"Typical Las Vegas," she said. "Even Bellagio's short-order cafe is majestically designed."

The ensuing conversation revolved mostly around her new television show.

"Sterling Hastings came up with the idea," she said. "He believes a program exposing tabloid slander will not only attract a sizable viewer audience but will also favorably launch my career."

"It sounds intriguing. Most of the trash you see on the tabloid covers is ridiculous, but as you wrote, their articles can also be ruinous. It's about time someone came up with some damage control. Movie stars and other celebrities should love a program like yours."

After they were served their luncheon sandwiches and shakes, Paula spoke of wining and dining with different movie and television stars. Richard was curious as to what they were like personally.

"As you can imagine, the younger ones can be self-centered and often live in make-believe worlds. But some of the more established stars really do want to connect with worthy causes. I was thrilled with how friendly they've all been to me. Seth says a major part of their attitude is because they consider me a stepping-stone to good publicity. I guess I must be gullible because they seem genuine to me."

Richard smiled and said, "What you've accomplished since last May is remarkable. It's as if you wrote an exciting script and now you're playing the lead role."

"And I have a more prominent position than some of the people who, only a short while ago, were telling me what to do. Having my own show will be financially rewarding, but it's riskier than a regular news reporting position. The show's success or failure lies in the hands of media critics and most important of all, viewer ratings."

"I'm sure you'll do well."

She changed the subject. "I called Juan after I talked to you this morning."

"I'm sure he was happy to hear from you."

"I expected he would be, but he seemed evasive, not at all like himself."

"He probably had people around him."

"No, he's always gone out of his way to make me feel special, no matter what. Maybe he's upset because I haven't had time to keep in touch."

"That could be," Richard said, although he knew exactly why Juan had been evasive.

When they finished lunch, she asked, "Could we take a drive around town? It's your turn to teach me about Las Vegas."

While she went upstairs to change into more casual wear, he went back to New Horizon for his raincoat and his car. Twenty minutes later he picked her up in front of the hotel.

She'd slipped into slacks, a sweatshirt, and a navy blue windbreaker similar to the one she wore the first time they met, except this time the inscription read: Paula Summers KHOL-NBC Television.

"What would you like to see first?" he asked.

"Could you take me out to your resort? It's becoming a major topic of discussion in Hollywood social circles."

He drove north on Las Vegas Boulevard through the Strip before turning west on Charleston. Twenty minutes later at the intersection of Desert Foothills Drive and Alta, he turned onto the access road leading to the site. Because of the recent rainfalls, work vehicles were standing idle. Well inside the resort area, he parked at the top of a knoll overlooking a large portion of the development.

She was surprised to see many resort building in the framing stages and several golf fairways partially landscaped.. Richard pointed to the approximate location of where his store would be.

"I had no idea this was going to be so enormous and two signature golf courses. That is impressive. You once said Mr. Forrester would give me exclusive grand opening story rights."

"He will, I'm sure. Incidentally, he wants to talk to you about becoming the resort's public relations director. He said to tell you you'd have extensive media exposure, and he's ready to make you a tempting offer. I told him not to bother because you couldn't be happier than where you are."

"Amen to that, but tell him I am honored with his consideration."

Light rain began falling again, and Richard drove back to the downtown area for a sight-seeing report. Cruising past government buildings and along the perimeters of the Fremont Street Experience, he revealed several construction alterations that were either underway or would be soon. He also talked about different entertainment promotions being planned.

Next she asked him to take her to the UNLV campus. By the time they arrived there, the drizzling had stopped, the sun was shining, and hefty breezes were busily sweeping away scattered cloud fragments. They left the car in front of the Student Union building and walked to the Greenspun building. On a Friday afternoon throughout the campus only a few folks were milling about.

Hoping to find an instructor she knew, they went to the Journalism and Media Studies offices, but the door was locked with no one inside. From there they walked back to the campus courtyard and sat down on a bench.

"This campus brings back some fond memories," she said, "but it seems as if I left here longer ago than just last spring."

"That's because so much has happened. Hold on, I just had a vision. When you become a famous television personality, they'll probably honor you with a plaque in this courtyard."

"I'm sure. Seriously, when I get back to the hotel, I want to call Jack Weatherford, my degree adviser. He's the one who made it possible for me to graduate without attending my final ten days of classes."

"I wasn't too happy with him back then."

"But thanks partly to him I have my position, and now you and I are together, so it doesn't make any difference, does it? Know what I'd like to do tonight?"

"Tell me."

"First I think we should have dinner at The Venetian. Remember our first night together at the restaurant in St. Mark's Square?"

"Yes, I do. I'll call and arrange for a table."

"And one of our stops this weekend has to be the Paradise Rendezvous, the place we used to go after hours to dance and relax."

"That's a must."

"I'll be meeting with a publicity spokesman for Mr. Wynn Monday morning, so I won't be leaving until Tuesday. Could you stay over until then?"

"I wish I could, but with the Christmas rush I'll have to leave Sunday."

It was late afternoon when he took her back to her hotel before going to his Paris room. All through his shower and dressing for the evening he couldn't stop thinking about her. *She really is even more beautiful than ever ... She seems unaffected by her success ... It's almost as if she's never been away.*

As he was walking out the door, he finally thought of Anita. *It's six o'clock, and so far she hasn't called. Things could not be better.*

Meanwhile, back in her suite Paula had styled her hair into a mini chignon with small, surrounding pearls matching her earrings. Other recently acquired jewelry included a gold watch bracelet and a diamond/amethyst ring. Her overall appearance, including her three-quarter length sleeveless emerald dress with matching heels, adequately fulfilled her desired Hollywood celebrity appearance. Whereas once she made a discount store overcoat look like Saks Fifth Avenue, on this night her white suede overcoat really was from Saks.

In line with his telephoned request, when they arrived at the Postrio restaurant their hostess took them to an outside terrace table. It was beneath a simulated street lamp and overlooking the Square. Through dinner, dessert, and the wine-sipping afterglow, time stood still as they recalled memories of their winter-spring romance.

By ten o'clock, however, Paula's second glass of wine was having the affect of a sleeping pill, and try as she might she couldn't refrain from yawning.

"I'm sorry I'm so tired," she said. "Please blame it on my lack of sleep last night and my early morning departure."

Cavalierly, Richard came to her rescue. "Hey, it's been a long day and you need some rest. I'll take you back to your hotel and we'll meet first thing in the morning for breakfast."

When they reached her suite door, with yet another yawn she said, "Is this all right, darling, because you can come in if you'd like."

"No, no, you rest those pretty blue eyes." He kissed her forehead, cheek, and lips before he said, "Sleep well, and I'll call you around eight o'clock."

As he was leaving the Bellagio, he felt a sense of relief. Their first day together was over, and he'd no more than talked with her, held her hand, and kissed her on only two occasions. Not that he didn't find her as desirable as ever, but he wanted to believe what he told Juan was true. His main purpose was to take his time to find out if the old chemistry was still there. Only then could he be fair to both her and Anita. He'd know much better, he figured, after the next day's events. Another thought occurred: *Tomorrow could very well be the most important day of my life.*

As soon as he entered his room, he called Anita.

Now it was she who was yawning as she inquired, "You're just getting home? It's after eleven o'clock."

"Yeah, I know. As I suspected, dinner with Maxwell Danforth turned out to be a long, drawn-out affair. It looks as if it's more of the same tomorrow. As I indicated earlier, he's a perfectionist who insists on covering every finite detail. Brilliant fellow, I must say, and we were still talking business when I took him to dinner at Caesars. Anyway, I'm tired and I'm going to bed. I'll call you tomorrow when I'm free."

"Sorry for being impatient before. Take care of your business, and call me whenever you can, especially when you finish tomorrow night. Promise me?"

"For sure."

Chapter Forty

PAULA'S SATURDAY SCHEDULE WOULD BE crowded with places to visit and friends and acquaintances to renew. She and Richard's first stop was for cappuccino and pastries at a Fashion Show Mall coffee shop. Afterward they casually strolled the hallways, their topics of conversation intended to make up for lost time. For lunch she would meet Cal Weatherford at Maggiano's. Afterward, her KHOL traveling companions would pick her up and take her to KBLV. There she'd spend time with former staff associates. At four o'clock Richard would pick her up and take her back to her hotel.

He, in turn, just before noon would leave her for his resort luncheon meeting, but in Anita's mind he would then join Juan for the handball match.

In light of the rainy week the Monte Vista meeting was primarily an uneventful review. When it was over, Richard called Juan, hoping he might have softened from his previous day's perspective. Juan confirmed that Paula had contacted him. He also admitted feeling uneasy talking to her.

Richard responded, "I really want for you to see her in person because you were right, she is more gorgeous than ever. What has surprised me is it's almost as if she's never been away." Out of context he added, "I don't know, is it possible to love—I mean really love—two women at the same time?"

"Fortunately, I have no experience on which to rely. Did you tell Paula about Anita?"

"Not yet."

"And when do you see Paula again?"

"Later this afternoon."

"And Anita?"

"Tomorrow, maybe."

Juan chuckled. "Tomorrow, *maybe?* Ricardo, this is getting messier by the minute. You need to come clean with both of these ladies before anything else happens."

Obviously Juan had not budged from his previous perspective so Richard kept the conversation short. "Listen, I have to go, but I am confident everything's going to turn out in the best interests for everyone."

As scheduled, at four o'clock he arrived at KBLV and took Paula back to her hotel where she would prepare for the evening.

An hour and a half later when he called on her, he was pleased because she'd slipped into the same ensemble she'd worn the first night they made love—the pink satin dress and the gem-like sparkling high heels he'd given her Valentine's night.

Those memory lane recollections continued with dinner at Mandalay Bay, namely because he remembered the Aureole as being one of her dining spots. Soon after they ordered, from the four-story wine tower a "Wine Angel" glided to their table with their pink champagne selection. With a cheery hello and a smile, she filled their glasses.

As they were partaking in their dinners and the champagne, Richard strayed from reminiscing long enough to completely disclose J.D.'s offer.

She responded, "You mean he wants you to move the company's central operations here, and you'd become an integral part of Monte Vista and their *entire* corporation? And you'd still be in control of your company? *And* you'd be the golfing operations chairman for a million dollars a year?"

"Basically that's the offer. So what do you think?"

"Of course, you'd have to think of your people back in Nebraska, right? I know they've always been a priority of yours."

"Absolutely."

"Well, Richard, I don't think you should let your personal feelings for them stand in the way of your business interests. If such a move would be good for you and your company, isn't it worth your most serious consideration? And if you did decide to relocate, and some of your staff chose not to, wouldn't such decisions be up to them? I think Mr. Forrester is offering you an incredible opportunity, not to mention we'd be only thirty minutes apart."

"I thought about that."

"Maybe what I have to say will help you decide. After we talked Monday, I took the liberty of telling Seth Greene about us, that we might soon be engaged."

"You did?"

"I told him all about you, and he's looking forward to meeting you."

She'd spoken the words he'd been waiting so long to hear. If they thrilled him less than expected, he assumed it was because she'd already indicated as much.

After dinner they moved on to the Paradise Rendezvous lounge on East Flamingo Road. On stage the Jethro Thomson Trio—piano, bass, and drum—had just started playing, and Richard found an empty booth near the dance floor. He ordered another round of pink champagne which, along with the relaxing mood music, this time encouraged more serious recollections.

"I knew for sure I loved you," he said, "Valentine's night when we were having dinner at the Top of the World. I didn't tell you then, because I'd only known you a few weeks, and Juan had advised me not to rush you."

With a smile she said, "And I knew for sure I loved you the first night we went to the Fremont Street Experience. Oh, and do you remember that was also the night the homeless man stopped us and asked for a handout. That old buzzard coming upon us like that scared me half to death."

Until then the discussions had been gliding along like a horse-drawn sleigh on a snow-packed country road.

Richard cleared his throat and said, "Actually the man you're referring to wasn't homeless, Paula. He had been at one time, but not on the night he stopped us. I know for a fact he had a good job then, and he still does."

She blew a sarcastic puff of air. "Are we talking about the same person? He didn't look as if he had a good job, and he certainly knew how to panhandle. How would you know about him anyway?"

"Well, it so happens one afternoon I drove down to the public library you once told me about, you know, the one close to downtown. He was also there and I recognized him and we talked for quite a while."

"That part of town is close to where many of the homeless hang out, all right, but what could you possibly have to say to him? I remember that night you gave him quite a bit of money, which surprised me."

"I gave him fifty bucks because he said he wanted to help a real homeless person. Remember? She was just a teenager, hungry and with no place to go for the night. When I saw him in the library, I was curious about what happened to her."

"Oh yes, the girl in the alley. Well, she got herself into that predicament, didn't she? Do you really feel sorry for people who make the kind of choices she made?"

Richard had all but forgotten Paula's attitudes toward the homeless. "Well, yes, I do feel compassion for the poor and homeless in general."

"Let me tell you something. In L.A. and Hollywood we have the same problems they have here—more and more of the homeless hanging out on the streets. The signs they carry asking for work are only ploys to get handouts from—I'm sorry—impressionable people like you. Whatever that old man told you he was doing, even if it was temporarily true, chances are he'll be without a job again. In and out of work, mostly out, is the stereotype for the homeless wherever they are."

This time her words struck a more discordant chord. He responded, "Sometime I'd like to take you down to the Salvation Army homeless center, here in Las Vegas, or in Omaha, or anywhere. Most of the people you'd see there are trying to survive with two strikes against them. I believe the position they're in could happen to anyone."

She shook her head, tsked her tongue, and said, "You mean most of them are just victims? I don't think so. What most of them should do is stop feeling sorry for themselves, stop making excuses, and start acting responsibly."

"I remember you saying something similar that night."

"In my family, Richard, we were all expected to do the best we could in whatever challenges we undertook. It's called work ethic and it helped me get my Hollywood position. I think it's a character trait most of the homeless never had, or if they did at one time, lost it and never seriously tried to recover."

"I disagree with you. I'd say a majority of the homeless have been good, dependable workers and would give anything to be that way again. As for the gentleman downtown, I'm sure he didn't want to ask me for money, but his concerns for the girl overcame his pride."

A part of Richard wanted the disagreement to end, but the verbal fencing and champagne led him down another path. "This is off the subject, but something is bothering me. When you went away last spring, did you feel the same way about me as you do tonight?"

Again she tsked her tongue and shook her head. "Now where is this coming from? I thought we had those matters resolved. I knew I loved you, and I felt miserable, and I've explained the circumstances several times, Richard."

"But in all those months after you left, didn't you think we should spend some time together? I mean, I'm just curious."

"Mr. Weatherford and I talked about those times today. We agreed I had to immediately accept the station's offer and do whatever was required." She reached across the table, took hold of Richard's hands, and said, "Look, we're together now, and remember what we said this afternoon? Those times are gone, forever. Okay?"

As if awakening from a bad dream, he said, "You're right, of course. What happened these past seven months should definitely be a closed door."

"Let's make that a forevermore closed door. I like the song they're playing. Could we dance?"

On the dance floor she put her head on his shoulder, and as the song was ending her eyes lifted to his and she said, "I think we should go back to my place."

Twenty minutes later Richard used her key to unlock the door to her Bellagio suite.

"It's almost half past ten o'clock," she said, "and the fountain show should be starting any moment now." Leaving only the entry light on, she walked over to the television set and turned to the guest service channel. "They televise the show on this channel," she said, "and the musical sound effects are fantastic."

She took hold of his hand, and they walked to the front of the window overlooking the lake. The observation deck below was nearly full, and moments later the fountains erupted into their latest choreographic splendor.

She turned to Richard and placed her arms around his neck as she sighed, "Now at last my life is complete."

Frank Sinatra's voice, filled with tender emotion, and Celine Dion's, just as appealing, added to the splendor:

"When somebody loves you,

It's no good unless she loves you,

All the way,

"Happy to be near you—"

The captivating scene and the voices reminded Richard of the night he and Anita were on the same observation deck, watching the same fountain show, listening to the same lyrics.

Responding to his surging emotions, he removed Paula's arms from around his neck as he said. "I'm sorry, but there is something we need to talk about and it can't wait."

"Richard, what are you doing? What is wrong?"

"What I have to say is important."

"Well then, tell me."

He walked over to the table next to the sofa, turned on the lamp, and turned off the television set.

Without the music his words took on even more meaning, "It concerns someone who means more to me than what's happening here."

Paula walked over so she could look directly into his eyes and responded, "Excuse me?"

"There are some things you should know, Paula."

"You said it concerns someone else? Who is this someone?"

"Her name is Anita."

In a state of shock Paula sat down on the sofa. Looking up at him, she said, "You're telling me you're involved with another woman? Have you completely lost your mind?"

"I'm beginning to wonder."

"Do you realize the gravity of what you've just said to me?"

"To tell you the truth, at this moment I'm not sure of anything."

"How seriously are you involved with this woman?"

"Perhaps more seriously than I realized. Strange as it may sound, I didn't completely realize it until just a few minutes ago. The truth is, I think I love you both."

Paula looked down and said, "I am deeply disappointed, Richard, to say the least. You owe me much better than this."

"Except for a long time we weren't talking, remember? From the moment you left for Hollywood, your main interest was your career, and things that meant a lot to me didn't seem to mean that much to you."

"What about these past two days? I thought we were coming together again."

He sat down next to her and said, "I figured once you and I spent some time together, I'd know exactly how I felt. It just isn't happening."

"How long have you known this person?"

"I met her last June and—"

"You mean you met her, and started caring for her right after I left?"

"No, no, it wasn't like that. I mean, I just met her then. It's a long story, but our paths crossed when she came to Las Vegas for a vacation. Then she came back here to work. You wouldn't believe me if I told you how we met, and it doesn't matter. All I know is one thing led to another, and by the time summer was over we were seeing each other, just as friends in the beginning, but after your Labor Day Vegas cancellation, I wasn't sure how you felt anymore. That's when she and I became more involved."

"Surely you told her about me."

"When we first met, she knew you and I were in love, and—"

"And she didn't honor your sentiments?"

"She did, but it was my fault. I only wanted someone to share some time with, but circumstances kept drawing us closer. She doesn't even know you're here in Vegas."

"What does she do? Where does she work?"

"She's a counselor in a high school."

Paula eyes scanned the ceiling. "A high school counselor? And what does she look like?"

"Well, she's attractive, and very intelligent, and—"

Paula surmised, "And I suppose she became your counselor concerning us."

Richard shrugged. "For a while she did, yes."

Paula rose and walked back to the window. Staring out at the now calm lake surface, she considered her options.

Still sitting on the sofa, Richard said, "I kept thinking you and I would be together as soon as you settled everything in Hollywood. Then we'd pick up where we left off. But a few minutes ago when we were close to making love, it didn't seem right, because I simply can't put aside how much she also means to me."

"I just took it for granted you'd wait for me."

"I'm not saying I've stopped waiting for you, but you put us on hold for a long time."

In anger she stomped her foot. "I'm sick of you constantly dwelling in the past and saying the same things. The station had to take into account my youth and inexperience, and they had to find out if I had the talent and depth for a high-level position. The work I was assigned to was demanding and did not allow for any screw-ups, professional or personal."

As if he hadn't heard, Richard said, "I never expected her to come into my life."

"So that's why Juan was different. And you and your counselor became lovers."

"I didn't say that."

"I know you did. You couldn't have let me go tonight unless something extremely personal was involved. I know you wanted to make love to me."

"I only know I'm in a serious predicament."

His continued confusion was resurrecting her composure. She walked over to him, and when he looked up, she said, "So it's not over between us. You still love me."

"I think I am still in love with you. I know I couldn't wait to see you and be with you. I think I want to see you again tomorrow, maybe even later tonight. No, it isn't over."

"But what about her?"

"Before anything else happens, I have to see her. I want to tell her face-to-face what I just told you."

Paula paused briefly before taking hold of his hands and tugging so he'd rise. Moving very close, she gazed into his eyes and in a feathery calm voice said, "You know how you felt about me these last two days. I want you to go and solve your problem with your, your, whatever she is. Find out which of us really means the most to you."

She put her hands on his shoulders, lifted on her toes, and pressed her lips to his, but not for long before she said, "Good night, Richard."

With that he picked up his raincoat and left.

All the way down the elevator and through the hotel lobby, every attempt at logic and rationalization became entangled in his swirling emotions.

Outside the Bellagio, the earlier relief from the harsh weather had only been the eye of the storm. Now the cold rain had returned, this time joined by blustery winds. He was unaware of the latest forecast of rain changing to sleet and possibly snow, a rare fall occurrence in Las Vegas.

Chapter Forty-one

BACK IN HIS PARIS ROOM, Richard substituted his raincoat and sport coat for a leather jacket. Then he called Anita.

"Rich, it's going on midnight. Your evening must have run late again."

"Sorry I couldn't reach you earlier. All right if I come over? I want to see you."

"Of course, but be careful, the weather's icky."

On the drive to her apartment, wind-driven sleet impaired his vision, and he thought the weather was a match for the way he felt. In his mind images of Anita and Paula vied for contention—first one, then the other, then side by side—each woman smiling confidently. He thought of the latest events and realized that before leaving for Omaha the next day, he would either have won or lost the woman he loved more than anything in the world. A bigger problem loomed; he wasn't sure which woman she was.

He focused on Paula. Like the perfectionist she was, she'd gathered the information she needed, cleverly placed the ball in his court, and made him feel she was confident he'd be coming back to her. Had he never met Anita, he'd still be with Paula, probably making plans for the future.

His focus switched to Anita. *I need to think of the best way to tell her the truth. I'll try to establish some common dialogue, like talk about her dad, or the weather, or about the meetings that didn't take place. Ooops, another lie. Let's see, I could ask her what she thinks of J.D.'s offer. She dislikes him intensely, and maybe that would rankle her enough to get most of the anger out of her system. She doesn't seem to stay upset for very long, so once she calms down, I can ease into the rest of it. I'll just say Paula called unexpectedly and I met with her—at her insistence, of course—but then how will I account for the rest of the time? Goodness, will I be glad when this is over.*

As soon as he parked in front of her apartment, he turned off his cell phone and hastened to her doorstep.

Anita, clad in a knee-length terry cloth robe and white ankle socks, met him at the door and said, "Get inside; that wind is cold!"

"Sorry to be coming over so late, but I wanted to see you."

"I'm glad you finally came."

She took his jacket and hung it in the closet. She'd never seen Richard so flighty as in the last couple of days, but she figured his actions were fallout from his self-described "concentrated sessions with Maxwell Danforth."

"I've missed you these last two days," she continued, then wrinkled her nose before inquiring, "Did you just have something to drink? You smell like champagne."

"I did have a glass a while ago. I've missed you, too."

They sat down on the sofa, and she tucked her legs beneath her. With a dimpled smile she said, "So tell me what's been going on with Mr. Danforth."

Trying to calm his rat-caught-in-a-corner heartbeat, he replied, "Mr. Danforth. Oh yes, well, I'll get to him in a moment, but first something of major importance has happened. I know how you feel about J.D., but I want you to hear about an outstanding offer he's made for me."

Her cute smile switched to an also cute frown. "Forrester has made you an offer? That I *definitely* want to hear about."

"Now please don't let your personal feelings for him influence your opinion, okay? Basically, he thinks we should relocate the Stewart Company central operations to Las Vegas. He wants us to become an integral part of Monte Vista, New Horizon, and Renzcorp. I would still have complete control of the company, of course, and he also wants me to become the resort's chairman of golfing operations."

Her frown changed to an expression of disbelief. "You did say move your company from Omaha to Las Vegas. For God's sake, Richard."

"That's what he's suggesting, but now listen to the details. They're really quite amazing."

Rising to her feet, she crossed her arms as she said, "I realize from the way you're talking, you didn't, but no matter how amazing the details may be, you should have instantly told him, 'No!'"

Weary from the events of the night and not expecting such an immediate negative reaction, he told himself to stay relaxed and think clearly. "I told him I'd think it over, but—"

"What is there to think over? Purely and simply, such a move would be ridiculous. Even I, an outsider, can see that."

"Now don't jump to conclusions. Why should this be so personal to you? A generous offer from someone like James Forrester deserves at least some degree of consideration. He's done an awful lot for me and our company."

Arms still crossed, Anita began pacing.

Richard also rose and hoping to avoid another interruption he spoke rapidly, "J.D. pointed out it would be easy to relocate, that it's done successfully all the time. The move would go smoothly because his entire corporation would be our support. Our company operations would remain the same, except we'd be bigger and better. Most of our staff who'd be willing to move would enjoy a more pleasant climate, with more to do here in the winter. You know, have fun in the sun. You yourself introduced me to a very wholesome style of living out here. And since you've been here you've learned Vegas is, for the most part, a family city filled with conscientious, upstanding folks."

Anita tsked her tongue and shook her head.

He continued, "Our company would have extraordinary expansion opportunities, and there's something else. As golfing operations chairman, he's offering me a one million dollar salary. That's right, yearly a million bucks."

She stopped pacing and said, "You can't accept such an offer. There are too many reasons why you can't. Your people in Omaha like being right where they are. You're the one who's always said they are the heart and soul of the company. Have you talked to any of them about this? Have you talked to Benjamin?"

Now they were both pacing and in passing barely missed each other.

She said, "Your silence makes me realize you are more than just considering moving, aren't you? And I would imagine without any input from Ben and Mindy. Your Christmas present for them, is it? You said *most* of your staff would be willing to move here. What does *that* mean?"

In the heat of the debate, he'd drifted from his original intent of defusing her anger, and then easing into his rendezvous with Paula.

He answered, "It means those who might choose not to move we would assist in finding similar positions in Omaha." Then he fabricated, "But when J.D. suggested in the future we might consider downsizing through attrition and retirement, I firmly told him I don't believe in downsizing for any reason."

"Oh, that was noble of you. Let me get this straight. You *are* thinking of moving here with *most* of your staff. And to top it off, future downsizing was discussed. What a thoughtful conversation you two must have had."

"I'm just repeating what he said. If you were in the world of business, you would realize an outstanding offer deserves at least some consideration."

"Richard, you can be so dense sometimes."

Side-by-side following her latest declaration, they stopped and established ground zero positions, face-to-face, inches separating their noses.

Thrusting her hands onto her hips, she said in a scratchy voice, "I know the influence Forrester has over you. In essence you're being lured by his materialistic, self-serving enticements. But you're not thinking of your own people; you're thinking only of yourself. You've been away from them too much."

"Hey, in spite of my absences this year, Ben has kept the company running like clockwork."

She turned and began pacing again, this time silently as she sought a sensible response. Finally she said, "I know something related to this. Many of your people in Omaha have been concerned this very thing might happen. I didn't tell you because I didn't think it was a possibility. You have never, *ever* hinted you might move your office staff out here."

"And I'm not saying I would. May I ask how you could possibly know they've been concerned?"

"Mindy talked to me about the possibility the night we were at the Century Club, and she's called me twice since then. She said there'd been talk, or better said deep concern, that there had to be—beyond what you were revealing—reasons for your continuing leaves of absence. That, along with your lessening concerns for the company. And who do you think was most concerned? None other than Ben. That's right, your best friend, and Mindy, of course. They're family, Richard. His dad needs them to stay right where they are. Mindy doesn't think Ken could survive losing them and his grandchildren. She thinks Ben will resign if you decide to move out here. You could lose him. Is this getting through to you?"

Straying further from his intended strategy, Richard brusquely replied, "I don't appreciate you talking behind my back, and I'd like to hear what you just said from Ben himself."

His growing feisty rebuttals further exacerbated her ire. She turned on her heel to face him again, and in a raspy voice she said, "So I'm making this up, lying to you?"

"I'd say exaggerating."

"So you are insinuating I'm exaggerating. Have you completely lost your mind? I can tell from this conversation you are not yourself. Something's very wrong here. How could you even consider Forrester's stupid idea?"

Slightly amused by the night's second assertion he'd lost his mind, he put his hands on her shoulders and said, "Anita, *please* calm down. The answer to your first question is I haven't lost my mind. As for future expansion, the company would probably be financially better off if we were to centralize from here. And the job he's offering me is, I must admit, at least thought-provoking. The answer to the second question is that I haven't decided to do anything. But you know, thinking back on the big blizzard that hit Omaha last week, and knowing on that day they were playing golf out here? Well, it gave me another reason to think about it."

She removed his hands from her shoulders and moved back a step. "You've always been proud of the integrity your father established within your company. And your people have always trusted in you to do the same. If you move out here on the whim of a big-time Vegas promoter, you'll take away more than you've ever given them."

"Anita, I think we need to—"

"Are you not who I thought you were? You're rich, but you want to be richer? Would you become a sacrosanct, inconsiderate, know-it-all executive of the twenty-first century? Would you sacrifice your own people's trust and put profits ahead of their happiness?"

"It's not as if it's taking place tomorrow, and you're being unreasonable. I just wanted your unemotional opinion."

The trigger of her temper began clicking faster. She threw her hands into the air and fired back, "You know what you need to do? Get off your exalted high horse. It's the season for giving, so try to think of someone besides yourself for a change. Think of helping, not *hindering* good people."

Before he could answer, she continued, "You were right a while back when you said you shouldn't be considered in the company of people like your father or Ben. I think it's time you personally volunteer for a noble cause, *Mr.* Stewart. You talk a lot, but only once have I seen you personally pitch in and truly work on behalf of others—on Thanksgiving Day, just that one time. Well, do everyone a favor. Go and play your stupid trombone in the Las Vegas Salvation Army band. March in a parade for the poor you claim to feel so much compassion for."

He grinned and said, "Did you say play my trombone in the Salvation Army band? As a matter of fact, they don't have a marching band. I asked your father and he said they have a music department, but not a marching band, at least not this year."

"Yes, they do," she said. "I've seen them marching in parades—the Salvation Army band—navy blue uniforms, hats, everything."

Capitalizing on what he hoped might become a catching point of humor, he said, "Well, at least there's no marching band here in Vegas. So I would, but I can't do what you're advising."

Again he put his hands on her shoulders, but not amused with his simplistic sidetracking, she pushed them away, and said, "I'm making a valid point, and you're mocking me."

Her uncompromising rebuttals were like increasingly stiffer jabs to his weakening patience.

There was a moment of festering silence until without forethought he said, "Not everyone agrees with you. Paula Summers thinks J.D.'s proposal has some merit." No sooner had the words left his mouth than he wanted to reach out and retrieve them before they reached her ears.

Her face went blank. "Did you say Paula Summers? How did she get into this? Did you call her and ask her opinion about such an important company matter?"

"Annie, stop this."

"Don't familiarize with me over this. Anita is my name."

The cat partly out of the bag, he tried to cover his tracks. "I merely asked her what she thought of J.D.'s proposal. She thought it deserved serious consideration, which makes sense to me."

"And who is she anyway, some kind of a business genius? I suppose someone as self-centered as she is would think such a stupid, greedy move was just great. But worse than that, I cannot believe you called her. That *completely* blows my mind."

Anita's flashing emerald eyes and parted lips reminded him of the way she looked the night of her MGM fight. Standing nearly a foot taller, he wanted to pull her close and comfort her as he did back then. The problem was that on this night her combativeness was aimed directly at him.

"I did not call her. She called me and said she wanted to see me. I felt I owed her a friendly, casual meeting, and one of the reasons I came here was to tell you that I have seen her."

"So you knew you were going to see her and you didn't tell me? Explain *that*!"

"No big deal. She wanted to tell me about her new job and so forth. Before I knew you, she and I were about to be engaged, remember?"

"You're saying you owed *her*? What about *me*? What about *us*?"

"That had nothing to do with it."

She blew a sarcastic hiss followed by, "And when did all this take place?"

He shrugged and shook his head to minimize the importance of the meeting. "Yesterday, and I saw her a while today, but trust me, they were just casual, friendly meetings." Quickly he decided not to reveal any more, especially that he'd left Paula only an hour before.

"And all that song and dance about you being tied up, and you and Juan having a handball match, and the dinner engagements with Maxwell Danforth, all of it out-and-out deception, because you wanted to see her this weekend, and you blatantly lied to me?"

Feeling as if he was stranded in a swarm of angry yellow jackets, Richard nonetheless realized her accusations were stingingly on target. He tried to stabilize his fleeting thoughts. *Continue lying rather than aggravate her more.* Lifting his palms, he said, "Look, Mr. Danforth was here. After this afternoon's resort meeting, she called me again. Juan's friends had to cancel our handball match, so I agreed to see her. I only did that because you'd already made plans."

Determined to pry open the black box of his mind, she forged on, "Don't lie to me, Richard. Where did you see her?"

"Well, she was here on assignment and stayed at the Bellagio. After she called Friday, we met there for lunch and we just talked."

Anita's voice became strangely calm. "Did you tell her about us?"

"I did tell her about you and me, not everything of course."

"You saw her, took her to lunch, and told her just a little about us? Did you tell her we've been making love since last summer? And you saw her both days, didn't you? And I was right. There were no Maxwell Danforth meetings at all, were there? Now I know why you kept calling me 'your friend' in Omaha. How disgusting."

"Anita, let me explain."

"And you went other places, didn't you?"

"Well, yes, we did go to a couple of places, just to talk some more. As I said, they were entirely innocent conversations, believe me."

"At what other places did you talk—at your place, at her place?"

He shook his head. "No, not at my place."

"So you were at her place. And did you make love to her? Damn you, Richard."

"No, I did not make love to her. I told her I was thinking of you, and I had to leave because I wanted to see you right away."

Anita's expression went frigidly blank. She walked to the closet and yanked his leather jacket from the hanger. With dangerous finality she said, "I've heard enough. Take your jacket. You have to leave."

Moving back a step, he refused his jacket, and said, "Please let me explain what *really* happened. Don't let the night end like this."

"No further explanations are necessary. We'll talk tomorrow. Good night!" She threw the jacket directly into his chest and face.

Flinging the jacket over his shoulder, he opened the door and said, "Don't listen to me then!"

She slammed the door hard behind him and seconds later she heard the MKS engine rev and tires squeal. Racing into the bedroom, she threw herself onto the bed and covered her face with her hands. Anita Stevens hadn't cried like that since she lost her best friend Paige.

Chapter Forty-two

OUTSIDE THE FICKLE STORM SYSTEM had moved on, and now stars were peeking through the last separating clouds. As for Richard, his thinking processes were oblivious to the weather or his excessive speed. His plan to glide into the soft-landing explanation his master plan called for had detonated—all of his strategies detonated and in a shambles. Juan's insight had been as precise as an F-16 laser strike.

Seeking some kind of catharsis to calm his emotions, by habit he turned the radio to his favorite FM station, but the music was ineffectual. All he could think about was his confrontation with Anita. Then it struck him head-on. *Since the moment I saw her tonight, all that mattered to me was how I could protect her from being hurt, even though it meant lying to her again. Anita is the woman I love. Anita, and Anita alone!*

When he reached his Paris room, he noticed the telephone light flashing. Hoping it was her, he checked the message and instead listened to Paula's voice saying, "Richard, I tried your cell, but you didn't answer. Call me as soon as soon as possible, no matter how late."

It was the only message, and more than ever he wanted to talk to Anita. He figured because she hadn't called she must still be very upset. *I'm sure it will be better reaching her first thing tomorrow.* He went into the bedroom and without undressing stretched out on the bed. No sooner had he closed his eyes than a tidal wave of stress and fatigue overwhelmed his consciousness.

At 7:30 in the morning the telephone on the dresser awakened him.

"It's me," Paula said. "Did I wake you?"

He cleared his throat and said, "It's all right. I'm glad you called."

"Adam and Curt from the station stopped by shortly after you left. They didn't have any luck gambling downtown, so they decided to come out here and asked me to join them. After they left, I couldn't reach you, and I couldn't sleep because all I could think about was what happened last night." In a sarcastic tone she added, "Have you talked to your counselor, friend, lover, whatever she is?"

"I did talk to her last night, and I've made up my mind about what has to happen between us, I mean you and me."

"You've made up your mind?"

"I wanted to tell you over breakfast, but maybe this is better. I'm afraid, Paula, whatever we once had can't be anymore."

After a moment of silence she said, "You're making up your mind rather quickly, aren't you? Have you completely lost your senses?"

Third time my sanity's been challenged. "To tell the truth, I think I have. Please believe me—and I say this with a sense of loss for me and deep respect for you—after I saw Anita last night I realized how much I love her."

"So you left here and went directly there."

"I had to see her right away, to tell her I had not been truthful about seeing you."

"Richard, you've been under a lot of pressure these past few days, and it's understandable you're confused. You used to say fate brought us together, and I know you were right. Do you remember how you felt the nights we made love? Well, if we'd made love last night, I don't think we'd be having this conversation."

He tried a new approach. "If you think I don't feel stupid, like an idiotic imbecile, you're wrong. Anita told me that's what she thinks of me, except in more candid terms. I'm in agreement with her, but I love her."

"So you two had a fight. That could explain why you feel the way you do. When you fight with someone you *think* you love, that person can dominate your emotional reactions."

"Whatever the explanations may be, I can't get her out of my mind."

"As I said, this is all happening very quickly. You may change your mind in a day or two. It happens all the time." Following another pause, she continued, but this time in a teary voice, "I don't want to love anyone but you, and I don't want you to make a terrible mistake for both of us."

"Believe me, Paula, I am deeply sorry."

"So you're throwing aside the way you felt about us yesterday and the day before?"

"As I indicated, I thought I was giving what you and I once had a chance, but now I can see my thinking was was short-sighted and inconsiderate of everyone. Call me selfish and deceitful. No, I'm worse."

"Listen to me, Rich. If I'd been here these past few months, *none* of this would have happened. She had the advantage of being with you when I couldn't be."

He had to smile at the irony of her reasoning. "There's no doubt you are right about that."

Attempting to hold on to something hopeful, her voice steadied. "If you change your mind—today, tomorrow, whenever it happens—call me right away, and I promise you, I will forget any of this ever happened."

"Thank you for the thought. Now listen to me. I'm amazed at what you've achieved, and I'm confident you are going to have a highly successful career. You deserve it. You're a beautiful woman with exceptional talents. I knew you were going to the top of your profession the first time we met."

After he bade her farewell, she said, "I won't say goodbye, because I don't believe this is goodbye."

"May I say again, I'm sorry."

Seconds later, with the click of her phone, he felt a sense of regret, but also one of relief.

Figuring early on a Sunday morning Anita would still be in her apartment, he called but only a busy signal greeted him. Ten minutes later, same result. *She must be talking to someone for a very long time. Maybe her dad!*

Richard tried Robert's number but had to leave a message. "Call me as soon as possible. It is urgent."

He turned the television to CNN Sports where three morning commentators were previewing the afternoon's NFL games. Completely disinterested and seeking escape from the serenity of his room, he headed downstairs for breakfast.

Just outside J.J.'s Boulangerie he tried Anita again and finally was able to leave a message. "I positively have to talk to you. I'm leaving Vegas this afternoon, so call me as soon as you can. Thanks. I love you."

At ten o'clock his cell phone chimed.

"Hi, Rich, it's Rob returning your call."

"Rob, have you heard from your daughter this morning?"

"Not yet. She said yesterday she was hoping you two would be going to church this morning. You do remember her birthday is next week. Because everyone's been so busy, I suggested we postpone the party for another week."

"Her birthday! I completely forgot. If she calls you, tell her I want to be in touch with her because it is very important. I'm leaving for the airport about one o'clock, but tell her she can reach me on my cell phone."

"So there's a problem?"

"We had an argument, a serious one in fact, and I want to talk to her before I leave."

"A *serious* argument you say. Hmmm, well, that's too bad. I'll try to find her."

With so much to do in Omaha, Richard knew he couldn't return to Vegas until Friday. And if Anita wouldn't answer his calls, they would be out of touch until then. He figured what it all came down was that even if her temper had abated, her disgust and conviction must have remained.

The possibility of canceling his flight until Tuesday crossed his mind. Just as quickly he dismissed the idea. He knew it was absolutely necessary for he and Benjamin to approve the final Christmas promotions no later than Monday. Their other major task would be to begin planning for the firm's biggest social event of the year, the Stewart Company Christmas party.

An hour later he called Robert again. "I'm sure you would have called if you'd heard from her, but I thought I'd check."

"I'm getting only her voice mail. Sorry."

"When you do reach her, tell her if nothing else to call me at home this evening. Tell her I—never mind. Just tell her it's essential that we talk."

"I'll take care of it, Rich, but aren't you overreacting a bit? Everyone has a little spat now and then."

Richard waited for her to call even as he was boarding the jetliner. Following its takeoff, the pilot circled the city so that passengers would have a clear view of downtown and the Strip. Richard wished he were somewhere down there with the woman he loved, or perhaps exploring in the surrounding mountains, anything just to be with her.

He recalled her saying she planned to stay in Vegas over Christmas. *If all else fails, I'll see her before then, even if I have to camp on her doorstep.* A positive thought was that so far Robert was supporting him. The optimism dimmed as he realized her father had not yet heard her version of the confrontation.

If he thinks I've been unfaithful to his daughter, I'll lose his respect too.

Chapter Forty-three

ALTHOUGH OMAHA HAD BEEN HIT with its first major blizzard of the season, the city was recovering quickly, and the snowfall blanketing the hillsides and valleys provided a cozy holiday season background. In the downtown area and within mall complexes, wreaths, bells, and resplendent Christmas displays mellowed the crisp December air. Front yards were embellished with Nativity scenes, Santa Clauses, reindeer and sleighs. Many fir trees—large and small, outdoors and indoors—were circled with sparkling lights, and church bells and choir voices resonated through normally quiet neighborhood settings.

In the last several years the Stewart family Christmas celebration had gradually diminished. A couple of the elderly had passed on, and other relatives had moved to other parts of the country. Much of the spirit was rekindled when Elizabeth's family came to town, but this year they would be with her husband's folks in Baltimore.

When Richard arrived home Sunday evening, he went directly to the family room. Without turning on the lights, he activated the fireplace with a remote control. With his cell phone he pressed Anita's number, and to his surprise she answered.

"Anita, thank goodness! I need to talk to you."

"About what, Mr. Stewart?"

The sound of her voice, though igniting his spirit, was anything but receptive.

"About everything that happened over the weekend, about how sorry I am for the misunderstanding I've caused."

"Misunderstanding did you say?" She tsked her tongue, sighed in disgust, and said, "I'm very busy tonight, and I'm expecting a call from home at any—"

"I know, honey, but just give me—"

The line clicked, and she was gone. Hopeful there had been an unintended disconnection, he tried her number again but got a busy signal. He couldn't believe he'd finally reached her and she wouldn't allow him even a few moments. Apparently she'd made up her mind to reject any and all of his reconciling attempts.

He sat on the sofa in front of the fireplace and tried to think logically. He remembered her saying when she left her former husband he tried several times to reconcile, but she would have none of it. "Actually I wanted to celebrate because Danny boy was out of my life forever." Now Richard feared it was he who was in the same position as Danny boy. *She's probably already thinking of me as Richie boy.* Trying to concentrate, he took a deep breath and closed his eyes. *There must be some way I can get through to her, some way to convince her she's misjudged my intentions.*

His conscience, nearly forsaken since Paula's first call, joined his mainstream thinking. *The fact is, Anita's assumptions are all too close to the truth. Admit it. In those two days you desired Paula more than once. And you also—*

A spirit of hope intervened. *The most important thing is that you did not make love to her when she wanted you to.*

But his conscience spoke again. *Ah, but with all your other lies, Anita will never believe you.*

In spite of the recurring dead ends, a spirit of hope pressed on in search of some way to connect with her. He recalled a lesson learned from his Creighton law professor. *In a critical case you think you are losing, rid yourself of the mistakes, pursue every positive angle, and remember to act on instinct. Never hesitate in a crisis when a positive instinct appears. No matter how contrary the odds may seem, grasp on to it and go where it will lead you.*

So far the only solution to his problem, trying to connect with her by telephone, had been hopeless. *What I need is an instinct.*

Attempting to arouse some kind of a slumbering instinct, he leaned forward and pressed his fingertips to his temples. Memories drifted to recent events—Thanksgiving Day, Paula's call, the two days they spent together, and the fight with Anita. The last recollection was the most vivid of all.

He rose and walked across the room before pausing in front of the walkout window panels overlooking the patio. Opening all channels of positive thinking to *desperation search*, he gazed out at the snow-glistening evergreen bushes and then into the star-filled night.

Suddenly from out of nowhere a bright instinct appeared. Like a fiery meteor the instinct image streaked across the deep blue sky before bursting into a magnificent star.

Quickly his mind grasped on to the instinct and held on tight. In a likeness of James Forrester, he struck his fist into his palm and said, "That's it! It may be a long shot, but it surely is worth a try."

The next day following a staff conference filled with Christmas promotional planning, Benjamin joined Richard in his office. Their new responsibility was to organize plans for the Christmas party. The event would bring together employees and families from every Stewart outlet.

Richard was obviously in a super mood when he said, "Ben, we need to make this year's celebration one our people will never forget. During this morning's meeting we learned our early Christmas sales are pointing to a record-wrecking fourth quarter."

Benjamin leaned back in his chair and nodded. "People seem to be in a terrific buying mood. I think they're going through relief reactions following the blizzard."

Richard also leaned back as he added, "Whatever the dynamics are, this organization is on fire. That's why this year won't be like the others. You know, getting together for dinner, the bonus checks, and a few prizes. This year we're going to dig deeper.

"First of all, Christmas is on a Sunday, so tell everyone they won't be working Friday or Saturday. On Christmas Day we'll celebrate at the Happy Hollow Club. We'll need lots of space, including fun and recreation areas for kids of all ages. The party will start with afternoon socializing in the ballroom, and then around five o'clock dinner will be served."

Benjamin had in the past cautioned Richard regarding "overzealous monetary expenditures." This time the vice president realized his best friend was not about to be denied. With a nod and a smile, Ben said, "I'm sure our people will appreciate such an arrangement."

"And I want The Improv to provide the music. Contact Sherrie and Alonzo and ask them to round up as many of our group as they can. We're going to give our folks a real holiday musical treat. During the afternoon they'll provide the traditional Christmas songs, and later in the ballroom the music will be for dancing and more socializing. You know, Ben, we should have thought of something like this years ago."

Still smiling, Benjamin shook his head, but Richard was far from finished.

"Now to the nuts and bolts. We'll want to have exceptionally nice gifts for all the younger folks—tricycles and bicycles, stuff like that. Staff members will draw for new televisions, and laptops, and other major ticket items. I'll let you handle the details. Just be very generous. And while they're enjoying their desserts, I want every employee to be delivered a bonus check for a thousand dollars."

No longer smiling, Benjamin rose to his feet and intentionally dropped his clipboard. "You mean across the board? That's twice as much as last year, Rich."

"And we're making substantially more than we did last year, Ben."

"Aren't we getting a little carried away here? Two work days off, an expensive country club party, $95,000 in bonus checks—not to mention thousands more in gifts?"

"Nah, we're fine. We're showing our people the kind of respect they deserve."

Benjamin picked up his clipboard and sat back down. "As long as you're feeling so generous, why not toss in a family vacation to Disneyland or tickets to the Super Bowl?"

"Hey, I like both of those. Put them down for grand-prize drawings."

"What? Are you're absolutely sure about all this?"

"And as long as we're on the subject, you personally will be receiving a $5,000 bonus check."

"You recently gave me a raise."

"I know, but now don't get too excited. There's a catch to all this."

"For a five-G bonus, on New Year's Day I'd join the polar bear club and jump into the Mighty Mo."

"That I would love to see. Just be sure when the cameras start rolling, you're wearing a large-monogrammed Stewart Company sweatshirt." In a more serious mood, Richard leaned forward and folded his hands on his desktop. "Now for the catch. Tomorrow I'm going to Vegas, perhaps for all of December. If things come together as I'm hoping they will, you will be the party's master of ceremonies."

"You're leaving already? And you're going for the entire month? And you won't be here for the party? It would be the first time you've ever missed."

"It all depends on what happens out there. Hopefully I'll be in the process of preparing an agenda for a venture which will tremendously benefit a whole lot of people."

Benjamin frowned as he said, "A new venture? You know, Rich, I've been somewhat concer—"

"Ben, don't worry about my going to Vegas."

"To be honest with you, I have been concerned and have been meaning to ask. You aren't by any chance considering—"

"I think I know what's on your mind. This venture has nothing to do with our company. Just remember, I will always consult with you regarding any decision that affects the firm's future. And you can be sure, I would never proceed without your 100 percent approval. You and I love living in Omaha, don't we? Need I say more?"

Noticeably relieved, Benjamin said, "So you'll be spending Christmas with Anita, right?"

"I'd certainly like that, but—"

"This is getting ver-ee seer-ee-us. Well, just to let you know, Mindy and I think she's quite a lady. Please tell her we're looking forward to seeing her again."

"Yeah, well, whatever." Hoping to avoid any further references to Anita, Richard continued, "If the venture—actually venture is not a good word. Let's call it a project. If the project I have in mind works, there'll be nonstop work for me out there."

"I assume your project has some connection with Monte Vista?"

"Nah, no connection with Monte Vista at all. I hope to be able to tell you what I'm planning soon, but my initial objective is to find out if I can even get my idea off the ground."

When Ben left, Richard called J.D. in Vegas. The discussion lasted forty-five minutes.

Next he called Robert, who answered, "Rob McGuire at your service for the future Monte Vista family resort."

"Rob, it's Rich. Have you heard from your daughter?"

The line was silent.

"Rob?"

"Yeah, sorry, I did talk to her last night, and now I'm trying to think of some euphemisms on your behalf."

"Skip the euphemisms and give it to me straight. What did she say?"

"Well, she's *really* disgusted with you. Now she's making arrangements to go back to Cincinnati for Christmas. She was sorry she couldn't be with me, but was too upset to stay here."

"What? She's going back there? Damn it. I'm sorry, Rob, it's all my fault. I know she was looking forward to spending the holidays with you."

"She was planning to all right, but she said she wanted to take no chances of seeing you. She said you helped her realize how much she missed her family and friends back home." With his voice rising in a mixture of confusion and agitation, he added, "What exactly did you do to her, Rich?"

Richard felt at least one respite of relief because obviously she still hadn't told her father her version of the fight. Now he could reveal the circumstances in his own way. "It was a tremendous misunderstanding. She thought I was indiscreet with—you remember Paula?"

"Of course, Blondie, Mystery Woman."

"Right, Mystery Woman. She came to Vegas last Friday, and I did see her, in fact more than once. It was stupid, thoughtless of me not to inform Anita, but trust me, nothing of a serious nature happened. I'll tell you everything when I see you. Does she always get this mad?"

"I can't truthfully say, because I haven't had any experience with her when she's really upset. When women in our family lose their Irish tempers, they've been known to say strange, insane things, and they are also apt to throw anything within reach. After the smoke clears, though, they usually regret it all and become marshmallow sweet. But last night she was determined enough to give me a parting message for you. She said not to come near her and not to contact her because you and she were history, period."

"Great, gave me all that leeway, huh?"

"What worries me the most is she might decide to take a job back in Cincinnati for the second semester."

"She might take a job there?"

"Well, guidance counselors do take maternity leaves, so if someone is—"

"All of this seems impossible."

"It certainly doesn't look good. We have to do something, Rich, and fast."

"Do you know which airline she's flying?"

"She said American."

"After the flare-up we had, I guess I knew something like this might happen. Listen, I'm returning to Vegas tomorrow, and I may need your help with a new project I'm planning. If everything goes as I'm hoping and praying it will, there will be a mountain of work ahead for both of us."

"A new project did you say?"

"I'll explain when I see you."

Chapter Forty-four

THE NEXT MORNING RICHARD'S VEGAS-BOUND 737 soared like an eagle over the majestic Rocky Mountains. He could no longer be despondent about what happened with Anita. He was embarking on what could be the most important mission of his life: a mission that would tax the limits of his physical and mental capacities; a mission that would require untold numbers of personnel; and finally, a mission that might go absolutely nowhere.

If he could get the right support for his project, for the entire month he'd be attempting to create a series of events that, as he told Benjamin, could tremendously benefit "a whole lot of people." So there was neither time nor space for despondent thoughts. There could only be the inspirations of imagination, diligence, and heaven-sent good luck.

As soon as he entered the McCarran terminal, Richard called Madelline to confirm his afternoon appointment with J.D., potentially the project's most important center of influence. Then he called Robert.

"Where is your daughter? What are you hearing from her?"

Robert took a deep breath. "Okay, she called this morning. She said she won't be back until the day before school reconvenes after New Year's. I told her how I wanted to celebrate Christmas with her, but to no avail. I even tried to sneak in a positive word for you, but where you're concerned, she still wants to be totally incommunicado. She doesn't want me meddling, and she said she hates your guts."

"If you're upset with me, by the way, I understand. But I want you to keep meddling, in subtle disguise that is. We don't want to lose her, do we?"

"For sure not." Although he was concerned with the circumstances surrounding his daughter's anger, Robert also felt deeply about his ties to Richard. He wasn't about to allow something he didn't understand to permanently damage their relationship. "Sorry, Rich, guess I'm talkin' off the top of my head."

"It's okay. I want you to call her again and plead with her. Tell her how lonely you are. Say you want her to come back a few days after Christmas. Tell her since you won't be able to see her Christmas Day, it would mean a lot to you, because for a long time you've been planning something *very* special for her.

"I went ahead and tentatively made a reservation for her with American Airlines the morning of the twenty-ninth. If you can convince her to come back then, I'll call the airlines to confirm. But it will have to be done today. Tell her not to worry about the reservation change because *you* are taking care of everything. It may be just enough to convince her she owes you that much. Do your best?"

"I'll try, but what good will it do if she won't see you?"

"You'll be with her, and if nothing else happens that's reason enough. I do know one thing. The project I have in mind is the kind of stuff your daughter takes to heart."

"I hope so."

Richard's afternoon meeting in J.D.'s office lasted ninety minutes. From her adjoining office Madelline could hear the men's voices rising and lowering with numerous intervals of laughter tossed in. She reasoned it had to be a highly thought-provoking discussion.

When the men finished the discussion and moved to the outer office, J.D. said, "We'll do everything possible to make it work, Rich."

He then summoned Cindy and Madelline into his office to tell them of their assignments in Richard's newly named O/R Project.

Richard, meanwhile, went to his office to begin outlining plans for a new Web site. His purpose was to initiate what would become a steadily growing network of O/R contributors.

Late in the afternoon Robert called to say, "I have the latest concerning Anita. Seems there's been an encouraging change in plans."

So he could hear the results face-to-face, Richard requested they meet at Starbucks just up the street from Robert's apartment. There over their regular coffee and coke drinks Robert delivered one of his patented run-on reviews of the latest events.

"I told her how I was thinking of all the Christmases I'd spent without her. You know, the old song-and-dance routine you told me to use. And I said I wanted her to come back here a few days after Christmas, because I'd still be in the spirit. I said I had something very special planned, and I'd bought her a nice gift, and my tree would still be up. All that kind of stuff.

"Then I told her I'd already made arrangements with the airlines for her to come back on the twenty-ninth. What a liar I am. I'm getting to be like you. Sorry, but if a lie is for a good cause—as you and I have always said—what the hell. Anyway, she seemed impressed with my diligence and finally gave in."

Richard's face lit up. "You mean she's coming back here on the twenty-ninth?"

"Yup, she sure is."

"Excellent!"

Richard immediately opened his cell phone and called American Airlines to confirm the reservation. Then he informed Robert, "She'll be leaving on a morning flight and will arrive here around 2:30."

"Good. I told her not to make any plans for the late afternoon and evening."

"I owe you for this, Rob."

Robert's happy expression faded to one of concern. "Hold on, that's the good news. She wanted to know if you were in any way connected with her coming back early, and I told her no, for sure not. Lied to my own daughter again. Jeeez! She said a while back you'd been calling her, to try to change her mind, and you'd been persistent. She made it very clear I had better not intervene. I could lose my daughter over this, you know."

"Don't worry, I'll be careful. So she said I'd been trying to change her mind, huh?"

"About wanting it over with between you two. She said you were being unfair to the people who work for you. Specifically, you were thinking of relocating your company here and hadn't been up front with them. Now level with me, how much of what she's saying is true?"

"Okay, first of all I told her J.D. was offering me some outstanding incentives if I'd move our central operations to Las Vegas. I said generous offers from a powerful man like him you don't just dismiss. As for not telling my people back home, I'd only known myself for a couple of days. I told her I just wanted to know what she thought of the offer, but everything I said seemed to upset her."

"Yeah, she didn't buy any of it. She said you were trying to portray an image of not having made up your mind to relocate, but you had either done so or were close to it. Now tell me about Mystery Woman. God, that really set her off."

"I'm more guilty there, Rob, than I indicated before. As you know, I was in love with Paula not long ago, but then I fell in love with Anita. I just didn't realize how much she meant to me until everything came to a head. It all started when Paula wrote to me and said she wanted to come to Vegas to see me. I wanted to see her too, and in fact I planned for us to be together most of the weekend. I lied to Anita about my weekend obligations, and when she found out she was furious. As the story unraveled, she assumed I must have had intimate relations with Paula."

"Did you?"

"We hugged and kissed a few times, and we danced once. Otherwise no, absolutely not. Before that could happen, I told her I was confused, and I had to see Anita because I wanted to tell her everything I'd done."

"I believe you, but remember when I told you a McGuire female can lose her temper uncontrollably, but usually will recover quickly? I don't think that would be the case if Anita thought you'd deceived her. As we know, she's already had one unhappy experience."

"I made some big mistakes, but I love Anita deeply."

"Good. I know it must be difficult for you, but for now let's put aside the fact she's so upset. Tell me more about this new project you're planning."

For the next hour Robert listened with growing excitement as Richard described the major facets of the O/R project.

"What a miraculous event it would be," Rob said, "if you can pull it off, that is. You'll need a lot of people to make it work and is there time?"

"By all means personnel and time are of the essence. With less than a month of preparation, I know it sounds impossible, but considering we're in Las Vegas, and knowing what can happen in this town when the right people are involved, I think it has a chance. Two things to remember. From every conceivable angle, this happens to be the perfect time of the year for what O/R will require. And consider this, James D. Forrester, right person number one, has offered his full-fledged support and influence."

"You couldn't ask for more, that's for sure. But I don't see what all this has to do with Anita."

"I can't tell you exactly because I haven't worked everything out. For now I just want her here with you on the twenty-ninth. With her in mind I also want you to help me with a sidebar strategy to the main event."

Later when Richard returned to his room, a single call from Paula was on the answering machine.

"Hi, I'm back in Hollywood. I wasn't sure if you'd want to speak directly with me yet, so I decided to leave you with this: I hope you've been thinking seriously about us, and if you're feeling differently than you did, I want you to come here next weekend so we can start all over. Call me tonight."

Her message surprised him. He had assumed that with her pride she'd probably already made up her mind to forget him. Whatever, he had no intention of calling her back.

The next day he and Robert proceeded with but one common goal—to do everything possible to make the project a living reality. With alacrity—minute by minute, hour by hour, day by day—they were on their phones, on their computers, and driving all over town for conferences. Thanks to J.D.'s connections and influence, they traveled to appointments made at city hall—the mayor's office, the police and fire departments, the department of public works, and the office of special events. They went to businesses and several city high schools where they conferred with school officials. Richard was the spokesman, and Robert took notes and helped answer questions.

Each morning they were in J.D.'s office to discuss current progress and assignments. Once again thanks to J.D. the men met with front office executives at the major Strip hotels—Circus Circus, Wynn/Encore, Treasure Island, The Venetian, Mirage, and so on down the Strip. Next came the downtown hotels—Binion's, the Golden Nugget, the Four Queens, Fitzgerald's, and the rest. They went to the Rio and the Palms. Outside the main peripheries they visited with key spokespersons at Sam's Club, South Point, the Palace Stations, and the Sun Coast.

J.D.'s message to his entire New Horizon staff was unequivocal. "Until you hear otherwise, everyone will be concentrating on O/R and O/R alone." He personally called into service his fifteen-member Monte Vista Committee, Sam Beesley, and key spokespersons for the Monte Vista construction development.

And so it went. During the next two weeks the response and momentum on all fronts were accelerating beyond what either Richard or J.D. had envisioned.

A week before Christmas Robert informed him that Anita had departed for Cincinnati.

Briefly worried, he asked, "She hasn't changed her mind about coming back early, has she?"

"Not yet. She should still be coming back, but then again you never—"

"Robert, will you stop being so flexible? Just say she's coming."

"All right, she's coming!"

Two days before Christmas, although most of the project objectives were falling into place, Richard also knew time was swiftly slipping away. That afternoon the men arrived at the Salvation Army homeless center for their final meeting there.

As they were about to enter the Lied building, a homeless man waiting in line for a meal called out to Richard. "Hey, Mister, remember me on Thanksgiving day? We talked about the Super Bowl."

Richard walked over to him, shook his hand, and said, "Sure I remember you, Al. You're the Packers expert."

"You plan to be here on Christmas Day?"

"I will be, and I'm looking forward to hearing your playoff predictions."

"I'll remember to come prepared."

Inside the building Richard and Robert met in an extended session with Major Benson and two other Salvation Army staff personnel.

Saturday at noon more than one hundred O/R contributors and participants gathered in the Versailles Chambers for the project's final meeting. Following a catered lunch and opening remarks from Richard and J.D., the floor was left open for questions and answers. It was four o'clock before the meeting adjourned.

When all the others had left, Richard, Robert, and Madelline sat down with J.D. in his Time-out Corner to reflect on the results. The New Horizon president was beaming.

"Was that a productive session or what? Did you ever see such spontaneous teamwork? And the little gal from Wynn promotions, has she ever been a workhorse. Just one of many, though."

Richard said, "James, we owe our organizational successes more to you than anyone else. With so little time available, only you could have made so many contacts and created so much enthusiasm."

"Nonsense, Rich, this was your baby. My contributions were only as good as our team efforts and the responses of our contributors." Rising from his chair, he continued, "I'm going to have to leave now. Our son Derek is flying in from Boston to join us. If you run into any snags from here on in, don't hesitate to call me. If I don't hear from you, Thursday evening Marjie and I will be on hand to offer our assistance."

Madelline said, "No one in my family is coming here over the holidays, so if you need me these next few days, I'm ready."

Richard gratefully accepted her offer.

Late that afternoon he took his two friends to a swanky Palms restaurant for dinner. In spite of the calm Christmas Eve atmosphere, discussion between the two men flittered around the possibility of last-minute problems.

Finally, Madelline intervened, "Would you two stop worrying? With all your efforts and with so many people on board, everything's going to go as planned. You'll see."

Their final stop was her two-bedroom ranch home in Summerlin. While the three friends were enjoying cups of eggnog, Rob presented

Madelline with a necklace featuring gold strips enclosing three sparkling diamonds. The men had purchased the gift earlier in the day.

"Our way of thanking you," Robert said, "for all you've done this past month."

As J.D.'s assistant, Madelline had enjoyed an interesting and fulfilling career. Since she lost her husband several years earlier, she'd also been lonely. In a year in which guardian angels seemed to have made Las Vegas their convention center city, now it was she who was sure one of them was watching over her.

On Christmas Day the three friends served on the banquet lines at the Owens Avenue Lied center. Although Richard was cheerful to those he was serving, flashbacks of Thanksgiving made him miss Anita more than ever. Several times he looked around the busy dining room, hoping by some miracle she might show up.

During the next three days the men visited every O/R setting and met with each central coordinator and team leader. Late Wednesday afternoon Richard finally realized nothing more could be done.

Chapter Forty-five

ON THURSDAY MORNING, OFFICIALLY O/R Day, Richard was showered and dressed by seven o'clock. He received his first call from Robert.

"I just talked to her and she said she was waiting in the airport to board her flight. There'll be a layover in Dallas, but if all goes well she should be here by 2:30. I told her we'd go to dinner late in the afternoon before taking in the special show. She wanted to know more about it, but I said I wanted it to be a surprise. By the way once she arrives, I probably won't be able to help you very much."

"Don't worry, we're ready to rumble. Just try to get her in a really good mood. Oh, and if you're taking Madelline with you to dinner, remind her not to connect my name with any of the proceedings. Okay, Rob?"

"That I *won't* forget to do. I don't want my daughter leaving on the next flight back to Cincinnati."

"Yeah, I'm afraid that could happen. Anyway, stay in touch to let me know what's going on. Maybe since she's been home, what with the Christmas season and all, just maybe she's had a chance to reconsider our situation. She didn't happen to say anything about me, did she?"

"She did. She said she wasn't hearing from you anymore. 'Thank goodness,' she said, 'and good riddance.'"

While Richard was still finding Rob's forthrightness sobering, at the same time Anita's blunt finalities were becoming somewhat amusing.

With a chuckle he responded, "Well, what can I say?"

"Sorry, but I don't want to build you up for a major letdown."

Anita's flight arrived on time. Soon after Robert met her, she said she wanted to rest at her apartment before going out.

When she inquired about the evening's special event, he responded, "All I'm going to say is, it will be something you will never forget. I'm in a nostalgic mood, so for dinner I'm takin' you to my old workplace at the Golden Nugget. I'll call you again before I pick you up."

As for Richard's afternoon, all he could do was wait and pray. Although never in his life had he worked so relentlessly on a single project, he knew if everything turned out as planned O/R's final outcome would be, in Robert's summation, "nothing short of miraculous."

It was 4:15 when Robert called Anita. "I was going to have Maddy join us for dinner," he said, "but she has something else going on. We'll see her later on for sure. In case you haven't noticed, she and I are very close."

"I have noticed, and I think it's wonderful. Maddy is a lovely person."

"Thank you. Remember now, this is my post-Christmas party planning, so just say yes to everything, okay?"

"Well maybe, go ahead."

"I'm leaving now so we can be at the Golden Nugget by five o'clock. That should be early enough for us to be seated without waiting. Oh, and along with dinner we'll also be ordering some sparkling champagne."

"Father, you can't—"

"Mine will be nonalcoholic, but you can have the real McCoy. It's going to be a little nippy outside for the downtown show, so you'll need something to keep you nice and warm. Also bring along a scarf and a heavier coat."

"You mean your special show is going to be downtown and outdoors?"

"I thought I might have mentioned it this afternoon."

"No, you didn't. What kind of a show would be in the evening and outdoors this time of year?"

"One in which many of the city's most renowned celebrities will be in the spotlight."

She paused in thought before she said, "Why is it I'm skeptical about this special show of yours? Before I went to Cincinnati, I hadn't heard on radio or television anything about a special show. I think I'll drive myself in case I want to leave early. Do you mind?"

"I'd be happy to pick you up, but it's your choice."

"And when will we be exchanging gifts?"

"We'll talk about it over dinner."

"I'm leaving here in twenty minutes then."

When Anita's Camry pulled into the Golden Nugget valet parking, her father was waiting on the adjoining sidewalk. Wearing a red leather coat, a multicolored scarf, and black French heels, she stepped from her car and sent him her prettiest smile.

Feeling like the luckiest man alive for the millionth time since June, he met her halfway and said, "The show starts at 6:30, so we better head straight for the dining room."

The second floor buffet was a cut above—carpet and tile floors, comfortable leather booths, tables with armchairs, and wrought-iron chandelier lamps. Their table overlooked a swimming pool surrounding a glass-enclosed shark tank. The entire atmosphere was, as Robert had said, "a perfect setting for dining pleasure and in-depth conversation."

As they checked out the various food offerings and Anita was filling her plate, he put only sparse helpings onto his, not at all his custom on previous buffet engagements. Her main selections included portions of seafood, potatoes, salads, and vegetables, while he settled for two thin slices of turkey and small portions of macaroni and coleslaw salads.

Back at the table she said, "You've always raved about the great food here."

"For some reason, I'm not very hungry. I can always go back for more."

While she was sampling her selections, he barely nibbled away at his. Apparently more interesting than the food was hearing about her Christmas stay in Cincinnati.

She said she'd seen all of her family except for Travis, who was celebrating the holidays with his wife's relatives in Indianapolis.

Robert said, "You know we've never talked very much about your mother. So tell me, how is she doing?"

"As involved as ever in the church, her bridge club, and the social committee at the country club."

"Sounds like Shelley, all right. Since you and I found each other, thanks to Richard Stewart, has she ever said anything about me?"

Hearing Richard's name touched off a fleeting frown, but Anita shrugged it off. "Yes, she did. The first night I was home, she and I stayed up late and talked and she was curious about your new life. When I told her how well you were doing and how much you enjoyed your work, she seemed content you were, in her words, 'making something of your life.'"

Continuing within the delicate confines of his preconceived strategy, Robert said, "So she's not so upset with me anymore?"

"I don't think so, Father. I told her you blame yourself for what happened back then. I said we all make mistakes and need to be forgiven, and she didn't disagree."

Robert's steel-gray eyes glistened. "Ah, I must say, a thoughtful assessment on your part, my dear. So you think there's a chance she really has forgiven me?"

"I think she accepts things the way they are. When I first came back here last summer for the job, she wasn't at all pleased, but now she doesn't seem so concerned. She definitely didn't think I should leave home a few days after Christmas, but she knows I think for myself."

"It makes me feel good to know she's not still bitter. You know, Annie, I know something relative to this. Although I'm fully aware anything concerning Richard is a touchy subject, may I say something I know about him?"

Anita put down her fork and her expression conveyed an unmistakable red flag warning. In a lower, scratchy voice she answered, "I don't want to talk about him."

"Remember what you said about your mother? I mean, about the need to be forgiven?"

Anita's eyes scanned the ceiling.

Nevertheless, Robert reached deeper into the heart of his strategy. "I talked to Rich concerning you two just a few days ago. He said he'd lost you because of what happened with Paula, how he met with her, and so on."

"Father, I said I don't—"

But Robert interrupted and plodded onward. "She contacted him, and he felt he owed her a face-to-face meeting, because they'd once been, you know, almost engaged."

Anita huffed a sarcastic breath and shook her head.

"Anita, please hear me out. This will just take a minute. He did not—I repeat, did not—make love to her. It didn't take him long to realize he'd made a mistake seeing her at all. He admitted part of his decision to meet with her was not just out of respect, but curiosity also played an important part. He said he hadn't been truthful with you. He said the gist of it was he wanted to find out if he loved her as much as he did you. Now think of it, that's a man telling the truth.

"She meant everything to him before she left for California, and he hadn't seen her since. When they did meet, she made it clear she wanted him back and he was confused. But when all was said and done, he told her he had to see you because he wanted to tell you everything. And when he did see you right after seeing her, he knew how much he loved you and you alone. He was crushed by what happened after that." Looking directly into his daughter's eyes, he said, "Does 'Everyone needs to be forgiven' and 'We all make mistakes' apply where he's concerned?"

Anita's voice remained scratchy. "You're talking about something entirely different, Father. We'd been talking about our own engagement, and he took advantage of my trust. He lied to me and he deceived me. I mean, *really.*" Slowly she added, "I don't feel forgiving. He doesn't have anything to do with you and me being together tonight, does he?"

Fearing she was ready to get up and leave, he said, "No, absolutely not. It's Christmas, the busy season for him, so he's back in Omaha. Listen, I'm sorry for interfering, and whatever you think is fine with me. I only know where I'm concerned he's a good man who loved you very much. And I promise you, that's all I'm going to say about Richard Stewart ever again."

Her irritated expression changed to one of relief as she said, "I hope so."

Quickly he shifted gears. "Now, back to tonight's show. I know you're going to love it, because it's your kind of thing. In about half an hour over on 4th Street, there's going to be a big parade with all the bells and whistles."

"A parade."

"Correct."

"And that's your special show?"

"Special, all right. Think of it as the opening act of a major production, a production dedicated to turning around the lives of the city's poor and homeless. The instigators named it Operation Recovery, O/R for short, and it all came together in just these past four weeks."

Realizing any overtures aimed at helping the less fortunate would make her father happy, she leaned forward and with her eyes searching his, she said, "How intriguing; tell me more."

"Well, the parade starts five blocks south of Fremont Street and will continue all the way to Ogden Avenue. It'll be comparable to a college homecoming—lots of bands, floats, clowns, beautiful girls, the whole shebang. When I said many of the participants will be entertainers from shows around town, I'm talking about dancers, musicians, and showgirls. Even some of the city hall big shots will be in the procession."

"You mean the casino bosses agreed to allow a big parade for the homeless this time of the evening?"

"They sure did, and with little opposition. The cornerstone people in the project reminded them that Thursday is the last evening before the big crowds start pouring in for the New Year's weekend."

Anita recalled, "On the radio coming down the announcer did say something about a parade, but I didn't hear the details. But a parade dedicated to helping the homeless? Who would have thought of that? Did you have something to do with it?"

"No, not me."

"The Salvation Army?"

"Not them either. As soon as I heard about it, I offered my services and was able to play a small part, but that was all. But listen to what else is going on. Where the parade ends, the city has cordoned off Ogden from 4th Street to Casino Center until ten o'clock. In the middle of the street there will be three large tents where volunteers will be providing the needy—hopefully a great many of them—with truckloads of new merchandise like clothing, blankets, and lots of daily necessities. But that's just to get their attention."

Anita asked, "How were the organizers able to get so much merchandise?"

"Most of the stuff came from retail stores that donated articles targeted for after-Christmas sales. But much more important than the gifts, inside the tents there'll be volunteers registering people for future job placement classes.

"The goal of Operation Recovery is to pave the way for opening up new educational programs. It will be similar to what the Salvation Army offers. Remember when I told you they helped hundreds of folks find jobs every year? Operation Recovery will be a concerted community effort dedicated to putting thousands into self-supporting positions."

"That would be like the miracle you've talked about."

"Wouldn't it be something? I've heard this town has a lot of spirit, and I've learned these past few weeks how true it really is. Behind the scenes, several bankers and financial planners are organizing programs dedicated to raise money. Community and educational leaders are establishing training programs leading to job opportunities. College students in the city are forming a coalition seeking job openings in and around the city. One of their goals is to connect with the government's infrastructure improvements for street, highway, and bridge building; updating park facilities; school renovations; and expanding community health centers. There will be a lot of workers needed within the program."

Anita said, "It truly is a community effort. But for the training programs they're going to need a lot of instructors."

"Yes they will. To cover that requirement, they're talking to educational specialists and public and private school teachers. And although the instructors will all be volunteers, the response has been overwhelming.

"One of the most pressing concerns was figuring how they could come up with learning centers and living accommodations for so many prospective workers. The city has agreed to open up vacant properties they own for the construction of dormitories and low-cost housing units. That opened the door for volunteer contractors and subcontractors to build not only the living units, but also educational centers with complete classroom facilities.

"Remember when I told you at least 75 percent of the homeless would be working if only the opportunities were there? The project's ultimate goal is to eventually move at least that many into self-supporting occupations. I'm sure you're familiar with Habitat for Humanity, and you've seen the *Extreme Makeover* show on television. That same spirit will be present within Recovery, but on a much larger scale."

"You still haven't said who's responsible for Operation Recovery."

"I can't think of specific names right now, but I do know there were some very important people involved. As I understand it, the idea started when one of the city's most influential promoters was called upon by the primary instigator. The promoter is said to be a very public-spirited and charitable. He became completely intrigued with the idea and offered to do everything within his power to make it happen. He and his business associates contacted all the right parties like the VIP's at resorts, churches, schools, and businesses all over town."

As soon as they finished eating, Robert checked his watch and said, "We better leave if we want to see the start of the parade."

Outside the Golden Nugget they hurried down Fremont to 4th Street. By then large numbers of spectators were gathering on both sides of the street. The evening air was crackling with parade anticipation, and included in the crowd were countless numbers of the poor and homeless—men, women, and children—not afraid to be downtown on this particular night.

On the west side of the intersection twelve rows of bleachers had been set up for members and guests of the O/R planning team. Robert took Anita's hand and they climbed to an opening at the second row from the top.

Minutes later they could hear the revving of engines and the distant sounds of brass, drums, and whistles. Visible to the south were the swerving headlights of police motorcycles urging spectators to move back onto the sidewalks.

Leading the parade was a City of Las Vegas fire truck, its siren echoing through downtown. Firemen aboard seemed as happy and carefree as the children they were tossing candy to.

Next came a forty-two member volunteer citizens' band preceded by flag-waving women dressed in slacks and sweatshirts. Just as the entourage was passing by the planning team bleachers, the musicians, also wearing street clothes, struck up a rousing rendition of "Stars and Stripes Forever."

"They're very good," Anita said.

"They should be. They're citizens and some of the show performers I was telling you about. I guess there wasn't time to come up with uniforms for this particular group."

A yellow convertible carrying a smiling, waving Miss Nevada was next in the procession. Then came two more convertibles carrying city hall and other government dignitaries, also waving and smiling.

One city government official who refused to participate had said, "Some of those homeless people will probably be under the influence and will cause disruption during the parade." He was mistaken. Those attending could best be described as respectful and thrilled.

A prancing majorette paced the superbly trained, purple-and-white uniformed Silverado High School band.

Following them, red-blue-and-gold uniformed members of the VFW marching brigade paraded in perfect cadence. Along the way a couple of their clowns played humorous shenanigans on parade viewers.

Adding to the parade attraction were a variety of colorful floats, compliments of several resorts, schools, and civic organizations. One of their banners read *Our Community, United in Creating Jobs for Everyone.*

Robert turned to Anita and asked, "Glad you came?"

"This parade gives me goose bumps."

To her delight she spotted the approaching orange-and-black uniformed Grant High varsity band.

Scanning their faces, she said, "There's Sally Herseth and Tim Gunderson."

Sally, playing her flute, glanced toward Anita and winked to let her know she saw her.

Twenty minutes into the parade, Robert said, "Remember I said a high-level Vegas promoter and his associates used their connections and influence to get O/R off the ground?"

"You never did say who it was."

"I guess I did say that, but I was just joking. Actually, it was someone we both know—namely, James Forrester from New Horizon."

She turned to her father and said, "Forrester arranged for this?"

Robert cleared his throat. "Ahem, I believe I also indicated he wasn't the *primary* instigator."

"Well then, who was?"

"He happens to be a friend of mine and a former friend of yours—none other than Richard Stewart."

Anita blinked in wonderment as her father continued, "He knew if anyone had the power and connections to make this project work, it was J.D. With him and his New Horizon and Monte Vista teams assisting, more volunteers than you can imagine began putting the pieces together. Just think of where this could lead, Anita. Quite an idea Richard dreamed up, wouldn't you say?"

No longer annoyed at the mention of his name, she said, "Hmmm, so he's responsible for this. Well, he certainly should be—" Suddenly her memory flashed back to the night of the quarrel, the night she told him to think of someone besides himself. "Oh, my God," she sighed.

The parade was almost over except for one final band marching up the street. A lead male star from an MGM show was the strutting drum major, a skill he'd perfected in his high school marching band days. Two majorettes wearing red-white-and-blue outfits carried a banner that read Operation Recovery.

They were followed by four similarly attired baton twirlers, their batons reaching nearly as high as the streetlights. The twirlers were dancing showgirls, also with previous prep band experience. Behind them came a marching band with thirty musicians dressed in glossy blue-and-white nylon jackets and red nylon slacks. The jackets were embossed with white *Operation Recovery* scripted lettering and their blue caps had a red *O/R* insignia.

Anita said, "That's the most brightly colored band I've ever seen. How were they able to get their uniforms so quickly?"

Robert shrugged and said, "That's a good question. I don't know."

Just before they reached the bleachers, the band started playing a Dixieland version of "When the Saints Go Marching In." On the far side of a middle row, three men were playing trombones.

She looked closely and said, "The taller trombone player looks like—Father, it is, it's Richard."

Robert squinted and said, "It certainly does looks like him. Well, I'll be damned."

"You told me he was in Omaha."

"I did?"

"I'm going," she said, and she scampered down the bleachers and then across the street until she was at Richard's side. Staying in step with him, she glanced his way. Still playing his trombone, he returned her glance and his eyes felt good touching hers for the first time in a long time.

The procession continued a half block more to Ogden Avenue. Around the corner band members stopped and began congratulating each other.

Trombone in one hand, Richard took off his hat and said to Anita, "You told me I should play in the Salvation Army marching band. I told you there wasn't one, but with their help we organized this one. You know, it wasn't all that difficult finding volunteers, including quite a few homeless musicians. We had to round up some instruments, and it took several nights of practice at the homeless center, but we had a lot of fun."

"How did you come up with your uniforms so quickly?"

"That was easy. Ben special-ordered them through one of our store catalogs."

She noticed on the lapel of his uniform an ID badge labeled Richard Stewart, Omaha, Nebraska.

The couple gazed into each other's eyes, and time stood still until Richard asked another band member to hold his trombone. Then he put his arms around Anita's waist, lifted her eye level and when their lips met, a cheer rose from the surrounding musicians.

He leaned back and said, "Anita, about Paula—"

"You don't have to explain, Richard. I know you love me and no one else."

Within the three huge canvas tents in the middle of the street, growing numbers of poor and homeless folks were choosing articles from tables stacked with merchandise. Circulating through the crowds were volunteers handing out information packets detailing a variety of job training programs. The volunteers seemed eager to answer questions, and registration tables were crowded with people signing up for classes.

Richard's memory drifted back to the March evening when—just down the street from where he was now standing—he met Robert for the first time. The realization of what had transpired since then caused his spine to tingle like wind chimes in a summer breeze.

Anita said, "I can't believe how many people are here tonight, and so many volunteers. It truly is a miracle."

"I'm sure your father told you they're from businesses all over town, many of them from the Strip and Fremont Street. I mean managers, entertainers, clerks, valet attendants, waiters and waitresses. Juan and Maria and Madelline are around here somewhere. Juan himself enlisted many volunteers from Bally's and Paris."

"And *you* are responsible for this."

"I just took to heart what you told me to do. The important thing is from now on large numbers of the poor and homeless are going to have many good job opportunities. We're hoping what's happening here will spread to other cities across America. Wouldn't that be a dream come true? Oh, and give much of the credit to James Forrester. He and his staff and others worked hard to make Operation Recovery a reality. By the way he's postponing work on Monte Vista until the developers and contractors finish constructing the O/R community. Mr. Renzberg and his board have agreed. They think it will be great publicity for the resort and Renzcorp nationwide."

Richard put his arm around her shoulders and pointed inside the first tent.

"See the third table from the front? There's J.D. and his wife Marjie registering people for classes." Richard chuckled, "Look at that Marciano hustle."

J.D. looked up and said something to Marjie who also looked up and they both smiled and waved.

"Guess I had Mr. Forrester figured all wrong," Anita said.

Richard turned to her and said, "Anita, I've missed you more than you'll ever know."

Just then Robert walked up with Madelline at his side. Robert tried to conceal the joy he felt seeing his daughter and best friend/boss together, but there was a revealing smile on his lips and a twinkle in his eyes.

"Oh, hello, Rich," he said. "Say, I want to talk to you two. See the sign in front of the tents?"

It read: "Welcome to the First O/R New Year's Day Banquet, Las Vegas Convention Center, 12:00 to 4:00 PM."

Robert continued, "The banquet will give us an opportunity to sign up many more people for job placement classes. I'm wondering if you two would be available to work on the serving line that day?"

Richard looked to Anita and she said, "Definitely."

About the Author

Paul D. Smith and his wife Bonnie live in Sioux Falls. Paul has a B.A. from the University of Sioux Falls and an M.A. from the University of South Dakota.

As a newspaper and television news writer, and as a public school teacher, he learned the plight of the homeless is one of America's most tragic, heart-rending, difficult-to-alleviate problems.